'A propulsive, neatly structured thriller' *Guardian*

'The veteran writer has rarely strayed from forging complex and innovative thrillers ... In *The Collaborator*, his professionalism ensures a forceful, kinetic narrative.' *Independent*

'Tight writing and meticulous research ... Seymour paints the streets of Naples and their dark denizens with an artist's brush that lingers equally on the grime, the glitter and the blood' *The Times*

'The pace leaves you breathless ... Once again, Seymour has proved that he is the master of the thriller genre.' *Edinburgh Evening News*

'Not only is this gripping from the first, as Seymour establishes a convincing human relationship in a way that many thriller writers don't, but it deals with a real entity that is as terrifying in life as it is in this absorbing book.' *City AM*

'The finest thriller writer in the world today' *Daily Telegraph*

'Topical, gripping and original ... Naples is vividly portrayed, a city rotting inside from crime, corruption and decay. The stink and fear of the gangsters rise off the pages.' *Economist*

Gerald Seymour spent fifteen years as an international television news reporter with ITN, covering Vietnam and the Middle East, and specialising in the subject of terrorism across the world. Seymour was on the streets of Londonderry on the afternoon of Bloody Sunday, and was a witness to the massacre of Israeli athletes at the Munich Olympics.

Gerald Seymour is now a full time writer, and six of his novels have been filmed for television in the UK and US.

Also by Gerald Seymour

Harry's Game
The Glory Boys
Kingfisher
Red Fox (*US title* The Harrison Affair)
The Contract
Archangel
In Honour Bound
Field of Blood
A Song in the Morning (*US title* Shadow on the Sun)
At Close Quarters (*US title* An Eye for an Eye)
Home Run (*US title* The Running Target)
Condition Black
The Journeyman Tailor
The Fighting Man
The Heart of Danger
Killing Ground
The Waiting Time (*US title* Dead Ground)
A Line in the Sand
Holding the Zero
The Untouchable
Traitor's Kiss
The Unknown Soldier
Rat Run
The Walking Dead
Timebomb

THECOLLABORATOR

GERALD SEYMOUR

HODDER

First published in Great Britain in 2009 by Hodder & Stoughton
An Hachette UK company

This paperback edition first published in 2010

I

A CIP catalogue record for this title
is available from the British Library

B format ISBN 978 0 340 91888 3
A format ISBN 978 0 340 91889 0

Typeset in Plantin Light by
Ellipsis Books Limited, Glasgow

Printed and bound by
Clays Ltd, St Ives plc

Hodder & Stoughton policy is to use papers that are natural,
renewable and recyclable products and made from wood grown
in sustainable forests. The logging and manufacturing processes
are expected to conform to the environmental regulations
of the country of origin.

Hodder & Stoughton Ltd
338 Euston Road
London NW1 3BH

www.hodder.co.uk

For Harriet and Georgia and Alfie

PROLOGUE

It was a hot afternoon, stinking hot, and the sun beat up from the concrete path, dazzling him. A ridiculous afternoon to be out in a London park. He'd met friends for lunch, arranged long back, on the south side of the park – two guys from college days – but they'd had their girlfriends in tow, like trophies, which had made him feel awkward, as if he, not they, were the intruders. And, truth was, he'd been bored because the togetherness of the couples seemed to shred the spirit of mischief that ran in him – some called it 'happy go lucky' and his dad 'Jack the lad' – and he'd wanted to be gone before the loss was terminal. It had all been too damn serious, which seldom fitted well with him.

He'd eaten the meal, coughed up his share of the bill, and walked away from the Underground station, had crossed Kensington Road and gone into the park, over Rotten Row, and been within a few yards of the dog-leg lake before his mind had kicked back into gear. By now, the couples would be talking mortgages and future prospects. He was in the park where heat reverberated off the scorched grass and concrete. There wasn't half a square centimetre of shade close to him, and it was a pretty silly place to be – no skateboarders or football to watch, no promenade of stripped-down girls.

He looked for a bench to flop down on. He wasn't stressed by the heat or the lack of entertainment – his own little world gave him no grief – but it was damn hot.

The bench he saw was blurred, but a haven. He heard, far away, the shouts of children playing at the water's edge, but round the bench there was quiet. His eyes were nearly closed as he sank on to the wooden slats, which grilled his backside and lower spine. Jumbled thoughts loitered in his mind – home, parents, work, food, getting back to the north-east of the city, money – all easily discarded. With his eyes sealed against the light, maybe he dreamed, maybe he dozed. Time slipped on a July afternoon on the last day of the first week in the month.

The idyll was broken.

'Excuse . . . please.' A clear, uncluttered voice, an accent. He jolted upright. 'I'm sorry. I . . .'

Eddie Deacon never considered that responding might change his life, push it on to a road unrecognised and unexplored . . . His eyes snapped open.

He saw the girl – dark hair, light skin, dark eyes. Hadn't been aware of her coming to the bench . . . might even have been there when he'd taken his seat . . .

Mutual apologies. Sorry that he had been asleep. Sorry that she had woken him.

She wore a cotton skirt, short, not much of it, a white blouse, brief sleeves, and a textbook lay open on her lap, with an Italian–English pocket dictionary.

Strangers pausing, wondering whether to go forward – and blurting together.

'What can I do?'

'Please, I am confused.'

'How can I help?'

'I do not understand.'

They both laughed, chimed with each other. Eddie Deacon pushed hair off his forehead. He saw that when she laughed the gold crucifix, dangling from a chain bounced on her cleavage. That was what he saw – and she would have seen?

Him writing the script: not a bad-looking guy, pretty well turned-out, good head of hair, a decent complexion and a smile to die for. And she would have heard? A laugh that was infectious, not forced, and a voice with a tone of interest that was honest and not patronising. Well, he was hardly going to short-change himself.

'What's the problem?'

'I don't understand this – "turn over".What is "turn over"?'

Eddie Deacon grinned. 'Is this "turn over" in bed? Or "turnover" in business?'

'Business. It is a book on auditing accounts in English – and it says "turn over".'

He asked, 'You're Italian?'

'Yes.'

He said, 'In Italian, "turnover" is *fatturato*.You understand?'

'Of course, yes, I do . . . and you speak Italian.'

He shrugged. 'A little.'

'OK, OK . . .' She smiled – her teeth glowed, her eyes were alight. She riffled again through the pages of her book. Her finger darted down and stabbed at a line. 'Here . . . For "balance" we have *soppesare* in my dictionary, but that is not the Italian word for the commercial balance of an account. What should it be?'

'To "balance" an account is *bilanciare*, and a "balance sheet" is *bilancio di esercizio*. Does that help?'

She touched his hand – fleeting, a natural, spontaneous gesture of gratitude. He felt the tips of her fingers on his skin. He liked girls, liked their touch, but would have admitted, if quizzed, that he was currently 'between relationships'. God, who needed commitments? He'd nearly been engaged, to a local-government kitchen-hygiene inspector, two years back but his mother had become too fond of her too quickly. He hadn't found a soulmate.

'I have a very good helper.'

Eddie Deacon said he should be good – he was a language teacher. He didn't add that if he'd put his back into it he might have made interpreter level and gone to Brussels or even the United Nations, but it would have been a hassle. He taught English to overseas students. His core tongues were German, French and Spanish but he also had useful Italian. She told him she was on two courses in London: in the morning she studied English language and in the afternoons she did accounting and book-keeping. Eddie Deacon wondered why a pretty girl in a tight skirt and a tight blouse, from Italy, bothered with any of that, but didn't take it further. The sun seemed, in mid-afternoon, to spear his forehead and shoulders. The men and women who walked past the bench wore floppy hats or had white war-paint daubed on exposed skin, while little parasols shaded tots in push-chairs. There were squeals and shrieks from the lake, and splashing. He assumed that swimming in the Serpentine was forbidden and that the *gauleiter* men would be there soon, yelling that it was *verboten*.

He stood up. 'It's a bit warm for me. I prefer to be out of the sun.'

She said, 'Where is to be the new classroom? I need all opportunities to speak English. I have a teacher. I do not wish to lose him.'

It was, he thought, a challenge. She must have realised he intended to walk away, but her chin had jutted, her shoulders were back and now she was almost blocking his path. He reckoned that she was used to getting what she wanted. He didn't push past her. Now, for the first time since he had woken up, he looked at his self-enrolled pupil. She was lightly built, had narrow hips, a squashed-in waist and a good-sized, but not gross, bosom. Her face fascinated him: a fine jaw, a delicate nose and a high forehead, the hair pushed back. But it was her eyes that caught him. They had authority, did not brook denial. As a general rule, Eddie Deacon did not fight authority. He was one to go with the flow. He didn't look at the hips, waist or breasts of the girl before him but was carried deep into her eyes.

He asked where she was heading, and she told him. He told her he lived nearby – a small untruth: it would probably have taken him almost an hour to walk from Hackney to where he lived on the west side of the Balls Pond Road. He suggested they find a pub, with open doors, big fans and a cool interior. There, he said, they could have a hack at any accounting or book-keeping language that was giving her grief. Her books were in a bag now, and he took it, slung the strap across his shoulder. She hooked her hand into the crook of his arm.

Her hips swung as she walked, and she threw back her head, letting her hair fall between her shoulder-blades where the blouse collar had slipped.

'By the way, I'm Eddie Deacon.'

Her name was Immacolata.

On the north side of the park they took a bus and sat on the top deck with the window open beside them so that a zephyr of cooler air reached them. She leafed through the textbook, found English commercial expressions and quizzed him for the exact meaning in her mother tongue. They walked a bit on his territory – Balls Pond, Kingsland, Dalston – reached a pub and sat in a corner of the saloon. Eddie Deacon sensed that she was the most special girl he had ever spent an afternoon and early evening with. He was captivated. Couldn't think what he offered her beyond a few words in Italian and explanations of a few phrases of more colloquial English, but she seemed to hang on what he told her. Precious few stayed around to listen to him on where he lived or where the language school was, his anecdotes about the daftest Lithuanian students, where his parents lived, what excited or what bored him to death, and when he made jokes she laughed. It was a good rich laugh, and he thought it was genuine, not produced to humour him; he decided, in the pub, that she didn't laugh often the way her life was.

As dusk fell, they left the pub, her hand again at the bend of his elbow. Now he called her 'Mac' – had drifted into it without a prompt from her – and she seemed amused by it.

He walked her almost home, but at the end of a street off Hackney Road, she stopped and indicated they would part here. Now, a streetlight beamed on to her face. He had been with her a few minutes short of seven hours. He wouldn't have known what to do, but she led. She offered her right cheek and he kissed it, then the left. She was grinning – chuckling as she kissed his lips, and her smile was radiant. He asked if they could meet again. She told him where and when, without asking if it was convenient – which didn't matter to him because any time and any place were fine. She turned and left him. He watched her going away down a street of little terraced homes that the new rich had taken over. She passed the low-slung German sports cars and the gardens filled with builders' skips. She was Immacolata, she was twenty-five, two years younger than himself, she was from Naples, and would meet him again in two days' time. What did he not know? She had not told him her family name, or given him her address and phone number.

She was between two lamp posts and the light fell on her hair and on the white blouse. She went briskly and did not look back.

Why had she spent seven hours of her day with him, laughed and joked with him, listened? Because he was attractive and handsome? Because he was a success and taught in a language school? Because of his humour and culture?

Eddie Deacon thought the girl – Mac – was lonely. Sad too.

He would count the hours till they met again, and thought himself blessed.

She was round the corner, gone from his view. He would tick off every hour until they met again and hadn't done that for as long as he could remember.

Eddie Deacon kicked a can down the pavement then across the width of the street, and was euphoric.

I

She started to run. There was no pavement, only a track of dried dust at the side of the road. She ran past the stationary cars and vans that had blocked her brother's little Fiat. Faced with an unmoving jam more than three hundred metres long, she had had no alternative but to get out of the Fiat and head on foot towards the distant gates of the town's cemetery. To be late for the burial would have been intolerable to Immacolata Borelli.

She had left the car door open. Behind her she heard it slammed, then Silvio's call, his head protruding from the sun hatch perhaps, for her to run. Everything about the day, and the schedule, had been – so far – a disaster. The call had come to her mobile the evening before, from Silvio, the youngest of her three brothers. He had told her of a death notice in that day's *Cronaca di Napoli* detailing the passing of Marianna Rossetti, from Nola, the funeral to be held tomorrow at the Basilica of SS Apostoli, followed by the burial. Immacolata had been in the kitchen of the Hackney apartment she shared with her eldest brother, Vincenzo, who had been shouting questions at her – Who was on the phone? – because he was paranoid about her using a mobile. She had told Silvio she would be on the first flight the next day; she had told Vincenzo that the language school had changed the time of classes, and that she was required early. She ran past the cigarette smoke puffed from the motionless vehicles, and past the cacophony of car horns.

She had not been on the first flight out of Heathrow: it had been overbooked. Her wallet on the check-in counter, opened to display a wad of twenty-pound notes, had not made a seat available. The second flight had seats, but its takeoff time had been put back forty minutes by a leaking toilet. Had anyone ever heard of aircraft stacking over the Golfo di Napoli before landing at Capodichino? There was work in progress on the runway, military flights from the NATO detachment had priority and . . .

She had not been able to find Silvio because some arrogant *bastardo* in uniform had not allowed him to park in front of the terminal, and that was more delay. Normally there would have been a minder to sit in the car and tell the official to go fuck himself, but this journey was not normal, had been made in secrecy and was far outside the business of her family. It was only twenty-five kilometres from the airport to the centre of Nola, but there were roadworks and the lights controlling the single lane of traffic were broken.

They had reached the basilica. She had grabbed her handbag off the back seat, snatched up the little black hat with the attached veil, flung herself out of the Fiat, dumped the hat on her head, glanced at her watch as she charged up the steps to the main doors, run inside, heard the crisp echo of her heels on the flagstones and allowed moments to pass before her eyesight could function in the gloom. The space in front of the high altar was deserted, as were the forward pews. A nun had told her that the cortège of the Rossetti family was now well on its way to the cemetery. 'Such a fine young woman, such a tragic loss . . .'

Immacolata had gone back down the steps at speed, had nearly tripped, had accosted three people – an idiot, a woman who was stone deaf, a young man who had ogled her – and demanded directions to the cemetery.

She hitched her skirt hem higher.

It was eight months since she had arrived in London with her eldest brother. They had driven all the way north to Genova, then taken a flight to Prague, driven across Germany to Hamburg and flown into the British capital. He had used doctored papers but her passport had been in her own name. In those eight months she had had no contact with her father – it would have been difficult but not impossible – had not spoken to her mother, which could have been arranged but would have brought complications, and had relied on rare, brief conversations with the teenage Silvio. She was now familiar with life in north-east London.

The heat of the summer had gone. Two days after she had met Eddie, the heavens had opened and a thunderstorm of epic proportions had broken, sheet and fork lightning, claps that shook windows, torrential rain, and then cool. The day she had met Eddie, London had been as hot as Naples. It was as if that storm, biblical in its scale, which had caught them out in the open space of Clissold Park, had severed a link with her home city. The deluge had drenched them and they had kissed, then gone to his single room to take off the sodden clothes . . . and she had lost the link to her city, with the roasting heat, the stench of the streets, the strewn litter, plastic strips and discarded paper, the dumped kitchen gear and the slow rot of dog mess. All were with her now, as she ran on the dusty verge towards the cemetery entrance, as were, ever sharper, her memories of the young woman she had once been proud to say to her face was her 'best, most-valued friend'.

By hitching the hem of her skirt higher, flashing more of her thighs at those gawping at her from the cars, Immacolata could lengthen her stride. It shamed her that in London her best, most-valued friend had almost slipped from her mind. She was within sight of the gates. Eight months before, she had promised to stay in close touch with Marianna Rossetti;

in London she could have justified the rupturing of the thread. Not now. Silvio's hesitant words resonated in her mind, and his stumbled reading of the notice in the *Cronaca*. She didn't know the cause of death, only that her friend had passed away in the Nola hospital. She assumed an accident had been responsible. There was, as she knew it, no history of illness.

Her heel broke. She had left the London apartment early, while Vincenzo still slept, but had taken the precaution of wearing clothes for a language class. She had put her black suit, stockings, shoes and handbag in a zipped holdall. She couldn't have guaranteed that Vincenzo wouldn't appear at his bedroom door, blinking and bleary, to query why she was wearing funeral best to go to the school. She knew about security, the care that must be taken. It was ingrained in her, like grime embedded in the wrinkles of a labourer's hands. She had changed in the toilet of the delayed flight and had looked the part of a mourner when the aircraft had dropped down to the tarmac at Capodichino. Her trainers were in the holdall, which was in the boot of the Fiat, which was stuck in traffic more than two hundred metres behind her. Immacolata swore, and heard laughter billow from an Alfa level with her. She scooped up the damaged shoe, from which the broken heel hung at an angle, and pushed it into her bag.

She hopped and limped to the gate, sensing the softness of baked dust against her left foot, then wincing pain, which meant a glass shard or a sliver of metal. At the gate three or four families were with the flower saleswoman. She barged in front of them, dropped a fifty-euro note on the table, took a bouquet of white roses and greenery from a bucket and kept moving. If she had queued and waited for the change, the flowers would have cost her twenty euros at most. In Naples, she had learned that she had no need – her father's daughter – to pay for anything. She headed through the gate, wiped her arm across her forehead and went in search of a burial.

The cemeteries Immacolata Borelli knew in Naples were on the extreme edge of the Sanità district, where her father had interests, and out beyond the Poggioreale gaol. Both sprawled over many acres, communities of the dead, with myriad buildings for the cadavers to rot in. This one seemed smaller, insignificant, but it served a town of only thirty thousand. A statue faced her, a life-size image of a young woman of the same size and youth as her best friend, with a fresh daffodil hooked in her bronze hand. Her name, set in the stone wall beside her, was Angelabella, and the dates showed that she had died in her nineteenth year. Her face showed innocence. Immacolata was jolted – she had thought too much of the filth on the verge leading to the gates, her broken shoe, the size of the cemetery, and not sufficiently of her friend, whose death had brought her here.

She didn't know where to go.

She tried, twice, asking: where was the burial chapel of the Rossetti family? A man shrugged. A woman grimaced. She ran up the steps of the Reception, noticing how acute now was the pain in her stockinged foot – saw a smear of blood behind her – and demanded an answer from an official who sat at a desk and sipped rank-smelling coffee. He, too, showed no interest. She told him that the burial was taking place now and his shoulders heaved, as if to indicate that many funerals took place *now*. She swore, that word for excrement from the gutters of the Sanità and the Forcella districts. The official pointed above his head to a chart that mapped the layout of the Nola cemetery.

Immacolata went past the family chapels, where small candles burned and plastic flowers bloomed, where photographs of old and young fought against time's ravage.

She crossed an open space where the sun shimmered on white stone grave markers. She went towards the far wall, using the pathways between the stones. She approached a small group, their backs to her. She saw two ladders above the shoulders of the mourners. An elongated bundle, wrapped in white sheeting, was lifted and two men climbed the higher steps of the ladders and took its weight.

Immacolata remembered the shape of Marianna Rossetti's body, where it was full and where it bulged, the width of the hips on which a skirt would twist when she walked, but the men on the ladders lifted her corpse as though it weighed nothing. The Rossetti family vault was on the fourth level. The bundle went above the names and dates of the lower levels, the plastic flowers commemorating strangers in life and companions in death, then was level with a gaping hole. It had been hard to believe, when Silvio had telephoned, that her friend was dead, harder now to believe it as her friend was lifted level with the hole, then given a decisive shove towards the back of the burial place. As the men came down the ladders, she heard women weeping. Now the men went back up the ladders and grunted as they raised the hole's cover, slotted it into place, then gave it two loud thwacks to satisfy themselves that it was securely fastened. Perhaps an aunt of Marianna Rossetti, or a grandmother, or an elderly friend of the family, would come to the elevated grave in two years' time to clean the bones of the last decayed flesh and gristle, then stack them in a small space further back against the rear wall.

The noisy weeping was over. The ladders were carried discreetly to the side and the mourners started to shuffle away.

They came towards Immacolata.

She wondered whether Maria Rossetti would hug her, kiss her, cling to her. She wondered, also, whether Luigi Rossetti would shake her hand, composed, or whether his head would sink on to her shoulder and wet it with his tears. She hardly knew them, had never been to their home – it would have been impossible for her to reciprocate Marianna's hospitality, for her friend to come to the Borelli clan's apartment – but she had assumed that a daughter would have told her mother of a friend. She thought she would be thanked for the respect she had shown their daughter.

Lopsided, balanced on one shoe, she waited for the little group to reach her.

Peculiar. They seemed not to have seen her.

Maria and Luigi Rossetti were nearing her – perhaps a few of their brothers, sisters, cousins with them – but none in the group smiled in the wan way of the grieving. She might as well not have been there. They came on. She did not know what to do with the flowers and they were in her hand, which hung against her hip, and her hat had slipped to the side as she had hurried through the cemetery – the veil no longer covered her left eye.

She had met – engineered occasions – Maria and Luigi Rossetti at the college where she and Marianna had studied. It would be hard for her to step aside without standing on a grave, and, if she wobbled – as she might without a shoe – she would knock over two or three vases holding artificial blooms . . . It was not as if they hadn't seen her. The parents' eyes were now wide open, assimilating who was astride their path.

Immacolata knew that she was seen and recognised and the greeting came first from Luigi. He stopped in front of her and, as she held out the flowers from which water still dripped, spat on to the concrete path, halfway between her feet and his own brilliantly polished toecaps. He looked into her eyes, unwavering, and the word came silently, so that his wife would not hear it cross his lips but Immacolata would read it. He called her a whore. He did not utter the word a historian would have used when lecturing on the sex trade in Pompeii or Ercolano, but the one that would come naturally to today's dockers in the port of Naples. To her best friend's father, she was a vulgar whore of no worth unless her legs were wide and her knickers dropped. And the father was a respected teacher of mathematics to eighth-year students. She gasped.

He stepped a half-pace to his right and made room for his wife to pass. His eyes were without life, as if grief had purged it. Not so the mother's. Her eyes burned with anger. Immacolata had a moment in which to evade the attack but her reaction was not fast enough. The mother was personal assistant to the manager of a well-respected insurance company and had a reputation for integrity, dignity and probity. She reached out and caught the tight-drawn lapels of Immacolata's blouse, ripping the buttons from their holes. Her other hand grabbed the pretty little lace bow between the cups of Immacolata's brassière and the fabric split. Immacolata fell back, feeling the sun's force on her bare skin before she ducked to cover herself. Then the mother said, soft and controlled, that a whore should display herself and feel no shame because she cared for nothing but money. Someone kicked her shin – she didn't know whether it was the father or the mother. She went down on her knees and saw the bouquet crumpled beneath her, the stems snapped.

The father snarled, 'You are a whore and you have no decency. I know everything about you. I know who you are, what nest of snakes spawned you, the poison that comes from you – which took the life of our beloved child. She died from leukaemia. We were told at the hospital by the oncology department why – how – she contracted leukaemia. You and your family are responsible. You may be welcome beside the *autostrada* as you wait for your clients, but you are not welcome here. Perhaps the only language you understand is that of the gutter – so fuck off.'

The mother said, 'For four or five weeks, she complained of tiredness. We thought she'd been studying too hard. It was only when bruises appeared that we went with her to the doctor. She seemed anaemic. He examined her closely, particularly her eyes. They are trained to hide anxiety, but he rang the hospital, told them she was a priority case and sent us there immediately. I rang my husband at work and called him out of his class.'

Around Immacolata, cold, harsh faces blocked out the sun. When she dropped her head she saw the men's trousers and the women's knees, and if she stared at the dust there were shoes, men's and women's, and she feared she would be kicked again. She tried to make herself smaller, dragging her knees into her stomach, her elbows across her chest, but she couldn't shut out what she was told.

The father said, 'Of course, we know of the Triangle of Death – we've read about it – but we don't talk about it. In Marigliano, Acerra and Nola we're familiar with its mortality statistics, and the criminality of the Camorra in our town. They are paid to dispose of chemical waste – and dump it in fields, orchards and streams. That is what the Camorra, those foul gangsters, do. For two decades – starting long before we knew of it – the ground and water table were contaminated with poison so that the Camorra could get richer. They and their families have the scruples and greed of whores. You are part of a family so you're guilty too.'

The mother said, 'They found her platelet count was low. They took a sample of bone marrow to evaluate her condition, but there was no need to do any tests because that first evening her condition was obvious. First, she had an agonising headache until she lost consciousness. We were in a ward of twenty beds, most occupied, and had just a curtain for privacy as we watched the team struggle to save her life. We could see that they knew it was hopeless because they work in the Triangle and had been in such situations many times before. A neuro-surgeon was called, but she died in front of us. They tried to resuscitate her, but within forty minutes she was gone, snatched from us in a public ward, festooned with cables and breathing aids. There was no opportunity for us to comfort her, or send for the priest because that day he had gone to Naples to buy shoes. Her death hurt too much for us to weep. We were so unprepared.'

The words rang in her head. She knew now that they would not kick her again. They would have seen her hands trembling as she covered her breasts and clutched the shredded blouse.

He said, 'A doctor told me she could have contracted the disease as much as a decade earlier, swimming in a stream, playing in long grass in a field or under the trees in an orchard . . .'

She said, 'I used to take her to the fields and the stream behind our home. She would swim, splash, play, then roll in the grass to dry herself. While I watched her, laughed, and thought of her as a gift from God, she was being poisoned.'

The father said, 'The doctor told me that the farmland around Nola and the water table are saturated with dioxins. If I wanted to know more, I was told, I should see the *carabinieri* . . . I didn't think they'd speak to me. But yesterday I saw a *maresciallo* – I teach his son. He told me of the Camorra's criminal clans who make vast profits from dumping chemicals in this area: they call them the eco-Mafia. He said the clan leader in Nola had sub-contracted the transportation of waste materials from the north to the Borellis from Naples. I believed him. You've prostituted yourself for greed. Go.'

The mother said, 'There's evil in your blood, but I doubt

you're capable of self-disgust or shame. Your presence here is an intrusion. Go.'

In all of her life, Immacolata had never before been spoken to in such a fashion. She couldn't meet their eyes but kept her head low as she bent to pick up the destroyed flowers.

She passed a young man with a tidy haircut and a suit but no mourner's tie. He wore dark glasses and she couldn't read his expression. She made her way out of the cemetery. She had known for a decade and a half that her father dealt in long-distance heavy-goods traffic, and for a decade that her brother, Vincenzo, was involved with northern industry, and she herself, had arranged the hire of trucks from far-away hauliers. At the gate, by the statue of Angelabella, aged eighteen, she dumped the flowers in a bin and hobbled out to look for Silvio.

She felt numb and shivered.

She looked at them from the door, but they seemed not to have heard her come in. She had got off the bus and walked the last mile, ignoring the drizzle. She had had no coat, and the shoes, torn blouse and black suit were in the holdall, with the ripped underwear. She was wearing what her brother would have seen her in when she had gone out early that morning.

Vincenzo and three friends were playing cards. She watched them through a fog of cigarette smoke, and waited for their reaction so that she could resurrect the lie and embellish it. Each held a fan of cards up to his face.

Since she had been dropped off at Capodichino to wait for the flight, she had thought of the bundle lifted by the men on the ladders, the accusation made against her, and had seen the crowded hospital ward as a life had drained away. The bundle had been so easy to lift that the wind, however slight, might have wafted it from the men's grip and carried it up and away into the cloudless sky.

Vincenzo was the heir apparent to their father. He was thirty-one, a target for the Palace of Justice, the detectives of the Squadra Mobile and the investigators of the ROS, the Raggruppamento Operativo Speciale of the *carabinieri*. He had made one mistake in the ten years he had spent shadowing his father, the clan leader: he had used a mobile phone and the call had been traced. The apartment in the Forcella district from which it had originated had been raided and scribbled *pizzini* had been recovered. From these scraps of paper, covered with microscopic handwriting – Vincenzo's – another *covo* had been identified and searched. There, a Beretta P38 handgun had been found stowed in greaseproof paper under a bath panel. It carried the DNA signature of Vincenzo Borelli, and the ballistics laboratory had reported that it had been used to fire the bullets taken from the bodies of three men. He would face a gaol sentence as long as his father expected when he came, eventually, to trial. Vincenzo had disappeared from the face of the earth, and so had his sister: he as a fugitive, she dropping from view and gaining new skills in handling money movements.

In the doorway, she could have recited every word that had been said to her as she had lain on the ground. Every last word. And she could remember how the aggression had cut into her, wounding her. Never in her life had anyone spoken to her with such venom, or made such an accusation, while seeming not to care for the consequences of denouncing the daughter of Pasquale and Gabriella Borelli, sister of Vincenzo and Giovanni. It should have meant a death sentence. To humiliate and abuse the daughter of a clan leader was the act of a man bored with living. If her father, in his cell in the north, or her mother, who flitted between safe-houses, had been told what her friend's parent had hissed at her, that man would have been condemned. If she had interrupted the card game to say where she had been and what had happened, within twenty-four hours blood would have run on a pavement, a body would have lain at a grotesque angle and the authority of the clan would have been preserved. She had not even told Silvio, who had looked curiously at her torn blouse but hadn't asked.

Her brother won the hand. He always won. The game was for small stakes, two-pound coins. The heap on the table in front of Vincenzo was four or five times greater than the piles in front of the other players. London served two purposes for him. He was out of sight of the magistrates and investigators in Italy, but he was also in a position to do good deals, exploit opportunities and build the foundations of networks. He dealt in leather jackets and shoes manufactured in the small sweat-shop factories on the slopes of Vesuvio, then shipped out of the Naples docks – in secrecy after the labels of the most famed European fashion-houses had been sewn or stamped in place – to Felixstowe on Britain's east coast, or to the Atlantic harbours of the United States. A leather coat, with a designer label, could be manufactured for twenty euros and sold in Boston, New York or Chicago for three hundred. Many opportunities existed for Vincenzo Borelli's advancement. The downside was that a prolonged absence from the seat of power – Forcella and Sanità in the old district of Naples – diminished his status and authority. His parents had decreed that in London he should watch over his sister while she qualified in accountancy. A clan needed trustworthy finance people. He treated her as a child, showing no interest as she stood in the doorway. The music billowed around her.

The cruellest images were those of the hospital ward. When Silvio had driven her away from the cemetery, down the via Saviano, they had come to the inner area of Nola and had gone past two of the hospital's entrances. It was dominated by a ruined castle on a hilltop. It was a modern building. Of any hospital closer to her own area, she could have said which clan had controlled the construction of it, which had supplied the concrete, and which had owned the politician whose name was on the contracts, but this one was too far from her home. She imagined the interior of the Ospedale Santa Maria della Pietà, death coming fast behind a cotton screen, a young woman's mother screaming as her daughter slipped away, the father beating clenched fists against the wall behind the bed, the equipment's alarm pealing because the medics couldn't save a life, the mutterings of a stand-in priest, the weeping of patients in the adjacent beds, and the squeak of wheels as the body was taken away, the medical staff shrugging . . .

Now Vincenzo looked up, gave a brief smile in greeting. He held up an empty beer bottle, then pointed to the kitchen door. Immacolata dropped her holdall, went to the kitchen, took four Peronis from the fridge, opened them, carried them back into the living room and found space between the empty bottles, filled ashtrays and cigarette cartons to put them down. She was not acknowledged. She closed the door behind her.

In her room, she lay on her bed. She did not weep. She stared at the ceiling, the lightbulb and the cobweb draped off the shade and didn't think of the boy who had made her laugh. There was music playing in the living room and traffic outside in the street, voices raised in the apartment above and a baby screaming below. They meant nothing to her and she shut them out, but she couldn't escape from the raised bundle, the spoken savagery and cruelty of death.

The young man found his *maresciallo* in a bar to the right side of the piazza in front of the town's cathedral. He was from the Udine region in the far north-east, where there were rolling hills and valleys, civilisation and cleanliness. He would have hated Nola, his first posting after training for induction into the *carabinieri*, had it not been for the gruff kindness of his commanding officer. He still wore the suit that had been suitable for the funeral service and the burial, but his dark glasses were high now on his hair.

He waited until he was waved to a chair, then sat and handed the *maresciallo* the plastic folder he had prepared. A waiter approached. He ordered Coca-Cola. The folder, with the name on it of Marianna Rossetti and that day's date, was opened. His report covered five closely typed pages. He knew that, two days before, the *maresciallo* had met with the girl's father and was aware of the circumstances and cause of the girl's death. He himself had been ordered to the basilica and the cemetery to watch, listen – it had been explained to him that the family's emotions ran high. Also, he knew that a researcher at the hospital had published material in the foreign-language edition of the *Lancet Oncology* under a title that referred to *il triangolo della morte*, and that in the secure archive section of the barracks there was a small mountain of files dealing with the area's contamination. The *maresciallo* had read the first two pages, and he sat in silence. The waiter brought his Coca-Cola, with an *espresso* and a large measure of Stock brandy. He had known the *maresciallo* always spent time here in the evening and that he could be certain of finding him. He tried to read the other man's face, but saw nothing. He had hoped for praise.

The question was as blunt as it was unexpected: 'Have you drunk alcohol tonight?'

And he had believed that praise was due. The father and mother of the deceased had made no attempt to lower their voices so he had heard them crystal clear. Within minutes what they had said was written in his notebook as virtual verbatim. He had the accusation, the condemnation and the name. An older man, jaundiced and cynical, from long service with the Arma – what the *carabinieri* called themselves –

might have hung back, lounged against a distant headstone, smoked a quiet cheroot and reflected on what a shit place Nola was. The young man had made certain he was close enough to hear every word and to see the violence shown towards the woman. He accepted that he would not be praised.

'No. I haven't had a drink for three—'

He was interrupted. The report was in the folder, which was pushed back across the table. The *maresciallo* had a mobile and was scrolling, then making a connection. The young man was shown his superior's back as a call was made. He couldn't hear what was said. The chair scraped as the *maresciallo* turned to him.

'If you haven't had a drink, you can drive to Naples. There's a barracks at piazza Dante. You're expected.'

'Excuse me.'

'What?'

'My report – is it useful?'

The *maresciallo* swirled the coffee, drank it, then some brandy, and coughed. 'I don't know. Perhaps, if you want praise, you should ask the officer I'm sending you to. My old mother does jigsaw puzzles to pass her time, and tells me that discovering where one piece fits will solve the rest. There may be a thousand pieces on the tray in front of her, but slotting one piece into its home makes the rest easy. I can't say whether or not what you have told me is that one piece. Twenty-five years ago I was at the training college in Campobasso with Mario Castrolami, who's waiting for you at the piazza Dante. He will decide whether or not you've helped to solve the puzzle or made it more difficult.'

'Thank you.'

He had the folder under his arm as he walked to the door. In the glass he saw the *maresciallo* wave to the waiter, who poured another measure of Stock. He went out into the late evening and felt the warmth on his face. He didn't know whether or not he had learned something useful that day. He started his car and drove towards Naples. He wouldn't be there, he estimated, before eleven, and wondered what sort of investigator was still at his desk at that time, and what a physical and verbal attack on a young woman at a funeral might mean.

'Fucking brilliant.'

He turned the third page, and started on the fourth. He saw, from the corner of his eye, the *carabinieri* recruit, the kid just off the training course, flush with pleasure.

'Not you. You want a lecture? I'll give you one. If you stand against the power of the Camorra clans, you'll have behind you tens of thousands of uniformed men. But still, I think, you'll hesitate. Luigi Rossetti – who stands behind him? Only his wife. But he had the courage, alone, to stand up against the weasel girl from a clan family. All you've done is listen. Don't think you have the courage of the Rossetti parents. Did the weasel swear at them when they attacked her?'

'She said nothing.'

'Did she challenge them? Do I need to offer protection to the parents? Can he go back to teaching, she to her work? Their courage was amazing, but should they spend the rest of their days in hiding? Are they dead already? What did you read on her face?'

'Humiliation.'

Castrolami finished reading and shuffled the pages, straightening them. He chuckled, but without mirth. 'Understand. This weasel is the daughter of Pasquale and Gabriella Borelli, the sister of Vincenzo and—'

The recruit interrupted him, which very few did. 'It was humiliation. Also, she's a member of the clan, yes, but also a friend of Marianna Rossetti. She came to Marianna

Rossetti's funeral and brought flowers. The Rossetti family have no connection – my *maresciallo* is definite on this – with the Camorra inside Nola or beyond it. This friendship crossed a divide.'

The pencil had a blunt tip and was chewed at the other end. Castrolami rapped it on his desk, found a small place, a few centimetres square, clear of papers and beat a tattoo. His forehead was cut with a frown. Mario Castrolami could accept preconceptions and believe them, but when he was confronted with a superior argument he could ditch them. The Borelli girl had been at the funeral.

'It's rare, but not unknown, for a member of a clan to have a friendship with someone outside it.'

'She didn't fight back. She was shamed.'

'I believe you.'

'Is it useful?'

On the desk, files and folders made foothills and mountains. Coffee had sustained him through the evening. Around his desk, against the walls, there were filing cabinets, some locked and others open, showing squashed-in paper. There were more files at his feet, and on the bookshelves that flanked the door. He could have pointed to them or to the chart Sellotaped to the wall on the right of the door, which listed the clans and the districts they fed off, with lines running between them, blue to show alliances and red to show feuds, or to the montage of mug-shots on a board that hung to the left of the door, a hundred faces, men and women, categorised as major organised-crime players. He could have waved his arms theatrically to demonstrate the scale of the war in which he was a foot-soldier, the numbers of the enemy, and spoken of a campaign without end. Had he done so, he thought he would have cheapened himself.

'In a year or two, what you've brought me may prove important – or in a week. I don't know . . . The problem is that you didn't see Immacolata Borelli arrive, and you don't know how she left. Where did she come from? What was her destination? You've given me a little, which is tantalising . . . Thank you.'

Alone again, he felt excited, which was unusual for him, after twenty-five years with the Arma, and seventeen in the ROS. But it was there, unmistakable. He sank down from his chair, was on hands and knees, and his stomach sagged as he burrowed for the file that held her photograph. When he found it and extracted the photograph – taken in Forcella by a long-lens surveillance camera – he stared at it. Could a woman from that family show remorse and be humiliated by the death of a friend? He gazed at the photograph and searched for an answer.

Time ebbed. Eddie was slumped on the bed.

Before getting back to his room, he had sat for three hours in the restaurant on the left side, going up, of Kingsland High Street. Opposite him there had been an empty chair and a laid place that went unused.

The heels of his trainers left smears on the coverlet. Her face would have puckered, a frown wrinkling her forehead, if she had been there to see them. She was not. Her picture, straight ahead of him, had pride of place on the wall facing the bed. The landlord's offering, a Victorian artist's effort at cattle grazing beside the Thames, was out of sight behind the wardrobe, Mac's picture in its place. She was in the Mall, in front of the Palace, smiling, her hair thrown back, T-shirt strained, and the sun was on her. It was the best photograph he had of her, so he'd taken the memory stick to the camera shop the Punjabis ran, in Dalston Lane, where they'd blown it up to thirty inches by twenty. The picture was stuck to the wall – if it was taken down the paper would come with it. He thought it was there in perpetuity and had come to believe that he and Mac were in it for the long term.

The Afghan place, which did a wonderful lamb dish, was their favourite, and they could make the food last for ever, as they gazed into each other's eyes and held hands across the table. It was as if they belonged in the place, and the people who ran it – from Jalalabad – welcomed them with an enthusiasm that lifted the soul. All the time he had sat there he had waited for her to push the door wide and come in, panting, then hang on his neck to whisper apologies and murmur some excuse. She'd have kissed his lips and he'd have kissed hers and . . . He had studied the menu as a break from watching the door – not that he needed to because he knew it by heart. He hadn't ordered food for one, hadn't even ordered a drink. He hadn't believed she wouldn't come.

To the left of the photograph was the door to his room, a flimsy dressing-gown – Mac's – hanging on it. She would have complained loudly, in a jumble of Italian and English, if she had seen the smears on the coverlet, because it was his and her bed when she slipped into his little home. Only one room, only one window overlooking an overgrown back garden, then another row of houses, chimneys and greyness. The rain had fallen more heavily as the evening had gone by and now it was spattering the window panes. They had made love on that bed, sometimes fast, sometimes noisy, sometimes slow and quiet. They had first been on it after their second meeting . . . not long then, maybe twenty minutes, until she'd said she had 'to get back', and had wandered over his threadbare carpet, retrieving the scattered, sodden clothes, and had refused to let him walk her to her front door. It had been the happiest two months in the life of Eddie Deacon . . . He lay on his bed and hated the world.

He'd left the restaurant after three hours because his was the only table with a spare place and two couples were waiting.

The owners had seemed to sympathise, but had made clear that his love life was his concern and their priority was to seat one of the waiting couples. He had shambled out, and for a while he hadn't noticed that the rain was persistent, driving. The misery had eaten into him. Nobody who knew him, who saw him with Mac, could believe that Eddie Deacon had landed a girl like her. Dear old Eddie, 'steady Eddie', one of thousands who drifted along and didn't stand out, who was better than bloody ordinary but who didn't bother to be exceptional, had a girl on his arm who was dramatic, impressive, head-turning . . . and a bloody good shag. He had shuffled home and the rain had dribbled down his face, and he'd been within a hair's breadth of being knocked over crossing a road because hadn't seen the van coming. He hadn't known such love or such unhappiness.

On that bed, her still astride him and him still inside her, his sweat running with hers, her hair in his face, his lips brushing the cherrystone nipples, two evenings ago, they had fixed the rendezvous time and place. Always, in the two months since the park-bench meeting beside the Serpentine, she had been on time for their meetings. There were magazines on the floor, dropped haphazardly or chucked, *Espresso* and *Oggi*, fashion magazines and home-refurbishment magazines, a pile of her textbooks, dictionaries and notepads. He liked it best when she wore the dressing-gown, nothing else, and sat cross-legged on the bed, close to him, and they worked on her English – he liked every damn thing about her. It was the first and only time she had failed to turn up.

He didn't have an address for her, only a sight of a street corner, no mobile number. It hadn't mattered before because she was always where she said she would be . . . He thought a disaster must have struck her, couldn't think of anything else. It hurt Eddie so much that Mac wasn't there . . . and he realised how little he knew of her, how much had been kept from him. Questions deflected. Subjects changed. He could have bloody well wept. She was smiling at him from the photograph, the dressing-gown hanging loose on the hook . . . Damned if he'd lose her.

He stood by the hut. The sun teetered at the top of the treeline, and was in his eyes. It was hard for him to see. Behind the open door of the hut, at his back, he heard crackling radio connections. He had a little Spanish, picked up on three visits here, so if he had strained and concentrated he would have had definitive answers to the two outstanding questions: how many were kicking and how many were not? He stared out over the trees and thought he heard the first sounds of a Huey's engine and the gentle chop of the rotors. When the bird landed and they spilled out he would know for sure how many were kicking and how many were not. He would know, also, whether the advice he had given to the captain was sound or horseshit. He lit another cigarette — he'd worked through the best part of a carton since the team had been lifted on to the plateau and set down in the clearing close to the hut.

His name was called. 'They are coming, Lukas. Two minutes, and they will be down.'

He raised a hand in acknowledgement and ash fell from his cigarette on to his boot.

In the middle of the plateau, a soldier in combat gear took something from his webbing belt, arced an arm back, then tossed whatever it was. When it landed, bright orange smoke burst from it, climbed and was shifted by the light wind, masking the sun. The noise of the helicopter was louder. He heard, behind him, the exodus from the hut and the communications. The captain reached him, took the cigarette from between his fingers, dragged hard on it twice, then replaced it. The captain was Pablo – probably a good man, probably an honest one. He couldn't have said how many of the others, those who had gone into the jungle or manned the communications nets, were good and honest. Too often a call was made, satphone, mobile or landline, or a message sent, and the storm squad found only a 'dry house', which had been used to hold some wretch but from which he had been shifted out. Pablo had gone past him and was yelling orders. Soldiers came off their asses and carried folded stretchers towards the orange smoke. He told himself it meant nothing. It was standard operating procedure.

The Huey came in low, doing a contour run over the canopy.

Pablo stopped, turned, shouted: 'Are you coming forward, Lukas, or staying back?'

He indicated, two hands up, that he was standing his ground. He dropped the cigarette, ground it out under his boot and lit another. He was not in an army so didn't wear a uniform. He had on a heavy wool blue shirt that was buttoned at the cuffs and kept him warm enough against the chill at this time of year and at this height above sea level. His trousers were heavy-duty corduroy, dun-coloured. His boots were not military but of the brown leather used by hikers, and hitched to one shoulder was a rucksack that held his spare socks, underclothes, washbag and the notepad laptop.

The Huey made the approach. Usual for it to do a circle of a touch-down point, give the flier a chance to check the ground, but it came straight in.

If the bird came straight in, and was dropping the last few feet over the dispersed orange smoke, it didn't mean his advice had been wrong. He gave the advice as best he could and sometimes the corks popped and sometimes the bottles stayed in their boxes. His advice, offered to the captain, given what he knew, given the location where the poor bastards were held and the near impossibility of maintaining secrecy, had been to make the strike. The Huey landed heavily on the skids, bounced and settled.

The light hit the bird's camouflage-painted bodywork and he had a good view inside the door, which was slid back. The hatch machine-gunner jumped down and went up to his thighs in the long grass, which made more room for the soldiers with the stretchers to pass them inside. Three were handed up. If, at that moment, it was a disappointment to him that three were needed, he didn't show it. His feelings of disappointment or elation, his thoughts, were not for sharing. They wouldn't be FARC guys, wounded enemy, on the stretchers: they'd have been tipped out. Two of the stretchers were lifted down, the orderlies holding drips high above them, the bearers hurrying as best they could. A doctor in a pristine uniform was between the stretchers and examining the occupants on the move. The wounded would be stabilised, then casevaced: it was the way things were done.

He saw the third stretcher lifted down, no drip. The body-bag rolled on the canvas as it was lowered.

The doctor came past him. 'They were spotted when they were almost on target, but it gave away the critical last thirty seconds. It's what it depends on – success, failure. I think, Lukas, it's neither . . . I hope to save them.'

He didn't look into the faces of the two men, just glanced and saw the long, wispy beards and hair, the blood of bullet wounds on filthy clothing, and the grimaces because they were in shock and the morphine had not yet taken effect. Three men now emerged from the Huey and they were helped down, then led away bent low from the spinning rotors. They looked weak and near to collapse. He did the equation. Intelligence had reported six hostages – a French tourist who was an irresponsible idiot, a Canadian water-purification-plant engineer whose light aircraft had come down three years earlier, a judge who had been kidnapped eighteen months back, two local politicians who had been snatched four and a half years ago, and a missionary who was said to have Peruvian papers. One dead, two wounded, three unharmed was a good return.

Two soldiers were walking wounded. Five bodies were dumped from the hatch; they'd be FARC guys. A Chinook was coming in now. Would have been called up when the 'Contact' report had come in over the communications. A monster with a double rotor system and a full medical team. It was a good return – he'd seen the missionary walking towards him, and had seen him also, politely, shake off a hand that tried to support him. It was all because of the missionary. It was not for the tourist or the engineer or the judge or the local-government people; they could have been forgotten and left to rot. If it had been Special Forces, Americans, on the ground, the message would have been sent out in clear to the FARC that the missionary tag was bogus. The man passed him and there was a murmur, lips barely moving, which might have been two words: 'Thank you.' Probably was. He didn't acknowledge. The captain, Pablo, was not inside the loop and didn't know that the freeing of an American asset was the sole reason for this mission. Lukas, no one else, would have been permitted by the Agency to give the crucial advice on the rescue of their man. He had the reputation . . . but he shunned pride.

There was a colonel on the Chinook. He slapped him on the arm, and bayed, 'Good work, Lukas. We lost a local politico, but he was a left sympathiser, and the Frenchman. We've saved the judge, who has good connections with central government, and God's man, the Canadian and a mayor from this region. The injured will live. Fine work.'

A hand was offered but he kept one of his in a pocket and the other cupped a cigarette end. He did not do courtesies. It was not that he intended rudeness, more that the pleasantries seemed unimportant, and he wouldn't have considered such a refusal might offend. Guarding the cigarette was a greater priority.

But, later, at the ramp of the Chinook, he permitted Pablo to hug him briefly.

It would be an hour's flight to the military base attached to Bogotá's civil airport.

He would be in time to catch the Avianca night flight out of the Aeropuerto Internacional El Dorado for the long haul over the wastes of the Atlantic before the European landfall, then the short commuter ride to his home. The families of the survivors would be at the El Dorado, with jerks from the embassy, flashlights, government ministers and a ratpack of hacks. He would be well clear of them.

He would sleep on the long-haul flight. He always slept well coming off an assignment: win, lose or draw, he'd sleep.

2

The glass-sided box of the public telephone was ahead. The pavement was crowded at that time of the early evening and it slipped in and out of her view but she kept her eye on it, as if it was the Holy Grail.

She had not slept the previous night and had not eaten that day. She had missed an all-day seminar on insolvency, had walked the streets and sat in a park, with Downs Road behind her and the open expanse in front where mothers pushed prams, smoked and gossiped, where kids threw off their hoods and kicked a ball, and where work-gangs – sullen, resentful and bored – cleared dumped litter under supervision. She had watched them all. Had seen the old walk arm in arm or dragged along by a dog on a tight lead and the young drift. She had watched the high windows and balconies of the tower blocks on the west side of the park, and seen wet washing put out on lines to dry and dry washing taken in. The hours of the day had been eaten up. It was about betrayal, a big word, as big as any she knew in its weight.

It had rolled in her mind. *Tradimento*. It had made her – in her bed, unable to sleep – shiver and feel dread, because she knew the reward that waited for those who betrayed their own.

Her hand was tight on her shoulder-bag as she walked down the shallow slope of the street towards the telephone box. It was occupied. Three boys in baggy trousers and oversized sweat tops were crowded inside it: she wondered why they used a public phone, not mobiles – and whether they bought or sold. She looked to see if any others were hovering to use the phone, and thought not. Where she came from, that culture and that society, the word *tradimento* had a taste as bitter as poison. Betrayal was an ultimate sin, was stamping on the face of Christ . . . and she had sat through today on the bench in the park. She had kept her hands tight on the bag's straps and had watched but not absorbed. She had agonised on the implications of betrayal. Her first act of betrayal had been that morning when she had come out of the bathroom, dressed, and had crossed the living room. Vincenzo was lounging in a chair, smoking, a towel draped across his stomach as he turned the pages of a football fanzine about Napoli SSC. She had gone into her bedroom and come out a moment later with the bag that contained the notes she took in her classes. He had asked, without interest, about her day. She had answered, a mutter, that she had a seminar on *insolvenza*. She had needed to carry the work bag if she was to support the lie that she was attending her classes. She had lied to her brother and started the process of betrayal. Vincenzo had grinned – the idea of insolvency amused him. He, his father and mother, his brothers, his sister were worth hundreds of millions of euros, would never know insolvency . . . She had sat on the bench and watched, her stomach had growled, and she had steeled herself.

Was there something else she could do to reflect her feelings? Like what? Join a religious order and say prayers? Become involved with a charity, and help the mentally handicapped, alcoholics or HIV sufferers? Sign up for a campaigning political group and attempt to bulldoze change through a ballot box? Walk out, lose herself, try to forget what had been a part of her life? As alternatives, they had all – during the night – seemed inadequate and degrading to the memory of her best friend. Immacolata had found the strength to go to the telephone box.

When the self-doubt was worst she would stare out over the trees and up into the clouds, feel the rain on her skin and take herself back to those hours. Not many of them. She had been able to look at her watch and think that twenty-four hours earlier she had been hurrying along the verge of via Saviano, or that it was the moment her heel had snapped, or that she was hopping, hobbling, along a path between the family chapels, or that she was in the centre of the cemetery at Nola, staring across white gravestones to a far wall where the family slots were. She had recalled the hands taking the bundle and carrying it up the ladders. Clearest were the images of her clothing being ripped, her shin kicked, and the denunciation of her family's part in the death of her friend.

Had she known of the trade in the disposal of toxic waste? Of course she had.

Had she known of the profits to be made from shipping contaminated rubbish from factories in the north to dumping grounds in the fields and orchards of the south? Of course she had.

Had it ever intruded into her thoughts that her family would fear responsibility for the killing of her friend? Never . . . She remembered the flowers, bent, worthless. What she remembered best gave her the strength to commit the act: *tradimento*.

She stood by the telephone box. She eyed the boys. Had she been at home, on her own streets, and *ragazzi* had used a telephone she was waiting for, she would have been recognised, the call terminated, the booth offered, and respect would have been shown to her. Maybe, even, one of the kids – had she been at home – would have wiped the receiver on his T-shirt to leave it clean for her. Two of the boys stared at her, challenging. Here, on Kingsland Road, in Dalston against the border of Hackney, the boys with hoods on their heads, Nikes and new tracksuits ruled and did not expect to be stared out. She thought they were shit. One, the biggest, seemed to make a decision about her. He didn't pull a weapon, but ended the call and dropped the receiver, letting it dangle on its cable, then slouched out, his shoulder brushing hers. It was probably the nearest he had come to a moment of submission. She heard, behind her, another spit at the paving-stones.

She lifted the receiver. She knew the number. Anyone in her family knew the number, and the occupant of the desk on which the call would ring out. She had not thought of the young man. Perhaps he, too, was betrayed. He was ignored, didn't matter to her, as she stood in the glass-sided box. The headlights of cars, buses and vans glistened on the street, the lamps above her were bright and threw an orange wash over the windows of shops, banks, building societies and betting shops – all closed now. The young man didn't matter to her and had no place in the fierce heat of the cemetery at Nola. She put a Visa card into the slot and the display panel responded.

She dialled. She would not have needed to know the number. Neither would any of her family have 'needed' to know it. Knowledge of the number was power. Having it showed the tentacle reach of the clan. The direct line would have been listed only on the most confidential sheets and would have circulated only among a chosen, trusted few. Knowing it was a demonstration of the power of the clan to which she was integral. She took a deep breath, allowed it to whistle shrill from her lips.

The call was answered. She thought she had interrupted a meeting in the office on the upper floor of the Palace of Justice and that a subordinate had picked it up. She named the prosecutor. She was told he was unavailable. Who wished to speak to the *dottore*?

The moment of betrayal came fast, stampeded her. For a moment she couldn't speak. Then she straightened her back and jutted her chin. 'I think he'll find time to speak with me. Tell him I'm Immacolata Borelli . . .'

He walked into the classroom. A chorus of voices, in scattered accents, greeted him. For Eddie Deacon it had been a bad day and now it was evening. The chance of improvement was minimal. The language courses often took place after working hours and his foreign students flocked in when their daytime employment, legitimate or not, had finished.

It had been a long-standing promise, made at least a month ago, that he would go in the morning by train from London to Chippenham. His father had collected him at the station, and they'd had a desultory conversation in the car about the state of the railways, the weather, the roads, his father's pension, and just as they had exhausted all common subject matter, they'd reached the family home.

He'd had to go. He couldn't have brought himself to call and tell them he had a problem and couldn't make it. He would have heard undisguised disappointment, in whichever of them he had spoken to, and he'd known that for the last two days his mum would have been planning lunch: she worked, front-desk receptionist, at the offices of a local building contractor and would have told everyone there that she was taking the day off because her lad was coming down from London. They'd be waiting the next morning for a bulletin on how it had gone and how he was progressing, and from the way she told it, most would reckon he was a college lecturer and something of a highflier, not a language teacher who helped a cocktail of youngsters to speak basic English, and wasn't concerned with chasing 'prospects'. His father had taken early retirement on his fiftieth birthday, and pottered round the house fixing things that didn't need fixing. Eddie Deacon had damn near nothing that connected with the lives of Arthur and Betty, his parents. What he couldn't deny was the love they had for him. A bit humbling, actually. Like having a pillow shoved over his face that half suffocated him. There was love and there was expectation for his future. After lunch, if he was lucky, he'd escape for an hour, put on the old pair of boots that were kept on the shelf in the pristine garage, and walk by the river, maybe see a kingfisher in flight, lean on a field gate and have a herd of heifers nuzzle his sleeve. Then a quick tea, a pointed look at his watch and talk about the train he could catch.

He'd been up early. He had walked across from Dalston into Hackney and had turned up at the college where she was enrolled on the accountancy/book-keeping course. He'd asked for her at the administration office. 'Something urgent,' he'd said, 'and I need to see Miss Immacolata Borelli. She's a student on the B4 course. It really is important . . .' They knew who he was because he was there three or four evenings or lunchtimes a week to meet her. Whenever she finished a class and he didn't have one, he was there. A shrug . . . She hadn't been in. Had she called in sick? She had not, just hadn't turned up. Another shrug . . . He couldn't go soft, begging and pleading, and ask for a sight of her home address. Couldn't, because it would have shown up the biggest hole in their relationship – no address and no phone number. Then, an escape route – a walk in the fields, where the heifers were grazing, and down to the river.

The former soldier, from a bungalow down the lane, had been on the bank. Eddie Deacon was a good listener and didn't reckon to wipe his own views over another's and compete in conversation. He didn't know the guy – Dean – well, but his mother had told him grisly stories. Not much older than Eddie, but there was a tattoo of a paratroop's wings, and Dean had been Special Forces. Now he did contract work in Iraq and was gone for four months at a time. Listening seemed important and he noted that by staying quiet and lending an ear, the guy's hands stopped shaking, the fingers didn't clasp and unclasp, and the voice lost its breathiness. He didn't hurry him or glance at his watch, and learned a bit about the airport road, procedures to counter vehicle ambush and command wires, things that had nothing to do with the river, the flight over the water of the kingfisher – twice – or the patrol of a heron. When it was done, the guy had gripped his fist – as if the listening had been important. At home, he apologised to his parents for having been away so long and told them where he'd been and why he'd stayed out. He'd sensed then that the world of a psychologically troubled ex-soldier was a route march away from that of his mum and dad, and his own.

He'd headed for Paddington and the main-line train, a later service than intended.

Not that Eddie Deacon knew too much about the workings of the KGB, old time, or the intelligence services, present time, but he liked to joke that his mum, Betty, would have had an interrogator's job – no messing – if she ever chose to turn up and offer herself. It was a routine area. 'Relationships'. The village seemed to him a rabbits' breeding warren. Everyone they knew had children who were shagging and producing, some in marriage and others not. In everyone else's house there were framed photographs of babies with red-eye. So, was there a girlfriend? Had he met anyone? Was there anyone important in . . . ? As if he had to shove his thumb in a fractured dike, he'd done what he could to cut off the questioning. Stupid, but it was what he had done. Eddie had opened his wallet and taken out a photograph – Mac smiling, close up. He had seen his father's jaw drop and his mother had purred in appreciation. Showed, really, what they thought of him . . . they could hardly comprehend that the layabout, the tosser, their only child, had a photograph of such an attractive, star-quality girl in his wallet.

To get to the river, he'd had to make a promise. Yes, next time he came down he was definitely going to bring her with him. Guaranteed, safe as a supermarket 'special offer'. He'd told them a bit, not much. She was Italian, she was clever, she was going to be an accountant. Didn't tell them he'd sat in an Afghan restaurant for three hours the previous evening with an empty place laughing at him across the table, that she'd stood him up. Did tell them that she was friendly, warm and made him laugh. Didn't tell them that she had skipped classes that morning and hadn't phoned in with an explanation . . . Didn't tell them she hadn't given him her home address or a contact number. Didn't tell them he'd never walked her home. Did tell them, with his eyes, his face, and with the way he held the photo, that she was totally important to him. The sight of the girl, Mac, had silenced them, and he'd escaped to his river walk. Said it out loud, 'Mac, for heaven's sake, where the hell are you? Mac, where have you gone? What are you doing?' Behind him, in the kitchen, the dishwasher would be churning, Arthur and Betty would be muttering about a girl coming at last into their boy's life. All the time, down by the river, listening and offering a shoulder, she wasn't out of his mind. He'd thanked his mum for lunch, promised again that he would bring Mac next time he came down, thanked his dad for the lift to Chippenham, and come back to London.

Hadn't known what to do . . . and had gone to work. She throbbed in his mind.

'Good evening, everybody.'

It came back at him, surf rolling on shingle. 'Good evening, Mr Deacon.'

'I hope everybody's had a very good day.'

'Thank you, Mr Deacon.'

He'd had a hideous day of hurt, wounds and anguish. No
Mac and didn't know where to find her. He was important
to her, wasn't he? Definitely he was, had to be. He knew it
because she'd told him so . . . had told him when they were
in bed. 'Right, settle down. We're going to continue this
evening with our Agatha Christie story, and we're going to
pick up on page forty-nine. Let's get there.' When they were
in bed, naked, ecstasy shared, she'd told him how important
he was to her. She wouldn't lie, would she?

It had been enough to bring Mario Castrolami in his car
through red stop lights, then to get him as close to running
along poorly lit corridors as he knew how.

Castrolami steadied himself, his hands clamped on the back
of a chair. The fog of smoke made his eyes water and irritated
his throat. Four men and two women in the prosecutor's office
had cigarettes alive. The desk and the mahogany table in the
window were scattered with open files. The prosecutor headed
the section in the Palace of Justice that attempted to combat
the power, influence and control of the city's Camorra clans.
With him were his deputy, who had responsibility for the
inner-city clans of Naples, his *carabinieri* liaison officer, who
worked from the palace, his secretary and the archivist he
most trusted. Castrolami knew them all, knew also that each
man and woman in the room could be trusted implicitly. The
liaison officer, Castrolami had heard, personally swept that
office each morning for electronic devices. And a radio played
– tuned to a rock programme on a commercial channel. The
screen on the prosecutor's desk showed the soft-focus close-
up image of a young woman whose features he knew, whose
history he had studied, whose importance he recognised and
whom he had never met.

The secretary handed him coffee, a thimble cup. Castrolami hitched off his jacket, the pistol in his waist holster bouncing on his hip, and loosened his tie. He would have described the prosecutor as neat, like a manicured garden; his shirt was freshly laundered and his shave that morning had been close enough to hold the stubble at bay. A man who cared for himself. The deputy, tall and angular, was also tidy for a man now into the thirteenth hour of his day. The liaison officer was not in uniform but wore a well-cut jacket of expensive Scottish material. The women, too, did not show the day's pressures, had probably changed in mid-afternoon . . . There was no fragrance about Castrolami.

A tiny cassette was loaded into a Dictaphone and a button depressed. He realised the machine had been activated late, after the call had been taken. '. . . him, I'm Immacolata Borelli . . . Do not interrupt me, Dottore . . . I am calling you from London, but I wish to return to Italy. It is my intention to collaborate . . . By saying that to you on the telephone, I put at risk my life . . . More important, I put at risk the possibilities of a successful prosecution of my family . . . I require immunity, and an officer who is trusted by yourself should meet me in the Hackney Downs park, in east London, and I will come to a bench at nine in the morning, London time, and will wait for one hour. He should bring with him a warrant for the arrest and extradition of my brother Vincenzo. Castrolami is an officer of the ROS whom my father respected. You should send him. You hold my life, Dottore. You hold also the prospect of the conviction of my family, the Borelli clan . . . Good night, Dottore.'

There was a click, then silence.

He looked at the photograph on the screen. Castrolami saw the haughtiness that verged on arrogance, that in the surveillance still she wore 'ordinary' clothes, and small, 'ordinary' trinkets, no lipstick or other makeup and her hair was tousled. He did not know when this photograph had been obtained, whether she had been on her way to terrify a shopkeeper who was late in filling the little envelope with twenty or twenty-five per cent of his takings, or to a meeting with the general manager of a cement-production company to tell him that her price should be accepted or none of his mixer fleet would reach the road again . . . The voice on the phone had made a play of being decisive and in control. He thought Immacolata Borelli had failed, was in bits, near to physical and mental collapse.

'What is she worth?' the deputy prosecutor asked.

Castrolami assumed he knew the response he would get, but needed confirmation of the obvious, and gave it him. His breathing had steadied and he lit his own cigarette from a heavyweight Marlboro lighter an American had given him. With the flame extinguished, he said, 'Only a blood member of a family has a near to complete knowledge of its affairs.'

'With her help, what might we achieve?' the prosecutor queried.

He thought the prosecutor the best and most dedicated under whom he had worked in Naples. The man possessed an encyclopedic knowledge of the city's clan structure and the principal players. He imagined that the call had come during a meeting, when the day was winding down and perhaps a whisky bottle had been produced, and that it had exploded among them, a shellburst, fazing them. He thought he understood. 'We could close down the clan. The whole mass of them would go into the net.'

The liaison officer ground out his cigarette, scratched the bald crown of his head, murmured, 'She telephoned from London. What happened there for her to attack her family with such venom? I find none of it credible.'

Castrolami told them of the young man who had come to his office late the previous evening, the barbarity of a street fight in a cemetery. His words painted a picture of a family's controlled grief melded with aggression, and their courage. He said, 'She could have reacted in two ways. She might have condemned that family to death for the insult, or crumpled under a burden of self-disgust. It's happened before but not often. They feel overwhelming shame . . . Can you get the warrant in the time?'

He was told that the paperwork would be ready in an hour, that it had been on file, then given a flight number and a departure time. He preached the need for secrecy, which was accepted. He was told who would meet his flight in London, but the individual would be outside the loop of confidences. In that hour he could have gone back to his office in the barracks on the piazza Dante and packed a travel bag – spare shirt, singlet, socks and toilet bag – but he did not. He slumped into a chair, which squealed under the impact of his hundred-plus kilos. He wondered how she would be and whether she would greet him as an ally or an enemy. Then he swept an armful of files from the table and started to gut them, learning the latest intelligence, sparse and hearsay, on a clan now stalked by treachery, and he was smiling. He tried to bring life, animation, to the typescripts, flesh and blood to the photographs. He thought he walked with them.

Pasquale Borelli went to the recreation hall. He was fifty-five, slight and bald, with a prominent nose and a scarred head. He was allowed one hour in the hall per day under the terms of the *pena dura*. He was a strict-regime prisoner, under the terms of the Article 41 *bis* legislation, had no access to a mobile telephone, few and heavily supervised visits, little time in the company of fellow inmates. He was held in the maximum-security wing of the gaol at Novara in the north; the city was near Turin and Milan, astride the route from

Genoa into Switzerland. It was a long way from his home in Naples, hundreds of kilometres, and the authorities had intended that his incarceration there would sever his links with the clan he had dominated for two decades. Their intention was unfulfilled – a prison officer carried out messages written on cigarette papers. He still controlled an empire that was worth, perhaps, a half-billion euros. He awaited trial, and the chance of him enjoying freedom again was small, but he was optimistic that the evidence and testimony lodged against him could be challenged. He had to believe that no further denunciations would cloud his horizon. For an hour he would play pool in the hall; the table, of course, would be occupied when the officer unlocked the last barred gate, but a prisoner would immediately give up his place for Pasquale Borelli. In his cell he had a photograph of his daughter – not his wife. He loved her deeply, his *principessa*.

Gabriella Borelli was six years younger than her husband. Since his arrest, when he had been dragged out of the underground bunker by the ROS bastards, she had been undisputed in her leadership of the clan. They had been married for thirty-two years, since she, at seventeen, was little more than a child, but decisions inside the core of the clan had always been taken after her advice had been heard. Now she was a *latitanta*, and her continued liberty depended on her moving from safe-house to safe-house, a network of covert addresses. As a fugitive from justice, she was unable to utilise publicly the vast wealth the family had accumulated. Since her husband had been taken and the flight of her eldest son, she had won respect from other clan leaders. It had come from her clear-headed ability to strike deals, open up new markets and act with cold ruthlessness when such was required. She was feared. She was a small woman, petite, dark-haired, and well kept for her forty-nine years, but she wasn't out to look for a new dress, as she would have liked, but to attend a meeting. She was an anonymous figure in the narrow streets, walking briskly and carrying an old shopping bag. She missed having the strengths and certainties of her eldest son close to her, but rarely thought of her daughter.

Vincenzo was in his thirty-second year, the eldest, and he was eating a pizza in a trattoria off Hackney's Mare Street. He always had the Margherita, with mozzarella, tomato and basil – the colours, white, red and green, were those of his country's flag. He was with friends, young men from the fringe of the clan, and together they dreamed of a day when they could return to the city and eat the best pizza from the via Duomo, the via Forcella or the via Ettore Bellini. He would go back. He would take authority from his mother. He would not be able to drive a Ferrari, wear Armani suits or have a penthouse apartment overlooking the Golfo di Napoli, but he would have power, and he would be careful not to leave a trail from himself to a killing hand-gun. Vincenzo faced four charges of murder if he was located and arrested, so it was important for him to maintain his unseen existence in London, but he was concerned that if he stayed away too long the fear in which he was held in Forcella, and the respect, would diminish. He barely noticed his sister, accepted the need for a member of the family to have a good knowledge of financial procedures and structures, but he expected her to clean the apartment they shared and to look after his laundry. She wasn't important to him.

Nobody loved Giovanni, he knew that. He was twenty-three. That evening he was on a girl's family bed. Her father and mother were in the next room and had the television on loud. He fucked the girl – a virgin until he had penetrated her the previous week – on her parents' bed because it was bigger and more comfortable than hers. They would not complain, and they would not attempt to throw him out of their home. He was Giovanni Borelli, the son of Pasquale and Gabriella Borelli. In the Forcella district, and in part of Sanità, his name gave him unquestioned power. He would not pay the girl under him, who was giving him as good a ride as he was used to. Neither would he pay for the meal he would have afterwards. He paid for nothing. The only man who had ever raised a fist to Giovanni was his elder brother, who had beaten him, split his lip and cut his eyebrow – the sister of a friend had accused Giovanni of putting his hand up her skirt. His father had not protected him from Vincenzo; neither had his mother. Now he grunted and cried out as the orgasm came, louder than was natural for him, but he knew the sound would carry into the living room and would not be drowned by the television. Good that they should know their daughter was a good ride. He was responsible for the collection of dues in the area north of corso Umberto, south of the via Foria, and between the via Duomo and the corso Giuseppe Garibaldi. The only excitement came when a smart-arse shite would plead poor business, inability to pay, and be beaten – as his brother had beaten him. He thought his sister, Immacolata, an arrogant bitch, and she had no time for him.

In his bedroom, Silvio Borelli read a comic and listened to music on his iPod. He was seventeen, the youngest of the tribe. He had been told by his grandmother, never one to mince words, the circumstances of his conception. Eighteen years ago, in 1991, his mother had been sneeringly informed that his father flaunted an *amante*, had been seen with her in an hotel on the sea front, the via Francesco Caracciolo. When Pasquale Borelli had next come home she had punched his head, scratched his cheeks, kicked him in the stomach and kneed him in the groin. He had suffered a tempest of abuse. He had crawled to Gabriella Borelli and pleaded for her forgiveness, promising abjectly that such behaviour would never be repeated. They had made up, her on top of him, calling the shots, at her speed and for her gratification. The result had been Silvio. He was a sickly child from birth, and was doted on by his mother, but he loved his sister. He told her everything. Giovanni sniped that he wouldn't wipe his arse without asking Immacolata's permission. He lived with his grandparents, above the via Forcella, and sensed their contempt for him because he was not blessed with the family's hardness. He wanted little more from life than to speed in narrow alleyways on his scooter, and to mess with old schoolmates – and almost resented that his name denied him friendships. He knew that some spoke of him as a cretin, but a reputation for stupidity brought its rewards, and the clan used him to ride round the district and drop off narcotics, cash, messages and firearms. He was unsettled. Driving back from Nola the previous afternoon, he had been bewildered by the transformation in his sister's mood – and her shoe was broken, her clothing ripped and her knee scraped raw. She had been near to tears. And she was the best person he knew, the most important in his life.

The parents of Pasquale, the grandparents of Vincenzo, Immacolata, Giuseppe and Silvio, were Carmine and Anna Borelli. They were both eighty-seven, though she had been born four months after him. They had founded the clan, given it teeth and muscle, then passed its control to their son. They lived now in via Forcella, and as she sewed a collar back on to a shirt, he snored quietly in his chair and . . .

The television screen in the prosecutor's office was blank, the photograph killed. The files on the clan family were back in the secure area of the archive. The office was darkened. He had gone home, as had his deputy, the liaison officer

and the women who ran his life; they were as dedicated as
he was to the extermination of the Camorra culture.

A car's tyres had screamed as it had headed for
Capodichino. The liaison officer drove Castrolami. No sirens
and no blue lights, but speed on the back-streets. They had
swept into the airport and the Alfa had rocked at the sudden
braking outside Departures. Then he was out and on the
forecourt. He slid the pancake holster off his belt, the loaded
pistol in it, and left them on the seat. No backward glance,
no wave, and he heard the liaison officer power away. He
scurried through the doors to Check-in. An officer of Mario
Castrolami's seniority could have demanded, and received,
preferential treatment at the airport – a ticket already
processed, a boarding card presented to him, a lounge to
wait in until the rest of the passengers had been herded to
their seats, a drink, a canapé and an automatic upgrade –
but such treatment would have been noticed. He went past
the site of the death – unmourned – from heart failure of
Salvo Lucania, known to law enforcement in the States as
'Lucky Luciano'. He thought that the pain of the coronary
was a fitting end for that man. He always noted the place
where that boss had collapsed.

He went to the communal lounge and had barely flopped
into a seat before the flight was called. He walked to the
aircraft, the last flight of the day to London Gatwick, in a
swell of tourists. Voices played across his face and behind
his head. He spoke quite reasonable English, and was able
to distinguish appraisals of the ruins at Pompeii and Ercolano,
judgements on the Capella Sansevero compared with the
Pio Monte della Misericordia, the merits of the Castel dell'Ovo
and the Castel Nuovo. He was happy to be among tourists.
He accepted that an army of watchers, foot-soldiers,
maintained a sophisticated web of surveillance over the city
and its suburbs. Every district would have entrances watched

by men and boys, and myriad mobile phones would report which policeman moved and the direction of his journey. The camera systems of the police and the *carabinieri* were sophisticated but could not compete with those of the clans. It would be a disaster if it were known that Mario Castrolami had caught the last flight of the night to Britain: warnings would have been issued, coded messages sent, and it would have been known in London before the Boeing's undercarriage had dropped that a Camorra hunter was travelling.

He eased into a seat. The watchers were everywhere – the policeman on the forecourt, the porters on the concourse, the check-in staff, the baggage-handlers, the cabin crew. He put his face into the in-flight magazine, but tapped his jacket to reassure himself – for the fourth or fifth time – that the envelope with the warrant folded inside it was still there. He sensed the admiration of the tourists for his city, and their ignorance: they knew nothing. The watches were still on their wrists, the wallets and purses in their coats and handbags, and Naples was wonderful. He thought that an ignorant man or woman was blessed. He could count on the fingers of his two hands all the men and women in the city whom he believed had no price.

Sicily was bad for corruption inside the forces of law and order, money changing hands in return for intelligence and warnings. In Calabria, little was planned that did not reach the ears and eyes of the criminal tribes. From his own city, Castrolami could not have put twenty men – police, Palace of Justice and *carabinieri* – in a line and sworn on oath that he harboured no suspicion against them. The fear of corruption and the suspicion it engendered against colleagues should be ranked as one of the greatest successes of the Camorra. He had not phoned his wife to tell her that he would be away, had had no need to: she had long ago left for Milan, taken the children, gone back to her mother. She had sworn that Naples was a *cloaca* and that she and they would never return to that sewer. There was, of course, another woman, for mutual convenience, and he hadn't phoned her either . . . As the aircraft thrust up the runway and lifted, he replayed in his mind what that voice had said.

I put at risk my life.

He would not dispute that. She might, the bitch, have changed her mind by morning – they did, often enough. But he could recall each word of that young officer from Nola and believed she would be there. He could sleep wherever he found himself so he threw back the seat, ignoring the protest from behind, loosened his trouser belt, and saw, in a dreamer's kaleidoscope, the features of Immacolata Borelli. He heard himself say, in a sort of wonderment, 'I don't intend to talk you out of this, but have you any idea at all of where this will lead you, what is at stake?' Not just wonderment: astonishment. It wasn't the face of a *camorrista*, it was a good face, with smooth skin, not a cheap whore's and pocked. Or did he delude himself?

They were bored but polite. It was as plain as a pikestaff to Eddie Deacon that Agatha Christie needed high-profile selling in Mogadishu or Lagos, Vilnius or Bratislava – anywhere they came from. Agatha Christie was not holding them.

But he ground a nail into his palm and kept going. He was talking about the author's sentence construction. All the language schools did Agatha Christie; she was supposed to be the route towards decent spoken English.

Maybe, he wondered, Agatha Christie was taking the blame for his own inadequacy. He was droning. He had as much interest in who was the murderer as they did. His students wanted to be able to do the business with a gang-master, a bureaucrat at the Job Centre, the warden of a hostel, while the brightest needed to be able to communicate in a good-quality three-star hotel. What they also needed, and somebody was paying for, was a teacher with enthusiasm who could concentrate on a text. It was as though he was on auto-pilot. He could hear his voice, monotonous and flat.

The straw he clung to was that his Mac would be back at his place. She had an outer door key and a Yale to his room. It was only a straw, a pretty thin one, but it was possible that she'd be there. They all liked her at the house – couldn't believe she was real. A guy who pushed paper for H M Revenue and Customs, another who waited at tables in a club on Pall Mall, the one who sold train tickets for Great Western, and the PhD student from Goldsmiths couldn't believe she was real because once a week she made pasta with a sauce to die for.

They would all have known when he and Mac were on the bed in his room, must have heard, through those walls and down those narrow stairs, enough noise . . . Then she'd cook. She always brought plastic bags of food, and would never accept money – it was the only time she splashed out and showed she was flush. When they were out, as they should have been in the Afghan place, they shared. It had been laid down between them at the start . . .

He ached for her . . .

He didn't care about Miss Marple, or Poirot, didn't give a damn who'd done it. He wouldn't wait for a bus: he'd run all the way back to the little house and pound up the stairs and burst through the door and hope, *hope*, she was there . . . his straw. He hadn't made the bed that morning, hadn't straightened the coverlet. Seemed to see it still in chaos. He said, 'I apologise to you all. I'm not myself today. I hope it's not the flu. Thank you for your attention, and I'll see you all next week.'

As he gathered together his dog-eared lecture notes, they

chimed, 'Thank you, Mr Deacon. A very good evening to you.'

He fled. Hit the pavement, at full stride, and tears blistered his cheeks.

She liked Salvo – always used the diminutive, not Salvatore, and never called him by his street name, 'Il Pistole' – more than any of her own children, and had since the day he had been introduced into the heart of the clan three years earlier.

When she reached the bar, she went inside and past the counter, the tables, and into the inner room. He was already there, and immediately stood up. Giovanni was at the table but did not get to his feet. She could accept her eldest, Vincenzo, because he possessed the dynamism of his father, and could feel affection for the youngest, Silvio, because he was helpless, devoid of authority and ambition. She had never considered her daughter of equal importance to the boys. She disliked Giovanni for his painful and prolonged birth, and for his conceit and exploitation of the family name. If he had not been of her blood and had behaved with such arrogance in her presence he would now, like as not, be dead. Dead at the hand of Salvo, Il Pistole. It gave Gabriella Borelli some slight pleasure to know that her middle son, Giovanni, not only loathed Salvo but also feared him.

And Giovanni had cause to fear Salvo.

When she had come into the outer area of the bar, the staff would have begun to prepare coffee for her, a variety that was gentler on her throat than the small, bitter measures the men swore by.

She thought Salvo was similar to a ferocious dog that ran wild and free at night inside the fence of a scrap-metal yard and showed obedience to none but his acknowledged master. Her husband had recruited Salvo and advanced him, had been that master, but on his arrest the young man's loyalty had turned to her. She believed his devotion to be as honest as that of any slobbering Rottweiler or German Shepherd.

At a light knock on the door, Salvo was up again. He opened it, took the cup and saucer and closed it. He put the coffee in front of her. Indeed, Giovanni had cause to fear Salvo. The young man, recruited and advanced by her husband and now only twenty-four, was a killer. He could kill with a pistol but, if circumstances warranted, he could kill more artistically. He was best known for the pistol. In the Forcella and Sanità districts, the kids had photographs of the Beretta P38 on their mobile-phone screens, and images of the weapon's owner. As the ultimate enforcer of the Borelli clan Salvo had accumulated enemies. Vendetta blood feuds were no longer practised in Naples, but there were enough stones in the cemeteries around that quarter of the city for many to long for the day when he was a corpse in a crimson pool, or at least looking at a maximum-security cell's bars.

She sipped her coffee, and her thinly applied lipstick left a pale smear on the cup's rim.

But hers was a city of betrayals. Gabriella Borelli did not trust readily, so she had brought the son she disliked to the meeting. There should always be a witness. She would never place her faith entirely in one man. She could smell the sweat of sex on her son, seeping through his shirt and off his chest; he didn't even have the respect for her that would have made him shower afterwards. He flaunted the smell, and she wondered which teenage whore had opened her legs for him. Since Pasquale had been flown north to Novara, she had not taken a man into her bed – had not, but wished she had when she smelt the sweat.

They talked. She controlled a huge financial empire now. It involved property in the city, in other parts of Italy, the holiday resorts of the Balearics and the Canaries, the South of France and on the coast east and west of Spanish Málaga.

It covered import and export of goods through the Naples docks and a dozen ports near and far from Italy. Gabriella Borelli, Giovanni and Salvatore could have talked of legal and illegal trading and mentioned millions of euros. They did not. They talked instead of the merits of a power supply. Which was better? Should a two-stroke petrol engine be preferred to one driven by mains electricity but needing a cable plugged into a wall socket? It was all a matter of the time available, the location and whether the power was within easy reach. They considered the problem of a cold petrol engine, and how many pulls there would be on the starter cord – and what if it flooded? Much of the Borelli clan's business utilised laundered cash and that could be done in the back rooms of a major bank – local, American, German or British – but other matters needed close attention in the rear room of a back-street bar in the depths of Forcella. It was the place to decide between electrical power or a two-stroke engine. Salvatore would not have been consulted on commerce or investments. It was the matter of enforcement that necessitated his presence.

Gabriella Borelli liked Salvo, but was wary of him. In the world of Forcella, and the clans that ran so much of the city and its population, enforcement was critical. Respect must always be secured; lack of respect must be answered. To ignore disrespect showed weakness. To show weakness, even in a trivial matter, was fatal for a clan leader. A moment of perceived weakness was enough to alert circling rivals. A position of power must be reinforced with decisive action. That was Salvatore's role. Most often the P38 was used for quick, clean intervention, but reputation required innovation. That evening the discussion was on power supplied by petrol or by electric cable.

The decision taken, with Giovanni as a witness, herself sanctioning it, Gabriella Borelli left the bar.

Because she had chosen her way of life, she never complained about it, not even in her thoughts. Her husband would be in gaol for the rest of his life, and her eldest son was a fugitive; her middle son was a vain bastard, and her youngest son was a useless idiot. Her daughter was intelligent but had neither her mother's commitment to the clan nor the determination to succeed. Gabriella was more than twice Salvo's age, and he had no future beyond a quick death from a gunshot, or arrest and a long sentence that was slow death. On the street, alone, hugging shadows, both hands gripping the strap of her shoulder-bag, she thought of the arms of the man who killed at her demand, their thin, hairless beauty, his light, narrow fingers, his waist, flat under the T-shirt, and the jeans that bulged when he stood to greet her, to collect her coffee or to escort her from the bar. It was unthinkable. She flushed and . . . returned to the image of her daughter. A scooter swept past her, its fumes flagged into her face, and the picture was lost.

Eddie had studied the Victorian poets, the Lakes people, and Byron, at the small, unfashionable university in the Thames Valley. If he'd managed the entry to a better university or worked harder where he'd ended up, he would have been qualified to teach those poets, as eventual head of department at a sixth-form college. He hadn't, so he taught basic English to foreigners, and his high literature was from Agatha Christie.

There was no poetry in his pain. Nothing noble, romantic, or edifying about it. The pain hurt bloody bad, and left an emptiness he couldn't fill. The hole in his life gaped.

She hadn't been there. He had gone through the front door, brushed aside the taxman in the hallway, met the man from the ticket desk halfway up the stairs and reached his own door, then fumbled so badly that he couldn't insert the key. He had started to kick it when the PhD fellow did the honours with the lock. He had snapped the light on, heeled the door shut hard enough for it to slam and had seen the bed, empty – unmade.

What to do?

Too much pain. Yearning for his Mac, not daring to believe she had just walked out on him.

Music was playing downstairs, soul stuff, as if the others had caught his mood and sought to offer solace. He had said it to himself so many times, but he had never felt so bad before. Girls? Yes. Before? Yes. Village girls, university girls and language-school girls? Yes. Kissing? Yes. Groping? Sometimes. Shagging? Not often. Really caring? Not even with the hygiene inspector. It had never really mattered whether he was hooked into a girl or not. He was cold, he was lonely – he was so bloody unhappy. Hadn't eaten and hadn't slept much the night before. He asked the question aloud: 'So, what to do?'

He could see her magazines on the floor, her dressing-gown hanging limp from the hook on the door. The scent of her was still in the room. He could have leaned over, buried his face in the sheets and she would have been there, the sweet smell of her. He did not. He stared at the wall, found her picture. Sat taller and straighter. He told himself, 'Don't know what happened, don't know why it happened – whatever. Going to find out. Going to go to work in the morning, hack the day, and track it down, the problem of Mac, in the evening. Promise? Yes, bloody promise.'

He'd thought he wouldn't go downstairs and face them. Wrong. He went down and put his head round the door of the communal living room. Eyes looked at him, then evaded him, as if he had the plague. They wouldn't have known how to react to his unhappiness. The TV was on, bloody football . . . Yes, they all loved her, as if she was Wendy and they were Peter Pan's kids – and she cooked wonderful pasta . . .

Eddie Deacon forced a smile. His voice quavered but he got through it: 'It's been a grim day, double-whammy awful. I don't know where she is, don't know anything. Tomorrow I'll find out. Right now I'm going out for a drink or three.'

They all went. They had their arms round his shoulders, in the rain, not a coat among them, and headed for the Talbot, the public bar, as if everything was all right. He'd know tomorrow evening if he'd kept the promise he'd made to himself.

She didn't sleep. She was in her room with the light off so there wouldn't be a strip showing under the door when the gang came back and she wouldn't be called to get up and make coffee or pour beer.

Immacolata knew most of the stories of betrayal in the folklore of her city, although her mother, father and brothers would not: she had gone to a school that had taught her more than how to write a police statement in an interview room. She had been educated. She also knew what happened to the men, yesterday, today or tomorrow, who betrayed their own . . . She didn't know what they did to the women. Her mind raced, flicked through a score of images, and glimpsed the nightmare sight of what might happen to a woman before it was superseded. She was in the crowd, at the back, and the *polizia* were unwinding the roll of crime-scene tape. She was on tiptoe and had just seen the blood and the white underwear, the tanned thighs, maybe black hair, and the blanket was cast to cover . . . Her mind had gone on.

She told herself that only one person would have understood what she had done in the public phone box on the Kingsland Road. That person was dead. Marianna Rossetti would have understood. But her friend was immured behind the concrete hatch with the marble facing, which might now have been sealed with grouting. She lay still and breathed quietly. She had heard her father speak of Castrolami, the investigator from the Raggruppamento Operativo Speciale, and she imagined a man of dignity, stature and bearing. She thought of how he would welcome her, show gratitude for the sacrifice she intended to make and talk to her of the nobility of what she did . . . He seemed handsome and . . . But she didn't sleep.

She was in that street again – in the via Foria, or the via Cesare Rosaroli, or the via Carbonara – and the pain bit into her toes as she struggled for greater height to see better the woman on the pavement, who had been accused of betrayal, and know what had been done to her. Always, shoulders and heads impeded her view.

The hours went slowly. They came in. They drank, talked, played cards, watched TV, then Vincenzo was alone. She thought he paused outside her door and listened. If she had moved in her bed he would have come in and talked to her – maybe he had some problem with money, foreign-exchange regulations, the opening of a new account or a transfer – so she lay still. After half a minute she heard him clear his throat and go to his room.

Her mind was made up, the seed sown in the cemetery at Nola.

He had stomach cramps. He walked down the long pier inside Arrivals at Charles de Gaulle airport. The pain snatched at nerves in Lukas's gut, made his mouth twitch and brought a frown to his forehead. The cramps had not been brought on by the landing of the aircraft that had brought him from Madrid to Paris, a catastrophic bump, leap and skid in a fierce cross-wind that carried driving rain. Nor were they the product of the food served on the long Atlantic crossing, or the result of the confined leg room – he'd gone steerage because business class was fully booked. He had not smoked since he had gone through the departure gate at El Dorado. He walked slowly and soaked up the ache in his guts. Within a few strides he had killed the pain, the twitch and the frown. Nothing about him was noticeable to a stranger. He would go through Immigration and Customs briskly. He didn't need a visa for France, living now on a UK passport, and had only the rucksack slung loose from his shoulder. He had been authorised, some months back, at permanent secretary level, to carry two passports; in Washington this had been endorsed by an under-secretary. The passport with the Colombian entry and exit stamps was at the bottom, under his laptop. The one he would show at Immigration bore only East European and north African stamps – nothing from the Middle East, or Latin and Central America – so his movements would not go down in the computers that tracked international travellers. It was important in the work he did that he left no paper trail.

He would take a bus into the city centre.

He'd have a chance at a bus stop, in the driving rain and wind, to light a cigarette. That seemed important to Lukas, about as important as gaining a return of three unhurt, two wounded, one fatality. He didn't triumph, nor expect hero-grams, only a long debrief with his employer when he would sift in his mind what was relevant and what could be discarded. Not something to boast about, playing God, making decisions that might cost the lives of men and women. He thought more about the cigarette he would light in the bus queue than about a return of five survivors from six . . . It had been about the one guy, the Agency man, but Lukas declined to recognise a stark fact. When the bus came, he would ride into the city, then get himself down into the late train on the Métro and walk from the subway at Solférino to his apartment.

If he had permitted it, a limousine would have been waiting

for him at the kerb outside Arrivals. The Americans would have sent one as a mark of gratitude. The company would have ordered one. He had, perhaps, a Low Church love of frugality. None of the good men, the ones to whom Lukas gave respect, sought greasepaint, flashbulbs and welcoming bands. It was just possible that he was the most competent of the 'good men'. If he was the élite figure among them it was not because of his crusading spirit but the attention he gave to detail, the depth of his experience and his rejection of conceit when he won through. It was said that many who knew Lukas waited to spy out his emotions and motivation, and still waited. No car, no congratulations. Might have been because he knew how fine the lines were between success and failure . . .

He had one regret that evening. It was a few minutes short of midnight and he was returning to Paris too late to meet up with his friends. By the time he had negotiated the bus ride, the Métro and done the walk, his friends would have gone home.

Lukas was back where he lived – would be there until the next time the phone shrilled in his ear. It was his life. As someone had once said to him: 'Lukas, you dance on other people's misery. If it wasn't such a crap world you wouldn't have work.' He hadn't disagreed.

3

He blinked to see better. He was under a tree. During the night the wind had taken off enough of the foliage for the rain to drip on to his shoulders and head. He squeezed his eyes shut, hoping to clear out the water and the bleariness of a bad night. Mario Castrolami was looking for her.

The Ministero degli Interni, the vast, creaking bureaucracy on the Viminale in Rome, had an officer seconded to the Italian embassy. He was a policeman, not a member of the *carabinieri*, so Castrolami regarded him as a lesser creature – good enough to meet him last night at Heathrow and drive him to a Holiday Inn, not good enough to be given advance warning on the identity of a potential collaborator with justice and the implications that might splinter from it. An ROS investigator from Naples, a front-line salient in the war against organised crime, would have little trust in the combination of policeman and Viminale. So, after his failure to sleep, Castrolami had left the heavy sealed envelope containing the arrest-warrant papers for Vincenzo Borelli at the hotel's reception desk, with the officer's name on it . . . Laborious, complicated, but necessary, and if the woman did the business the officer would be told to collect the envelope and act on it. Trust, the lack of it, always governed Castrolami's actions.

He searched for her. He had never seen her in the flesh, but had the surveillance photograph to remember. Rain spattered his head and jacket. He saw some old people, mostly men, many meandering with a toy-sized dog on a lead, and some youngsters of both sexes who wore tracksuits and earphones, and ran in a trance. The most exercise Castrolami took was to walk, via a bar for an *espresso* and a pastry, to the station for the Funicolare, and after his descent to the Stazione Cumana, he would cross via Toledo and reach the barracks at piazza Dante. He thought it sufficient exercise for any man in the morning, but if it rained he brought his car. Twice, while he had waited under the tree, a dog had come to the trunk, cocked its leg and pissed. On neither occasion had the owner apologised.

He couldn't see her. He wondered if she was standing back, hesitating to show herself. He moved clear of the tree-trunk so that he was more visible. Put simply, there would be only one swarthy middle-aged Italian waiting at two minutes past nine – yes, he had remembered to alter the time on his watch – under a tree in diabolical weather. The city authorities in Naples were about to declare a drought: the skies had been clear for weeks and the temperature in late September still reached the high eighties. In his apartment he had a raincoat, unused and forgotten. Behind the front door umbrellas stood in a stand, also unused and forgotten. Maybe he'd drown. Maybe he'd catch pneumonia.

She appeared.

He could see her face. She had a small umbrella up, with a pretty flower pattern, but held it back over her head because at that angle it shielded her better. She wore a light plastic coat that came to her hips, but her legs were soaked, though she seemed not to notice it. He knew what he would say. Unable to sleep in the Holiday Inn, with the walls seeming to enclose him, a sealed tomb, he had passed the hours in deciding the tone he would take and the relationship he would create with her. Perhaps because she was here, not in Forcella, she seemed more vulnerable than he had expected. At home she would have known every trick in the game of counter-surveillance – had been born with the tactics in her genes. Anyone from the Borelli clan – other than the young idiot, Silvio – knew the craft of criminality from the moment they dropped out of their mother's *utero*. A man had said that the Camorra would live until every woman in the clans was sterilised and every man castrated. She did not use any counter-surveillance tactic: it was clear that she knew she was late for a meeting and was looking for the second party.

He knew, too well, the enormity of what she had done, but Castrolami reckoned she knew it better than he did. Should he wave or hold his ground under the tree? He had thought she looked vulnerable, but this was Immacolata Borelli, daughter of Pasquale and Gabriella, sister of Vincenzo and Giovanni, educated and intelligent, granddaughter of Carmine and Anna, being groomed in financial management so that she could clean dirty money. Vulnerable . . . not innocent. She saw him.

She stopped. She was on a path and a cyclist swerved past her. Then two runners divided and went either side of her. The wind took the flaps of her coat and opened it as far as the lower buttons allowed. Castrolami noted the vivid orange blouse; he thought it was her statement. He smiled grimly to himself. She was entitled to make a statement, but this was the easy time. She would know the threat to her life if she came close to him, talked to him, did as she was instructed, but he doubted she had grasped the pressures that would now build in her mind. But that wasn't his problem.

He came out from the shelter of the tree. The rain in the wind layered on his face. His collar was damp, his tie bedraggled and the jacket's shoulders were sodden. His hair was flat, and drips fell off his nose. He murmured, 'Come on, you little bitch. Come and do the business.'

She did. She had a good swing to her walk. She was the

daughter – clear to him – of the clan leader and the clan leader's wife. The child of the *padrino* and the *madrina* locked eyes with him and closed on him. The vulnerability was now hidden. She stretched her stride. He believed then that she hoped to dominate him because that was her culture. She could wish it, but it would not happen.

She stood in front of him. She could have tried to use her umbrella to shield both of them, but she collapsed it, shook it, pocketed it. If he could be wet, so could she. She spoke coolly: 'I am Immacolata. Are you Castrolami?'

He reached into his pocket, lifted out his wallet, flipped it open and showed his identification. He put it away.

He knew what he would say.

Over his shoulder, she saw a kid kick a football. So normal. She saw a man throw a stick for a yapping dog. So ordinary. Far behind him, kids were skiving from school and dropped sweet wrappers as they fooled. So predictable.

He said, 'You asked me to come and I came. You can beckon once and I'll run, but it won't happen again. If you flick your fingers or whistle, a dog will come to you. I'm not a dog. So, I'm here. What do you want to tell me?'

'Two days ago, I was at the cemetery in Nola for a funeral, my friend's funeral, and—' she stammered, uncertain.

He was harsh and his voice was cutting. 'I know about Nola, Marianna Rossetti and the Triangle. I know what happened to you there, what was said and what was done. I repeat, what do you wish to tell me?'

She had thought there would be a car, a big Lancia or a Fiat saloon, and that a call on a mobile would bring it hurrying to the nearest kerb, that she would be whisked inside and away to an embassy house. She had expected a tone that was at least respectful, if not deferential. She wanted control and couldn't find it. 'I'm Immacolata Borelli, I—'

Withering: 'I know who you are, who your parents are, who all of your family are.'

'I am part of the Borelli clan, and—'

'Of course you're part of it.'

'I said in my call to the palace, I wish to return to Italy,' she blustered.

'Then return to Italy. Does the Borelli clan not have sufficient funds to permit you to purchase an airline ticket? If you wish to return, then do so.'

'I want protective custody.'

She saw his eyes roll and his lips moved on those words – *I want protective custody* – but soundlessly. The rain was harder now but he seemed not to notice its new intensity. He stared down at her, his eyes never off hers. Nobody had ever stared challengingly into the face of Immacolata, daughter of Pasquale Borelli. Then: 'Why?'

'And I require immunity from prosecution.'

Now his head shook, a comedian's exaggeration, and she thought she heard a click of his tongue. 'I very much doubt we would consider that. I presume we'd be talking through the statutes concerning money laundering, extortion, tax evasion – maybe not acts of physical violence – membership of a criminal conspiracy. We do reduced sentences but not immunity in circumstances such as yours. What would justify protective custody, a reduced sentence? What chips can you place on the table?'

'It's because of what my family has done.'

'Indirect responsibility for the poisoning of your friend.'

'I wish to do something in her name.'

'Your friend was poisoned by the contamination of the water table with toxic waste illegally dumped.'

'So that I can look, in my mind, into the face of my friend and not feel total shame.'

His expression showed no enthusiasm – rather, boredom.

'That would be excellent. You do *something*, we're not specific but *something*, and you can go to a priest, squat in the confessional box: "Can't really tell you too much about all this, Father. Wouldn't be healthy for you to know, but I'm doing *something* to right a wrong. My family did the wrong, not me personally, but I want overall forgiveness, and more sunlight in my life." How gratifying. What are you prepared to tell me?'

'I can tell you about my family.' Her voice was little more than a whisper.

He lifted an eyebrow as a slow smile curved his lips. 'I had difficulty hearing that – again, please.'

'I said that I can tell you about my family.' She had spoken boldly.

'Did I hear that correctly? I'm not sure. Again.'

She knew he was toying with her, that he was the cat and she a small rat. The amusement was in the mouth, but not in the eyes that looked down on her. She broke. 'I'll tell you about my family,' she shouted.

'Better. Again.'

She yelled, over him, past him and out across the worn grass of the park, at the trees, the walkers and joggers, the talkers and the kids who should have been at school. 'I'll denounce my family.'

Many in the park had heard her. Some merely turned their heads but went on their way, others stopped to gawp. 'I hear you, but do I believe you?' he said softly.

'You have my word.'

He allowed the irony to run over her: 'I have the word of the daughter of Pasquale and Gabriella Borelli?'

'Everything.'

Now he was an uncle to her. As a *zio* would, he tucked her hand into the crook of his arm and walked with her through the rain, their shoes squelching on the grass and the mud. 'You travelled to Nola, Signorina, you were late, for whatever reason, and did not reach the basilica in time for the funeral mass, but you travelled on to the municipal cemetery. There, you were humiliated, and subject to the emotional experience of parting from a friend. You flew back to London. You didn't sleep. The accusations are alive in you and guilt haunts you. You pick up the telephone. None of this, yet, is difficult. You make a statement to the prosecutor's office that is laced with dramatic intent. You put down the telephone and imagine champagne corks pulled, an executive jet on stand-by and that you will be brought back to Naples to be met on the tarmac with a red carpet, the cardinal in attendance and the mayor. No, it hasn't happened. They sent Mario Castrolami, as you requested, and the flight home will be in economy where there is little leg room, the food is foul and English barbarians are talking about the culture fix they'll get in our home over seventy-two hours. You will then, Signorina, be surrounded by strangers – and don't expect them to regard you as a resurrected Mother Teresa. They will try to leech from you every scrap, morsel, titbit of information so that they can shut away your family for even longer – the family who has trusted you with their lives, and whom you will have betrayed. Many months after you've taken that flight back to Italy you'll have to appear in court. At one end of the room there will be the judges, in the well of the court the ranks of the lawyers, and at the other end a cage. Behind its steel bars you will see your family. Will you turn to me then and say, "Dottore, I have doubts now on the course of action to which I was committed last September. I've changed my mind. I don't wish to go ahead with this. It was a mistake. I want to be reunited with my family. I want the love and warmth of my gangster father, my ruthless, vicious mother, my murderous eldest brother and my

psychopathic middle brother. I want to return to them."
Will you turn your back on the court? Many do, Signorina.
They climb high, survey the view and scramble down. Their
nerve doesn't hold. Will your nerve hold?'

She lowered her head and looked at the toecaps of her
shoes. She allowed him to lead her along. 'It'll hold.'

'They all say that, but many fail to deliver.'

She stopped. She felt his fingers drop from her arm. She
faced him and tilted her head. She could see the cage, their
faces, the hatred that beamed at her, and the contempt. 'My
word should be sufficient guarantee.'

'You will never be forgotten, never forgiven. You will never
again walk the streets of your city as a free woman. Can you
turn your back on Naples?'

It was her home.

Those Greek traders who had first anchored their boats in
the shadow of the great mountain, mid-eighth century BC,
had called it Nea Polis, the New City. The Romans came
later from the north and corrupted the name to Napoli. Now
it is a city adored and detested, admired and despised. It is
one of UNESCO's proudest World Heritage Sites, and is
regarded by Interpol as having the greatest concentration in
the world of Most Wanted organised-crime players. Horace,
the Roman poet, coined the phrase 'Carpe diem', 'Seize the
Moment', and it is still the maxim of Neapolitans.

Many cultures have left their mark on Naples. After the
collapse of Rome's civilisation and its hold on the city, the
occupying army was that of the Ostrogoths, then the
Byzantines from Constantinople, the Normans and the
Spanish. There were Bourbon satraps and Napoleonic
revolutionaries. Admiral Nelson's fleet covered the port with
cannon, the *Wehrmacht* and the Gestapo sought to control
it, after which the Americans gave it military government.

In the last century, Communists, democrats and Fascists have attempted to bring Naples to heel, but failed.

At the university, the academics seek to excuse the inner city's million people for its ungovernability. They quote the actual and the potential. The actual is the Camorra, the generic name for the criminal families that are the principal employer and major pulsebeat in Naples. The potential is the lowering image of the mountain, Vesuvio, with its volcanic capability and history of destruction. The criminality survived the most savage reprisals of the Mussolini era and now cannot be beaten: the threat of the volcano mocks any who look far to the future: it may erupt at any time and warning will be minimal. Those same academics point proudly to the magnificent churches and palaces, and strangers flock there from across the world.

John Ruskin, the English art critic and reformer, came to the city in the late nineteenth century and saw the Naples that has attracted the first overseas tourist industry. He wrote, 'The common English traveller, if he can gather a black bunch of grapes with his own fingers, and have a bottle of Falernian brought him by a girl with black eyes, asks no more of this world or the next, and declares Naples a paradise . . .' But he would not be seduced and continued, '. . . [Naples] is certainly the most disgusting place in Europe . . . [combining] the vice of Paris with the misery of Dublin and the vulgarity of New York . . . [Naples] is the most loathsome nest of caterpillars . . . a hell with all the devils imbecile in it'. Outsiders may come, criticise and leave, but those who are bred and live in Naples are held by loyalty, as if in chains, to the city.

The gulf makes a perfect natural harbour. The sea ranges from azure to aquamarine. The churches are noted for their splendour, and the castles that defend the shore are reassuring in their strength. It has the best of everything – architecture, painting, sculpture, music, food, vitality, and the refusal to be cowed – with the biggest open-air narcotics supermarket ever created, the wealthiest criminal conspiracies ever known, and a degree of violence that makes both the brave and the cynical cringe.

In the heart of the old city, where the streets were laid by Roman road builders, then wide enough only for a handcart to pass and now for only a scooter, is the district of Forcella. The Borelli clan ruled Forcella.

'Can you do that, erase that place from your mind?'

'I hope . . .'

'What's hope? Useless, inadequate. Either you can or you can't.'

She flared. 'I am Immacolata Borelli. You offer me no respect.'

Castrolami shrugged, as if she had scored no points. He said, 'I see so many of them. This isn't Sicily. The vow of silence doesn't exist in Forcella, Sanità, Secondigliano or Scampia. In the far south, the gangs are linked by blood. It's impossible to consider that a family would turn in on itself. But you're not Calabrian – I'll get to the point, Signorina – or Sicilian. The clans of Naples have greed, brutality and no honour. Do you understand? We have more men and women offering to collaborate than in any other part of Italy. They're practically queuing outside the palace. Sometimes the prosecutor has to check his diary to make sure he has a slot for a new one. Many are rejected because they have little to offer that we don't already know, a few because we don't believe they can sustain the pressure of their treachery. I offer no informer respect, and I'm used to rejecting them. Don't think, Signorina, that you have earned my admiration or have my gratitude.'

'You insult me.' She tried to stamp her foot, and mud

spattered out from under her shoe. No avenue of retreat was open to her. She knew it, and so did he. She couldn't throw a tantrum, spin on her heel – slip probably – and walk away. She had met him. Perhaps she had been photographed with a long lens from a car among those parked bumper to bumper around the park. Perhaps he had a wire strapped to his chest and a microphone in one of his jacket buttons. Did she believe that – if she walked out on him – the ROS would not allow a photograph limited distribution among the journalists accredited to the palace, or not make available a snatch of her voice to the RAI correspondent in the city? On Sunday mornings priests talked often about taking personal responsibility for one's actions, the need to consider consequences beforehand. She couldn't meet his eyes and dropped her head. It had stopped raining, the wind had freshened, and she shivered.

He said, 'You know better than I do that the name for such a person is *infame*. That person is not a patriot, a hero or heroine. Disgrace walks with them, and the *infame* who betrays his or her family is the lowest of the low. You could never stand, Signorina, on a box in the piazza del Plebiscito and attempt an explanation of what you have done. You'll become a pariah and be forced to make a new life.'

Her lip trembled and her voice, to her, was hoarse. 'I will.'

'Never go back?'

'I won't.'

'If you're found again in Naples, what will happen to you?'

'They'll kill me.'

'What do they do, Signorina, to an *infame* before he or she is killed?' He was relentless. 'What do they do?'

'I don't know what they do to a woman. I know what they do to a man.'

*

The crowd was four deep in places where the best view was to be had. The girl reporter from the crime desk barged her way through, offered no apologies and kicked the ankle of an obese man who didn't shift out of her way. When she was through the spectators, she looked for her photographer, located him and went to his side. 'My car wouldn't start,' she said.

'Your car's shit and always will be. My cousin deals—'

'Yeah, yeah. What have we got?'

Relaxed, the photographer smoked a small cheroot, took it out of his mouth and blew smoke, then used it to point at a space on the pavement between two parked vehicles. A checked tablecloth that doubled as a shroud filled it. The feet of the corpse, its shoes and blue socks, stuck out from the covering, and she could see where blood had diverted round sprouting weeds to dribble into the gutter, where it was dammed by a plastic bag. Beyond the cars, half hidden, a police scene-of-crime technician manoeuvred a camera fixed to a tripod, other officers standing around languidly, and an ambulance was parked further down the street. She stretched up, laying a hand on the photographer's shoulder, and could see better past the parked cars. A woman sat on a straight-backed wooden chair no more than two metres from the body. She wore a nightdress of thin cotton with a dressing-gown, as if she'd been roused from her bed, and cradled a child – a boy of perhaps four – as she stared blankly ahead.

The photographer said, 'I done her – she's the wife – wrong, the widow. I done her when she first came, bawling and screaming. That was before they covered him up.'

'Do we have a name?'

'The police have, but they haven't shared it – you'll get it off the street or, officially, at the Questura.'

That was where she worked, on the ground floor of the police headquarters, off via Medina and down near the sea front, in the cavernous Mussolini-era building in the room where the crime-desk hacks fed off the information they were given. She was relatively new to the city but her father had a business partner who had an uncle who had influence at the newspaper, and it had always been her ambition to work as a crime reporter. The link had secured her the job – the normal way of things in the city. The more senior staffers on the team were out of town because a supplement was being prepared on the Casalesi clan operating in Caserta, so her phone had rung – and her car hadn't started. She might well take up the photographer's offer to introduce her to a cousin who dealt in secondhand vehicles. What they said in the newsroom about the photographer told her that a car from that source would be cheap, but the chance of paperwork to accompany it was slight. She had her notebook out and a ballpoint pen.

'So, what happened? Was he shot?'

'You sure you want to know?'

'Of course.'

'Have you had breakfast?'

'No – because the car wouldn't start and I was late and—'

'Better on an empty stomach. It's not pretty.'

Most of the murders she had covered since she'd joined the crime desk had been pistol shots into the head of a man eating in a trattoria, drinking in a bar, sitting in a car, playing cards with associates. 'Tell me.'

'You asked. See there, behind where he's lying? There's a grocery. The *drogheria*, of course, has steel shutters down at night. The padlock was cut and the shutters lifted enough to get a man under. They needed electrical power. They took the cable in with them, found a point and plugged it in. Then they went two doors down, called at the place and the wife said her husband wasn't in and went back to bed. They waited for him to come back from wherever, jumped him and dragged

him to where the shutter was up. He would have seen – not
much light on the street but enough – what they had waiting
for him and he'd have been shitting himself, too scared to
scream, and they'd started the engine – can you take this?'

'Try me.'

'They'd plugged in a circular-blade tile-cutter.'

'Jesus, help us.'

'One of the cops told me before the big apparatchiks took
over. There's no pretty way to say this, but they cut off his
balls first, then put them in his mouth – forced open his
teeth and shoved them in. This is the twenty-first century,
this is Naples, a cradle of civilisation. You doing all right?'

'Fine.'

'They put some euro notes in too. Then they cut his head
off. The blade can go right through a bathroom or kitchen-
floor tile, so it wouldn't have had a problem with a neck.
They took his head off and laid it in his crotch so it covered
up where his balls had been.'

'Did you say "a cradle of civilisation"?'

'They did all this on a pavement and there's a streetlight
no more than fifty metres away. People must have passed
him in the night after they'd driven off. They must have seen
him with his head in his crotch, gagging on his balls and
the money, and must have stepped round him, kept going.
People live over the *drogheria* and alongside it, but they never
heard anything. Nothing heard and nothing seen. The
grocery owner came to open the shop before going to the
market and found him. What more do you want to know?'

She swallowed hard. If she had thrown up, she would have
demeaned herself, and it would have gone straight round
the city's newsrooms and the hacks' room at the Questura.
She swallowed, gulped. Then she looked hard at the face of
the widow, and thought she saw acceptance, not anger. She
wondered if she could write her piece on the expression of

fatalism, base it round the mood that seemed to grip the woman. She didn't keen and the child didn't weep.

'I want to know what he'd done to be punished like this.'

'He was a carpenter.'

'Why was he killed like that, though?'

'The policeman who talked to me said that the Borelli clan, who have this territory, wanted the *pizzo* from him.'

'So they extort cash from him — a hundred euros a week?'

The photographer lit another cheroot, puffed at it, shrugged. 'He shouted his mouth off. He said he'd go to the palace, inform – the police have that from the woman. Maybe he'd already made a statement to the prosecutor. Maybe he'd only said he would. In some districts you can do that and survive, but not in Forcella or Sanità. He'd threatened it, and that was enough.'

'So that's what they do to an informer?'

'Yes. And nobody reported any noise or the body in the street, because they were frightened, and because nobody values an informer. He has the status of a leper.'

The scene-of-crime technician had folded away his tripod. The ambulance crew had carried the body on a stretcher to the vehicle. The woman and the child were escorted by a priest to their door, and the owner of the *drogheria* lifted his steel shutter, uncoiled a hosepipe and sluiced the pavement. The crowd dispersed. The reporter and the photographer drove off, to write copy, check pictures and hear the police statement in the Questura. Within minutes, there was no trace – on the pavement or in the street – of where an informer had been killed.

He glanced at his watch. She had promised detailed information on the functioning of the clan, her mother's role in the running of the organisation, the dealings of Vincenzo, and the work Giovanni was put to in Forcella. What she had told him was merely headlines, but to an investigator it was mouthwatering, not that he showed enthusiasm. He took no notes, and didn't wear a wire. He thought it important to be indifferent at this stage of his linkage with Immacolata Borelli.

In his mind were the bullet points of what he needed, and two were outstanding. He asked where Vincenzo had been that day. Did she know anything about his diary? Where could he be found after midday? She was vague. It was difficult for her, she said, to know her brother's schedule. She gave him the address of the apartment they shared, his mobile number, the name and location of the cafe-bar he most often patronised, the warehouse where he stored the coats and shoes he imported and exported.

'I emphasise and repeat, Signorina, that intense pressure will be applied to you when your family learn what you've done. In the first period, before a legal process, we will protect you, but we can't protect all those who may be dear to you. Could they find, hold and hurt, maybe murder, a lover?'

'No.'

Put a second time, the question was redundant, but it was his practice to examine the face rather than merely listen to words.

'In Naples, there's no lover, no boy?'

'No.'

'In London, are you in a relationship with someone you met here? An Italian boy? A boy from the college you attend?'

'Is that important?'

'It is, Signorina, because you'll be sequestered, perhaps for months, in a safe-house and under protection. A boyfriend won't be able to visit you. You can't get on a plane and come back to London because you want him, because—'

'It won't happen.'

'So there is a boy here?' His eyes bored into her, looking

for truth, demanding it, and he towered over her. He was aware then that the first thin sunlight had broken through the cloud and played on her cheeks. 'I have to know.'

'Yes, but not significant.'

'What does that mean – *significato*? Is there or isn't there a boy?'

'We go to bars, we go to films, we go—'

'You go to bed. But you say it's not "significant" – yes?'

'He's just a boy. We met in a park. It doesn't mean anything.'

'You won't pine for him?'

She threw back her head and raindrops cascaded from her hair, the sun catching them to make jewels. 'I'll forget him – maybe I have already.'

He looked into her eyes for evidence of a lie and couldn't find it. Her eyes were clear, bright and unwavering. Mario Castrolami knew little of love. His wife and children were in Milan, lodgers at her mother's home. There was little of love that he could remember – it might have been his uniform that had attracted her when he was young, slim and straight-backed, but now he no longer wore it, his shoulders were rounded, his stomach pushed at his belt, he was edging towards his forty-seventh birthday, and he slept with a loaded handgun in the drawer of his bedside table. There was a woman with whom he shared a restaurant table and the couch in her studio, but only once a month, never more than twice. She painted aspects of the great Vesuvio, exhibited some and sold a few, and he was fond of her – but it wasn't love. Most of the time he forgot his wife and children, and if his friend, the artist, moved on, she, too, would be forgotten. He did not challenge her again. He believed he had found honesty in her features.

Not that honesty would help her. Deceit was a survivor's weapon. Away from her, Castrolami used his mobile phone.

A new day, and Eddie felt better. Last night was gone.

Better and freer.

He had had breakfast with the others in the house, toast
and cereal, and Eddie had said his piece about losing track
of Mac, and there had been, almost, a collective howl. She
was part of them all. Down the pub, and the laughter. Back
home, her cooking lasagne or cannelloni, or making a sauce.
Coming out of the bathroom with maybe just a shirt on, or
the see-through robe, and fluttering her eyelashes at them.
It just wasn't possible. Eddie had thought that each of the
others would have looked back to the last time they'd seen
her, mentally stripped her mood and looked for indicators
that she was bugging out on him – and them. He had said
he was going to teach and that at the end of his working
day he was going to find her. Didn't know the number, but
had dropped her off that first time at the end of a street –
a bloody long one – and he'd find her if he had to bang on
every door and ring every bell.

He taught with enthusiasm, was maybe at his best. He
had ditched Dame Agatha, and had gathered up an armful
of weathered, much-used digests of Shakespeare, condensed
anthologies. Eddie himself, quietly and with sincerity, had
read Sonnet 116:

> *Let me not to the marriage of true minds*
> *Admit impediments. Love is not love*
> *Which alters when it alteration finds,*
> *Or bends with the remover to remove.*

And a Lithuanian car mechanic had read aloud:

> *O no! it is an ever-fixed mark*
> *That looks on tempests and is never shaken;*
> *It is the star to every wand'ring barque,*
> *Whose worth's unknown although his height be taken.*

The classroom had rung with applause and he had blushed. A Nigerian who wanted to nurse but needed the language before she could enrol was next:

> *Love's not Time's fool, though rosy lips and cheeks*
> *Within his bending sickle's compass come.*

A Somali man who washed dishes in a hotel but wanted to be a street trader stuttered through

> *Love alters not with his brief hours and weeks,*
> *But bears it out even to the edge of doom.*

An Albanian needed more English if he was to get customers for a delivery service up in Stoke Newington. He was last to be chosen and looked about to opt out but Eddie wouldn't let him, so he tried:

> *If this be error and upon me proved,*
> *I never writ, nor no man ever loved.*

Then the class stamped and slapped their palms on the desk tops. He thought a Hungarian girl, plump, with Beatle spectacles on her nose, was savvy enough to take stock first, and she said to the Algerian next to her, in halting English, that the sonnet was not performed for them but for their teacher, it was his love they had recited, and what she had said went on down the line, behind her, in front of her, and the room echoed with giggles.

They did more extracts and his medley of students, gathered from across the globe, played Ferdinand, Miranda and Prospero, Lysander and Hermia, Juliet and her Nurse, Lorenzo and Jessica. He ended with Sonnet 18, and had the Hungarian girl read it:

Shall I compare thee to a summer's day?
Thou art more lovely and more temperate . . .

He let her read alone and her delivery grew in confidence, but he brought in the whole class to echo the final couplet and make a chorus:

So long as men can breathe or eyes can see,
So long lives this, and this gives life to thee.

It had been a unique class. He doubted it would be repeated.

He would find her, his Mac. He had promised to.

Eddie walked to the staff room and the coffee machine. He felt that purpose had returned.

The bustle of the prosecutor's office was stilled. He was at his desk, which was littered with a carpet of opened files and more lay on the wood tiles beside it. The deputy prosecutor had a cigarette in his mouth, the lighter lit but left to burn ten centimetres from the tip. The liaison officer winced, air hissing between his near-closed teeth. The personal assistant to the prosecutor bit sharply at a pencil and looked up from her screen. The archivist was halfway across the office from the door to the desk and carried a load of cardboard file-holders that reached from her stomach up to her chin. They were the inner cabal. The call had come, faint and with a poor signal, from Castrolami. The prosecutor looked around, into each face, and they nodded, accepted his judgement: Operation Partenope, named after the mythical daughter of a goddess, who had drowned in the Gulf and was regarded as a symbol of deceit, treachery, was launched.

Now he spoke softly: 'Let's get to work. I want on the telephone the extradition team of the Metropolitan Police, if they're not too arrogant to speak to me. I want the operations director of the Squadra Mobile, and the duty officer, ROS, here for fourteen thirty hours, with arrest squads on stand-by. There must be no breach in security and no names of targets given. We have a small window and must jump through it. And—'

His desk phone pealed. His assistant passed him the receiver, and mouthed that the caller was, again, Castrolami. The prosecutor began to scribble names and addresses, the light of triumph in his eye.

She dictated. Castrolami repeated into the mobile phone what she told him: all of the addresses used as safe-houses by Gabriella Borelli; the location of the rooms where Giovanni Borelli slept; the apartment, off the via Forcella, that was the home of Carmine and Anna Borelli, and where Silvio Borelli stayed; the rooms off the piazza Mercato, a street behind the via Polveriera and an alley to the north of the vicolo Lepri that Salvatore, Il Pistole, used. She gave the last streets with dry relish and had long believed that the clan's principal hitman fancied having his hands in her knickers, her stomach against his, and wanted to put a ring on her finger, thus ensuring his advancement in the clan: family would bring him that. She felt no emotion as she spoke. All the time she had clear images in her mind. They were not the faces of those she denounced. Or the features of Castrolami, jowled and clumsily shaven, with raw, bloodshot eyes, his sparse hair whipped up by the wind.

She saw the cavernous space in the basilica, empty because she had been late. The face of an innocent carved in stone, Angelabella, with the single flower, as she had hurried past with one foot bleeding. She heard everything that had been said to her, and named the streets where the safe-houses were. She had done it.

He cut the call, put the phone back into his pocket. He said quietly, almost conversationally, 'I hope, Signorina, you aren't fucking with me. This is big. We must win or be laughed at. If we lose because you're fucking with me then I'll put you into the sea, off the rocks, and hold you down.'

She looked at him. 'I'll go the course, whatever they throw at me.'

She stood then, feet a little apart, shoulders back. Her coat was now open and had dried on her, her blouse stretched across her breasts. She slipped her hand into the damp crook of his arm and they walked together.

It was a good morning by the river. The rain and cloud had cleared and Lukas was hunched on the step with his friend.

Squatting on a canvas stool, Philippe drew with crayons on heavy white paper pinned to a wooden board. With midday coming, it was close to the high seventies and in the afternoon the temperature might hit eighty. But where he had taken his pitch there was shadow from the doorway. Down and across the street, there was a footbridge over the river, marked by a larger-than-life-size statue of Thomas Jefferson. Lukas didn't know much about Jefferson's life and times, but it was a good place for the artist. Tourists from the United States came and took photographs of the statue, then seemed to want to remember the place with something more authentic, so they purchased his crayon drawings of the statue, the bridge, the river, and the Louvre, which was on the far side of the Seine. Usually, when he was at home, Lukas would come to that doorway and settle beside his friend. If his friend was concentrating, he would sit quietly and do some thinking of his own.

If they talked it was about little things. The price of bread, the state of the football championship, whether the weather was lifting or closing in. He would never pry into Philippe's life, and in return he was not asked, when he came back after a week or three, or a month, where he had been or why. There

was always, in late September, a strong odour rising off the
river because its level was low, and when he looked upstream
he could see the little island covered with Notre Dame. He
came to this place, unwound his emotions, let them slacken,
and was distanced from where he'd been – Afghanistan, Iraq,
an Uzbek or Tajik city, the jungle of the high mountains in
Colombia – and Philippe wouldn't press him. Why was the
man his friend? In one limited area there was total and
compelling frankness between them. Philippe said his work
was shit, and Lukas never disagreed. He valued honesty –
men and women died when assault-squad commanders or
hostage negotiators and co-ordinators fought little patches of
territory and declined to be truthful. The work was shit, but
it sold and fed his friend, and meant there was a place for at
least another month where Lukas could find company.

He was anonymous here, which suited him. He didn't
carry a mobile in Paris, but the way he lived his life meant
he was seldom far from the telephone on the small table
inside the apartment's front door, and a light flashed if a
call had come in and a message had been left. He always
hesitated a couple of seconds, no more, before he picked it
up when the light flashed red.

They'd gone round it for a long time and had now reached
consensus. Philippe, busy on Jefferson's face, the second
work since the discussion had begun, was certain who would
win the weekend's football games, and Lukas agreed. In his
own trade, he knew that disagreement killed.

Three times a day, Lukas was out of his apartment, but
seldom for more than two hours. It was always a stampede
to catch up when the call came and the light flashed red.

Philippe shared his flask – it was good coffee, as always.

4

He disliked to ask a favour, to place himself in debt or obligation to any man. He hadn't asked one but Castrolami had endured an uncomfortable, awkward day, but now he had purpose. They were out of the city and on to the motorway. It was not yet dusk, but the sun was sinking and it would be evening when they left Heathrow, night when they reached Fiumicino. The man from the embassy drove.

In the hours since they had left the park, they had shopped – underclothes for her in a chain store. He had passed her euros from his wallet, which she had placed in her purse, then used British currency – he thought her the daughter of her father because she hadn't given him change for what she had purchased. He had hustled her. They had been brought fifteen minutes in the car away from the park and he thought they were nearer to the heart of the city but distanced from where she lived and where her brother might be. Then she found a nightdress, a washbag and the items to go with it. For himself there was a sandwich in a cardboard and cellophane wrapping. He had not discussed with her the possibility of her returning to the apartment and packing a bag: it had been stated as fact that there was no question of her going near her street. They had stopped outside a railway station near the shopping area, and she had walked with him to a fast-photo booth and done portraits. Then they had killed time.

Had Mario Castrolami been prepared to ask for favours a choice might have presented itself.

He could have used the embassy man to contact the London police and request a secure room – in a police station, wherever – for them to wait in. In Naples, it was common talk among the Squadra Mobile and the *carabinieri* that the British police, in particular the London force, were self-serving and unhelpful to the point of obstruction. They lived, it was said, in a fantasy land of imagined and patronising superiority . . . So he had no secure room with the London police. He believed he must take precautions against a collapse of her determination, a sea-change in her mood: he couldn't rely on her to say where they could lie up for the day – there might be a back doorway on to a street through which she could slip and disappear. Nor was he prepared to take Signorina Immacolata into the embassy to wile away the hours. He didn't know the personnel so he didn't trust them: he had had the driver from the ambassador's staff park a block away from the embassy; then had given him the photographs of her from the booth. The man had been gone for half an hour, then returned with the new passport. It was not yet noon, so they had gone to another park. She had said it was Hyde Park. The rear doors of the car had been locked, and the radio turned up.

It was slow on the six-lane motorway.

Castrolami couldn't have taken her out on the first available flight with seats free. He wasn't prepared to move her until a signal came to him, via his mobile, that the extradition unit had eyeball on Vincenzo Borelli. She had not complained, had accepted what was incarceration, had refused food, had not asked for a lavatory, had not made empty conversation. It suited him that he was not required to do small-talk, and that others would begin the detailed debrief. He was not much more, really, than the bag-carrier. He neither liked nor disliked her, was neither attracted to nor disgusted by her. Her breathing was steady, giving no indication of stress . . .

but he kept an eye on the front windscreen. The driver had a day-old copy of *Corriere della Sera*, and had heaved the news and arts sections over his shoulder and into Castrolami's lap while keeping the sport pages. But Castrolami hadn't looked at the paper and neither had she. They had watched the movement in the park – pedestrians, pram-pushers and horse-riders – and hadn't talked. The call had come. His bladder had hurt, but he had known the vigil was near to its end. He didn't know how she felt now that the surveillance team had eyeball on her brother, and didn't ask.

They were leaving behind the tower blocks of London and the sun was dipping down. He had half expected her to crumple and look for comfort from him – she'd get fuck-all if she did. A bag-carrier didn't do nurse. She sat bolt upright and her lip wobbled occasionally, but there were no tears.

Further out of the city, the traffic speeded up. The mobile-phone messages had told him of the eyeball in London, the readiness at the palace in Naples, the teams gathered in briefing rooms at the Questura and at the barracks in piazza Dante. He had gutted her for headline information before they had gone on the shopping jaunt and that information had gone. He doubted that she could, now, step back.

He had made one accommodation to his principle of refusing to ask favours. At the terminal the car was met – only a protocol chief, but sufficient, carrying the printouts of two tickets.

The plastic bag dangled from her fist. It was the symbol, he reckoned, of how far she had come. Her possessions were in one cheap bag, and they consisted of underwear, washing kit and a nightdress. Then there was whatever she had in her handbag. Castrolami handed his passport and the one she would use to the protocol guy. They were examined, the title pages flicked, and they were taken through locked doors and into hidden corridors where only permanent Heathrow staff had access. They emerged into a departure area, were given the printouts and brought to a Passport Control desk – one at the end, which had a Position Closed sign but where a young woman sat. She looked at the pages, at the faces, handed the documents back. There was a screen ahead, and he saw that the Rome flight had been called. He had been told that if the traffic was heavy on the motorway, and they were late, the flight would be delayed. He had a hand on her arm and steered her towards the pier, then hooked out his mobile, dialled, waited, was connected.

He said where they were, confirmed the schedule. He was told the operation had been named Partenope. He shut the mobile and switched it off. They came to the last exit off the pier. He thought she had walked well, not stumbling, not faltering. Maybe she was, as he had suspected, a hard bitch under the veneer of sadness at the death of a friend, hard and uncaring.

Would she stay the course? They all said they would, but only a few did, and were alive, able to build a new life, when the trials were over.

He stood aside and let his hand fall from her arm. He couldn't read her, couldn't pierce her thoughts. She stepped from the pier inside the aircraft. Castrolami had had to stifle the urge to shove her the last metre, but it had not been necessary. He showed the boarding cards and a woman led them into business class, then to the front row where no other passengers would need to pass them and look at their faces.

The door was closed, the engines gained power. She had her belt fastened. 'Aren't you going to ask me how I feel, whether I am strong?'

He shook his head, then turned his face away and closed his eyes, as their speed on the runway gathered.

★

He put the phone down, gave the order of confirmation. Operation Partenope was named after the Siren woman who seduced men having lured them on to rocks and then killed them, and who had ultimately failed and had committed suicide by drowning and who lay in a pauper's grave, if mythology were believed, among the sunk foundations of the buildings between the via Solitaria and the via Chiatamone. Operation Parthenope had legs and ran.

The prosecutor eased his hand off the receiver and saw that his palm had left a sweat sheen on it. He believed he presided over the dismantling of a clan. It would be, he could predict, an opportunity for a minister in Rome to speak of a blow of the 'greatest significance' to the heart of the city's criminal activities. If it worked well, he would receive a congratulatory message from the minister. He could reflect on a durable heart, because many times central government had claimed such blows against it, and on the columns of men and women in patrol cars and riot wagons leaving the yards behind the Questura and piazza Dante. In London, more officers and guns would be moving into position to arrest the eldest brother. It was synchronised, choreographed. The silence fell over the room. They must wait. He was brought coffee. He pictured now the columns of vehicles snaking across the city – routes would have been worked out so that they seemed to head away from target locations, then swing back, giving minimal warning of their approach – and only now, inside the cars and wagons, would the officers know who they moved against. The prosecutor hated the lack of trust, was shamed by it. He regarded it as the single most impressive creation of the clans.

At about this time in the evening, the curtain would have been rising for the second act of the opera, a Mozart, for which he had begged tickets from a cousin. He had cried off in mid-afternoon and his wife had sighed and said she would find someone else to take with her. He was marginally disappointed to miss the performance. Opera soothed him. He believed fervently that whatever hours he worked at the palace he must enjoy something of life beyond.

Silence was good because words – at a moment such as this – were inadequate.

She was said to be strong – Mario Castrolami's verdict – and she would need to be, if the arrest programme was successful.

A battering ram broke open the street door, forcing the lock. A small boy, reared on extravaganzas of video-screen warfare, watched big-eyed, in fascination. What he played at was happening. He was across the street, had a vantage-point between two parked cars and was almost hidden by a lamp post. He watched the uniformed guy with the ram step aside, and a charge of black-clad police plunged through the broken door. The boy recognised the firearms they carried in Hackney, east London. They were on display often enough. If he had had a friend with him he would have been able to report that the men were from the specialist firearms team, CO19, that they had Heckler & Koch machine pistols and Glock 9mm handguns, and one at the back had a Taser immobiliser. Now he heard wood splintering, oaths, frantic shouting, then quiet. Up on the first floor, a policeman drew the curtain, denying the child a clear view into the lit room.

He didn't have to wait long. The prisoner was hustled into the doorway, out on to the step, then brought fast down the flight to the pavement. The boy knew him.

All the kids of his age knew Vincenzo – Vinny to them. His sister, too. They ran messages for Vinny, the Italian, would take a piece of paper to the other side of Hackney, up to Seven Sisters or south to Hoxton, a tiny scrap of cigarette paper that was folded up smaller than the bitten-down nail on the child's little finger. They were paid for taking messages. This boy, and all the boys, knew the Italian as a gangster of style . . . real life and bigger than in the games they played in the arcades and on their machines. They idolised Vinny but were never close to his sister. She wasn't there – only him. There was a moment when he could see, so clearly, Vinny's face. The streetlight he was under threw enough illumination to reach across the street, and the blue lamp was circling on a police car. Plenty of light fell on Vinny's face. Magnificent . . . 'Fuckin' fantastic,' the child thought. Then the police gloves, black leather, came down on top of Vinny's head and pushed him into the car. Handcuffs on his wrists – had seen them as Vinny was brought down the steps from the broken door – but not a mark on his face. There were no cuts on his mouth or round his eyes and his shirt wasn't ruffled. The boy understood. To fight would have been pathetic. Scum would have fought.

The child reckoned he knew about gangsters, and had no ambition in his life but to have the status and stature of Vinny, the Italian. If he had fought they would have belted him, like they did the big black guy, bouncer at the club off Kingsland Road. It had taken eight pigs to get him down, and then they'd kicked shit out of him and more. He caught Vinny's eye. The child was nine but thought himself the friend of Vinny, the big man from Naples that was somewhere way down south. In that moment, he was certain that the Italian gave him the slightest nod of recognition. Then a policeman was in front of him, telling him, 'Go and get fucking lost, kiddo.' The car had gone down the street, and the guys in black were spilling out down the steps from the main door.

It was a big man's cool, a top man's, that he didn't fight and didn't get himself thugged. The child thought that Naples, wherever it was, was a prize place if it was where Vinny had come from – proud, not frightened, ignoring all the guns round him and going at his own pace into the back of the car. He wondered where the sister was, and whether she would go in the cage with her brother. The car had gone round the corner at the end of the street, headed, he thought, for Lower Clapton Road and the Hackney police station.

The policeman was blocking his view of the front door, so he got 'fucking lost', but only to the corner. There, he sat on a low wall near to the Kentucky Fried Chicken place. He'd wait there for the sister to come and warn her not to go in the cage.

A window exploded out and glass crashed down into the street, which was enough to tilt eyes upwards. Heads were already craning at the block's front door where *carabinieri*, in protective gear, stood guard. A flashlight was aimed up three storeys and locked on to the window. The man appeared and screamed.

The crowd knew who the *carabinieri* had come for.

In that narrow street, spanning the top end of Forcella and the southern extremity of the Sanità labyrinth, they all knew who Giovanni was. Before the first of the attack wave had levered themselves out of the wagon and sprinted for the door, on the warning of their approach the street had been blocked with boxes, cartons from shops, pallets from building sites, rubbish and debris. Gas canisters were loaded in the barrels of some of the rifles confronting the crowd of local people and plastic baton round launchers were aimed at them. The second wave had had to negotiate a storm of abuse, and when the crowd had heard the door broken down above them, the first rocks had been thrown at the men in the cordon.

There was a gasp. He was naked. His body glistened. Giovanni had screamed, but now he swung clear of the window, evaded a heavy gloved fist that attempted to grab his arm, reached out and caught the downpipe from the gutter. His legs hung free, and the crowd saw the hair between them, at the trunk. A half-brick arced up and reached the broken window. The crowd heard the oath of a casualty. It was encouragement.

The fugitive slithered up the pipe, then took hold of the old ironwork guttering and the two nearest stanchions. Rocks and cobblestones, apples, potatoes, melons rained against the *carabinieri* at the entrance and at the window where arms attempted to grab Giovanni. Obvious – he'd been in the shower. As he sought to lever himself on to the gentle slope of the tiles, high above the streetlights, the beam still held him, and there were flashes from a score of mobile phones. His genitalia wobbled, danced, girls screamed, mothers giggled and old women shrieked happy obscenities. It was a huge effort, but he succeeded. Giovanni lifted a leg high and lodged his foot on the tiles. Then he was up, and standing.

At shouts from below, he turned and saw the black-clad *carabinieri* on the roof ridge. Then he would have known he was as trapped as if he had stayed in the shower cubicle or his bedroom. He ripped out a single tile and threw it viciously, two-handed, at the hunters.

It was theatre, and the crowd's participation in the performance was demanded. Forgotten: the *pizzo* taken from every shopkeeper, every small man trying to build a business, the extortion that robbed them. Forgotten: the conceit and bullying by the son of a clan leader. Forgotten: the weeping mothers, wives, sweethearts, sisters of those slaughtered to create discipline. Giovanni Borelli had milked the moment.

They had him. His wrists were wrenched behind his back and handcuffed.

Who ruled here?

One *carabinieri* vehicle was overturned and torched before

they brought him out. Three volleys of the plastic baton
rounds were fired and a dozen gas canisters. Men in full riot
gear, the masks distorting their faces, used their clubs to
batter a passageway to a vehicle with mesh over its windows.
By then they had found boxer shorts for Giovanni Borelli.
The *scugnizzi*, the urchin kids of the street – the watchers,
couriers and wallet thieves – cavorted near to the burning
truck. Giovanni was driven away. More gas was fired, but
with him gone, the anger fled. Show over.

It was said that, within an hour, half of the kids on the
north side of Forcella and the south side of Sanità, had
transferred the image of the naked Giovanni Borelli to their
mobiles' screens, and that the penis, hair and testicles were
in good focus. He was, if briefly, a hero.

A police team from the Squadra Mobile knocked at the door
of the old couple's apartment. When it was opened, they
stood back respectfully, as if apologising, and Carmine Borelli
stepped aside and allowed them to pass him. The detectives
wore their own clothes, rough-wear garments. Their jeans
were faded, some torn and ragged at the knees, their sneakers
had not been cleaned and their T-shirts were sweat-streaked
and creased. They had on, also, lightweight plastic tops with
Polizia emblazoned across the chest, and holsters that pulled
down their belts. Carmine Borelli, founder of the clan, was
treated with deference. The detectives used the mat inside
the door to wipe their feet before they went further inside
and, in the living room ducked their heads to Anna Borelli,
who sat and sewed and watched television, a hundred-
centimetre-wide screen that dominated the small room, the
sound turned high. She did not acknowledge them and kept
her eyes on the needle.

He was given respect because he was of the old guard of
clan leaders. His fortune had been founded in the weeks

after the Allies had reached the city in the autumn of 1943 when a *mercato nero* had run free. Its profits, from trading in every commodity that commanded a price, had been huge. It was long ago, and actuality was blurred. Pimping, prostitution, the corruption of medication, the purchase of politicians, the killing of rivals, the theft of funds sent by the military government for the restoration of utilities were unknown to these young detectives, who saw a humble, bent old man in a cardigan, a faded shirt and trousers, with scuffed leather sandals. He was in his eighty-eighth year, and his marriage to Anna had been celebrated, and consummated, sixty-eight years earlier. Together they had chased money and tracked power and . . . He was asked where his youngest grandson was.

Silvio was brought from his bedroom and was not handcuffed. Now his grandmother discarded her needlework, rose stiffly from her chair and smoothed his hair. The detectives took him down the flight of stairs from the apartment – Carmine and Anna had lived there since their wedding day and it was furnished in the fashion of four decades past – to the lobby on the ground floor. The door was closed quietly by the last detective to leave.

There was no riot. Carmine Borelli was as good as his word. A crowd was outside now and resentful murmurs eddied. The police stood nervously, defensively, around their vehicles and the outer door, with gas loaded and baton rounds. The grandfather came to the window. He opened it wide, pushed back the shutters and his arms were out – as if he were Papa, the place was piazza San Pietro and it was the Sabbath. He made a calming gesture with his gnarled hands. His word, in Forcella, carried weight, and had done since American troops had released him from a cell in the Poggioreale gaol after he had told the intelligence officer that he was a political prisoner, a youthful but implacable enemy of Mussolini's Fascism. He did not wish a disturbance outside his home because it might aggravate his wife's heart condition. The *scugnizzi* were denied their hour. They let the rocks drop to the cobbles and put the fire bombs – petrol in Coca-Cola bottles – in shop doorways. Not even they, feral and wild, would ignore the demand of Carmine Borelli.

Silvio was driven away. His hair was in place, and no missiles were thrown or gas fired.

When they had gone and the street had emptied, Carmine Borelli leaned against the living-room wall. His jaw jutted, his face was set and the blood drained from his bitten lips. He knew, and Anna knew, that they couldn't use a telephone but must wait for news. How great was the attack on the clan, his family?

She had the shop, its owner and contents to herself. In the salon, below the piazza dei Martiri, Gabriella Borelli was queen. It was in the folklore of the family that she had spent sixty thousand euros on dresses, chosen, purchased and carried away on the afternoon that her husband had stalked, confronted and shot a man from the piazza Garibaldi who had ambitions to reach into Forcella. Also in the folklore of the family, but not talked of, was the stacking of the boxes containing the dresses in a lock-up garage for a full half-year before Pasquale had decided it safe for her to wear such expensive clothes at a hotel south of Sorrento where, under false names, he had taken her.

The obvious shops for her to visit, the most exclusive in the city, were down the hill from the piazza dei Martiri in the via Calabritto where there were the outlets for Valentino, Prada, Damiani, Gucci and Louis Vuitton, and shoes from Alberto Guardini, but she preferred a smaller street behind the via Calabritto. She was, of course, one of the wealthiest women in the city, and had control of sums in excess of half a billion euros. Price was immaterial to Gabriella Borelli. What mattered to her more was that she could not drive a top-of-the-range Mercedes sports to Capodichino, book a first class air ticket to Gran Canaria, stay at a hotel with a hundred luxury rooms, take a suite, then soak up the sun during the day, dance in the evening, and strip for the night in a king-size bed with Pasquale or . . . It was not possible. She stood in her underwear – brassière and knickers – in front of the full-length mirror and held up to her the dresses and pirouetted, letting the music, a string quartet, waft over her.

She had no stake in the shop, minor or major. Could have bought it outright, and not noticed the price. The family owned hotels, apartments, time-share blocks, offices and many shops. However, it was more satisfactory to have a straightforward commercial arrangement to buy clothes even if they were seldom on her back.

Those she didn't like – too small or tight, too revealing for her age, she threw on the floor. The owner could pick them up, smooth and rehang them. Those she liked she laid across a chair. She could have had any of the dresses she tried – which were a genuine label from Paris, Milan or London – manufactured for her, exact imitations, in the sweat-shops on the slopes of Vesuvio. The little factories, hidden among villages on the slopes, were the responsibility of her eldest son, Vincenzo. She yearned for Vincenzo more than she did for her husband, suffered from her inability to talk to him, to hear his certainties. In fact, she purchased the label, not the dress. It was an escape for her.

Discarded dresses lay on the carpet, but she had chosen four. Perhaps one more would go on the chair. She was, normally, a middle-aged woman scurrying alone on the streets, or driving a small car with plates that showed it to be old. There were the boxes in the lock-up garage, and more in a basement, and she had had an air-conditioning system fitted in a cellar behind the Duomo where more clothes were stored, unworn, and in three of the safe-houses she flitted between there were wardrobes filled with dresses, skirts, light jackets and blouses. The escape was to dream, and dream alone. The money the clan had accumulated brought power, influence, control and authority – but the opportunity to pamper herself was remote. She smiled cheerfully and the owner clucked with enthusiasm. The dress was turquoise, not so close round her waist as to accentuate the first traces of flab, neither a tart's dress nor a matron's. It covered her knees. It would have looked well on her daughter, Immacolata – it was the first time that day she had thought of her. It would have fitted Immacolata but she wouldn't have chosen it. There were girls at the heart of the Contini clan, the Misso clan and the Lo Russo clan who would have worn that dress, turned heads and stopped conversations, but not her dull, dreary Immacolata. She held the dress up to her and the owner – with skill – gave a small squeal and clapped her hands. Gabriella Borelli turned the full circle, then laid it on the chair with the others. She didn't know when she would wear it . . . she saw herself – made up, with jewellery from strong boxes in two of the safe-houses, or the diamonds kept for her by the few she could depend on – as she walked on the young man's arm past the small orchestra, the restaurant manager grovelling a greeting, and was taken to the best table. Above her was the suite, and in the suite was the king-size bed, and the young man who admired the turquoise-silk dress was— A telephone rang.

She felt a chill and shivered. She recognised that call tone. It had no romance, no style, was not stolen from an opera aria or something popular. It was piercing, like a car's alarm. Brief, then silence. She turned her back on the clothes and went to the chair where her coat and bag were.

Salvatore had that number, the young man who . . . and Umberto, the lawyer long used by the family. It was for times of emergency.

A text message waited. 'Three run, Four run – Bravo five boxes – Twelve walk – block 5 alpha.' She studied the text, memorised and deleted it.

She said to the owner that she would call for the dresses she had chosen and would then settle the account. The owner was at pains to indicate that settlement was a small matter and should not concern the *signora*. Gabriella Borelli left the shop the way she had come, through the staff area, past the toilets and the storeroom, then went out into the street through a reinforced door. She waited. She listened. She looked from a corner for a loose cordon, for men who lounged and smoked or sat in parked cars. The text messages she sent and received on her mobile were always coded: 'Three' was Giovanni, 'Four' was Silvio and 'run' was arrested. She was 'Bravo' and 'boxes' were safe-houses that had been hit. 'Twelve' was Salvatore and 'walk' meant still at liberty, while 'block 5 alpha' told her where he would be and at what time.

She was a woman in a dowdy coat because the chill came in from the sea with the evening, and slipped among shadows. Dreams had been curtailed and an escape cut short. Fuck Giovanni and fuck Silvio. If five of her safe-houses had been hit, searched, then the security of the clan, on which she prided herself, was split open. How was it possible? Almost – not quite – fear held her.

The pictures came on the screen. There were digital images of Vincenzo Borelli in the custody suite at a London police station, full face and profile. They were replaced by a photograph of Giovanni Borelli being brought out of a door, wearing only boxer shorts. An officer behind him carried a bundle of clothing. The youngest, Silvio, walked meekly, appearing confused, between two towering men. The locations followed the individuals, a sequence of smashed-down doors, succeeded by an interior of a living room or bedroom.

The deputy prosecutor, unable to mask his disappointment, said, 'We have the three cubs, but not the vixen. We were given five safe-house addresses, have hit each of them but she wasn't there. Possessions? Yes. Recent clothes down to dirty ones? Yes. Jewellery not put away? Yes. She was due back at one of them. I suppose we have to query the tactic of overt hits.'

The liaison officer smarted. 'We agreed on simultaneous strikes and—'

'And we do not have Salvatore, Il Pistole.'

'We were given five locations for the vixen, and couldn't have delayed the lift.' The liaison officer was prepared to rebut any criticism of the operation, which he had overseen.

The deputy prosecutor, maybe from frustration or tiredness, or from the simple matter of dashed expectations, snarled, 'You had a free hand. They were your decisions. Where is she? Under your leadership we were the Gadarene swine in a headlong dash. Perhaps – and I say this with all charity – a calmer approach and surveillance stake-outs might well—'

'We had to act in concert.'

The prosecutor thwacked a fist on his desk. 'If we're divided, we lose. I believe we'll have the mother within hours. The plane is now, I estimate, thirty minutes away. We'll push the girl harder.'

The prosecutor reckoned it was not his optimism that won a truce in the recriminations, but his mention of Immacolata Borelli. They had all been in the room when the tape was played and her tinny voice, with traffic noise surging across it, had told them a plain truth: 'It is my intention to collaborate. By saying that on the telephone to you, I put my life at risk.' The voice, the memory of it, might have shamed the protagonists. The deputy prosecutor shrugged, and the liaison officer went for water. They were all thinking of her, the prosecutor decided, and the enormity of what she had done. He was offered a biscuit, but waved away the plate. He said, 'I don't know how, but we'll have the vixen.'

Two and a quarter hours of street tramping, and failure. Fortune did not shine on Eddie Deacon. He had started so brightly, full of hope and anticipation, when he had reached the street corner to which he had brought her from the pub. There, she had slipped her hand off his arm, grinned, waved and wandered down the street under the streetlamps. She hadn't looked back. He had stood on one corner and she had disappeared round another. He had never been back. Always his Mac had turned up on time, punctual as a digital clock. He knew only that she had turned off to her left. He had stood there and had seen a pretty much main route with bus stops, and smaller streets going off to right and left. There were shops with flats above. There were smart little residential roads where professionals from the City or the Law Courts had come with their Polish builders, and there were bollards at the end to stop rat-runners and twockers. There were streets where there seemed to be more bell buttons on a pad by the front entrance than windows. She might have gone to a high-grade road, or to a couple of rooms above a launderette or a travel agent.

What to do? He could hardly stop anyone he saw going about their business: 'Excuse me, have you seen an Italian girl in this street/road? We have this big thing, but she never gave me an address or a phone number, and she stood me up for a meal in the Afghan up Kingsland Road. Do you know where I can find her?' He had walked – had been into Pakistani-run shops that sold everything and takeaways that did chicken or curries, and at first he had shyly shown the photograph he kept in his wallet, but for the last two hours he had just walked, peering into every young woman's face, and found that he was doubling back on himself.

He went past a doorway, Edwardian, set in London brick, between a Turkish bank and a charity shop. Both had been open when he'd gone by the first time but now they were closed and showed only security lights. A pair of police stood outside, a regular officer and a Community Support girl. He remembered now that the door was covered with tacked hardboard.

His feet hurt, but not as much as his mind. He kept seeing her. Every time a girl materialised, round a corner, off a bus, out of a shop, into the throw of a streetlight, Eddie Deacon stared her out. Worst was when he had run after a girl – had seen the swing of the hips, the straight back, the chuck of hair over a shoulder – had caught her, gone in front of her, damn near blocking her on the pavement and she'd been reaching into her handbag – could have been a nail file, a personal alarm or even a pepper spray – when he had seen the spectacles. He had apologised, grovelling, had just about scraped the knees of his jeans on the pavement. She had walked on after one glance that measured him up as a sad thing or maybe a lowlife pervert. He stopped. Everybody watched policemen. Everybody pretended policemen standing on the first step of a flight were interesting, and doubly interesting when the door was opened, two men came out with filled plastic bags and put them into the back of an unmarked van, then went back inside. So interesting . . . and it rested his feet, which hurt bad. He looked down at them, and noticed the glow beside his legs.

The kid smoked. Eddie Deacon thought he was about ten, but the face was too near the pavement for him to make out the features. He sat on the kerb and his feet were in the gutter. He couldn't have been seen by the police across the street.

The kid asked if he was looking for Vinny.

He said he wasn't. It was just good to stop walking and rest his feet.

Was he looking for Vinny, the Italian? He heard a tremor of worship in the kid's voice, as if he was talking about a footballer.

Eddie Deacon took a deep breath and told the kid he was looking for a girl – an Italian girl. Then he had his wallet out and bent down with it. The kid struck a match, and Eddie showed him the photo.

'She's Immacolata,' the kid said, reedy, then coughed and flicked away his cigarette. 'She's Vinny's sister. There's filth here. They took Vinny, and I stayed to warn her if she came so they didn't lift her. They put a girl's bag and clothes in the van. Then I heard them talking and one said to a sergeant who came in a car that her bag was for shipping home to her. That was all.'

He thanked the kid. It was an afterthought but he asked him if he'd still be there later.

'Something of yours in that place? Something important?'

He said there might be. Then, 'I have to get inside.'

Was he a friend of Immacolata? He was.

A good friend?

He thought so.

'Did you shag her?'

Eddie Deacon looked at the kid crouched on the ground, his shoulder level with Eddie's knees. He said quietly, 'Not your business. Important? Maybe. How do I get inside? God – you'd know, wouldn't you?'

'I would, too.'

He tried to sound authoritative: 'Then you'd better take me.'

A smile slashed the kid's face and Eddie saw it when another match was struck and cigarette lit. He was told to give it a couple of hours, then come back – and that it would cost him.

He had no doubt that the kid would have the skills to break into a property that had a police guard on the front step.

Salvatore felt her tremble. He had not known Gabriella Borelli, *madrina*, leader of the clan, show fear, but she shook and couldn't stifle it. He held her close to him and the warmth came off her body. One arm was close round her shoulders and the other round the small of her back. She was twice his age. She was the most feared woman in the city. He could feel the straps of her underwear, and she would have felt the hardness against her belly. He could have pushed aside her coat, lifted her skirt, pulled down the panties, then flicked his own zip and hitched her up so that her arms were round his neck. Could have leaned her back against a wall and gone into her. Had he, it would have been – sad – the stupidest action of his life. Against a wall of old brick, put up by craftsmen centuries before, to have fucked a *madrina* while her husband was in gaol in the north and subject to Article 41 *bis* would have condemned him. Already Salvatore, Il Pistole, was a marked man and could live with it. If he fucked Gabriella Borelli he was a dead man and walking nowhere. And yet . . . He let a hand worm round from her back along the top of the pelvis, let it slide down and heard her breath quicken. And yet . . . He was not stupid.

He kissed her lightly on the forehead, at the hairline, and eased back from her. He thought – could not see in the darkness – that she clenched her fists and maybe drove the nails into the soft palms. He was glad, then, that he had backed off first. Her face would have hardened, and her jaw would be out.

The moment – body against body, juices aroused, heat rising – would not be referred to again. She would show no sign in the future of that intimacy. Neither would he. He thought she would have been a good fuck, better than the daughter. Salvatore knew that if ever she believed he was conceited enough to think he had any hold over her she would destroy him.

She touched his arm. It seemed to acknowledge a moment of weakness that was now stamped on, bagged, disposed of. She said, 'They have searched five addresses I use. Who knew five of my addresses?'

No cheek, no attempt to joke. 'I did.' He knew she would consider him as much of a suspect as anyone else. She had the ability to detach herself, analyse, and act. It was not necessary to bluster innocence to her.

'Who else?'

The wall behind her was high, dwarfing them, and above it was the Certosa di San Martino, of the fourteenth century, and behind the monastery, the fortress of Sant'Elmo, whose first stones had been laid eight hundred years before. That he was in the deep shadow of two of the most remarkable buildings in a city that was, itself, a miracle of history did not impress the clan's principal killer. He had one boast only: he would never be taken alive. Coming after him were the police detectives and the ROS investigators, the families and associates of those he had killed on the instructions of the Borelli clan, and if he rose too fast that clan would destroy him.

He had been found and taken in hand by Pasquale when he was a *scugnizzo*. The *padrino* had lifted him off the street, where he thieved, conned and tricked for food and money, no family to care for him, and created a ladder of advancement for him to climb. He had done street-corner spotting – who came into Forcella, what was their business and where they went – message-running, with tiny scraps of paper, sealed in plastic and secreted in body orifices, and had given out beatings when monies due were not paid. When he was eighteen, Pasquale – identifying talent where he could find it – had put the P38 into his smooth hand, had driven him to a disused quarry beyond Acerra and let him fire two magazines at rusty cans. A week later he had been given his first living, walking, breathing, spitting, cursing target. He had money and status, and wouldn't see his thirtieth birthday, which he accepted. He would be dead, and would not have – at his last breath – a regret.

'All the brothers, they knew.' He had taken instructions from Vincenzo before his flight to London but always after a moment had elapsed as if clarifying that his obedience was considered, not automatic, and instructions from Giovanni only if they were prefaced with 'My mother says.' He was contemptuous of Silvio and had never received an instruction from him. It did not cross his mind that he should include the sister, now gone eight months, with the brothers in having knowledge of the safe-houses.

'Yes – and who else?'

'Did Carmine and Anna Borelli know the addresses?'

Her father- and mother-in-law might have known two of the five, three at maximum. Not all.

'Did Umberto know?'

The lawyer, used by the family for more than thirty years, was now elderly, run to obesity and looked a fool, a pompous one, but his intellect was sharper than any other city lawyer's. He was skilled in the manipulation of court processes, the transfer of monies while they were rinsed clean, and the avoidance of surveillance. Umberto, perhaps, was a more significant aide to the clan than Salvatore, the killer.

She thought briefly, then replied that the lawyer might have known two addresses, no more.

'Did Pasquale know?'

She did not dismiss it. Her body seemed to stiffen, tighten, then a coil was loosened. She relaxed. She said that however desperate her husband was to regain his freedom, he wouldn't dare to betray her – and he would have known three addresses, but not five.

He shrugged, had no more to offer. He took out a small pocket torch and flashed it three times down the lane. He heard the response, the gunning of a scooter engine. It came forward, no lights shown. Did she want to be taken somewhere? She shook her head decisively. Who now to trust?

She walked away. He thought her wealth could have provided her with a Bentley, a Maserati or a Porsche, a driver in uniform and a guard to protect her. The scooter came up and collected him, the lights were flicked on and he saw her trudging the other way, along the rough track that would bring her out on the corso Vittorio Emanuele. He didn't know where she would head for but he reckoned it an hour's fast walking to get back to Forcella and Sanità.

He sat astride the pillion, slapped his man on the shoulder – he called him 'Fangio' – and they powered away. He did not look down from the track at the beauty of the bay and the reflections on the sea from ships' lamps and portholes or up at the illuminated ramparts of the castle. He let his mind scratch at the problem. Who had betrayed the clan? Who had earned death – not the fast death of the P38, but slow, stretched death? Who?

The aircraft landed, hit hard. She reached out, instinct, as the wheels bounced and the aircraft seemed to fly again, then the impact was repeated. Her hand took his. The fingers did not close on hers, and there was no comfort from them. Then she realised Castrolami thought nothing of her and had no concern whether she was terrified on landing or not.

They taxied, turned, idled and then, with a last lurch, the aircraft braked and was still. A ripple of applause shimmered behind them: it had not been a smooth flight, with turbulence over southern France, then powerful cross-winds as they had descended on Fiumicino, and the landing had been rough. Immacolata Borelli did not join in. She had only once, while they were in the air, left her seat. Then she had gone to the toilets in front of Business and had changed into the few new clothes she had been permitted to buy. She had washed her face and hands and had looked at herself in the mirror. She had tried to smile – and could not.

She had returned to her seat. Castrolami had not spoken to her. She thought he reckoned it enough that he had her on the plane, out of British jurisdiction and on her way to Italy, home. He hadn't asked if she was comfortable, if she was hungry, if she wanted a drink or a magazine. He had scribbled on a pad, might have been his report or his expenses, and she thought his socks smelled worse in the cabin than they had in the car.

She heard, behind her, a stampede. She had expected that she would have to wait. Castrolami squeezed his bulk past her, no apology, stood in the aisle and successfully blocked any passenger wanting to short-cut through Business to the forward door. Then he flicked his fingers – as if he had called a dog. She didn't move. Heard the flick of the fingers again, louder, more insistent and closer to her ear. Sat, didn't shift. The hand came down – the one she had clutched when the plane hit – caught her coat and yanked her up. Her waist snagged on the belt, still fastened. His other hand came across her thighs, almost groping her, and opened the catch. She thought he wouldn't have noticed where his hand had been. She stood.

She saw that two stewardesses and a purser eyed her, almost stripped her. It was obvious that she was a fugitive returning. No sympathy, no clemency. She had been offered a rug for her knees and had declined it, also earphones for the stereo. The trolley had come with newspapers – *Corriere*, *Messaggero* and *Repubblica* and she'd said she didn't want one. A few remarks only, and she wondered if they were sufficient for the cabin crew to know she was Neapolitan. If she was from Naples and in custody, she was a *camorrista*. She understood then that few shoulders would offer her a place to weep.

He had reached into his pocket and produced a pair of dark glasses. He handed them to her. The lights were poor in the cabin and outside it was late evening. She shook her head.

Castrolami said, 'Maybe there's a photographer. How do I know, when I have no control over it, what the security's like? I'm off my patch. Maybe this place leaks. Maybe your name is out. You want to make it easier for them? Put them on and turn up your coat collar. I don't want you dead, Signorina . . .'

She put on the glasses and pulled up the collar so that it half covered her cheeks. She thought, was not certain because his voice was only a murmur, that he added, 'Not before we've had you in court and testifying.'

He took her arm, led her out through the door and on to the pier, then down a flight of side steps into the night. Two cars waited, and men had sub-machine guns. The rear door of the lead car was open for her. Fingers lay on trigger guards. She was from a clan family and couldn't play at ignorance, and she understood the reaction towards a traitor and knew their fate. She attempted to bring to mind Marianna Rossetti's face, the last time she had seen it, without the ravages of leukaemia.

Immacolata Borelli had completed the first stage of her journey home. She dropped her head, sank on to the back seat and the crackle of radios was around her as she was driven away.

Music played at one café and the last stages of a soccer game were on a television at the other. Lukas was about halfway between the soccer and the music, and had yesterday's *Herald Tribune* in front of him with a month-old copy of *Match*.

Most evenings, when he was in Paris, he walked down the rue de Bellechasse and on to the rue St Dominique. There, he would pause outside the building with the double gate wide enough for a carriage and pair to go through, and he would take a moment under the plaque to consider the life and work of J. B. Dumas, *Chimiste-Secretaire Perpetuel de l'Academie des Sciences*, and note a date carved in the stone that put recognition of this man at 209 years ago. It was important for Lukas to stop for those few seconds, break his evening walk to the Bar le Bellechasse, the Drop Café or the Café des Deux Musées, because then he placed matters in his life into a correct perspective, one that he could manage to be alongside. There would be no plaque erected in Kabul, or Baghdad, up in the forests of the Midwest or in the triple-canopy jungle high in the Cordillera Central east of Cali for a co-ordinator who made the judgement – weighed lives and deaths – between the arguments of the negotiators and the storm-squad commanders. Nobody would read a plaque naming Lukas *Sometimes a Saviour and sometimes a Killer, Federal Bureau of Investigation and lately of Ground Force Security (London)*. Lukas did not rate himself important enough to warrant a plaque.

He thought them good people who served in the cafés and bars he patronised. They were ordinary people, who would not know of the situations that confronted him when he worked. It was better not to bring back to Paris with him, in his rucksack, the situations and knife-edges on which he operated. If business was slack they talked to him about the concerns and excitements of 'ordinary' people, and did not push for entry into his life – his unexplained absences – or pry, and they brought him beer and he gave them tips in midsummer and before Christmas. He paid always for what was brought to him unless the *patron* came with the drink. They could all set agendas and choose the subjects – had free range – except one area. He would steer the talk away from sons: he didn't welcome chatter about the triumphs and failures of sons. It was an area of pain suppressed, not shared, and he managed the deflection with subtle skill. In the bars and cafés, wiling away the evening hours, he never drank so that his mind clouded: the telephone in the apartment could ring at any time and activate the voicemail.

There was agitation at the far end of the bar. His name was called by a white-aproned waiter and he was told that the game had gone to penalty kicks and he should come for the death throes, but he smiled, shook his head, stayed in his chair and nursed his beer. Tomorrow, he thought, he would go to the museums – first the Musée d'Orsay and then that of the Legion – if the telephone had not rung and no message had been left.

5

The kid hissed, 'No lights, only the torch. And no torch till the curtains are done.'

Eddie Deacon could honestly have said that never in his life had he done anything that warranted the intervention of the police. Maybe he was a bit drunk sometimes on a Friday or Saturday night, rolling along the street and using a lamp post as a crutch, but he hadn't done anything that required an officer to get stuck into him. It didn't make him special, just ordinary. If a policeman's torch had lit him now, it would have been handcuffs, the back of a wagon and a cell door slamming.

The kid had asked for fifty; they had haggled. He had settled for thirty. Eddie thought the kid might be as young as nine. Newspapers he glanced at in the staff room carried interminable features on the spread of hooligans on the capital's streets. Thirty pounds had been passed, and to make it up Eddie had had to empty a pocket and dig up pound and fifty-pence coins. It was big money to him, but he didn't think it was high-value work to the kid . . . He rather liked him.

They had gone to the parallel street at the back. The kid had led and Eddie had followed. There was a locked iron gate at the side of a four-house terrace, and the kid had unfastened the lock as if it was easier than opening a toothpaste tube. They had edged along a garden, while inside a baby cried and a television played, and Eddie had been

helped over the end wall. They had dropped down into a
yard filled with sodden cardboard cartons that would have
come from the shop alongside the steps to the door used
by Immacolata and her brother. Next, up a drainpipe using
a dumped stool to get clear of the ground, then a window
ledge. The kid used a penknife on the window while Eddie
tottered beside him. The kid was sure-footed and showed
no fear. The window was levered up and a small thin arm,
width of a broomstick, came down, a hand took Eddie's and
wrenched it through the gap. Funny thing. When the small
hand took his weight, Eddie never doubted that he was safe.

What he liked about the kid was his sheer anarchy. Didn't
do arithmetic, as nine- or ten-year-olds should, but did
burglary. Didn't do joined-up writing and reading aloud but
did house-breaking. And smiled: wasn't sour-faced, but had
an openness and a sense of untamed rebellion about him
that were captivating. They stood statue still in the darkened
room, listened and heard nothing. Then the window was
closed and the kid said – still a treble voice – his friend
Vinny had boasted that a new alarm system had been
installed, had cost a grand, that the system couldn't be
interfered with by an intruder. The kid said, shrill whisper,
that the system was shit and he'd gone into the apartment
by this route, disabled it and brought out a leather-covered
Filofax by way of proof and carried it to the trattoria where
Vinny ate his pizza. Eddie hadn't understood how the circuits
could be blocked but Vinny had. He had given the kid fifty
pounds.

The kid worshipped Vinny. Only when he was talking
about him did the anarchy light go out of his eyes. He had
looked away just once, not done eyeball-to-eyeball, when
Eddie had asked what work was Vinny in. The kid had said,
'Business,' and looked away. Eddie remembered how he had
been at that age – guarded, protected, supervised, bred on

a wish-list of ambition and success, and damn near frightened of his own shadow.

The curtain was drawn. A palm-sized hand torch was passed to him. 'Is it in her room?' the kid asked.

He nodded. The kid took his arm and took him across what he now realised was a spare room, storeroom, into a central corridor and then the living area. The torch beam raked it. It was chaotic. Every drawer was out and upturned, the contents on the carpet. Every cushion was off the chairs and dumped. Pictures hung at wild angles, and Eddie thought they'd been shifted to see if they concealed anything. The magazines had been opened and dropped. He asked, confused, why it had been done. The kid told him, matter-of-fact, that there must have been a problem with the VAT. Then he repeated that he had heard police talk of the girl – Immacolata – who had gone back to Italy, her bag to follow. The kitchen was more chaos, plates scattered, saucepans on the floor or in the sink, refrigerator left open, sachets of pasta sauce slit as if they might have concealed something. The kid now amplified explanations and Eddie made out an exaggerated wink when he was told that people in 'business' sometimes forgot what VAT they owed.

Eddie didn't use his brain to analyse, then challenge. The kid seemed to glide over what was on the floor; but Eddie didn't. He kicked a china cup and heard it disintegrate, glass crunched under his feet. Then the small hand was tugging him and he was facing a closed door.

'She's lovely, isn't she, Vinny's sister?'

'Leave it.'

'Did you really do it with her – shag her? I used to watch her – I was out the back, and her room light would be on. Maybe she didn't think anyone was there. I used to, you know – when she was taking them off. I did.'

He didn't think of the kid as a dirty-raincoat man, or a

voyeur: they all did it. At his house, with a few beers taken, he and his friends had lined up to see across the garden to an upstairs window. He wasn't proud of himself, but didn't reckon it a hanging offence. Eddie thought that here, at least, the precocious adulthood of the kid came up short. Wouldn't have had sex, not at nine or ten. He was let into the room. The door had been locked and no key in it, but the kid opened it with a fast movement and Eddie didn't see whether he used a hairpin or a plastic card. He could smell her.

'Not your concern . . .'

Her perfume scent and slight body odour mingled. To smell her hurt him – like a kick, sharp, on his shin. The first thing that Eddie Deacon realised was that the room was only untidy. It had not been searched. The wardrobe doors were open but the dresses, blouses and skirts were on the hangers, and the drawers were not dragged open, tipped out. He hurried to the window, drew the curtains and switched on the torch.

It was a single bed, unmade, the duvet pulled towards the pillow but not straightened and smoothed. He let the beam sweep the room. He knew what he was looking for, had not promised it to himself but had hoped . . . He was disappointed. He had wanted to find a photo frame on the little pine table beside the bed, on the chest, or the bookcase to the left of the window, with a picture of himself inside it.

He set to work.

Nothing in the room shouted that Immacolata Borelli was the lover of Eddie Deacon. His own room, on the other side of Dalston, had the blow-up image of her, and her dressing-gown, which she put on when she came off the bed and went to make tea or coffee or to bring him a beer. He had precious little money each week after he'd paid the rent, and presents for her were his definition of mild extravagance, but the last thing had been a scarf – silk, a sale in Regent

Street, price slashed – and she'd said it was wonderful. He found it in the top right drawer of the chest.

He had been three, four minutes in the room when the kid came to the door. He made a sucked sharp whistle, as if he wanted to be gone. As yet Eddie had found nothing. There were three more drawers in the chest, on the left side. He went through them faster as the kid watched.

Nothing. Nothing in the pockets of clothes in the wardrobe. Nothing in the drawer of the bedside table. The kid came further into the room, snatched away the torch as if that were his right and shone the light into a wastepaper bin, picked it up and tipped it out. Eddie saw a ripped packet for tights, the wrapper from a tube of strong mints, two or three squashed paper handkerchiefs, a torn blouse, shredded brown paper that might have been used on a small parcel – and a plastic tray for sweet biscuits with Italian markings. The kid bent and sifted through what was on the carpet. He gave a scrap to Eddie. 'About all there is.'

Eddie Deacon held a piece of jagged paper, the tear running through a handwritten address – not the destination. Where the tear was, to the right, there were four scrawled lines. On the top line was 'elli'. Below it was 'cella'. Under that line was '157'. At the bottom was 'poli'. He was trying to decipher it when the torch beam was cut.

He was led, as if he were the child, out of the room and the lock was refastened. They went on tiptoe across the debris on the living-room floor to a window facing out on to the street. He was gestured to look down. There were two police officers on the front step, rubbing their hands and talking quietly. He realised then the quality of the kid's anarchy.

They went as silently as they had come. Down the drainpipe, across the yard and over the wall, through a garden and a side gate, supposedly fastened, then out on to a lit street. All tarted up, this one. Signs in the window proclaimed neighbourhood security co-operation, and alarm boxes winked lights.

The kid turned to him. 'Don't give me any shit about what they call love. It's all because she's a great shag, yes?'

He wondered if, one day, the kid might learn what was shit and what was something else, but was not confident of it – and he thought the boy didn't want to hear about the pain of separation, the hurt of his Mac going out of his life, about fighting heart and soul to win back the one person, in his world, he could not be without. He had the scrap of paper in his pocket and knew where he would take it. The kid, at nine or ten, was riddled with cynicism, and love hadn't reached him. Why disabuse . . . ?

'A great shag,' Eddie Deacon said.

They did high fives, whacked their hands together, and he watched the kid walk off. Just a kid, but with a bounce and a roll in his stride. There was the flash of a match, and a wisp of smoke curled away from his face.

Couldn't help himself. Eddie Deacon called, 'She's fantastic, the light for me. Thank you for helping me. She's more important to me than anything.'

If the kid heard he gave no sign of it but kept going towards the corner. Daft to have confided that to an urchin, a thief, but it was heartfelt.

She stood by the window, full length, with a sliding door that led to the balcony. The nightdress, bought in London, was shorter than she had thought, thinner, and hung tight on her. She had no slippers, sandals or flip-flops so Immacolata was barefoot on the marble flooring. She assumed that any of the penthouse apartments in such a block, in such a location, would have a veneer of marble in the living room. The sun was up, just above the distant mountain range.

She didn't know Rome, had been there once with her mother, years before, to stand on an Easter Sunday in the piazza San Pietro and see the tiny far-away figure of the Holy Father. So she had not recognised the route taken by the two cars as they had sped towards the centre, then veered away, crossed the river again and climbed a hill. The headlights had speared up and caught pine branches. No sirens and no blue lights. Nothing to indicate that the passenger in the lead car was a *collaboratore di justizia*, was protected, a *pentita* who would give evidence against her family in return for clemency, an *infame*, who would be despised in the streets where she had been reared. She came unheralded and unannounced. She had been hustled out of the car, and the guns were there, but under draped coats. She had been bundled into the lift, then almost pushed the few steps from the lift door into the penthouse.

She had been ignored at first by Castrolami, who was on his mobile – she'd heard him swear – and eyed by the two men who were to mind her.

Cold cuts of meat, a salad, fruit and cheese, laid out on plates, were taken from the refrigerator.

She was told nothing, shown to a bedroom with an en-suite bathroom, and had heard the door locked. It was done quietly and she reckoned it was not intended that she should hear it. A poor night's sleep, almost nightmares when she did drift off, able now to comprehend what she had done. At half past six, according to her watch, she had heard the key turn in the lock. She'd gone into the living room. The two men were up, smartly dressed, shirtsleeves and ties, shoulder-holster harnesses across their chests with weapons.

In case she had forgotten overnight, she was told – after the hope was expressed that she had enjoyed a satisfactory rest – that their names were Giacomo Orecchia and Alessandro Rossi. She'd nodded, then gone to the window.

Gerald Seymour

She had intended to provoke them.

Immacolata wore only the flimsy cotton nightdress, white but with flowers at the collar, and stood in front of the window as the sun came up over the rooftops, towers and spires. She eased her feet apart, let her heels be half a metre separated. She could feel, through the pane, that the sun already had the power to warm and would have lit the outline of her body. It was not normal for Immacolata Borelli to glory in her body, to use it as a tool or as a weapon. She imagined the way the light silhouetted it. Then she turned.

It would have been their skill that they moved in silence; neither watched her. The younger was out through the door, in the kitchen area, and sat at a table, looking at a newspaper – he was Rossi. The older one, Orecchia, was in a bedroom, again with the door open, smoothing a duvet and straightening a coverlet. It had been for nothing, her gesture. She had flaunted her body, to tease or confuse, and it hadn't been noticed.

From the kitchen, Rossi: 'Would you like coffee, Signorina? And we have *panini* or bread, fruit, and cheese. Some of it or all?'

Whatever. Did she care? Hardly. 'I don't know . . .'

Orecchia said, 'Do you want some coffee before you dress or while you're still almost naked?'

She met his eyes. She realised then that he had taken a gamble with her: that he could ridicule her, showing he recognised the game she was playing and would not tolerate it so had laughed at her. She flushed and twisted away from them so that neither would see, through the flimsy material, the curve of her bosom, the cherrystone nipples or the hair above her thighs. Orecchia reached behind the bedroom door and his hand appeared with a heavy towelling robe. He threw it at her. It landed on the marble beside her so she had to bend to lift it up, with an arm across her chest as she did so. She slipped into the robe, belittled and angry.

Rossi called, 'I make good coffee, Signorina, and I bought the bread this morning while you slept. My suggestion: breakfast now, dress afterwards. Then we have visitors and work.'

She believed they were treating her as they would a spoiled child, and seemed to have set guidelines. They had not leered at her or been shocked by her. They had, with laid-back politeness, almost taken her legs off at the knees. She stumbled across the marble, bare feet slipping, losing her poise, to her bedroom door. She showered – found a small bar of soap there and a sachet of shampoo, and she had her own washbag. She barely allowed the water to run hot, then was out and drying herself viciously. She dressed – new underwear, the same outer clothing she had travelled in, and left her hair damp. She could smell the coffee and the warmed *panini*.

Beyond the window there were similar blocks to the one she was in, surrounded by high steel fences with sharp spikes; the walls had broken glass embedded in concrete on the brickwork. She saw a maid beating a carpet on a balcony, and a man, who wore only shorts on another, was smoking and scratching his chest. A woman watered her plants with a hose. She did not belong in their world. Perhaps she belonged to no world. Her nakedness had been her attempt to take control of the void into which she had thrown herself.

She was as much a prisoner in that apartment as she would have been in a cell in the Poggioreale gaol. They might have read her.

'Signorina, the coffee is ready.'

'Bread and fruit are on the table, Signorina.'

She went into the kitchen and sat with them. Rossi was the heavier and she imagined he worked out in a gym. His arm muscles bulged in the short sleeves of his shirt, he was clean-shaven and a little gel had gone on his hair. She recognised the pistol in the holster as a Beretta. He poured her coffee.

Orecchia pushed the fruit bowl towards her. He would have been fifteen years the elder, wiry thin, and his shirt seemed a size too large and fell loose from his shoulders, except where the holster harness trapped the fabric. His tie was the more vivid. He had a worn face – had been there, had done whatever, had seen it. She gulped coffee, snatched up a roll and tore it into pieces.

Rossi said, 'Signorina, we are from the Servizio Centrale Protezione, under the authority of the Interior Ministry. You will be given later a form in triplicate that you will read and sign. By agreeing to the conditions laid down by us, you commit yourself to obeying instructions and following the advice we will offer. You are not a free agent. You have made an agreement with the state, and we expect you to honour it. We're a specialised team, trained to handle and protect collaborators. We're not nannies, chauffeurs, psychiatrists or servants – and, most certainly, we're not friends. It was your decision to be where you are today. You were not under duress to take this course. From us you can expect dedication and professionalism.'

Orecchia said, 'It was not thought, Signorina, that you needed a female officer attached to you. There are very few. Those we have are allocated to women we consider inexperienced in the role of a *pentita*, and the pressures that will inevitably be exerted. I have read the file. You are from a family high in the ranks of the organised-crime clans in Naples.'

Rossi: 'We don't think you're fragile, Signorina.'

Orecchia: 'As tough as the boot on an artisan's foot.'

Rossi paused, eyed her, without charity or respect, but his tone was as correct as if it had been taught on a course: 'Nothing about you, Signorina, is unique. You're one of many we have overseen. We understand the psychological stresses you will endure. You will believe you can escape from us, go home, walk on your own streets, explain and be forgiven, then forgotten. They'll kill you, Signorina. You'll lie in the dirt of a street among dog's mess and rubbish, and you'll bleed. A crowd will gather to stare at you and not one person will shed a tear of sympathy. And you can put the scum where they belong – in maximum security, and under Article 41 *bis*, and you can be born again. You will not run from us.'

Orecchia scratched a mole on his nose. He wore a wedding ring, narrow, and she wondered if he went home often and if, when he was at home, he told his wife the secrets of his work. He spoke quietly and she had to lean across the mess of crumbs and orange peel to hear him. 'In a few hours, Signorina, it will be realised that you have collaborated, become an *infame*, and they will search for you. Alessandro has talked about a shot in the head fired from the pillion of a scooter as you walk a street in Naples – or Rome, or Milan, or Genoa – but he's told you the minimum. To me, from what I know, it's predictable that they'd wish – before killing you – to hurt you, but you're of the Borelli clan and you know what happens when a message is to be sent. In the most recent killing – the funeral is today – the victim's testicles were cut off and placed in his mouth, then his head was cut off and placed in his groin. That is reality.'

'We're not bullet-catchers or human shields.'

'We know our trade. We'll do all in our power to protect you.'

She poured more coffee for herself, slurped it. The doorbell rang. Orecchia glanced at his watch, was satisfied. Rossi took his hand off the pistol in the holster and went to the hall, but Orecchia stayed in front of her, blocking a view of her from the archway linking the kitchen to the hall. His hand did not leave the pistol in his holster.

Immacolata was introduced to the prosecutor. She had

seen him many times before – on most days his picture was in *Cronaca* or *Il Mattino*, or his image was broadcast on the local RAI channel, and he had been in court when she had seen her father brought in chains to the cage. He was slighter than she had imagined, his hair was thinner and his checks had the pallor of exhaustion. She thought of the magnetism in her father's eyes, the way they mesmerised and captured attention. Ash stained the front of the prosecutor's jacket and he dumped a heavy briefcase on the kitchen table.

He pulled out a file with her name and photograph on it. She thought of the cemetery at Nola. The table was cleared. She was told that the woman with the prosecutor was his personal assistant. A tape-recorder was laid on the table and wires were connected to a small microphone. She noticed now that the plates and cups had been stacked in the sink, and the guns had gone.

The tape-recorder was switched on, there were the briefest preliminaries. Immacolata kept the cemetery in her mind, the statue of Angelabella, the screams directed at her, the anger, and the pain inflicted on her. She started to talk.

Gabriella Borelli needed to work. There had been La Piccolina a decade earlier, and before the Little Girl, as Maria Licciardi was known, there had been Rosetta Cutolo, known as 'Ice Eyes' in the city. There had been Carmela Marzano and Pupetta Maresca. All had been figures of consequence on the streets of Naples, as was Gabriella Borelli. She had to work if she was to cling to the most important strand in the life of a woman who craved and valued the title '*la madrina*', which was power. The gaining of it far outstripped the acquisition of money. Power came, primarily, from the ability to do successful deals.

She could not hide in an underground den, as Pasquale had been able to. She needed meetings, and to be at them without the clay of the countryside on her shoes or the dust of cement-floored bunkers on her skirt. She was in the back room of a pizzeria on the northern side of the via Foria, one of the busiest streets in the city for traffic and pedestrians, where noise and movement were constant, overpowering and engulfing. She had slept fitfully at the home of the mother of a man who drove cement-mixing trucks for the clan; had arrived on the doorstep, had been admitted in time to see the midnight news on the local RAI channel, had seen tape of Giovanni and Silvio paraded past the ranks of the *paparazzi*, an old monochrome picture of Vincenzo, had heard the mayor in front of the grand building on piazza Municipio speak of a 'great blow against the heart of the evil of the criminal culture' of the city. She had been brought fruit and cheese and had been offered the woman's big bed, had declined and slept on a settee, with her handbag on the floor beside her head, the small pistol in it within easy reach. It was the first time she had used that address as a refuge for a single night: it would not have been known as a place of importance to her – as were the safe-houses that had been raided. She understood that she had been betrayed from inside the clan, but did not yet know by whom. She had been gone early in the morning, as the city's life returned, and had walked to the pizzeria.

Salvatore was outside the inner door.

She met with Albanians. They talked of the movement of girls – none, she demanded, to be more than fourteen – who would be taken from Moldova overland to Tirana, then brought to the Adriatic coast to be ferried by speedboat to a fishing village north of the Italian port of Bari, then driven to Naples. She was firm on the price, would not haggle. She demanded also that the girls be made available for medical examination to prove virginity, then stared at a dull ceiling light while they bickered among themselves. She presumed they would have learned that she was a police and *carabinieri* front-line target, that her organisation was in danger of being successfully dismantled, and that they might believe she was vulnerable.

The matter of the girls was dealt with. Brusquely, she continued with the agenda: refined heroin – the poppies from Afghanistan, the chemical from the laboratories of Turkey, then shipped from the Balkans and Montenegro to the port of Naples. The price of the heroin. Again, no debate permitted. She said what she would pay. Monies were agreed, delivery dates accepted.

Her meeting broke. She shook their hands formally to bind the agreements.

She went out of the pizzeria's front door on to the street.

She did not, of course, carry a diary. Everything was in her head. Meeting locations and times, rendezvous points, market prices. The next meeting – in another back room, in a bar on the via Arenaccia – was to determine the volume of hardcore stone for the foundations of a new apartment block on Cristoforo Colombo, then the amount of concrete required for the six-storey construction, the prices for the materials and the fee for the men in the *municipio* who would give permission to build. It was a normal routine for Gabriella Borelli.

The sun was warm on her face. She felt as if a winter frost thawed. By the conclusion of the meeting the Albanians had shown her the necessary respect. She wondered if those who had guided them to the rendezvous had shown them a half-page of yesterday's *Cronaca* and translated a report on the death of a man in a street, the meal made of his testicles. She walked briskly, Salvatore, Il Pistole, behind her, and felt she had regained control.

They broke. The recorder was switched off and a new tape inserted. The prosecutor's assistant went to the toilet.

She looked up into the prosecutor's face and hoped for a smile and praise. Immacolata Borelli had been prompted to talk about her brother, Vincenzo, who was to appear before magistrates that morning and would then be transferred to a maximum-security facility. She was confused. 'You haven't mentioned my mother.'

'That is correct,' the prosecutor answered gravely.

'You took her?' she pressed.

'We did not.' A small frown cut into his forehead.

'Because you couldn't find her.'

'She wasn't where we looked for her.' The prosecutor's tongue licked his lower lip.

'I told you where to go.'

'You did.'

'She was the principal target.'

'She was one target. We regret she isn't yet in custody. She will be, very soon.' He smiled wanly. The assistant came back to her chair and the recorder was switched on again. 'It shouldn't concern you whether or not your mother's in custody.'

The gesture was fast, instinctive. Immacolata hit the table with the heel of her hand. The impact bounced the tape recorder and spilled the prosecutor's coffee. There was a flicker of movement in a doorway off the hall as if a watcher had been alerted. She said, 'I won't talk to you until my mother has been taken. I trusted in your competence. You have failed.'

'Do you imagine I travel lightly from Naples to Rome to hear the tantrum of a woman who overestimates her own importance? I can cut you loose and—'

'You won't take my mother.'

She stood and the chair fell behind her, clattered. She didn't look at them, didn't see the slow turn of the spools in the tape-recorder. She went to her room and slammed the door. It was her mother's face, lit by camera flashes, that she wanted to see, her mother's face, in shadow as a cell door closed on a corridor's lights, and her mother's face, when early sunlight caught the cell windows and the bars made stripes on her skin. Her strongest emotion that morning was not love but hate. It went so deep. It covered a mother's apparent indifference to a girl-child, the failure of the parent to rate the achievements of a daughter. Immacolata had been denied attention, denied praise, ignored. She lay on the bed. There had been hate for her mother, but now there was fear at the reach of her arm.

'Is that what he said?'

'It's what I was told he said.' Salvatore was at Gabriella Borelli's shoulder. His voice had been a murmur and his lips had barely moved. While he had guarded the inner door of the pizzeria, the *scugnizzi* had brought messages to him. Lower in the chain than the foot-soldiers were the kids who watched entrances to the quarters of the city and reported, listened to conversations in bars and reported, sat in the gutter opposite police stations and *carabinieri* barracks and reported.

'Say it to me again.' She spoke from the side of her mouth, a whisper, as the traffic roared by, horns blasted, men and women walked along the pavement, and her words were lost to all but Salvatore.

'He was in the bar at the top end of Casanova, Luigi Pirelli's bar. He was in a group and the TV was on. The arrests . . . Alfredo's youngest heard him. He said, 'The Borelli clan is history. They're finished, old, shit and soft. They have no authority now. Count the days, they'll be gone.'

'That man, he is not to say that again.'

She walked on. Salvatore dropped back. He was soon fifteen or twenty paces behind her. He had much to think about. He was the enforcer of the clan and answered only to Gabriella Borelli. He had taken on, also, responsibility for her security and the offshoots of the group. Three years ago, before he had been arrested, Pasquale Borelli would have had the last say on security. Eight months ago, before his flight to London, Vincenzo had been given that responsibility in his father's absence. He did not know where such leakage of information had come from: the faces of men bounced in his mind, called forward, then discarded. He kept her back in his sight, and the pistol, the Beretta P38, was in his belt. He wore a loose-fitting jacket to conceal it.

She was tough, and her walk showed it. The weakness of the last evening had been short-lived. Salvatore thought Gabriella Borelli magnificent as he tracked her, watching her back.

He asked, respectfully, if Lottie would join him in the staffroom alcove. Eddie Deacon hardly knew her, had offered her no friendship, but now he needed her. She was – and the young guys who taught at the language school tittered over it – shyly lesbian. Obvious, but never confessed. Lottie had not outed herself. She was reluctant to come with him, suspicious, but then he did what he reckoned was his best imitation of 'Labrador eyes' and she would have seen it mattered to him. There was no snigger on his lips.

Eddie said, 'Sorry and all that, but I need help. I've lost a girl. It's really hacked me off. Don't know where she is, other than gone home, and she's Italian, from Naples. Says on Google that a million people live there, that the city is a hundred and twenty square kilometres. I have to find her, but I don't know where to start.'

Lottie looked at him in the marginal privacy of the alcove, perhaps remembered slights that were not imagined, remarks behind hands and little darts of cruelty. 'What if little Miss

Perfect doesn't want to be found – at least, not by you? . . .
All right, all right. What have you got that might help?'

Eddie had the torn scrap of paper in a see-through plastic
bag, as if it was priceless. He seemed reluctant to give it up,
share it, but did so.

'You didn't answer me. What if she rates you a pain, and
wants shot of you?'

'I'll have her say it to my face,' Eddie said. He shrugged,
then did the smile he was famed for – it implied that no
woman could possibly want shot of him. Lottie grinned, then
looked at the handwriting. He had gone to her because she
had spent time in Naples, at the university, and spoke the
language fluently. He tried to joke: 'I really don't understand
why any female of the species could want shot of me, let
alone rate me a pain. Just not on the agenda.'

She studied the paper as if it were a crossword puzzle,
then gazed at him. 'I'm wondering, Eddie, if you're behaving
like an adult or reverting to teenage male, all acne and
infatuation – or is that not my business?'

'Just a little old cry for help . . . please. If it wasn't for her,
it's you I'd be chucking red roses at.'

She rolled her eyes, almost blushed. 'What's her name?'

'Immacolata Borelli.'

She breathed out hard. 'Right, line one, try Borelli. Line
two, go with a number and via Forcella. Line three will be
the zip code, four more preceding digits, then 157, for that
part of the Forcella district that runs between via del Duomo
and the Castel Capuano. The last line is Napoli. It's hardly
Enigma code-breaking but, then, you're only a man.'

'A specimen to be pitied.'

After she'd repeated it, and he'd written it in ballpoint
on the back of his hand, he surprised himself, and her, by
taking hold of her shoulders and kissing her hard on both
cheeks.

He was turning away as she said, 'Are you really going there?'

'Too right – what else?'

Eddie Deacon set off down the corridor for the principal's office.

Twenty metres had become forty. They were on via Carbonara, close to the old castle that had doubled as a courthouse. He understood the route she had taken. In Salvatore's mind many issues competed for prominence: the man who had said the Borelli clan was 'finished, old, shit and soft', a leak in security, his job as protector to Gabriella Borelli. Any could have claimed priority, but he didn't make that choice. Then he looked at his watch, saw the time, recognised he was late for the rendezvous with his scooter driver, Fangio, and smiled. Gabriella Borelli was at the lights, waiting for the pedestrian green and would cross via Carbonara above the castle. He smiled when he remembered 'Fangio', who had done a 'Wall of Death' stunt in a circus, had crashed spectacularly in front of five hundred punters, or more, and would not have had the money to buy a new bike. He had always enjoyed the memory of Fangio's face when he was offered the post of scooter rider to Salvatore, Il Pistole. Fangio had been in Poggioreale and Secondigliano, was no altar-boy. There were few Salvatore trusted, but Fangio was one. Many people were waiting to cross at those lights, then the traffic slowed and the charge started. Not for Neapolitans to wait. Sinewy lines of pedestrians wove among the vehicles. He could barely see her.

She had heard doors close, and a minute later a car had revved outside the block. Then music had started in the apartment, and the only voices were those of the minders.

She lay on the bed, her head on the pillow, straining to

hear what was said. The music was opera and distorted the
voices. She realised the prosecutor had gone, would now be
on his journey to Naples. There had been no soft knock on
her door, and no discreet voice – maybe that of the woman,
his assistant – had urged her to come out of her room, to
co-operate. She had been abandoned.

She had convinced herself that walking out on them was
justified by their display of incompetence. They had failed
to arrest her mother.

The doorbell rang.

They were at the bottom of the seniority heap. He was
twenty-four and she was his senior by three months. They
had started at the training school on the same Monday
morning, had been posted to Naples on the same Monday,
accepted and begun duty with the Squadra Mobile on another,
very recent, Monday. To survive, they stayed close, had
volunteered to work together. Around them there were men
and women who were prematurely aged, jaundiced and
pessimistic, who preached that ambition was heresy in the
team. They had been up all the previous night and now
headed for their homes out to the south on the sea front
and sleep.

He had driven one of the Alfas carrying a senior man to
a block where, on the third floor, they had hoped to find *la
madrina*. She had driven a car filled with officers to another
of the addresses given by an informant – not identified at
the briefing. Now she drove and stifled a yawn, changed
down and braked. Pedestrians flooded the roadway around
them. The photographs, blown up, of Gabriella Borelli, the
target, were in the car. He cursed. Both were hungry,
exhausted; both, for the operation the night before, had
studied the photograph long and hard.

The curse became a gasp. He jack-knifed and snatched

up a picture that had been on the rubber matting, smoothed it, gawped. He elbowed her hard in the ribcage below her right breast, jarring his bone on her holster. For a moment the photograph was in her face. She nodded. They had the certainty of youth, and neither would have considered their judgement flawed, their recognition wrong.

Weapons drawn, they ran from the car, left the doors wide. The crown of her head bobbed in front of them and the gap closed.

Not hate, but fear. After the doorbell had rung, Immacolata heard a bucket, water splashing, a woman's voice, and laughter from the minders. She thought a maid had come to clean, and she was ignored.

She realised the weight of her fear.

No warning. No shout to alert her that police with guns drawn were immediately behind her. No opportunity to raise her hands as the pistols were aimed at the point in her back where straps and shoulder muscle met.

Salvatore saw a small tableau in front of him that seemed mimed.

He was used to making calculations, those that involved a reasonable chance of survival within a time frame of a second or two. He could cruise on the pillion his chest and stomach against Fangio's back, have the P38 in his fist inside the right pocket of his leather jacket, and he would see the target – darkened by his helmet visor – walking, sitting or eating, on the pavement, in a car or at a pizzeria table, and he would know whether or not that was the moment to strike. If he went in for the kill, he would rap his left hand on Fangio's shoulder, the scooter would swing and take him close, then stop for the few moments he needed to aim and achieve a clean hit. If he hit Fangio's shoulder twice, Fangio would take the scooter past the target and the hit was aborted: might be an escort in place, a folded windcheater on a table when the temperature was high that would conceal a firearm, might be that a *carabinieri* or police vehicle was following or approaching. He wouldn't intervene if he couldn't succeed.

She was pitched over. The young man stood, legs apart in a movie pose, his weapon aimed – two-handed – at her. The young woman had launched herself and landed on Gabriella Borelli's back – a she-cat on prey – had wrestled her down and, with one hand, had wrenched an arm of *la madrina* behind her back. The other held a heavy pistol, big in a slight fist, so that the barrel pressed against the neck. Salvatore had the Beretta half out of his waist belt, and the moment was gone. The man no longer covered Gabriella Borelli but the people – men, women and children – who scattered away from where they had their prisoner, as cars and vans veered to the side. It was as if a cordon was around them, an exclusion area. He thought she would have said, and perhaps stroked his arm as she did so, that she trusted him alone. Because of the open area between him and them, he would be seen and identified if he ran forward, and would have to enter the space to be close enough to fire killing shots.

It could not be done.

He thought that she looked old with her face crushed down on the sand and shit and weeds of the little island where once there had been a traffic bollard. There was dirt on her face, her hair had lost its shape and there was shock in her eyes. He had broken the trust, had failed her.

She was dragged to the car. Her feet did not get a hold and a shoe came off, but she was pulled there and the door thrown open. The young man thrust her in and threw himself on top of her. Fumes spewed from the exhaust and the car sped off. Salvatore saw, before he lost it, a hand clamp a light on the roof and the blue flashes that spilled from it. He heard the siren wail.

He walked away, more alone than he could remember at any time since Pasquale Borelli had chosen him, had taught him to kill, and taught him well.

Flashes in her mind of the moments of fear. A girl left to mind a slow-cooking meat   baby lamb – in the oven, told when to take it out, forgetting, and coming back into the kitchen to see the smoke then cringing from her mother's beating, a hard one. Her mother made fear, and the hate was secondary. There was no love in her life, not from her family. Love was sealed away from her in the cemetery at Nola. She knew only hatred and fear. More laughter came through her door, but Immacolata did not share it.

He put the phone down, ended one of the calls that seemed to consist of almost endless silences. The display panel told him the connection had been for four minutes and nine seconds, but it had seemed to Arthur Deacon a fair imitation of eternity. He walked slowly from the hall table towards the kitchen. He couldn't go in as Betty was washing the floor but he came to the doorway and coughed, as if that was the best way to gain his wife's attention.

She squeezed out the mop, quizzed him with a glance. 'Well?'

'It was Edmund.'

'I know – what did he want?'

She used a mop on the kitchen floor three mornings a week, then went to work at a family firm of builders, and would tut if he stepped on the clean tiles and messed up. He was watching her, thinking how to relay what he had been told.

'Have you lost your tongue? What did he want? Money? At his age he ought to be able to—'

'Listen. Just for once. Listen. Thank you.' He saw astonishment on her face. His boldness, almost, surprised him. She liked to say that her mother had told her on the eve of their wedding, 'Always remember, Elizabeth, a husband is for life but not for lunch.' She was at work over lunch time and he made himself sandwiches. She liked also to remind him that she was now the principal breadwinner and he was a pensioner who had taken the early bullet. 'Yes, best if you simply listen. Edmund has resigned from his job.'

'What for?'

'He packed it in as of today. He's going tomorrow, or this evening if he can arrange it, to Naples.'

'I don't understand.'

'Listen, and you might – after a fashion. That girl he spoke of, the one he promised to bring to meet us, she's gone. Gone home. No warning, no explanation, but gone. Sadly, he intends to follow her.'

'What did you say?'

'I said there were other fish in the sea. Apparently not. I said he'd run the risk of hurting himself. He said he was hurting enough as it was and wouldn't notice any more pain. He'd never said anything like that to me before, bared himself in that way.'

'Extraordinary.'

'I don't want to be rude, Betty, but I'm wondering whether either of us would have gone chasing halfway across Europe if the other had done a bunk. I doubt that's unfair. I said I'd look after his Visa bills – and couldn't think of anything else. Oh, yes, I wished him luck. It didn't seem sensible to be parental, old and cautionary. That's it.'

His wife said, 'No, I wouldn't have followed you. She must be very special, that girl.'

*

At that time in the morning, the tourists had not yet come to the museums. Lukas had. The bars, coffees and beers were for later in the day, while squatting close to his friend who drew the river, the Louvre and Notre Dame was for the middle. Early, he came with a plastic bottle of fizzy water to sit on a bench and watch the first arrivals. Most would not know a Millet from a Manet or a Monet, but Lukas had no sense of superiority, and could not have made the distinction himself. He came to see people and search their faces, the better to understand them.

The science he practised affected humble people, average people, ordinary people. It was they who looked at the great statues, the bronzes, outside the former railway station that was now a museum and gazed at the massive charcoal grey bulk of the rampant elephant with flared ears and the rhinoceros that looked ready to charge, both larger than life. It was those people – businessmen, teachers, backpackers, engineers, charity workers, and those of whom it was said 'Wrong place at the wrong time' – whom he worked to liberate, to keep alive.

When the buses came he would settle back and stare into the faces, but not be noticed himself, and he would play mind games. How would they respond, hooded, bound, beaten, videotaped with guns at their heads and knives at their throats as they parrot-spoke denunciations of state policy? His interpretation of how they would react, in circumstances of the greatest stress would govern the guidance he gave and the decisions he took.

He had no favourites. He was no more on the side of the pretty slim blonde girl with the denim mini-skirt who came off the bus with the Hamburg plates than he was on the side of the guy who walked behind her with a stick. All were equal. So, he was not summoned to the great offices of authority in the power centres of the world. He did not walk echoing corridors, was not brought into carpeted offices and offered sherry or Scotch, because their occupants did not know his name. He worked in dark corners, that were – except once – beyond the reach of long-lens cameras.

It was rumoured, though five years later it remained unconfirmed, that a photographer from a German news agency had snapped him on a street in Baghdad when he was with a Special Forces crowd. The photographer had been embedded with a marine unit or would otherwise have been hotel-bound. Rumour ran that the sunlight had nicked the glass of the Leica camera so he had seen its owner and strode up to him. He had half strangled the snapper when he pulled off the strap and broke the camera open by stamping on it, destroying maybe fifteen thousand dollars' worth of equipment. He had taken out the memory stick and had chucked it into the middle of a wide sewer, then had gotten on with his work. The photographer had been told by a gofer alongside Lukas, from the Green Zone, that if he talked about the incident his safety could not be guaranteed. It was a rumour. In the work he did, his anonymity was precious, perhaps even more so than that of an élite bomb-disposal operative. If his face had been known to the enemy, with his reputation, he would have been a prime target, and his usefulness in the field minimised. And, which he had not admitted to another soul he had a rooted aversion to the limelight, almost shyness, disguised under brusque indifference.

He had no medals, but the people – ordinary, average, humble – coming off the bus of a Hamburg tour company, pretty and ugly, young and old, did not have medals. Most of those freed from the hell-holes, the bunkers where they squatted in excreta and urine, listening for footsteps and wondering if a weapon was loaded or a knife sharpened, would never know of Lukas's existence. It was better that way. No handshakes at the end, if it had gone well, no hugging and kissing, no names and promises of cards on the anniversary. The only way.

So, his imagined friends queued in front of him to enter the museum, and one of his real friends sketched in crayon by the river, and several more cleaned café tables and swept floors – and all would be wondering if he would stroll by, spend some time, or whether he was gone, wherever and for whatever.

That morning he left his bench, went to the kiosk and bought a pistaccio ice-cream. It was his favourite. He thought about it when he was in places that didn't do that flavour or any other. Some said he was a screwball and unhinged, others that folk should be goddam grateful the lunatic stayed on call and was never far from his phone.

When he had finished the ice-cream and wiped his mouth, he would head into the museum for the Legion of Honour, and the impeccable garden in the central courtyard with the fine red roses. It was where he went when he had tired of the mind games, and it was where heroes were. He did not see himself as heroic, and if a medal had been offered he would have refused it.

Many, meeting him for the first time, defined him as 'that screwball'. A major in the Rangers had. It was Baqubah and they'd helicoptered in from Camp Liberty at the Balad air base between Baghdad and Samarra. There was a single-storey house, breeze blocks and tin roof, on the extreme edge of the place near fields, and the asset handled by Task Force 145 said it was where the hostage was – a Greek-born engineer and expert in electricity supply, and how many guys held him. Difficult to get close, and the usual thing would have been to do three or four days' reconnaissance, learn the movements and do it from a distance. Lukas was at the command point, four or five klicks back, and was barely tolerated by the major who rated him – FBI background and all – as an unwelcome shoe-in. A forward covert observer would have been on a telescope, reported a jerk coming to the building cautiously and that he carried a canister of milk and a metre-wide roll of clear plastic sheeting. Only Lukas – in the command centre – had reacted. He had demanded – not asked or suggested but *demanded* – that the storm squad assault the building immediately. It had been agreed. Would have been Lukas's damn near manic certainty that had won the day: an attack without sufficient preparation, without a model of the interior, and in the bright heat light of the middle of the day.

Twelve minutes after Lukas had made his demand the first men in the Ranger platoon hit the doors front and back, than the windows, and chucked in stun grenades and gas canisters, like it was Christmas and they were giving them away. They dragged out the Greek, and brought him back from the dead. The Greek said he would have been dead in five minutes, was shouting it because of what the grenades had done to his hearing and choking because of the gas. Then the major asked the man designated a 'screwball' how he'd known the attack had to go in without the necessary preparation. Lukas had said: 'Because they took the plastic sheeting in.' Would he explain? Lukas had said: 'They always spread plastic sheeting out on the floor before they saw a guy's head off with a serrated blade to keep the blood off it.' There had been a camera, with a charged battery, mounted on a tripod. The major had been awarded another ribbon and his storm squad had commendations, and none of them had ever seen Lukas again. Maybe by now the major had made brigadier or even general, and maybe the Greek had a good position in power supply at the ministry in Athens . . . and Lukas wandered into the courtyard of the museum for heroes.

It was how he liked it, staying unknown but being on call.

6

He had been lucky. He told himself that luck had dictated that a lorry should spill its load on the M11 just north of Harlow, the northbound carriageway, and that a tailback of four miles should delay a family on a budget break to Rome while the rail service had sailed past unaffected. Eddie Deacon would have slept on a bench at the airport, Stansted, but instead found himself aboard a 'cheap and cheerful' flight going to Ciampino.

A rush to get himself on board, a chase down corridors and piers, and he had been the last on to the aircraft. He was not even in a seat before the doors were closed and it was taxiing. He told himself then that he was blessed.

He had not bought a book, and they didn't do freebie newspapers with that airline. The child on his left ate chocolate messily and concentrated on a GameBoy, and the woman on his right was rigid with nerves – he reckoned he might have her hand in his lap, for comfort, when it came to landing. Eddie didn't buy anything from the trolley and sat still, upright, stared ahead and made no contact, eye or physical, with the woman or the child. He thought he might just as well have pulled a pin and rolled a pineapple grenade into his parents' living room: his father had been monosyllabic and breathing hard, but had coughed up the offer to look after his plastic bill, which was decent, but afterwards they would – together – have been in shock. He had switched off his mobile before catching the train to Stansted. He reckoned

they would have tried half a dozen times to phone him, to
try to dissuade him, to tell him he should go to the language
school and request his job back. His parents, and all their
friends, would never march out of regular paid employment
without having another position to move to on the following
Monday morning. So, the concept of what he had done left
him vaguely light-headed. His mind danced.

What was bizarre about the choreography was that he
had not stopped – he hadn't since he had sat alone in the
Afghan restaurant and waited – to consider that Immacolata
might have decided that he was a boring no-hoper, a saddo
and a loser, and that a summer fling was over as autumn
came on. Never thought of it. He had a BA (Hons) in Modern
Languages, only a 2:2 – they called it a Desmond at that
university in the Thames Valley – and at the end of four
years' study was supposed to possess some capability at
analysis. He had left with a good knowledge of German, fair
French and some Spanish, with a smattering of Italian, which
might take him over the front page of a newspaper.

He knew Berlin, having walked the pavements and worked
in all-night cafés during summer vacations, and could get
himself around Paris without glancing every five minutes at
a map, and he wouldn't have been lost in Barcelona. He
didn't know Rome or Naples, but he had once spent two
days in Milan, having climbed on the wrong train in Geneva
when he should have been going to Montpellier in France,
coming from Munich. It mattered not. It was not in the
temperament of Eddie Deacon to worry at a problem, as if
he needed to untie a tight knot in a length of string. He
either ran from problems or tilted at them. If she had indeed
walked out on him she could say so to his face: clear, one-
syllable words. Not possible, not his Mac. Second point,
chewed on briefly in the aircraft cabin: police at the flat, a
brother taken away, the flat searched, everything about her

hidden from him like her address. Was she 'dodgy', or 'bent'?
Weighed it. Didn't care. She was his Mac.

There was no doubt. He had to go to Naples. He had to
find her. He'd pull a face, she'd grimace and shrug a bit, ask
him what the hell he was doing there – in a street, whatever
it looked like, whatever via Forcella looked like. He'd say he
wanted a fresh roll for his breakfast, maybe some *croissants*.
She would look surprised, astonished, then grin. He'd laugh.
Both laughing, hugging and holding tight. It was what he
thought. Nothing about a broken door, police on the step,
a wild kid who was expert on breaking and entering, maybe
no more than ten years old. Nothing about sitting for several
hours in a restaurant, hurting, and hurting worse in his
bedroom where her dressing-gown hung and her magazines
lay about. Nothing about talking to, pleading with a blow-
up photograph on a wall. They would do it, meeting again,
just casual, as if nothing had happened and no wounds had
been cut into him. He never saw her solemn, sullen, serious,
because Mac was always the photograph on the wall.

Who knew what love was? They didn't talk about love in
the little house they shared in Dalston. Love was not an
agenda area with the guy from HM Revenue and Customs,
the club waiter, the rail-ticket seller or the perpetual student.
Love was in movies, books, magazines. Screwing and shagging
were real – rare but attainable with a good alcohol flow –
but love was off-limits. The definition of love, as known to
Eddie Deacon, was an ache in his guts, a yearning and the
bloody awful misery of not seeing that face coming round
the corner and the little wave, then feeling her touch . . . And
the bloody child had put chocolate on the sleeve of his jacket,
and the bloody woman's hand was on his knee and her
fingers were tightening. They were long over the Alps.

The light was failing, and the sun had dipped below the
wing. The child was gobbling chocolate to get the box finished

and the woman was going into white-knuckle time because the engine pitch had changed, and Eddie sensed that the descent had started. At that time, he should have been educating a roomful of immigrants – all his chums from the Baltics, the Balkans and North Africa – on the intricacies of *Murder in Mesopotamia* or *Death on the Nile* or *Murder on the Orient Express*, didn't really matter which. Like pressing a button on the staff-room computer keyboard, he deleted them, erased them.

It was early in the evening and a city's lights were on. The aircraft yawed and the undercarriage rumbled as it was lowered. Of course he had come. He was Eddie Deacon, and he wanted nothing more than to see her, hear her, feel her – and there was no logic in it and no more analysis of what he knew.

The wheels hit, a good landing, feathered, and he didn't know of anything he should fear.

He came out of the car fast, slammed the door, waved off the driver. For Mario Castrolami this was foreign territory. What he had seen of Collina Fleming was enough to curl his lip. He tasted the first trace of bile in his throat. He had heard it was a hill for millionaires, the big ones, and the apartments were broad built, their balconies had expensive plants on them and the plots were surrounded by barricades. Dogs barked behind electronically controlled gates and porters patrolled the front doors. He thought the hill was about privilege and wealth. Castrolami, investigator in the *carabinieri* ROS, detested privilege and lacked wealth. Could have done . . . Could have blocked enquiries, made files disappear, given advance warning by public phone, with a handkerchief over the mouthpiece, of a raid planned for the following dawn. All of that would have filled an offshore account. He lived in Vomero, the comfortable area of Naples, but on the north side of the Castel Sant'Elmo, and he needed to be a gymnast and to stand on tiptoe on a chair to peer through a skylight for a minuscule glimpse of the sea and the east promontory of Capri. He thought the hill oozed money.

A woman passed him as he went to the gate. It was late September and Castrolami's tie was loose and there was sweat in his armpits. She wore a fur coat, and carried a dog under one arm. Where Castrolami lived, on the wrong side of Vomero, there were stray cats that would have killed that toy dog and eaten it. She looked up, saw him, dismissed him as irrelevant and went by – probably thought him a plumber or an insurance salesman. There was no porter on this block and he rang the bell, gave his name and the gate was unlocked. He carried a thin cardboard file and a small overnight bag. He loathed Rome, and hoped the bag would be needed for a night or two, no more.

He was admitted.

He asked how she was. Rossi, the young one, gestured – something of amusement and something of frustration.

The older one was Orecchia. 'She stays in her room. It was about her mother. We find it often enough. There's the excitement and drama, the centre-of-stage hour, then the moment of reality and the fear. She's frightened of her mother. You understand, we're not interrogators. At this stage we're here to protect her and maintain the security of the safe-house. She wants to stay in her room, hide at the back of her cave so we don't drag her out. She won't eat, she won't talk, she won't . . .'

Castrolami smiled. He did a grim, dark smile well.

He went to the door. It was less than twenty-four hours since he had brought Immacolata Borelli to this address, and less than twelve since he had been told she had refused to speak to the prosecutor, and only half a dozen since the file had landed on his cluttered desk. They used him, at the

Palace of Justice, as a bulldozer. That evening, he should
have been with his friend, who painted views of the mountain,
at an exhibition of modern art in a church on the riviera di
Chiaia and afterwards . . . They took for granted, at the Palace
of Justice, that the bulldozer did twenty-four/seven.

He didn't knock.

The light was off, but the blinds were not drawn and the
street lamps far below threw up enough for him to see her.
She lay on her back, her legs together, staring at the ceiling.
She didn't turn to face him but said quietly, 'I don't want
anything to eat or drink.' He put the light on, hit all the
switches, and she jerked her head sideways. He went to the
table and put the file on it. Then he walked towards her. He
took her right arm at the wrist, heaved her off the bed and
she nearly fell. He said nothing and dragged her to the table,
her feet slithering on the floor. He kicked back a chair, made
room for her, pressed her down on the seat.

He flicked open the file cover, and spilled out the photographs.

She saw her mother. Immacolata held the photograph under
the table light. She looked at the wife of Pasquale Borelli,
the leader of the clan and controller of most business activities
in Forcella and Sanità, the woman who did deals that had
relevance in the north of Italy, in the South of France, in
Spain and Germany, who had ambitions for the opening of
opportunities in Great Britain, who aspired to be a player
on the east coast of the United States and had links with
organisations operating in the west of the former Soviet Union.
She looked at the photograph of her mother.

A little gasp.

Her gaze slipped to Castrolami. If he felt sympathy for
the fate of her mother he disguised it. His expression was
blank. He showed neither clemency nor triumph.

She matched his mood.

Her mother, whom she had feared, was on the ground – on concrete built up a few centimetres from the street – was helpless.

For a moment she wondered, and then she asked, 'Is she dead?'

He shook his head.

In the black-and-white photograph, enlarged to twenty centimetres by twenty-five, her mother was prostrate. A man was poised above her head, his pistol drawn and aimed at her. A woman crawled on her back and had wrenched up one arm so that the hand almost touched the neck, and held a pistol against the neck so that the barrel dented it. Her mother wore the dead look on her face. She was supine, had no fight, did not cringe. It was as if she was comatose from shock. She had fallen awkwardly under the weight of the woman, then must have wriggled backwards to get further clear of the man with the aimed pistol. The effect of that movement had been to ruck up her skirt. It had ridden up her thighs. Immacolata gazed at the photograph. It was the indignity . . . Her mother's thighs were white on the grey concrete, but not as white as the knickers she wore. Immacolata had a glimpse of them, frozen by the camera. She thought of the respect her mother demanded – from her children, the clan, foot-soldiers and associates, from businessmen to foreign gang principals. She thought of when a stick had been taken to her, aged twelve, when she had refused to leave her bedroom to sweep the floor in the living room and hall, and when her face had been slapped, a stinging blow, as her mother had announced to her brothers that she was to be *la madrina* and Immacolata had not suppressed a giggle – of nerves at her mother's self-elevation to such a height. She thought of the verbal criticism, offered in a café, when she had failed to bring back all the protection-payment envelopes from the via Casanova. It was her mother, humiliated, who lay prone in the road, and at the periphery of the camera's view a small crowd had gathered and formed a wary half-moon. She believed, from the greyness and distortion of the picture, that her mother's arrest had been captured on a mobile phone. She realised she had been brought this particular photograph – not one of her mother being led through *paparazzi* and cameramen, flashes and arc lights, able to use the haughtiness of a Pupetta Maresca, a Rosetta Cutolo or a Patrizia Ferriero – to see her mother laid out in a posture of vulgarity.

'Did I do that?' Immacolata asked, almost in awe.

Castrolami: 'Alone, nobody achieves anything. Together, much. You were part of "doing" that. A big enough part, when your involvement is known, to guarantee that the sentence of death is passed on you.'

'What do you want of me now?'

'I want you, Signorina – excuse me – to stop trying to play games with me. You should now consider your situation as set in stone. You see the photograph of your mother. I don't think she'll be pleased to know that her picture is now a source of amusement throughout Naples. When she knows, and she soon will – it's inevitable – that her daughter has collaborated and is in part responsible for her being photographed with bare thighs and most of her arse on display, I believe she'll feel resentful towards you. But there's no turning back. And she's behind bars, in a cell. She's beginning the process of rotting.'

'Do you know, Dottore, what it's like to die of leukaemia?'

'No. I would imagine, though, that it's worse than being in a cell and rotting.'

'I think so.'

'I rarely offer advice, Signorina, but now I'll break a habit. Don't waste my time again, and don't forget your friend's suffering.'

'Where do we start?' she asked, pushing away the photograph.

'We should talk again of Vincenzo.'

A corridor led from the staircase to the basement cell block and the interview rooms where prisoners met their lawyers. One of the detectives who had arrested Vincenzo Borelli accompanied the custody officers who escorted him from the cell along the corridor. Even for this short walk from a departure point to a destination deep inside a protected police station – and Paddington Green was a fortress, designed to hold resourceful terror captives – he was handcuffed to an officer. Since his arrest, he had seen no lawyer, no detective, only the uniformed men entrusted with guarding and caring for him. He knew nothing.

He was Neapolitan, a man – it was right that strangers should see he cared. He asked softly, with concern, 'My sister, Immacolata, where is she? Is she held?'

The detective behind him sniggered. He would have thought, Vincenzo recognised, that he dealt with crap, with an Italian. 'Not *held*, friend, not here and not likely to be. Actually, friend, she's shafted you – she's singing like a whole damn choir . . . Sorry, did I say that? I don't think I did.'

Vincenzo thought it was arrogance. The detective needed to appear a mastermind, senior, and to have detailed knowledge of an extradition case. Vincenzo looked blankly ahead as he was led down the corridor, and mimed being simple, fitting a stereotype, not understanding.

In an interview room, he met a lawyer. The lawyer offered him cigarettes, said he came from Catania in Sicily, was based in the British capital and dealt exclusively with cases – criminal and civil – in which Italian citizens needed representation. He said, too, that he had been appointed to act on Vincenzo's behalf by Umberto. He gave the name of a street and quoted a telephone number as verification that he knew where the clan's lawyer lived and the number of his personal mobile. Vincenzo told him to call it and deliver a message urgently.

The message was in English: *The diva performs with rare beauty and is hired for many performances.* He told the lawyer that the message was to be spoken once, fast. That was all he wished to say. He wanted the man gone.

Vincenzo, in his cell, believed that within half an hour the message would be on Umberto's desk. Umberto would have recorded it for safe transcription, memorised it, then destroyed the tape and the typescript. The door shut on him, a key turned in a lock. He leaned against a wall, much scribbled on and graffiti-strewn, then beat the painted brickwork with his fist till the bruising came.

His own sister . . .

He left the ticket window and ran. He was last on the train, and he thought that, too, was luck. Eddie Deacon had managed to rip open the heavy door while the uniforms shouted, waved their arms and blew hard on whistles, but he jumped aboard, closed the door after him, they did a sweet smile for the man who reached the window and glowered.

The train rolled out of Rome.

He had come into the city on an airport bus, and had suffered a sea-change. Realised it now. He didn't have a seat, but stood and rocked with the motion of the carriage. The engine gathered acceleration. The sea-change was in him. Luck was sprinting with him, and he was thankful for it. Darkness flanked the train as it cleared the Roman suburbs, and then he made out the tight clusters of lights high up, and imagined the track had been routed between hills and their old villages. He felt exhilaration, as if he challenged himself. Not bad, was it, getting himself halfway across western Europe on the same day that he'd jacked a job, cleared a bank account? He had plastic his family would guarantee, and was hightailing through the hills south of the Eternal City. Excitement, adventure: they wouldn't have contemplated it – 'they' being the HM Revenue and Customs clerk, the waiter, the ticket man and the student. One would be dragging himself back to the house after a day of staring at a screen with a head fit to bust, the next would be making polite noises to pompous farts in the club and bringing them drinks, the ticket man would be on late shift and counting the minutes till he finished, and the last would be buried in some damn book about manorial field divisions in the Tudor period. They would find his note, hasty, scrawled, and would each feel – Eddie reckoned – a spasm of jealousy – but not half of the jealousy they'd feel when he brought her back. It was excitement, adventure, and he felt himself lifted, almost euphoric.

It was a brilliant line, so fast, so modern, so smooth. It was as if he had entered true civilisation. Didn't have a line like this, or a carriage, on the route to Chippenham. He knew of nothing now that could block him. He was on a pedestal, had placed himself there.

He would find her.

'Incredible! It's Mac! Wow! Fancy bumping into you here. Just happened to be passing.'

'Did you now? Funny old world, yeah?' And hearing her voice, the accent and the lilt, and knowing she damn near laughed – not at him, with him.

'Like you say, Mac, "funny old world". Shall we go and get a beer?'

'Can't think of anything better.'

Didn't know where he'd find her, couldn't picture it – or where she'd lead him to find a beer. Didn't care. Excitement was the narcotic in Eddie Deacon. On this train, on the new track, it would take ninety minutes to travel from Rome to Naples. Everything went for him, and luck smiled. Why should it not?

He read the note that the child had brought him. He needed a magnifying-glass to decipher the tiny characters. It was Carmine Borelli who had first taken the young lawyer, Umberto, inside the clan's affairs. He had spotted the overweight and indulgent rookie with no resources of his own, and no family to keep him in a fitting standard of living, and had backed his intuition. It had been forty years the previous June since he had made the approach, and the youthful Umberto had virtually kissed his hand in gratitude. It astonished him that Umberto's ponderous, stubby fingers were capable of writing in such a delicate minuscule style. He would have thought the lawyer too clumsy to fashion it. The magnifying-glass made the message clear.

Clear, but almost unbelievable.

Your daughter-in-law arrested, your grandsons also arrested.
Your granddaughter collaborates with the Palace of Justice and has been flown to Rome.

He couldn't complain that four words were used when one sufficed. So few words and so great this effect. He was breathing hard, with wheezes and bubbling gasps. He understood. It was a situation as critical for the clan he had founded as that which had confronted the brothers in Sicily during the Fascist regime and the rule of the brutal 'prefect of iron', Cesare Mori, when the Cosa Nostra had been closest to defeat, and no different in Naples during the time of Mussolini. But Mussolini had fallen, and the Allies had landed first in Sicily, then on the mainland at Salerno, and a new era of opportunity had arrived. Carmine Borelli had seized that opportunity, had begun to form the apparatus of the clan that bore his name. It had survived, with respect, on the streets and in the files of the Palace of Justice for sixty-six years. He had been married to Anna only two years when American troops had entered the bombed streets of Naples. Everything he had built – according to the note a street child had brought him from the lawyer – was now at risk.

A convulsion of coughing shook his body. He spat phlegm into his handkerchief and the irritation passed. He sat still in his chair with the scrap of paper in his palm and the magnifying glass. He did not call his wife, but she had admitted the child and would have known that the much-folded piece of paper was of importance so had allowed him to digest it first, then would come to share. He had known, of course – as she did – that the boys were held, not merely Silvio, that Gabriella had been taken in the street and her photograph circulated in the day's newspapers. The bite of the *vipera* was *your granddaughter collaborates*. If he smoked more than a full carton in a day there were pains in his chest – but no worse than those now in his mind. He could think of so many clans in which a member of the inner family had taken the *pentito* programme of the Palace of Justice, and he had always – in the fifteen years since the programme had been launched – felt a sense of superiority over those who had not been able to hold the loyalty of sons and daughters, nephews and nieces, brothers and sisters. It was his own *nipote* who sat now with the men who were his lifetime enemy.

Much for him to reflect on.

He remembered the contempt he had larded on those clans cut deep by the testimony of their own: the sneer, the retort, the shrug, and the secret feeling that it was but for

God's grace that . . . It could have been his brother, now long dead, or his brother's son, shot and left to bleed to death on the via Carbonara, or his grandson, the least liked among his *nipoti*, Giovanni. It was none of them. Immacolata was accused.

He let his mind rove. His wife, Anna, had brought the newborn granddaughter to the visitors' hall at the Poggioreale gaol. In that place of dirt, noise and despair, where he had been held for four months before the charges of extortion were dropped, the infant had slept, as if unaffected by where she was, had made a little island of calm in the clamour. Her christening had been delayed until his release. He had been present in the church at the top of the street in Forcella, and the priest had been his friend. The child's father had been one of the many *latitanti* in the city, in flight from the prosecutor, and Carmine had replaced Pasquale in the place of honour at Immacolata's first communion and had hosted the celebration lunch. The child became a teenager, then a young woman, and he would sit her beside him and give her the benefit of his experience, and she would listen. He would have said that her affection for him was great – greater than she harboured for her mother and father – and that her respect for him was total.

Anna came into the room. She had poor eyesight, poorer than his, and her chair was always by the window. She reached out a hand and he passed her the scrap of paper and the magnifying-glass. She glanced at the note, then shook her head sharply. It was for him to tell her what was written, and to repeat it would be another wound, cut ever deeper. He used the zapper to turn on the big TV and raise its volume. There had been police in the house so recently and not a chance of observing them: he would say nothing of importance without turning on the television and increasing the volume. She leaned close to him and he to her, his lips little more than ten centimetres from her ear. He could see each of the cancer marks on her skin, the wrinkles at her throat and the hairs on her upper lip. He told her everything, and always had.

He said, 'The boy came from Umberto. Umberto writes, "Your granddaughter collaborates with the Palace of Justice and has been flown to Rome." Umberto denounces Immacolata. She is, Umberto says, an *infame*. Immacolata seeks to destroy us.'

She gave no answer. Carmine could see only the chill slab of his wife's face, devoid of expression. The child, Immacolata, had spent as many of her waking hours in this apartment as she had in her mother's. It was personal, the hurt. Anna gave no answer, he believed, because she still pondered on what her response should be. She would not speak unless there were words of substance to say. He felt the damp on his face. A tear trickled down his skin to the thin stubble on his cheek.

His shin was kicked.

A sharp blow with a heavy lace-up shoe, which stabbed pain into the bone.

He thought she might as well have condemned their granddaughter. It had taken five or six seconds for him to relay the message, and twenty-six years of love, commitment and caring were obliterated.

He looked into his wife's face. Many times in those sixty-six years of marriage she had worn an expression that frightened him, and so it was. He saw in that face a terrible, but controlled, hatred. Where Immacolata was involved, he could be soft – but his wife could not.

They had broken. Castrolami came into the kitchen to make tea and left Immacolata Borelli to sip a glass of juice.

It was different. He had fastened the photograph to the

wall. From where he had sat her at the table, the microphone close to her, she faced it. He was to the side of her. It was natural for her to look up, to be certain that a point made was assimilated, and then she saw her mother – on the ground, in humiliation, the skirt pushed up, white skin, whiter underwear, dignity and control stripped. It was different because the Borelli girl now talked, and during the time he had been there he had used three spare tapes from the stack he had brought. They had moved beyond Vincenzo, enough on the first two tapes to ensure an extradition case to go with the evidence already laid before the British courts on charges of murder, and the third detailed the control of Gabriella Borelli over the clan, not mere supposition. Supposition would have been that Pasquale Borelli slipped out messages from the gaol of Novara through a route in the gaol's catering; detail was that the route, whereby the husband let the wife have his advice, involved the man who brought the flour, yeast, salt, olive oil and cheap dried milk to the prison bakery, and was a facilitator for the communications of two maximum-security Sicilians. Supposition was that the contract for a new sewage works at a town inland from Naples had corrupt political involvement; detail named the men who had granted the contract in the local town hall, what they had been paid for their co-operation, how the payment was made and how that contract would be shared between different clans – who had trucking, who had labour, who had cement. Castrolami needed to break the meeting for tea.

Orecchia took milk from the refrigerator and poured it. 'You're pleased with her.'

'More so than before.'

Orecchia's smile was cold. 'You were hard on her.'

Castrolami said, 'Because I feel nothing for her. She is not a true *pentita*. There is no sense of penitence. The death of a friend, linked to her, and an attack on her at a cemetery, her being too late to attend the funeral Mass combine to create a sense of guilt. She seeks to redress the guilt, but that's not penitence. Revenge, anger, dislike for her family, who may not have valued her as she thought she deserved . . . Many things. But it's not a road-to-Damascus conversion.'

'She's not Paul,' Orecchia murmured, 'but few of them are.'

'And no shining light, only little grievances topped by the friend's death. No sense of outrage at the criminality of the Camorra, what has happened to the city, Naples distinguished by callousness. Shit, that's boring.'

'Excuse me, have you no sense of sincerity? You see her as shallow?'

'You know better than I, friend, what she'll face. When the pressure crushes her, we'll see sincerity or not . . .'

Orecchia handed him the cup, no saucer, and a sweet biscuit. 'Me, when I go home – not often – I stand in the shower for a full fifteen minutes and the family screams there'll be no hot water for the rest of that day. They say I'm mad, that I sup with devils. I say I eat with a long spoon. You know what's worse? The collaborators believe they do me, Rossi, you, society, a great favour by coming to us. I despise them.'

Castrolami smiled grimly. 'Maybe you'd find spiritual fulfilment as a street sweeper. Thanks for the tea.'

Orecchia said, 'I'm not joking. I trust this one, all of them, as far as I can kick them. They entangle people, squeeze and suck the goodness from them.'

'I hear you.' Castrolami couldn't have argued with a word he'd said, but he wondered how a man survived in his work if he saw only bleakness. Did he laugh at home? Did he follow a football team with the fanaticism of the Mastiffs in Naples? Did he pay tarts? Castrolami wondered if Orecchia

was ever saddened when a collaborator was cut loose from
the protection programme and left to fend for himself – did
he ever respect them? That evening he would talk to
Signorina Immacolata about her mother's hard-drugs-
importation programmes and . . .

The voice droned again at him: 'To be touched by them
is to be contaminated.'

More luck. He was told that a single room was available, the
last, and that it was the first day after the end of the high-
season rate – big luck double time for Eddie Deacon, innocent
and ignorant.

The accommodation desk at the city's railway station had
found him the room. A pretty girl had circled the hotel on
a map and confirmed it would not be expensive. He had
slung the bag over his shoulder and started to walk, making
his way – only two wrong turnings – from the wide square,
the piazza Garibaldi. He had tasted the heat, the noise, the
smells and the chaos of traffic and scooters, and had known
the first pangs of nerves. He had stood outside the hotel
door and the neon above him blinked without pattern. Kids
stood on the streets, smoked and didn't talk but eyed him.
More nerves. They spoke some English inside, and the man
who gave him the key had a squint, a khaki mole on his
cheek and a stutter. Eddie spoke kindly to him. He thought,
then, that he needed a friend – any bloody friend from any
bloody place. Maybe the excitement, the adventure, the
exhilaration, like the neon, blinked.

He went up to the room. His step was heavier and the
bounce had gone. They were saving on power for the stairs:
the bulbs were low-wattage and made the shadows longer,
the greyness of the walls and ceiling deeper, the lack of light
accentuating the scratches in the paint. He was no longer
within the civilisation boundaries of the train carriage that

had brought him south. He heard a couple row in German about the cost of the meal that evening and the budget being blown. Another couple on the next floor up grunted, squealed and worked the bedsprings, and there was a tray outside the door on which was a barely nibbled pizza: the sex sounded good but the pizza had dried out. He had been told by the girl at the accommodation desk at Napoli Centrale that this *pensione* was the best he could afford. He went on up the staircase, the carpet thinner, more faded and worn with each flight.

The key was on a chain that hooked on to a small wooden ball. He slipped the little card that had come with it – his name, room number, the hotel address – into his trouser pocket, opened the door and groped for the switch.

The room was smaller than a prison cell, with a wardrobe, an upright chair, a table hardly deep enough for an A4 sheet of paper and a single bed. Beside the wardrobe there was a square section of transparent plastic for a shower, basin and toilet. Only a damn small cat, a kitten, could have been swung in it. Had he expected a Marriott room, or one from a Holiday Inn, maybe an InterContinental? Old story: in this world, Eddie, you get what you pay for. Eddie Deacon, in Germany or France, had never felt himself a stranger, had not been the lonely foreigner.

He pushed open a window and the sounds of the night buffeted against him – cars, screaming, music turned up high. He knew he was in a street behind the piazza Garibaldi because it showed up on the map he had been given. He had asked the girl if it was near to the via Forcella and she had shrugged as if to indicate that only an idiot needed that information, and then she had agreed it was. Another visitor to Naples, with a rucksack on his back, had elbowed Eddie away from the desk. He felt an increase in those nerve pangs.

So, he slapped his face with the palm of each hand, then unfolded the map. He didn't feel good, he didn't feel right, but he didn't feel as if he was about to bloody lie down and cave.

He mapped out a route.

A man had said – in public – that the family was shit, finished, a spent power. Might have been right. Salvatore walked into the bar.

He wore no face mask. The room was brightly lit and his face, features, identity were clear. The clan of which he was the enforcer was worth – if all property investments, treasury bonds and shares in a half-dozen of the leading money markets were added up – in excess of half a billion euros. As an enforcer, he could have been directed to a penthouse apartment on the Côte d'Azur or a villa in a smart, protected suburb of Frankfurt, and his target would have been a banker or investment manager who had misappropriated tens of thousands of euros, or a hundred thousand, or a million. Also, his work was to maintain the respect and dignity the clan family needed. He handed down the justice of the Borellis to those who were high and mighty, to the potential informer who refused to pay a hundred euros a week – and to the braggart in the bar. He looked around him.

He was seen, noticed. He didn't want anonymity. If many saw and knew him, the word went faster. His eyes fastened on the man.

It had always surprised Salvatore that when he confronted a victim, they seldom ran or fought. They were, almost all, helpless and trapped in terror. This one was no different. He would have said it, that the family were shit, would have repeated it, would have gone home and lain beside his whore-wife in their bed, and the bravado would have oozed away. He would have known that within hours, a few days but less than a week, the enforcer of the clan would come for him. He had nowhere to hide. A victim, a man of forty, would have been familiar with only the few streets that surrounded the districts of Sanità and Forcella, and the labyrinth inside the area of two or three square kilometres. He was, and would have realised it, a dead man walking from the time his mouth had opened and his tongue had flapped, who lived out the final stages of his life in a small flat with his wife and children, in a bar where others were cautious of his company, who was in *la cella dei condannati a morte*. Others now backed away from him. His jaw was slack, the spittle was white against dark lips and sweat gleamed on his high forehead. He would have felt his legs sag under the weight of his body.

He did not have to show the pistol, the Beretta, at his waist. Salvatore flicked his fingers. He gestured with his head to the door. At that moment some men – bankers or street scum – wet their trousers in the crotch or fouled their seat. Some closed their eyes and began to pray. Some wept, some pleaded. Some spoke of their children, their wives. Some went as if they sleepwalked.

This one did.

Salvatore also knew that the man he had called out would have friends in the bar with whom he had played in the street as a child, sat in schoolrooms, talked and watched football in that bar for an adult lifetime, and none would help him now. Perhaps in a week . . . not yet. Power not yet gone: a photograph in a newspaper of the thighs and the covered arse of Gabriella Borelli, more photographs of her children in custody, but no certainty, *yet*, that power was in new hands. None of those friends, once valued, would block the door, defend him.

It was the way of Naples. The authority of the clans, even one seriously wounded – weakened – ruled.

And none in that crowded bar would say they had seen Salvatore's face. Within two minutes the bar would have emptied, well before the first sirens and lights arrived. Only the staff would be there. All would claim to have been facing the far wall, or busy at the coffee machines, or in the rear store for more milk. That, too, was the way of Naples, unchanged and unchanging.

Clear of the bar, he pushed the man across the broken pavement, a vicious shove. Where a slab should have been there was a pit and the man's shoe caught in it and he fell forward. He was half in the street and half in the gutter. Salvatore kicked him in the buttock and the man crawled limply forward. He had chosen this place because he knew that no street cameras covered the stretch of road between the Porta Capuana and the via Cesare Rosaroll. He had the pistol out of his belt. He fired one shot and the bullet went into the back of the man's knee and there was a little limp scream of shock, then another, shrill, from the pain's spread. Salvatore waved up the street.

Extraordinary – true to Naples, Palermo and Reggio Calabria in the toecap of Italy's boot: traffic had disappeared from the road. It had been there, a constant, hooting snarl, but was gone. The road was empty but for a white van, old, rusted, with no registration plates.

It could accelerate. The man would have seen it, heard it, but with his leg shot away at the knee he could not avoid it, and squirmed on the tarmacadam. He was in an oil slick now, his shirt smeared, and the van went over him, cleared him. No one saw. No witnesses in the bar, on the pavement or in cars on the road saw the van go over him. Perhaps it crushed his back or broke his neck. Perhaps it left him grievously injured but still living. It braked.

It reversed. It came back up the road and the rear tyres lifted as it mounted the body a second time. When the body was cleared and the van stopped again, there was no movement.

Salvatore climbed into the passenger seat. His driver, whom he called Fangio, went away down the road.

He thought that the clan, those still at liberty, clung to power by the thickness of the string used to bind a birthday present.

An hour later, a boy came to him. He and Fangio, for speed, shared the shower, scrubbed and washed. Their clothing was bagged for disposal. Few knew of that address. The lawyer was among the few. The child brought a scrap of paper and left, running. More than adults, Salvatore, Il Pistole, whose face was on their screensavers, trusted the kids. He had to wipe soap from his eyes before he could read the compacted handwriting. He shuddered.

He crumpled the paper, threw it at Fangio's feet and saw it carried in the torrent of soapy water down the drain. To shoot a man in the back of the leg meant nothing to him. He was unaffected by the sight of a van speeding down a road well lit with high lamps, then bouncing over a sprawled body. He felt almost a tremble in his legs, under the damp towel.

He would have said he could believe anything of Naples – *anything*. He had been wrong. He could not have believed, if he hadn't seen it written in the spider hand of the lawyer, that Immacolata Borelli had collaborated.

Not the thickness of string – the thickness of one strand woven to make string.

He didn't know, then, what he could do, should do, without the power of the clan at his back. He, too, was dead – squashed, broken, bloody. He didn't know where he should turn.

He couldn't still the trembling – or the image of Immacolata Borelli – and he couldn't believe.

*

He was at the end of the street under the sign that said it was via Forcella. He saw nothing familiar and nothing that offered a welcome. The light was poor, the shadows harsh. The spearing headlights of weaving scooters caught the shapes of men, women, kids, then lost them as the riders powered away. Eddie Deacon had told himself that it was important, before he went to sleep, to know where via Forcella was, how far away, how . . . He felt intimidated. There, at the head of the street, and he thought it hardly wide enough for two cars to pass, he realised that a group of kids watched him and he wished he hadn't brought his wallet with him. He believed himself evaluated as worth a hit or not worth a hit. Nothing he saw reassured him. He was beside a church, but it was darkened and he sensed that the doors were bolted, locked, secure against the night and strangers.

He turned away.

It was as if he backed off.

The street corner seemed an interface. When he retreated he was on the via Duomo, and the map said that the city's principal cathedral was there, and the shops had lights in their windows. There, he felt fine. Down that street, he had felt a cloying nervousness. It would be different in the morning, of course, and he would be back in broad, warm, sunshine-laden daytime. He trudged back to his bed, and was troubled that he had suffered what was bloody nearly a panic attack. He had thought, till then, that luck rode with him.

He would be back in the morning to find her.

Eddie was serenaded to faltering sleep by sirens – so many of them and for so long – and the vehicles came, raucous, to a street near where he was. Only when the sirens had died did the restlessness and tension drain away. Then he could think of her again, as she was in the photograph on his wall.

'Fancy bumping into you here. Just happened to be passing.'

Because of the work he did, Lukas had long ago shed a body clock. He could work in the night, sleep in the day, just as he could type on his laptop in the back of a bucking Land Rover or Humvee in half-darkness.

He typed his report on Colombia, what they had achieved and whom they had lost.

He was as happy working late into the night as in the morning, was not fresher at the start of a day than at the end.

No drama would creep into his report, no descriptive factors and no *colour*. He would list briefly what he had known, and the advice he had offered on the basis of facts available. Nowhere in the text would there be disguised praise for his own part or criticism of others.

Only a professional could make sense of it. Only those who employed him now, the chief executive officer at Ground Force Security and the director of operations, or those who had employed him in years past – the Federal Bureau of Investigation and the Department of Defense – could have made drama from the few pages on offer. The descriptions were clinical, and he used the short-hand jargon of his trade. Men across the globe who dealt with the high-risk stakes of hostage rescue and negotiation would read the pages and know that Lukas had written them, and they would pray to God that the next time he was needed they found him available to travel and not marooned in some other shit-heap place.

Home for him, where he typed, was an apartment under the eaves on the top floor of a street off the rue de Bellechasse. The mother of the CEO of Ground Force Security had lived and died there, and when Lukas had come on the firm's

books, it had been offered to him. The French capital suited
him. He had no wish to live in the UK when he was employed
by a British-based company, and less to be resident in the
United States after twenty-two years with the Bureau, the
last two on secondment to the Department of Defense. He
craved to be distanced from his work, and the Paris apartment
satisfied him. Little more than a shoebox, it comprised a
cramped living room and a kitchenette behind a chipboard
partition, a bedroom under a sloping ceiling but that had
room for a big bed where a man with nightmares could toss
in the darkness, a bathroom with a power shower that could
wash off Iraq's sand and Colombia's mud, and a hall with
a table and the telephone. It might not ring for a week or a
month, but a red light would flash if he had missed a call.
Lukas did not like being far from the telephone.

He was finishing off the report. Ground Force Security
would be heaped with praise by the Agency because their
man had survived and cover had been maintained – 'goddam
brilliant, a mother-fucker of a triumph,' his CEO would be
told by Langley. His own view: pretty much OK – not
desperate and not wonderful. Some whom Lukas dealt with
at field level regarded him as a lunatic. A few told him he
was a lunatic. He didn't take it personally, or when a Spanish
diplomat had tried to punch him after calling him a lunatic.
He had written it up in the usual laconic way afterwards.

*Negotiations with a tribal leader had been ongoing for
excess of three days. Much reliance placed on the talks;
my view, too much reliance. Asset intelligence reported
the hostage held in a six-storey block of twenty-four
apartments plus basement. Exact location of hostage and
hostage-takers in the building was not known but we
had electronics in the stairwell. A male – not seen before
at the building – approached and carried a plastic bag*

containing one large potato. I advised readying the storm
squad for immediate intervention. Spanish diplomatic
personnel in the command centre took a contrary
position. The electronics in the stairwell indicated the
unknown male to have gone to the second floor, right
side of staircase. I urged an instant assault . . .

No mention of the attempt to punch him, the screamed
accusation that he cared nothing for the life of a Spanish-
born expert in antiquities on attachment to the National
Museum. No mention of a diplomat having to be restrained
while frothing with rage. No mention in the report of an
expert's experience. A big potato, weighing more than two
kilos, had been the trigger for him. The diplomats believed
negotiation would free their national, that a premature assault
endangered the captive's life. To be told that a man carrying
a potato into the building was reason enough to abandon
the talks that had been so difficult to initiate had caused an
explosion of fury.

The assault was successful. Four Iraqis were killed by
troops from the Polish special forces team and the
hostage was freed. He would have been dead within the
hour. Signed, F. Lukas.
    NB A large potato was used as a pistol's silencer in
the assassination of a British national, the barrel tip
being indented into the potato and the killing bullet
passing through its bulk.

A British co-ordinator – one whom Lukas admired – had
told him about big potatoes. It didn't offend him to be accused
of lunacy because he understood too well the stresses they
all felt. The Brit had given him a cassette and Lukas had
gone off to watch, alone, the video of a killing. The potato

as the end of an automatic-pistol barrel, a Makharov, had dulled the noise on the soundtrack of the firing. He had seen the body collapse – not fall forward but go down like one of those big old cooling towers that were dynamited. The co-ordinator, tough, hard, had seemed badly cut by that loss. They were all in the same club, limited membership, and all felt badly when they lost out. He had failed to save the life of a European tourist who was a damn fool stupid guy to think he could walk those mountains without having looked through websites and Foreign office advisories – but it still hurt. It just seemed cheap to Lukas to show the world what hurt.

From his living room, he often looked out into the hall, but no red light winked and no bell rang.

7

There were kids at the top of the street. They wore a uniform of faded T-shirts and tracksuit bottoms or denims and scuffed trainers, had close-cropped hair that made them look as though they were recovering from a louse infestation. They had darting eyes that crossed over the pedestrians who came off the via Duomo, turned and headed on down the street. When the T-shirt of one was lifted in a sudden arm movement, Eddie Deacon saw the handle of a knife and the upper part of its sheath. The kids did not kick footballs. Behind them, astride a scooter, smoking, was an older boy, maybe fifteen or sixteen, and he kept the engine idling. Against the wall two more boys, maybe seventeen or eighteen, had mobile phones clamped to their faces.

Eddie Deacon was not an idiot   some said he was bone idle, that he lacked 'drive', that he was short on ambition – and nobody had ever called him 'stupid', but he had common sense, 'nous'. He had realised that everyone who went down that street was visually checked over. There was a rhythm to it. A man or a car appeared and the kids seemed to rush in front of him, maybe to slow him. The scooter's engine speed quickened and the mobile was spoken into. Once he had seen the scooter pull out and go down the street, and a signal must have been sent because, within seconds, another scooter had taken over sentry duty. He had walked past two other streets leading into the district and there had been kids, a scooter and mobile phones at the top of each. He could recognise it, could not deny it. Eddie had slept poorly because of the nerves. He was as intimidated by the street, hesitating and hovering at its mouth, as he had been in the darkness the night before. He felt his intelligence dulled. But it was what he had come for, to go down that street and find Immacolata Borelli.

Nobody had accused him of cowardice, or ever mocked him for fast-fix religion.

It might have been the nerves. On the via Duomo, before he reached the junction with via Forcella, he had found himself outside the cathedral. He had gone inside and lingered there. He had read that the huge high interior was built four hundred years ago after earthquake devastation had brought down the thirteenth-century building, and that under the most recent foundations were a Greek temple and a Roman-era rainwater canal. He'd read, too, of San Gennaro, who protected the city from disaster and whose blood, kept here in a vial, liquefied each first Sunday in May and each 19 September. The saint had died in 305 – he did a simple sum fast – 1704 years ago, beheaded after torture as punishment for his beliefs, and his blood was a dried cake for three hundred and sixty-three or -four days of the year, but went liquid on those two days. If Eddie Deacon had told the guys in the house off the Kingsland Road this story, and that he didn't doubt it, he would have been laughed all the way to the pub, to do the first round and the second. Flowers were being arranged near the altar and he imagined there would be a wedding later. A scattering of chairs was taken by crouched figures. He was happy to have been there, yet he never went into the church on Hoxton Street or the one on the other side of Dalston at Middleton Road. Being there, hearing a choir of treble angel voices rehearse, settled him a little.

So, best bloody foot forward.

The light didn't come down the street. The alleyways leading off to the sides, spars off a mast, were narrower and dim, and above them washing hung. There were shops: for hardware, groceries, bread, cheap clothing. The façade rendering had peeled away and the paintwork was chipped and flaking. Often, in the first few paces, he reached back and touched his hip pocket, where the slim wallet was. He wore faded jeans, trainers and a short-sleeved shirt; he had left his passport, his plastic and most of his cash in the little safe in the *pensione* room. It seemed necessary for him – under the gaze of the kids, the boy astride the scooter and the older boys with the mobiles – to feel for his wallet.

He said softly to himself, 'For fuck's sake, Eddie, get with it. Where are you? In western Europe, the cradle of civilisation. Why are you in western Europe? To find Mac. What are you? A bloody wimp. When are you going to grow up? Now . . . now.'

A woman carried two thin plastic bags that were heavy with vegetables. Eddie asked her – in stuttered Italian – if she knew where Immacolata Borelli lived. The woman looked through him, as if he didn't exist, and he repeated the name, but she walked past him.

He didn't know where the street ended, where the vicolo Vicaria began, but he did not think via Forcella was long, maybe two hundred yards. Everyone should know her . . . A man stopped in the centre of the street, a dog squatted and defecated, a cat crouched at his feet and chewed gristle from a bone, and a scooter swept by them. The man had paused to light his pipe. Eddie asked if he knew, please, where Immacolata Borelli lived. The man gaped at him. Eddie said the name again. The match burned until it touched the skin of the man's fingers, then the man pushed past. He stepped in the dog's mess, four square in it, and seemed not to care.

The kids were behind and level with him. If he faced
them, they met his gaze. They made a cordon behind him
when a car came down and it had to hoot for them to give
space. Two men sat at a table on the street, and the car
slowed to get past them. Eddie saw they had dominoes. He
stood over the table, waited for a play to be made, expected
that one would look up, but neither did so he interrupted
the game. He asked once more: did they know where in the
via Forcella the home of Immacolata Borelli was? He couldn't
read the faces, tanned, cracked, as if the skin was old leather,
or the eyes, but one spat and the brightness lay on a
cobblestone beside Eddie's trainer, and the game went on.

He was confused. He didn't understand why she lived
there. It was poverty. So were parts of Dalston, corners of
Hackney, Hoxton and Haggerston, but he did not see any
of the pockets of wealth, anything of quality – the small areas
that had been tarted up – as there were in his corner of
London. He thought he sounded like his father. But it had
been clear enough on the scrap of paper – *Borelli,Via Forcella,
Zip code, Napoli*. He stood outside a shop that sold bread,
rolls and cake. He was taken inside as the queue moved in
and the kids were left on the pavement. Now the scooter
was with them and the engine was gunned. He reached the
counter. He asked for the home of the Borelli family, said
that he was looking for Immacolata Borelli. The woman heard
him. Eddie thought she considered what was requested of
her. He spoke the name again: Immacolata Borelli. The woman
looked away from him and her eyes went to the next in the
line, her smile broad. What did that customer want? Eddie
went out of the shop.

Bells clamoured in his mind. A broken front door in a
north London street and a police guard, his Mac never giving
him an address or a phone number, and she had disappeared.
This was her home, and he was watched, and no one in the

street responded to his request for information. The bells rang loudly. What to do?

Should he stop, turn, walk away and quit? He didn't doubt that each person he had spoken to had known of Immacolata Borelli. He swore. Stop? No. Turn and walk away? No. Quit? He went on down the street and looked for the next man or woman to ask, the kids and the scooter trailing him.

She talked of her mother, had done since she had woken. She had taken a perfunctory shower, gobbled a roll, gulped coffee and sat at the table, drumming her fingers for the tape to be switched on.

'An account she values is that with the Dresdner Bank – I can't tell you the number. It's at fourteen, Karl-Liebknechtstrasse in Leipzig. It's the first place cleaned money goes, fixed-rate deposits for six months. She goes in October, doesn't stay overnight since my father's arrest. She has a travel agent that routes her from Reggio Calabria to eastern Germany on budget flights for German tourists. The turn-round time for the aircraft is sufficient for her meetings. There's never less than eight million euros in the Leipzig account, and she's a generous supporter of the bank's nominated charities. You understand?'

Castrolami sat opposite her. He was swivelled sideways and did not look at her, or at the picture of Gabriella Borelli on the wall. He didn't look at her because he was shaving. Had he faced her, the action of the battery-powered machine would have interfered with the recording. She couldn't tell, with his cheeks and eyes away from her, whether he was impressed by what she said, or indifferent to it, but he didn't prompt her. Perhaps, Immacolata thought, he had turned on a tap and preferred not to interrupt the flow. He shaved, working the machine with three heads across his face, his throat, below and above his lips, and she talked about the distribution of money. Where were the accounts placed? In what banks in what cities? She spoke of huge sums but he never raised his eyebrows in astonishment or disbelief.

The sun shone on her.

A maid sluiced the tiles of the kitchen floor.

Orecchia lounged on a settee behind her and read his newspaper – a socialist one that her father, Pasquale, said was fit only for wiping a backside. He never spoke or coughed or intruded in any way, but his holster harness was round his shirt.

Rossi was on the balcony and swept up dried leaves that had fallen from the plants in the ochre pots. He would have been aware that he could be seen by the residents in other blocks so his holster was hitched on a chair. She had fired a pistol, but never at a human target. Had her mother? Perhaps, but she didn't know. She couldn't have said whether her mother killed by proxy – Vincenzo, Giovanni, or the cold, creepy one they used – or had done it for herself. It didn't matter. After she had talked about money, she would go on to killings. With killings she might raise Castrolami's eyebrows. Rossi swept diligently, but sometimes she looked up and out through the opened glass doors to the terrace and she thought he watched her, and each time she set her shoulders back and allowed her blouse to be stretched. Then he swept some more.

There had been no views from the apartment her brother rented in London or from the buildings they had occupied in Sanità and Forcella: roofs, water tanks, satellite dishes, and glimpses of the great mountain where the cap was missing. Here, from Collina Fleming, the view was exceptional. Clear skies above, trees and an *autostrada* link below, and a distant horizon of grey hazed hills on which clouds perched. Maybe she would live here . . . Have a maid who came in and cleaned . . . Finish accountancy courses and have diplomas . . . Set up in a small business with money provided by Castrolami's people, or the prosecutor's people, until she was able to support herself . . . A new name . . . And maybe meet someone, have babies, maybe . . . The warmth filled the apartment but a small zephyr wind came with it. Immacolata had dreamed of her future and talked of her mother.

'Every April she goes to the Société Générale bank on the road called La Canebière, number fifteen, in Marseille. She is driven to Bari, then flies to Milan and connects to Marseille. She starts early. She has lunch with her manager, and is back the same evening. They think she's a resident of Milan. That account is for more than two million euros and—'

A plastic bucket on the balcony toppled. She realised then that Rossi had swept and now watered the pots. He had kicked over the bucket. She stopped. That brought a reaction from Castrolami, a little hissed curse because she had been interrupted and the flow broken.

'How am I doing?'

'You talk and we listen. That's what's expected.'

It was the place, in a dream, that she might live, away from the dark, drear streets of Naples, beyond the reach of Sanità and Forcella – and the gaols at Poggioreale and Novara – beyond the reach of the hands that would be scrabbling for her eyes.

'Please, I want to go out.'

Now wariness clouded Castrolami's face. 'You know what's dictated. No phone calls, no meetings, no contacts. Signorina Immacolata, they'll kill you.'

'I want to buy food – I want to cook.'

He sighed. She thought him confused. He had finished shaving. Now he opened the head of the machine and blew the mess out on to the floor. 'What other banks outside Italy does your mother use?'

'And we'll shop and I'll cook?'

'Yes . . . The other banks?'

'She doesn't visit it but meets a representative in Turin each January, the Danske Bank in Stockholm, on Norrmalmstorg. In Spain, in Madrid, the family uses the Banco Santander for fixed-term deposits.'

Her mind had drifted. It was where she could be, could settle, could live, could make a new family.

His mobile rang. The noise, insistent, clamoured in his pocket: he had tried to emphasise that he shouldn't be called when he was with the *pentita*, Immacolata Borelli, unless to be given information of seismic importance. They had gone beyond European banks, were now in the Cayman Islands – a Swiss bank – and had just talked through Greek Cyprus, a Larnaca branch. She stopped and he switched off the tape.

He listened. It was the message he had expected – he might have been surprised had it not surfaced the previous evening.

A Naples newspaper, *Cronaca*, had telephoned the Palace of Justice and asked for guidance on a rumour in the Forcella and Sanità districts that Immacolata Borelli, twenty-five-year-old daughter of Pasquale and Gabriella Borelli, was collaborating. Was the rumour confirmed or denied? He was told that time had been bought, that the prosecutor was unavailable, in meetings, and that the press office could neither confirm nor deny – but only a few hours could be bought. He thanked the caller and pocketed the mobile.

They had had the gentle hours. He imagined the word racing through the district of her birth and childhood – as it had with an Alfieri, a Contini, a Misso and a Giuliani. But for it to be a girl, pretty, educated, intelligent, would captivate the city. He did not hide news. Good or bad it should be spelled out.

He said, 'It's rumoured in Naples that Immacolata Borelli is an *infame*. Word is out and on the streets. They would spit at your picture, if they had you in via Forcella, they would stamp on you until your breath had gone. If you ever believed there was a time for turning back it's gone. Now I shall ask you a very serious question.'

'What?'

'Is there anything in your life that I should know about which you have not told me? Signorina Immacolata, is there anything that can be exploited, a weakness?'

'No.'

'Should I believe you?'

'You insult me.'

She looked at her best when she was angry. But, and it troubled Castrolami, the sunlight was reflected on to the white marble floor and her eyes, making them black pockets. He liked to look deep into the eyes when he was deciding whether a suspect was truthful or lied. He could not see hers. He thought her strong, and that she would need to be strong.

He said, 'In an hour, maybe, we will go to the piazza, where the stalls are, and you can shop. I think you'll find that a chic corner of Rome is more expensive than Forcella or any part of Naples, and probably the produce is inferior. That we give permission is a gesture of trust.'

She didn't thank him. He thought her an enigma: tough and vulnerable, resolute and frightened, hard and pliant. He didn't yet know her, didn't know whether he ever would – whether a gesture of trust was misplaced.

She had shuffled towards him. Salvatore watched the approach of Anna Borelli, grandmother to the family and icon in the clan. He had heard she had been the strength behind her man, that the clan would not have prospered without her and that she was the worst woman in Naples to make an enemy of. He knew her to have been born in 1922, the year Mussolini had launched, from Naples, the march on Rome that elevated him to power. He knew her to have been married in 1941 when her husband had come out of hiding from military conscription and posting to Montenegro. He knew her to have stepped back from the running of the clan in the middle 1980s when its strength was assured and Pasquale was given authority, knew that she had paramount importance in the clan's territory. She came close to him.

She was frail, with bent shoulders, and walked with a stick to mitigate her rheumatism. She had cropped white hair, but her clothes were always ebony black. If she ever smiled he hadn't seen it. If she ever laughed he hadn't heard her. She paused outside a hardware shop and he saw her examining brooms, weighing the advantages of one against another: she was worth, by whatever calculation, millions of euros, but fingered brooms to decide whether one that cost three euros was as good value as one that cost five. He came close to her, and the owner of the shop, who had been solicitous and grovelling as if to royalty, stepped back to give him room and privacy.

He said, 'Grandmother, it is a time of maximum danger to the clan. Nonna, the wolves circle because they believe us weak. Nonna, without Pasquale, Gabriella and Vincenzo, and with the bitch Immacolata whoring with the palace, we need leadership or we'll disintegrate. Everything you and Carmine achieved will be lost. Unless you lead now, your lives will have been wasted. I beg you, take control. Fight. Umberto can find me, but in extreme emergency call this . . .' He slipped a piece of paper into her clawed hand. He relied on her memory, in her eighty-eighth year, to absorb the number. He was satisfied she would have done so within an hour. With total sincerity Salvatore said: 'We depend on you, Nonna, and on Carmine. If we're led we'll follow. If we don't fight, we're dead, and the whore has killed us.'

He walked away from her. At an entry fifty metres down the via Forcella from the hardware shop, he paused in the shadow. The priest passed her, the bastard priest from the church of San Giorgio Maggiore – should have been shot – and she didn't acknowledge him. Salvatore thought she bartered with the shop owner for a discount on the broom, and – for certain – she would be given it. There were many who would delight in dancing on his corpse and many who would queue for the privilege of dropping him. He reached his man, Fangio, put on the helmet with the smoked-glass visor and was gone.

It was perplexing to him. Frustrated, annoyed, failing and unable to get sense from anyone, Eddie Deacon beaded on the priest. Perplexingly, the priest walked in the centre of the street and scooters swerved to pass him, going either way, and the street was lined with shoppers and gossipers, old and young, and no one spoke to him. He was young, no more than thirty, with a rounded, chubby face but there was no cheer in it: pallor and tiredness characterised him. He had come out of a courtyard through tall iron gates. The school had the name 'Annalisa Durante'. Eddie sidled towards the priest.

A quick side-step, like a soccer player's swerve, and the priest had passed. Eddie called after him. No response, but the priest's step quickened. He fastened on the back of the man – had to: he had been the length of the street and must have asked a dozen people where the Borelli home was, and had not received one coherent answer. The kids followed him still, but not with intensity. He didn't think they regarded him as threatening, more as a curiosity, but they were behind him and he'd noted that each time he asked, the boy on the scooter quizzed the person he'd spoken to.

The sun came higher. He sweated. Strips of light and warmth knifed on to the street from the alleys. More people were out. If he met eyes, they were averted. If he smiled, it was not returned.

He didn't know what else to do, but followed the priest. The spark had gone out for him, as if hope was extinguished. So alone. The priest went up the steps of the church and into it. Eddie had that sense of being the stranger and unwanted. In the stone slabs beside the main door, at about the level of a man's head, there were chip marks, two scars where the stone had been gouged. He followed the priest inside. Cool and quiet enveloped him.

They walked. Rossi led and he wore a lightweight poplin jacket so that his shoulder harness was covered. She followed, with Castrolami alongside her, Orecchia behind. They went down a side-road from the block, where the parked cars had been in place all summer, the bonnets and windscreens coated with the fine dust that came from the north African deserts, carried on the winds. The hill where they had brought her was empty of residents, still holidaying in the south or at the Sardinian resorts. That would have been why they had shipped her in here. There were so few people in the apartments and on the roads.

The dogs had not been taken to the southern beaches, but abandoned to the care of maids and porters. They threw themselves at the balcony railings. Immacolata had forgotten, almost, the ferocity of the sun – but there were many things to be forgotten. She walked with a good step and Rossi had to sense her pace and stretch his stride to keep ahead of her. They went past the entrance to a tennis club and she glimpsed the pool, azure blue, and the loungers; the Borelli family had not been able, in Naples, to belong to a club where tennis was played and there was a pool, so Immacolata didn't play tennis and couldn't swim. Different worlds, and this one closed to her by the dictate of the clan's security, but there were clubs like this in Posilippo and Pozzuoli north up the coast. There was a clinic, and more apartments set back, with different dogs and different porters, then the road ducked down and ran beneath a roof of pine branches.

Castrolami said, conversationally, 'We put you in a tower block on the north side or on the east side of Rome and on every floor women are looking to see who is new. It's an intelligence-gathering system, unavoidable – you know that. It's the same in a tower in Naples. We put you in a small town near Firenze, Pisa or on the Adriatic, you open your mouth and they hear you, Naples, and they hear us, outsiders, and they think that Mafia scum is being hidden among them, and there are demonstrations, perhaps violence, because they despise you and believe you contaminate their society. It's good here because we're among the people who don't know the Mafia but hate the VAT officials and the Revenue investigators, and who seek to live in privacy. If, however, they believed that a collaborating criminal had been brought here, there would be outrage and the accusation that we've reduced the worth of their property. We don't flaunt you.'

'And when they come back from holiday?'

'We'll think again, look at the budget and—'

'Move on?'

There was an old bridge over the river ahead. They had left the shade of the trees and gone under a six-lane road. She could see over the parapet wall that the Tiber's level was down. It looked played out, not like a famous river. He didn't answer her. She thought they would keep her in the fine apartment while they stripped the meat of what she knew, then ship her on when only the bones remained.

Castrolami said, 'The bridge is the Ponte Milvio, one of the most important in the city. It was built by Gaius Claudius Nero more than two thousand years ago. Constantine won a great battle at the bridge in 312 AD. It's been repaired many times, then a new phenomenon. Three years ago, young people in love were attracted to it, put padlocks on the lamp post and threw the keys into the river. So many padlocks – the bigger and heavier they were, the greater the love – were fastened there that the lamp post collapsed. For a few months there was a virtual lamp post, on the web, but now the mayor has put steel columns on the bridge and it's possible to fix padlocks again. Do you find that interesting?'

She shook her head decisively.

Quietly, his response: 'No, you wouldn't because you assured me that you do not, at present, have a lover. You told me so. We should cross the road.'

Rossi had already done so.

It was a fast thought only, a brittle image – of him in a park, and in a small, grubby house, then laughter, the smoothness of skin and . . . She followed Rossi, and Castrolami was holding her arm. She didn't think she was a prisoner but that he guided her between cars and vans. In her mind she had a list.

She had shopped twice every week for food to cook for Vincenzo and his friends, and once a fortnight she had gone to the street market to buy enough to make a meal for *him* and *his* friends. It was a market far superior to those in London, laid out in splendour, stalls stacked high, every variety and every choice, but of a lower standard to that of the piazza Mercato and what was – had been – her home. She turned, tapped her hip pocket to show it was empty, pulled out the lining of a side pocket, grimaced, laughed . . . Orecchia passed her a ten-euro note, and Castrolami was taking his time, pecking in his wallet, so she leaned forward and took a twenty from it. Rossi gave her a ten. Immacolata chose veal and was about to point out the size of the fillets she wanted when she felt the pressure of Castrolami's fingers on her arm. She indicated, and he spoke. She had learned. She selected potatoes, spinach and green beans, and Castrolami took the notes from her and paid. She bought tomatoes and peppers, button mushrooms and onions, and at another stall there was cream and cheese. On the way out at the far end of the covered market there were wines and spirits, and Castrolami bought one bottle, from Friuli, and she queried it with a gesture, then pointed to him, Rossi, Orecchia and herself. One bottle? He tapped his own chest, and the other men's, then shook his head. She could drink; they would not.

They didn't take the bags from her. She carried three and Castrolami two. It was hotter, might have reached the eighties, and no breeze came off the river. In London, if she had shopped with *him*, *he* would have carried the bags. In Naples, a foot-soldier would have carried her shopping, just as he would have parked the car and waited a respectful pace behind her as she chose. Perhaps it was the glance she gave Castrolami that prompted him. He said, 'If they carry your shopping it would impede their shooting. If they had to shoot it would be in your defence. A shopping bag doesn't help in aiming and firing.'

She thought, again, he had insulted her. She walked faster, away from him, and slowed only when she was a pace behind Rossi. The padlocks on the bridge were in her mind: if she'd been there with *him*, which of them would have taken the key, made the statement of love, and thrown it out into the slack water?

Castrolami was with Orecchia. They were fifteen paces behind the young woman and kept that distance, and Castrolami listened to the older man, who lived and ate with the criminals who collaborated, and slept near them – and held a grip, maybe a loose one, on sanity.

'You ask me how she'll be. You want to know if she'll fall early or late, or stay on her feet and be strong enough for the court.'

To Castrolami it was a pain to be endured. Some investigators and detectives were easy in the company of criminals, could go to weddings and birthday parties and survive allegations of corruption. Not Castrolami. He detested being with them.

'I was with one from your city and you'll have known him. He walked out of the door one morning and the next we heard he was in the Secondigliano area of Naples, or perhaps Scampia, whichever. He had taken a train from the north. A week afterwards we heard he'd arrived home and was on the street, dead. One bullet, middle of the forehead. We'd been with him for four months. Time and resources wasted.'

Castrolami remembered him. Police, not *carabinieri*, had handled his defection. He walked slowly, felt burdened.

'There was another. We had him in Genoa for a whole year, with his wife, his mother, his aunt, her mother and three children. We brought him to Caltanisetta to give evidence against twenty prime Sicilian fuck-pigs. We dressed him in his good suit, a clean shirt and a tie and drove him to the courthouse. He smiled and said he now wished to renegotiate his terms – like his evidence was a piece of goddam property. More money, a better allowance, or no evidence. We had twenty men in the cage and were waiting on his testimony. We agreed the new terms, won the conviction. Then the agreement was torn up. I don't know now whether he's alive or dead.'

Castrolami knew there was a segment of opinion,

influential, which believed too many had been allowed to become a *collaboratore di giustizia*, that too much was given them. It was an easy way to win convictions. With the crimes of the Camorra or the Mafia, there was little opportunity for gathering forensic evidence, less chance of finding eye witnesses prepared to face down intimidation and go public in court. The collaborator, the *infame*, was an attractive solution.

'I've seen little of her, but we were given some notes before her arrival. I read of the leukaemia death, her supposed friend. Perhaps it was merely that the guilt needed a trigger or perhaps the emotion was real. Now you talk to her about her mother, her brothers, but you haven't played a big card. It's there.'

Castrolami faced him. They were now on the rough, narrow road that went up beneath the pines.

'I'm not trying to teach you your job but I'd milk the disease. To be verbally abused, physically assaulted in a cemetery at a burial, is no small matter. Use it, twist it, work it. My advice, Dottore, there isn't a living human being whom she loves. Make good with the dead.'

They trudged on. Orecchia was fitter than Castrolami and climbed the hill easily. He could see, in front, the haughty swing of her hips.

The priest came from a side door. A cleaner who polished the altar silver had said he would be there soon, but it had been an hour. The measure of Eddie's stress, lethargy, lost nerve was that he had been prepared to sit out the hour on a shadowed pew, only moving to do something he had not attempted before: he had made a donation, taken a candle and lit it, then sat some more.

When the priest came through the side door, the cleaner went to him, pointed to Eddie and returned to his polishing.

The priest approached. His short hair, rimless glasses and creased cassock made no concession to style. He sat on the bench beside Eddie, who introduced himself, then asked for Immacolata Borelli. Oh, yes, the priest knew Immacolata Borelli. His eyes flashed and his back straightened. Eddie warmed. Where would he find her home? There was no immediate response. He thought the priest considered. Eddie, ignorant, didn't understand. Why, if the priest knew, should he hesitate? Eddie, innocent, did not comprehend. Sadness fell on the face of the priest, as if he had made a decision that wounded him. He sighed, stood up, and the sadness was wiped away. The face was devoid now of expression. He took Eddie down the aisle, and Eddie paused to put a five-euro note into the box for the repair of the church. He was led out into the brightness. The kids waited on the far side of the street and watched, with the boy on the scooter. The priest pointed far down the via Forcella. Eddie could just make out the fruit and vegetables stall that protruded into half of the street's width. Beyond it was the fish stand. The priest said that the door between the fruit and vegetables and the fish was the home of the grandparents of Immacolata Borelli. For a moment, his head was beside the two scars on the stone, then he backed away. Eddie had been past those stalls twice, had asked in the *tabaccaio* opposite and been ignored. When he turned to thank the priest the church door was already closed.

What should he have done? What should he have said to the foreign boy, a fool, who came to Forcella and asked for the home of Carmine and Anna Borelli? What was his responsibility? Too tired, he had deflected the problem – had done as he was asked and had not accepted responsibility. The foreign boy wanted to meet Immacolata, and he could picture her, the granddaughter of Carmine and Anna Borelli:

it had been her brother, the middle of their three grandsons, who had fired the two pistol shots at a predecessor. It was too much for him to take on as personal responsibility.

Fear stalked him. Fear corroded principle, decency, courage. He had no stomach for the war on the streets. He had crumpled. Predecessors had fought the culture of criminality in Forcella and been broken, or had moved away in indecent haste, or were in Rome under police guard.

He could justify to himself that he could have done nothing to divert the foreigner from visiting the grandparents of Immacolata Borelli – and she was the only one of them with, perhaps, a thimbleful of charity and goodness. He felt cold in the church, shivered and crossed himself.

The Allies had reached Naples. The Fascists had fled. An opportunity had arrived. The troops, British and American, reached the city on 1 October 1943, and within a week the fortunes of the infant Borelli clan had prospered. Carmine, out of gaol, would never deny that the first moves of Anna, his young wife, were integral to them. She had opened the brothel.

It was the first to function within a short walk of the seafront where American officers were billeted in the sequestrated hotels. She brought in women from all classes of Neapolitan society. They shared common features – acute hunger, extreme poverty, the ambition only to survive. It was on a small courtyard where the walls of two buildings were held up by timber supports; a third side had taken a direct hit during a bombing raid. It was within a stone's throw of the Palazzo Sessa – home of Sir William Hamilton, Emma, and Horatio Nelson – and the officers trooped there. The women Anna Borelli recruited began work with the puffiness in their faces that came from near-fatal starvation, but food supplies came with the patrons, and silk stockings, lipsticks, chocolate and cigarettes. They were the wives of stall-holders and lawyers, of labourers and advocates, of street-sweepers and civil servants. Soon they had colour in their cheeks, and they started to eat well, their families too. There were mornings when a queue of women, dressed in their best, had formed outside the heavy front door to plead for the opportunity to be fucked by GIs, and Anna took the most attractive, the most sexually experienced. She did not employ uninitiated teenage girls: the GIs wanted women who did not waste time, were easy to penetrate, who knew the trade. It was said – among the women who came to work at noon and went home at midnight – that in the first days Anna Borelli herself had lain under the gross belly of an American lieutenant colonel, that she could make him squeal like a spiked boar, and the security of the building was guaranteed.

The war of Carmine Borelli was fitful. Called up on his eighteenth birthday, the papers instructed him on which barracks in the town he should report to, and the day after he went into hiding, courting Anna while he was on the run and dodging raids by the Fascist police, coming out of hiding for the day, his marriage to Anna in the church of San Giorgio Maggiore, being informed on, and arrested the following evening. A question never asked and therefore never answered: how was Anna Borelli so skilled in lovemaking, after one night with her nineteen-year-old husband, that she could so successfully entertain the American lieutenant colonel? After two years in Poggioreale gaol, he was freed by Allied forces after he had woven a tale of a young, persecuted liberal democrat imprisoned for his beliefs. He had found the first employees of his wife in cubicles wide enough for a bed, a chair and a narrow table for a washstand, and had shaken the hand of the lieutenant colonel in the hallway, ignoring the man's apparent intimacy with his wife. They had, together, not looked back.

Within weeks, she had opened two more brothels. Within months, he had become a king in the black-market sale of goods brought by the Americans into the Naples docks, and he had started his *mercato nero* with those stockings, cans of food, packs of cigarettes, coffee, sugar and chocolate that the first customers had given his wife by way of a gratuity. First a handcart, then a small closed-sided van, then a flatbed lorry, then many lorries, and always protection from the military government – and the question he never asked of his wife.

It was in the bloodstream of both: the search for power, authority and wealth bred microbes in their veins, which they had never lost.

He had walked down the street from the church, past the shops that were now familiar to him, past the men who sat and played cards or dominoes, and past the Madonna figures in niches in the stonework where candles burned and flowers drooped. He had paused beside the fish-seller's stand and had watched water from a fine spray fall on the swordfish. He had never seen a swordfish, and this one was more than five feet long, its sword another four, and . . . he realised the outer door was open. He could have sworn on oath that it had been closed the previous times he'd gone by. He had known then that the kids or the scooter rider had forewarned them.

He said simply, 'I came to find Immacolata.'

The old man had American-accented English. 'You knew her in London? You knew her well?'

The old woman had a crow's croak, and spoke English. 'Do you sleep with her? Do you do fuck-fuck with her?'

He blushed. Eyes pierced him. The coarseness of the question neither unnerved him nor seemed peculiar – almost, in this place, natural. They were both, he estimated, in their eighties. He sensed that they moved with difficulty, were in pain, and near the door there had been a stand of walking-sticks. The room he was in was furnished, Eddie thought expensively, but with hideous taste – chrome, plastic, fluffy, pinkish. The PhD man in the house in Dalston would have called it kitsch, and his mother's lip would have curled in disdain. He noticed there were no photographs. Not a picture of Immacolata, or of a man who would have been her brother, or of her parents. Everyone his mother knew, all her friends, had homes littered with photographs of grandchildren, shelves and surfaces groaning under them.

The question, its vulgarity, almost amused Eddie, but the eyes of the old woman pierced him with a brightness that suggested she harboured a degree of humour. He would not have dared to lie to her. 'Yes.'

The old woman shrugged. 'There are many girls. Why come to find Immacolata?'

'I think . . . because I love her. You know . . . what I mean. Yes, I love her.'

She said something to the old man, Eddie didn't know what. She reached up from her chair, caught the collar of his shirt, tugged his face down and spoke into his ear, then moved her head to let him speak into hers, but her eyes stayed on Eddie.

The old woman asked if Immacolata loved him. He thought she used the word 'love' as if it was strange to her, but he reckoned that was because she was struggling with the language. He wondered how she had learned English, what call this peasant woman had had to speak it. He repeated and amplified. 'I hope she was in love with me – at least, very fond of me. We were very happy together.'

She tugged again at her husband's shirt collar.

Her small spider fingers scratched at the material of his shirt, pulled and jerked his head down. She was, like him, in her

eighty-eighth year, but her memory was as sharp as the day
he had come back to her from the Poggioreale and she had
told him – without a balance sheet to read from – the finances
of the brothel. She murmured the numbers given her by
Salvatore. He would have had to write them down. Her
mouth to his ear, her ear to his mouth as he repeated the
numbers. She told Carmine that it was equal to a gift from
the Virgin and ignored his shock at what he considered
inappropriate, almost blasphemy – that leverage against the
bitch had walked through the front door, presented itself,
gift-wrapped. He understood. Anna would go to the kitchen,
make coffee and take cake from the tin. He, Carmine, would
go into the hallway and telephone. He repeated the number
again.

What they knew of the English language, American, was
from the days when the troops had been in Naples. Good
days, the best, he a king and she a queen. The fingers loosed
his collar. He smiled at the young man, hoped it a smile of
friendship, and there was a girlish charm about his wife's
smile, which he thought as insincere – and sweet – as the
smile she had used for her customers more than sixty years
before. The same smile and no truth in it. She said she would
make coffee and bring cake, and she said that Carmine would
go and telephone, that there was a man who knew where
Immacolata was and, please, would the young man wait a
little. There was an image of long ago, never forgotten. A
shared cell in the south-west block of the Poggioreale. A
spider, huge, whose territory was the angles between the
brickwork, the bars and the grimy glass of the window. It
had a web that extended nearly a metre across and half a
metre high and the prisoners bet each evening, in cigarettes,
how many new flies would be trapped in the daylight hours
and eaten at night. The spider was esteemed and admired,
its body the size of a matchbook. It trapped the ignorant

192   *Gerald Seymour*

and the innocent. She went to prepare coffee and bring cake,
and Carmine went into the hall, leaving the young man alone.
There was excitement on the young man's face.

Always, to fight against the testimony of an *infame* – the
bitch whore who was his granddaughter – there must be
leverage. Only that, applied with extreme violence, could
destroy the most feared threat to the clans: the informer,
turncoat and traitor.

His was the cleanest and best-polished window of any in the
long line looking out on to the central walkway on the third
floor of the Sail. He was Davide. He spent many hours each
week with a bucket and a rag washing his windows, outside
and in. He used warm water and soap, then a disintegrating
cloth to dry them. He sprayed them with polish, then used
a dry cloth to take off the last of the filth that had
accumulated on the glass. Those who lived in the box
apartments, crumbling from neglect, on either side of him
regarded the occupant of 374 with tolerance and amusement.
Many in the Sail – a gigantic architectural monstrosity –
existed with mental aberration. It was a dumping ground
for the socially challenged and the medical misfits. On the
eastern extremity of Naples, the district of Scampia had
achieved notoriety as a supermarket of drugs, a killing ground
in clan warfare, and as a place where the city authorities
could dump the detritus of the city's population. Davide was
among the rubbish placed there, and he seemed to eke a
minuscule living from delivering messages and packages for
one of the Comando Piazza, who flourished around the Sail,
and small handyman tasks.

Davide's home was on one of the lower floors of a building
that had become a cult symbol of ugliness. The lower floors,
where No. 374 is found, represent the hull and level decking
of a yacht, with ten storeys of floors. Above the deck there

is a towering sail-shaped construction, vertical at the mast on the far end from Davide's location, but terraced down for another ten levels. It has always been known as the Sail. Of the seventy thousand listed in the most recent census as living in Scampia and its tower blocks, some eleven thousand are in this architect's eccentricity. Some call the different levels and ends of the Sail by colours, and others know each block there as a *lotta*. Davide was a resident of Lotta H, which was Green, and which had the franchise to market heroin, already refined. Through his well-cleaned windows, Davide observed much of the trade and the sight of him in his handkerchief-sized living room, the television blaring and only a side light on, was familiar to the lookout, the seller and the Comando Piazza who ran them, and to the *magazzinieri* who held the stockpiles of the narcotic, and even to the level of *aquirenti* who purchased in bulk, and bought from the *capo* of the clan that had authority in the Sail. All, from the top of the tree to the bottom, knew of the demented old fool who spent hours on the windows, bringing them to a brilliant shine, and left his apartment not more than once a week. He was almost always there and when he was not outside and window-cleaning, he was hunched in a chair with the curtains open.

To others, he was Delta465/Foxtrot, and valued – too valuable to be burned by the routine of drugs trafficking.

Salvatore came. He had left the van, with dark bloodstains on the tyres from where a stomach had burst when it was driven over, and was at the door. He was met by Carmine Borelli. He was briefed. He thought the old man panted as if some rare delight hooked him, anticipation . . . Sometimes Salvatore found that his own breath spurted in the moment that he lifted a pistol and aimed it. He thought it would have been, perhaps, before he was born that the old man had last made operational decisions. He was revelling in the chance to live again. The talk was short, as it should have been. He broke away, chuckled to himself: the young man who had screwed Immacolata in London, who *loved* her, would find that the bitch's sweat, the bitch's caresses and the bitch's groans came expensive. Carmine Borelli had said the young man, screwer of Immacolata, was an idiot and would not make any difficulty. The radio that morning had quoted an unnamed official in the Palace of Justice as stating, no equivocation, that the Borelli clan was history, a broken reed. He saw nothing in the street that gave cause for anxiety.

The fish-seller, Tomasso, had had the pitch in the via Forcella for twelve years, his father for the twenty-three before him. Short but broad-shouldered and thick at the waist, he had cropped hair, controlled stubble, good jeans, a good-quality shirt and good shoes. What he wore was good because he sold fine fish fresh from the market that morning. There were, however, matters relevant to the state of mind Tomasso enjoyed that were not generally known to those who dictated the economics of his fish stall. His father's cousin had a boat that fished from the harbour at Mergellina, but two years before Tomasso had been told by the Borelli clan that he must only buy fish landed from the boats they owned. He had not complained and had acquiesced because his chance of obtaining another pitch was minimal. Now, also, he must pay to the clan a hiked *pizzo* for the right to put the stall in that place. Also, now, he must supply fish at cut-price to the trattoria two streets away, at less than cost, because the trattoria was owned by the clan. The *pesce spade*, huge, with the malevolent eye, frozen, would have been taken by Giovanni on a normal day, and not paid for: that had happened more often in the last months.

But the shit-face hadn't come, was in the cells at Poggioreale, and the cow who headed the clan was also in the cells, and Vincenzo had sent the message by courier telling him where he could and could not buy. They were, in his opinion, fucked, but he knew what had been done last evening to a man who had shouted it. Tomasso kept quiet, sold where it was possible, but impotent anger burned in him. Where he stood, close to his till and scales, he was, perhaps, two metres from the door of the house where the old goat lived with his woman. He had seen the young man go into the building, had seen also that kids had come with him, and a scooter boy, and he had thought the young man a stranger. The kids had still been in place, on the far side of the road, till two minutes ago. Everyone knew Salvatore. Everyone who worked in the via Forcella or in the Sanità district knew the face of Il Pistole, who had come and talked inside with the old goat, had waved the kids away and gone. He felt the tension ratchet, and he was aware that the street, quietly and without fuss, was emptying.

The grocery was down the rue de Bellechasse, and Lukas – as was usual for him – bought only the bread, milk and eggs that he would eat in twenty-four hours, nothing that would go sour or stale in the fridge if the apartment was indefinitely abandoned. The red light had not been blinking when he had returned.

He had checked his post before he started on the cleaning, as he did every day. Nothing that needed attention. There was little enough for him to collect from the box by the main door: a few utility bills, offers of health insurance and holiday brochures, never anything personal. When he was away, in a war zone or counter-insurgency theatre, he always noted how men and women, far from home, yearned for mail from their families, emails or phone calls. Didn't matter whether he yearned or not, he wasn't getting any. No envelopes came with spidery writing, copperplate, a big fist or one that was near indecipherable. It was as if, wanting or not, he had no home and no folk who cared a shite. So, he built a wall, surrounded himself and . . . Lukas cleaned.

He did the cleaning, too, about every day, because he had the feeling always that he would go out through the front door, lock it behind him and might survive or might not. Might go down in a Black Hawk over a Shiite city in Iraq, and might get blown off a road by an IED outside Kandahar, and might fall off some dirt track in the mountains of central Colombia. He was like many of the gypsies who serviced the dirty little wars: he didn't want to think of anyone making an entrance to collect his effects and puckering a forehead as they wondered where to start, thinking that the man was an untidy jerk and had left a mess. He might only have ten minutes between the telephone ringing or coming back in and having the red light alert him, dragging the bag out from under the bed, locking the door and starting the sprint for Solferino Métro. He kept the place neat and just about in a state that no one could be sure that anyone had recently lived there. All his washing went most days to the launderette, even if it was just briefs, singlet, socks and a shirt.

When he had finished the cleaning – it took all of a quarter of an hour – he checked the laptop. There were copies of the fulsome praise from DC that had come into Ground Force Security, and gratitude for his report. The company didn't give him saccharine accolades for what he had achieved in the last trip, knew that the sweet stuff was unwelcome. Lukas could have reeled off the story of disasters in the hostage-rescue trade. He didn't do celebrity and didn't want back-slapping. Truth was, the fear of failure gripped his gut more when he was in the field than the demands of success. Failure was a body-bag. There had been enough for them never to be forgotten.

He wound up the cord of the vacuum cleaner that did the living-room rugs and the bedrooms' carpet. Ruby Ridge was in Lukas's battle honours, and nobody was keen to shout that one up to the clouds. Lukas, if he had engaged in a discourse about his work – which he never did – would have said that Ruby Ridge, up in the forests of Idaho where it was wild enough for mountain lion, had been the first pinpoint lesson of where a screw-up had happened. An innocent woman shot dead by official marksmen, and a child, and in return fire a US marshal killed, then the circus of a full-blown FBI-controlled siege of ten days' duration, with a cast of maybe five hundred agents, and millions paid by government in subsequent compensation. Lukas had not been senior, had been then a marksman with the Bureau's Hostage Rescue Team, and had seen a cock-up played out close enough to smell the shit that emanated. A good lesson for a rookie. He had been far back from the front line overlooking the cabin, and his Remington Model 700 had never been out of its bag, let alone loaded, but he had seen, played out before him, how bad it could get. He knew he walked a fine line between Ruby Ridge and the broken careers, and the hero-gram stuff on his laptop.

He watched the telephone and thought it might be an opportunity to go visit his friend who did the artwork down by the river, shit work and without talent, but by a good friend. The artist would never have heard of Ruby Ridge – or seen the face of a hostage when it was frozen in death, attached to or severed from the neck, or incoherent and trembling in the moment after liberation. Lukas played the strings, did God, and he went round a last time with a duster.

When he closed the door he stood in the lobby for a moment and listened. The bell did not ring. He went off down the flights of stairs.

8

Eddie came out of the main door on the ground floor. He had been told he would be met and taken to Immacolata. He saw a great deal in the moment he was on the outer step but he assimilated the importance of nothing.

The door swung shut behind him. He caught a glimpse of it and the grandfather's old hand, pocked with cancer scars, that had heaved it: too fast, no chance to thank. A van was parked on the street as if about to unload, but nothing was taken from the tail doors and nothing was carried to them. A pavement opposite had bustled and was now still. The kids were not crowded in the street but further up the slope of via Forcella and further down, as if they formed a cordon and made a perimeter. A man came forward and did not play-act friendship, a frown puckering his forehead. A hand from the interior slid open a side door of the van. The guy on the fish stall caught Eddie's eye, the swordfish in ice beside him, and held his gaze.

Eddie had his hand in his pocket, was reaching for a handkerchief – must have been dust, up his nose and in his throat. He was about to sneeze. A man closed on him, came from the van, and behind was a dark interior, and sacking, a rope trailing out of the opening. The man on the fish stall held Eddie's eyes. So much, then, for Eddie Deacon to assimilate. Time slowing. The man coming slower. People in the café opposite pirouetting their chairs to face away from the street, but the pace of the movement slackening. Trying to understand . . . The fish-seller had that look, unmistakable, no argument with it. Like a warning shout, but nothing passed his lips. The quiet, like fog, settled on him but the sights were clearer.

He could not comprehend why the fish-seller should give the warning. He could only react to it.

The hands of the man reached towards him. Not open, not in greeting, clenched. The veins stood out in his muscled arms, like highways through the hairs. Eddie ripped his hand from his pocket and moved into that defensive stance, as a boxer does, trying to go forward on to the balls of his feet. He had never, since he was a child in a tantrum, hit anyone. He had never punched, kicked, gouged or bitten another adult. He had only once intervened in a fight and played a hero and— So fast. His hand was only halfway up to protect his chin and throat when the fist of the man came at him. He felt himself buffeted. Pain riddled his nostrils and there were tears in his eyes. A grip tightened on his shirt and he was dragged forward. He was pulled past the fish-seller and saw nothing but a face without expression. Should he have tried to run? No chance: blocked by the van and the fish stall on its heavy trestle legs. Could see only the backs of the heads in the café opposite.

He was dragged forward and when he was close enough the man's knee exploded into Eddie's groin.

About the end of it, his experience as a street-fighter. Real pain now. He tried to double up, which merely offered his jaw, the chin, to a short-arm hook punch. He went into the side hatch of the van.

Eddie was face down, his head buried in a heap of loose sacking, foul-smelling and tasting – hard for him to breathe, and he struggled, but one fist was clamped in his hair and the other whipped his face, used it as if it was a boxer's training gear. He stopped the struggle. The door was slammed. Then all light went and a hood was over his head. His arms were snatched down into the small of his back, handcuffs snapped on. He heard the tearing of heavy-duty tape and his hood was lifted, the tape fastened over his mouth, and the van was moving.

The hands were at his legs and rope was wound round his ankles. He heard the oath when the van must have hit a hole, perhaps where a cobblestone was missing. Then the rope was lashed tight and tied.

He was helpless.

He wondered if he would hear sirens, immediate pursuit. There had been people in the café, people further up the street and down it. He imagined a phone call on a mobile, alerting police to what had happened. The hope died pretty bloody soon.

Eddie realised that the van was not speeding. There was no chase. The driver went at the normal speed for morning traffic, didn't hoot, didn't weave, didn't chase back-doubles and rat-runs.

He thought the worst. He was gone, lost, and it was hard to drag air into his lungs, and could hear the breathing of the man sitting on the van floor close to him. He didn't dare move because that would get him another thrashing. Truths came.

Eddie Deacon, bloody idiot, had blundered on to territory where he should not have been. Way back, he should have walked home from the Afghan place, should have reached up and taken down the blow-up of Immacolata, his Mac, folded it and put it deep in a drawer, maybe under his socks. He should not have gone with a street kid and burgled, should not have jacked in work and taken a budget flight, should not have walked down a street where no smile met his and no help requested was given. He should not have trusted the old couple, grandparents and providers of coffee, cake and betrayal. Pretty damn obvious: keep the idiot in place and send for the heavy squad.

What to do? Important – not important: why it had happened. What to do mattered.

Bitch and fight and get another beating. Go passive, supine and give up the ghost. Lie still, let the world move and try to bloody think. He gave himself three alternatives. He was bound at the ankles, handcuffed at the wrists, his mouth was gagged and a hood covered his face. He had to make choices between alternatives, would have to.

He did not know how long he was in the van, lost track of time, and would lose also the pain in his wrists where the cuffs bit. He never heard a siren.

The fish-seller, Tomasso, came round his stall and bent low. He believed it would be thought he retied the knot in his lace. He hadn't moved from his place beside the cash box and the scales until life had returned to the via Forcella. Chairs in the café had swivelled, the pavement was filled, and scooters swerved along the length of the street. Children poured out of the big gates of the school named after the girl who had been shot in cross-fire, Annalisa Durante; a murder gang had come to kill the son of a more minor clan leader in the district. Tomasso watched the children – six or seven, the only evidence of innocence in the street. He knew her parents, who lived a dozen doors up, and he knew what had been the fate of the priest then at the church on the corner with the via Duomo who had denounced the clans and called for their elimination from the community. He had seen the street return to normality, then moved round his stall and bent to tie his shoelace. He could reach, also, a few centimetres to the right of his shoe and slide his palm over the piece of paper that had fallen from the young man's pocket. It had been at the moment that the hand came out fast, in response to Tomasso's silent warning, that the piece of paper had been dropped. He slipped it into his breast pocket after glancing at it and realising what it was.

The priest who had stood against the clans and their culture, after the killing of the teenager Annalisa Durante, had had two shots fired at him when he paused on the steps of his church and now lived in Rome. He came back to Naples rarely, but always with an escort of police bodyguards. There would be protection for a priest but not for a fish-seller, so he was careful in his movements. He telephoned his uncle and asked him to come – quickly, *subito*, immediately – and mind the stall. The paper in his pocket gave the name of a hotel and the room number. While he waited, he considered which route was quickest, and hoped he might help – when no other would – a wretch in the gravest of danger. To ring the police direct was a step too far.

Immacolata was permitted to prepare the food.

She had heard the courier's motorbike outside the main gate to the block, then the doorbell. She had seen the plastic sack of tapes Castrolami had taken across the living room into the hall, and the door had been opened. She had seen, from the kitchen's balcony, the courier in black leathers load the sack into a pannier, then ride off at speed, spitting dust.

She washed vegetables, scraped potatoes and brought the *penne* down from the upper shelf where the pasta was stored. She had turned up the radio and did dance steps between the sink and the surfaces where the food was laid out. For a few minutes she felt freedom, perhaps for the first time. Orecchia and Rossi had left her to herself, and in those minutes she had expelled from her mind the scams, deals, fixes and hits of the clan, and had filled the void with . . . nothing. She delighted in the emptiness of the black hole.

Castrolami was at the door. She was sluicing the spinach

leaves, had been measuring the *penne* in her mind, was deciding on the mix of tomato purée and cream for the sauce.

She turned once, saw his face, must have had a smile on hers and the music from the radio lifted her. Her mother was gone, her three brothers were gone, via Forcella was gone. Castrolami was at the door, leaning on the jamb and watching her, not sharing any form of pleasure. He had destroyed the mood. She saw no thanks, no gratitude. He looked at her as if she was a child, wayward and not to be humoured.

'Yes?'

'We go back to work. Now.'

'I need only a few minutes and then I'm—'

'We start now,' Castrolami said. He reached across the work surface to the radio and killed the sound.

'What is so important that it can't wait five minutes?' Her hands were on her hips, her feet apart, her chin jutted. She barked: 'Well, what?'

He scratched his leg, then let his teeth run across his lower lip, looked at the ceiling, then said coldly, and without apology, 'It's time to talk about leukaemia and about the death of a long-standing friend.'

Everything gone, broken. 'Yes, of course.'

She threw the kitchen gloves into the bowl where they sank among the spinach leaves and the potato peel. She yanked the tie loose on the apron, hitched the strap over her head and let it fall to the floor. She turned her back on the sink and the work surfaces and strode towards the door, but he made no effort to back away.

Almost, she had believed she would be among colleagues. Now she realised she was alone.

'Enough,' he said. 'We'll eat first.'

★

The fish-seller, Tomasso, spoke with the day manager of the *pensione*, Giuseppe. They had not met before, but in the sparring for mutual contact – for guarantees – it was learned that a cousin of Tomasso had been at middle school with Giuseppe's niece. Everyone who lived at street level in the city knew that there were times when a man took a grave risk, times when he relied on trust.

He showed the piece of paper. It was a big decision for him to say what he had seen, but old enmities, long-festering slights and past wrongs encouraged him. The fish-seller was rewarded. The day manager had an address on a card filled in by a young Englishman, a point of contact. He had done his bit, played his part, and was assured of virtual anonymity. Tomasso believed he had done right, which was important to him.

Giuseppe did not pay the *pizzo*. The night manager did. Sometimes it was Giovanni Borelli who came for the small envelope, and sometimes it was the younger son, the little bastard, and once it had been Gabriella Borelli, who had been rude, boorish. First it had been the daughter. Immacolata Borelli had arrived with a pocket calculator and demanded to see the books. She had sat with the owner for an hour in the office at the back. Two men – thugs – had been with her and had loafed in the reception lobby. They had known, the night manager, the day manager and the owner, of a shift in authority in that district and that the Borelli clan was now supreme. There had been photographs in the *Cronaca* of bodies lying in the streets. The books had been shown to the daughter, and the owner had not considered refusing to pay and informing the police. Immacolata, with her calculator, had decided how much should be paid each month. The day manager was from Genoa, and worked in Naples because his wife demanded to be near her widowed mother. Giuseppe hated the corruption of the city.

He found a number in England from the address given, rang it and steeled himself for what he had to say.

There was the sound of a trapdoor slamming above him, then a bolt's scrape. The impact pushed air across his hands, but not through the hood covering his head. He was on concrete. Now that the trapdoor was shut, and the air from above was gone, Eddie sensed dampness around him. For a while he lay still. He tried to learn. There were sounds, at first clear, and he thought feet moved immediately beside the trapdoor, then heard low voices, but the footfall and the words were soon muffled, then gone. He was uncertain as to whether he had heard an engine start – the van's or a smaller, noisier one, like a scooter's. Silence fell.

The quiet frightened him. It was more intimidating, he thought, to have a curtain without noise draped around him than it had been at the moment of his capture – violence, speed, pain, scrambled, tumbling images and thoughts. The intimidation of the silence was intensified by the hood, the gag, the cuffs, but the rope at his ankles had been untied. He could, after a fashion, relate to his kidnap: nothing like it had happened to him before, obvious, but it did in movies and books. Books didn't do the darkness and films didn't do the silence. He could move on his backside, could wriggle forwards, backwards and sideways.

He started to explore.

The concrete floor was not wet but moist. He had been dragged out of the van and had slipped. His head had careered into the bottom of the side hatch and the impact had dazed him, but the hold on him had not slackened. He had heard a door unlocked ahead and had been propelled through it, then down some steps. On the steps he had stumbled again and fallen forwards unable to use his arms to protect his face. The hands gripping him had let him go, and Eddie's shoulders had taken his weight against the wall, but his nose had bled. He had been held upright in a room, a basement or, more likely, a cellar, and the trapdoor had been lifted and his ankles freed. Hands had held him under the armpits and he had felt his feet dance in a void, like a hanged man's. He had been lowered into the space and then, as his feet had made contact with concrete, he had been shoved violently sideways so that he collapsed and was prone. Then the trapdoor had been shut. Now he moved, with the grace of damaged reptile, across the floor.

To learn about his surroundings, Eddie had to manoeuvre himself backwards so that his fingers could touch and feel. He made calculations. He reckoned he was in a bunker dug into the earth below a cellar, and that its dimensions were six feet by eight. The sides were of breeze blocks and the mortar holding them was crudely applied. In a corner there were two sacks, heavy-duty plastic and well filled.

Something now was worse than the darkness and the silence. He imagined the hood over his head had once been a pillowcase on a child's bed. Maybe since then it had been used as a rag to clean floors, windows or lavatory seats. The smells in it were deep in his nostrils. Bad enough not to be able to breathe through his mouth, worse when the passage into his nose was clogged with the hood's stench. Eddie found he could tilt his back against a wall and wriggle his body downwards while his head and the hood had contact against the roughness of the mortar. The movements eased the hem of the hood upwards. He scratched his shoulders against the barbed edges of the mortar and might have drawn more blood, but the hem was lifted from the nape of his neck, then to the back of his skull and on to the crown. It was important to him that he did this. Since the street, and the slamming of the door behind him, the eye-contact with the fish-seller and the raising of his hands, Eddie had done nothing for himself, had been like a bloody vegetable. He shook his head violently. Rotated it, waggled it. The hood came off. A different air and a different smell were on his face and in his nose.

He thought it a victory. There was no light in the bunker. All he could see now, with the hood off, was a thin outline where the trapdoor sides met the ceiling it was set in, and one pinpoint where there must have been a flaw in one of the trapdoor's planks. He stood. He couldn't straighten to his full height – and reckoned the bunker was five feet high. It was a victory that he had shed the hood, and the guys in the house in Dalston would have rated it. A Revenue clerk, a clubland waiter, a ticket seller and a work-shy PhD student would have seen the value of success.

Shortlived, the sense of that victory.

Eddie wanted to pee. He had crawled backwards around the bunker's walls and found the filled sacks, but no bucket. With his wrists held in the small of his back, he couldn't drop his zip. He hadn't wet his trousers since he was five, on a school outing. Also gone, with the sense of victory, was the belief that the guys in Dalston would have the faintest comprehension of being in darkness and feeling the urge to wet their trousers. He slumped.

He could hear nothing – no vehicles, no music, no voices and no sirens. It was as if he had gone off the face of the earth. Fight, be passive or think. Time for Eddie Deacon to face the alternatives and make a choice. Time to wonder *why* it had happened.

He sat against the sacks, with only the bloody darkness and the bloody silence for company. The bladder pressure grew, and he knew that the fear would return.

It was a gesture of his new-found defiance. Carmine Borelli left his stick propped in the corner inside the doorway. He had swallowed three Nurofen tablets – the strong ones –

washing them down with cold water. He knew that Anna
would watch him from a high window and he would be
tongue-whipped if he failed.

Between the clans that were labelled 'Camorra', there was
no overall authority, no consensus of leadership. On the
island of Sicily, Cosa Nostra groups acknowledged the
disciplines imposed by a *cupola*, a cabinet of principals; there
was a predictability and a certainty about the future. Not so
in Naples. A clan was dead when power was lost . . . Now
the Borelli clan teetered on the brink of oblivion.

The drugs compensated for his leaving behind his stick.
The pain from his rheumatism was controlled. In old age,
Carmine watched much daytime television and flipped
between the satellite channels – so many dealt with the big
animals of the African plains, elephant and lion and buffalo.
When their teeth failed and they could no longer forage, or
when their muscles and strength failed, or when their eyesight
was gone and their keen hearing, the great beasts were pushed
aside by the young. Many afternoons he had sat in his chair
and watched as an old elephant, lion or buffalo was killed
or pushed aside and left to starve. As brutal as Naples. He
had shaved closely, and wore a suit with a laundered shirt
and a tie. His thick hair was slicked back with gel, and Anna
had wiped the dust off his shoes.

He felt himself born again.

He walked down the street where a man had been taken
from a bar and shot in the leg, then driven over. Salvatore
was a half-pace behind him, while a dozen of the young men
who wanted to be enforcers and had tried to find favour
with his son, Pasquale, and daughter-in-law, Gabriella, fanned
out around him. Carmine wore his suit jacket open, the jacket
flapping from his walk, the butt of the pistol in his waistband
there to be seen. Salvatore had a fist buried in a deep pocket
that bulged, and some of the young men carried wooden

staves or pickaxe handles. If he was not on the street and not exercising authority, his clan area would be lost. It would not be gone over a year or six months, but in a day. His right hip hurt in a throbbing ache. To compensate he put more weight on his left knee and experienced stabs of pain there. He kept walking, his smile broad.

Some of the older men gathered in doorways. They had been on the payroll in the early days of power when the city was devastated by bombing, the sewers were fractured, epidemics rife and money was to be made. Now they called the name he had once been given. Then, now, he was 'Il Camionista', the Lorry Driver, because he had had the first fleet of trucks on the road, the permit, the petrol and the goods they transported from the Americans. He had skewered his way into so much in those incredible, prosperous days. He had been told, and had believed it, that a third of all cargo landed by the Americans ended up on the stalls of the street traders in Naples, a good proportion of it in the via Forcella: food, clothing, oil. Best of all was the copper wire used for the Allies' telephone communications – it fetched massive prices: his people cut down the wire before the first connection was made. He acquired good business from funerals. He could arrange, for a price, to summon that 'successful cousin from Rome whose intellect and wealth enhanced a sad day', and therefore lifted the prestige of the bereaved family. Nothing had been beyond Carmine Borelli, but it was sixty-five years ago that he had been known as Il Camionista. The younger men looked at him questioningly.

They would have thought: Pasquale Borelli already in gaol, Gabriella Borelli also in gaol, Vincenzo, Giovanni and Silvio in gaol, and the whore of a granddaughter singing to the Palace of Justice. Where was the power? Would the Misso clan take it, or the Contini clan, or would a new boy come out of the shadows? Was the old guard already dead, or moving only

in the last spasms? At the café, from which a customer had
been taken and killed, the owner brought out a small tray of
bogus silver with coffee and a brandy apéritif. Carmine drank
the coffee first, then the alcohol, and stifled successfully the
choke that rose in his throat. Further down the street, a
haberdasher who was three days late in payment of his *pizzo*
thrust the envelope into Carmine's hand, murmured apologies
and said he had put in extra. He had been on the street for
five or six minutes, and little time was left.

Had the man actually said that Carmine Borelli was an
old drunk and useless, fit only to pleasure himself in a chair?
Had he? Who had heard him? He had been kept for an hour,
to wait and sweat, in a lock-up behind the butcher's, would
have squatted among the bones and offal waiting for disposal.
Some had said they had heard him say Carmine Borelli was
fit only to take his penis in his own hand. It was enough
that a rumour of what the man had said was abroad. Carmine
Borelli had not risen to the position of clan leader by clemency
and charity. It would be done on the street.

In his time, leading the clan, he had killed, it was estimated,
thirty-six men with his own hand, and had ordered the proxy
killing of at least another sixty.

It was high risk.

It was about authority and respect. It would be done on
the street, in public view, in daylight, so that none could say
Carmine Borelli slunk in the shadows. The man was brought
out. Carmine recognised him. The man knelt on the pavement.
Two of the foot-soldiers produced plastic bags – for garden
fertiliser – and held them close to the man's head. He gibbered.
Carmine had known the man's father, his uncles and his
mother's family. Many said he was an idiot and certifiable.
But he shot him. He had not killed for twenty years.

He shot him low in the forehead at a point equidistant
between the eyes. Blood spouted but was trapped by the

plastic bags. Had Carmine wanted to run, he could not have. The damaged joints in his knees and hips prevented it. Salvatore took the pistol from him and was gone.

He turned his back on the man, who should have been in an asylum and was crumpled on the pavement, and made his way back to the via Forcella. He hoped he had sent a message or he, too, would be on the pavement. He would not give up the clan, would not see it cannibalised. His hand shook from the impact of the pistol when it had fired. He was out of the street by the time he heard the sirens. They would take the corpse to the Ospedale degli Incurabili, then to the mortuary. The police and the *carabinieri* would come. If he, Carmine Borelli, was named by a witness as the killer, his authority was sand dribbling between his fingers. If the investigators and detectives met the familiar wall of silence, there remained a small chance he could resuscitate the clan . . . meaningless, if the whore didn't break with her interrogators.

He stopped at several more shops, small craftsmen's businesses and showed himself. He thought it the best of fortune that a fool had come from England and had talked the rubbish of love for the whore. By the time he reached his main door, beside the fish-seller's stall, he would not be able to hide the limp. The whore was the key; the fool was critical. He would go first to the home of a dear and long-standing friend and there he would strip and shower. The fine suit and the shirt would be bagged, and the change of clothes brought for him there by Anna would be neatly laid out. His friend would burn the clothes that carried the residue of the pistol's firing, his body would be clean of such traces, and then he would go home – after visiting a café where many would swear he had spent two hours . . . if his authority held up. As he walked, Carmine Borelli shook his head. It was so hard to believe that Immacolata was the whore.

★

She wanted to dance. Orecchia refused and Rossi declined more politely but as firmly. She did not ask Castrolami.

She had had the music up, high volume. Castrolami had pushed his chair back from the table, gone to the radio, turned the volume down and talked of unwelcome complaints from the floor below. They had said she cooked well, that it was a fine meal, and she had thought the praise insincere. She did not dance in Naples, had not danced in London. She was not trained to dance. If she could dance with Orecchia or Rossi, she thought she might dominate whichever man held her.

They had eaten what she had put in front of them, but not had second helpings. It was not disguised: she believed they would have preferred to hit the freezer and do defrosts in the microwave.

She stood up, went round the table, worked her hips and let her hands drop first on Orecchia's shoulders, then on Rossi's. Neither reacted. When she was opposite Castrolami, he looked at her. She stared at him and undid an upper button on her blouse. He looked away.

She fell back on temper.

She didn't wait for them to clear the table of glasses and the cheese plate, she scooped up what she could carry, and made as great a noise as possible by dropping them into the bowl in the sink, on top of the pans she had used for the meat and the pasta, the knives, forks and spoons. She expected them to come running. Their voices were low in the dining room. Immacolata went back for the wine bottle and her glass, then stalked again to the kitchen. There was enough in the bottle to fill her glass: the men had only drunk water. She ran a tap noisily, put the soap in. Everything could, of course, have gone in the dishwasher, but then there would have been no noise, no possibility of reaction. She had noise, not the reaction. She sang, made more noise.

Immacolata washed and stacked.

Songs from Naples – where else could they be from? She only knew songs from that city. It was her life. She heard him wheeze and turned.

'Tell me how it was for her in the last twenty-four hours of her life . . .'

'I want to know about the last hours of Marianna Rossetti's life.'

He stood in the kitchen doorway. He was not, then, proud of himself. Seldom, if ever, was. It was a job. He couldn't bring himself to show sympathy or humanity. Had he done so, the emotions would have been fraudulent. The course he took was necessary for the job. He gave nothing of himself to Immacolata Borelli.

She reacted. Was a little drunk. It had not been a strong wine, but she'd put down most of a bottle. She stared hard at him and her lips moved, but no words came.

Castrolami said, 'I want to know about the last hours of Marianna Rossetti's life. If you've forgotten what you were told I can remind you. Would that be a good idea? Should your memory have failed you, I have a note of what was said to you in the cemetery in Nola. I ask again. Tell me how Marianna Rossetti died, what the leukaemia had done to her, about the contamination. Does your memory need prompting?'

The reaction was not aggression but as if a deep wound had opened, the rawness exposed. There was, he thought, an inner struggle.

'Do I have to?'

'Yes,' Castrolami said. He squeezed it out of her, as if from a tube that needed folding over and pressurising. He heard how the father had spat beside her feet, how her offer of the flowers had been rejected, and she was called a whore.

He heard how the mother of her closest friend had used her fingers to rip her blouse and underwear, had kicked her, and she had fallen, crushing the flowers.

'Don't gild it. I'm not interested in *you*, how *you* felt, what they did to *you*. I'm interested, Signorina, in the last hours of your friend.' He said it harshly, and had no regret.

'Her last days were marked by exhaustion, very tired, very lethargic, no energy . . .'

He thought she spoke like a machine, and no emotion showed.

'Then bruises appeared all over her body, but she had not hit herself or been hit. The bruises were there. She was very pale. It was high summer in Nola – hot sunshine – and she was so white, anaemic. She was taken to the doctor. He knew immediately. As soon as he had peered behind her eyes, used that little torch, he made the call to the hospital.'

'You miss nothing, and you spare yourself nothing. Continue.'

He tested her, her toughness and resolve. He had to strain to hear her, but he didn't lean forward: he stayed propped against the door jamb. 'The doctor thought it too urgent for Marianna and her mother to wait for an ambulance. Her mother drove her, and they called her father from work.'

He was told of the fast collapse of the patient, the pain in the skull, the uncontrolled internal bleeding, the neurosurgeon arriving too late, the failed resuscitation.

'How did she contract the disease that took her life, that left her in her last hours without dignity and peace? How?'

'Being in the fields, bathing in streams, having gone close to where toxic waste was dumped.'

'Who dumped the poison?'

He was told that the father of Marianna Rossetti had said that the clan at Nola had, for more than twenty years, paid for the toxic waste to be left in the fields, the orchards and the riverbeds around the town.

'The question I asked was "Who dumped the poison?" You have not yet answered it.'

He was told that the transportation of the waste from the north was sub-contracted to the Borelli clan in Naples who had an empire of lorries and trucks. Her father had arranged the transportation. Her brother and her mother had banked the money paid for it.

'The food on your plate, Signorina, was the blood money for the poisoning of your friend. That isn't a question. It's a statement.'

She nodded. All the time she had spoken, and he had listened, she had washed plates, knives, forks and glasses. He hadn't noticed. It was as if they were tied together, bound by what he said and what she said, and all else was shut out.

'The clothes on your back.'

Again, she nodded, then tipped out the water from the bowl, but did not face him.

'The classes where you have learned book-keeping, the basics of accountancy, so that you can more successfully launder the cash from poisoning others.'

She peeled off the rubber gloves, threw them into the bowl, then nodded – accepted what he had said.

'You should know, Signorina, that the Camorra has a profit of three billion euro each year from this trade. That is a vast amount of food, clothes and classes. Cancer rates are up in some categories – liver, colo-rectal, leukaemia, lymphoma – to levels three times that of the rest of Italy. It is the Triangle of Death, Signorina Immacolata. Do you accept responsibility?'

She was staring out of the window. From the little movements of her shoulders, Castrolami thought she might weep. 'I do.'

'I care little for the killings in Naples. Bad guy kills bad guy. Excellent. Fewer bad guys to pollute the streets. Marianna

Rossetti was not a bad guy. I seldom do speeches, Signorina. This one is about those already dead, those already condemned and those yet to be contaminated, all innocent. A whole district, hundreds of square kilometres, is poisoned and no one knows how to clean that ground and filter that water. For generations to come there will be the misery of the visit to the doctor, the rush to the clinic, the failure to prolong life – and for your like there will be meals on the table, the best clothing on your back and a fat bank account. You confirm to me that you take responsibility?'

She had lifted the glass. Drained it. Held it up so that not a drop of the wine should be left in it. 'Yes.'

'And you will see this through?'

'I will.'

'Whatever?'

'Correct.'

He heard the glass fracture. He realised she had crushed it in the palm of her hand. She opened the rubbish bin with the foot-pedal, let the shards fall into it and blood dripped. He thought he'd done well. Theatrical, but acceptable in context. Castrolami's opinion: it had been necessary to cut away the bullshit in her and break her. Having broken her, he could rebuild her. He thought her stronger now, and focused. He believed she would, as she had said, see it through in the face of whatever was thrown at her.

The policeman stood on the step and the porch light played on his shaven scalp. His suit was crumpled, his shirt was second-day-on and the tie was loosened; he should also have smeared some polish on his shoes – shouldn't have been there, should have been in Salisbury at County Headquarters, should have been changing into the best suit, clean shirt, best tie and better shoes, should have been focusing on the seminar kicking off that evening: 'Terrorism – Tackling the

Reality of Today's Threat'. Was, instead, at a bungalow in a village outside Chippenham. The rain was tipping down.

'We have to look, Mr Deacon, at the actual world – as it is, not as we'd like it to be. Do we have at the moment – I'm just repeating what I've already told you and your wife – the resources to look into this, as you would like us to? We do not. It's a matter of priorities, Mr Deacon – difficult as that may be for you to appreciate – and what you've told us doesn't top the priority ladder. Then there's the cutbacks. If we could link your son's disappearance to international terrorism, it's a different ball game – could probably send an aircraft-carrier down there. Sorry, not appropriate, Mr Deacon . . . Look, I understand how upset you are, but see it, please, from our viewpoint.'

The father said, 'I'm sorry if my son's situation is inconvenient.'

'I think you're getting the hang of ours, sir. He's gone off, your boy, to try to patch up a scene with a girl who walked out on him in London. You get a garbled call, all the language difficulties thrown in, saying your son's been kidnapped. Who says? You can't tell us. What's the source? You don't know.'

'I'm probably keeping you,' the father said evenly.

'We've called the *carabinieri* – those people in pantomime uniforms – in Naples. They have no report of a kidnap. We've not been idle. We've called the consulate there and they've checked with the police. Nothing heard. I'm being frank with you, sir. It's about resources and priorities – and also about our pretty desperate relations with Italian law and order.'

'I'm sure you've something more important to be getting on with.'

He saw the brief smile of relief and watched the man scuttle to his car, which was parked in the lane. He checked his watch. It had been twenty-eight minutes of pass-the-buck messing.

From behind him, Betty asked, 'Arthur, what's Eddie worth?'

He looked out on to the lane, then the darkened outline of the hedges and fields, hearing the smack of the rain around him. 'Pretty much everything we have. That's what Eddie's worth to us. Not the easiest boy, but the only one we have.'

'A difficult enough little beggar.'

'But he's our son.'

'Can be infuriating. What do we do?'

'Can be an utter wretch. I was thinking, top of my head, of going down to Dean's. Hear what he has to say.'

'You should. Eddie met him, didn't he, last time he was here? Had a good talk. A pretty sensible chap. Just troubled . . . I can't think, right now, of anyone better – or what else to do.'

He came inside and – as if it was something he should do more often and had forgotten for too long – gave his wife a brush kiss on the cheek. He dialled a number, and spoke to Dean Weymouth's partner at their home a quarter of a mile up the lane. He wouldn't have gone near the man without first checking that it was a good time to call. All the village knew Dean Weymouth had bad turns when he came back from the three-month visits to Iraq, and his space was respected – but he had always said the company he worked for was the best: efficient and dedicated.

Arthur Deacon didn't know where else to go. But it involved his son so he had to go somewhere.

'Each time I go back, Mr Deacon, it's worse. But I keep going . . . Doesn't make sense, does it? I go back because there's nothing else. Going back is my way of saying I'm not history, not scrap, not finished and chucked out. I'm a soldier, Special Forces, that family. I have no other skills. I'm diagnosed PTSD – my stress levels go up to the top of the gauge – but I keep going back, have to.'

They were outside, in the wilderness of the untended back garden. Dean Weymouth was happier there than in the house.

'I'm not accusing anybody, certainly not you, Mr Deacon, but I hear the word is, round here, that I'm "peculiar" or "unpredictable" or "difficult" . . . maybe just round the twist. People don't understand "traumatic stress" and don't see it as a medical affliction, like a worn-out hip or a hernia. They cross the street, pretend to look anywhere else, find excuses not to talk. You're almost crying on the Black Dog days for someone to talk to – but people haven't the time or the inclination.'

He wore only a T-shirt on his upper body and it was short-sleeved. The rain ran down the decorative lines of his tattoos, and was in his cropped hair. Mr Deacon had on an anorak and a cap. Dean Weymouth spoke softly and without rancour, in a flat, almost lifeless monotone.

'All right, wrong. Most people haven't. Your boy, your Eddie, he did, he made time. We didn't talk stress, trauma, disorder. He let me ramble on down by the river – only last Sunday – about that new weed that's taking over on the banks, and we saw the kingfisher fly, and I told him about the fish in there and . . . It was nothing talk. Would have bored a saint half to death. He gave me time, not many do. It was precious.'

He lit a cigarette. It took three matches because of the shake in his hands – he remembered his hands hadn't shaken when he'd been by the river and given time. The trembling was always bad when the end of a home leave was in sight.

'I'm going back in a couple of weeks. What spooks us most there is the thought of getting lifted – being taken. It's

like your worst nightmare but ratcheted up. We do close
protection, usually of civilian experts. We have to take them
to work. Could be lifted in the office, hoods in bogus police
uniforms, or blocked in on the road and not able to shoot
a way out of it. We know about kidnapping. It scares the
shit out of us. If that's happened to your boy, Mr Deacon,
in Naples, then I'm sincerely sorry.'

He threw the cigarette on to the uncut grass.

'There's a man who works for our company. I've not met
him. He's a sort of freelancer and gets hired out to
corporations and governments, and to people with big bank
balances. I don't know if we can fix something. We say, out
in Baghdad, that if ever we're lifted, we'd pray this guy isn't
on another assignment, that he's sent for. He has a gold-
plated reputation – a nose for what to do and what angle to
come in from . . . but I've not met him. Have to see what's
possible.'

The rain was across the face of the father and dripped
off the cap's peak. In the half-light from the kitchen window
he couldn't tell whether it was only the rain on his cheeks
or tears too.

'I'm going to make a call for you. It's the best shout I can
do. Your boy had time for me. I'll let you know.'

His hand was gripped, held tight, as if Dean Weymouth
was a lifeline.

'I hear what you say, Dean. My dad, and your dad, my
mother and your mother – just the same – and worried sick
as yours and mine would be. To expect help from the boys
in blue, well, that's asking too much. Yes, I'll ring. Are you
resting up? Good to hear it. Look after yourself, and we'll
see you before you go south again.'

He was Roderick Johnstone. He opened a file on the screen
of his computer. The abbreviation of his first name, and an

exchange of one letter gave 'Ruddy'. There was a duck with that name. He was known therefore, to his face and his back as 'Duck' and had been since school. Most casual observers of Duck rated him stereotypical: a mane of blond hair, a public-school education but few academic qualifications, a commission via the Royal Military Academy into a good cavalry regiment, a middling career, then into the outside civilian world, a pinstripe suit and a Mayfair office. Such observers would badly have misread the man. He had formed a private security company, had drawn around him a kernel of experienced men, mostly with the hallowed Special Forces background, had shown rare business acumen and had landed major contracts in Iraq and Afghanistan. He did protection of property and personnel, and used UK nationals from the Regiment at Hereford, the Squadron at Poole and from the Parachute Regiment. He had built a reputation for the delivery of what he promised, value for cash and discretion. His payroll was small, but he was expensive, and clients queued for his services. Among illustrious clients, among those requiring total anonymity, was the Central Intelligence Agency, and Duck's email in box was filled with 'sincerest thanks' and 'deepest gratitude' and 'top to bottom appreciation from those inside the loop here', and on his payroll there was a hostage co-ordinator. He was searching that file.

Why did Duck bother with a matter so seemingly trivial? Where were the rewards?

Would he involve himself in something so lacking in fact and intelligence?

There was about Duck a quirk of anarchy that had made him a second-rate soldier and an alpha-class business operator. He liked to say that 'ordinary' people used the same hand, same paper, same technique to clean their backsides as the self-appointed élite, and those that his teams protected were 'ordinary' – ordinary accountants, ordinary telecom engineers, ordinary electricity-supply managers, ordinary sewage-treatment technicians, ordinary advisers on hospital management – and his teams, too, were made up of ordinary people, as Dean Weymouth was, and had ordinary parents and . . .

Duck's care for men such as Dean Weymouth, the men on whose backs – and guts – the company prospered, was utterly sincere. He valued them, listened to them and tried damned hard to stay loyal to them. His own company had not – thanking the good Lord – had an employee kidnapped. He'd met other CEOs, whose firms had. He understood the awfulness of it, and he had on the books a bloody good man. The file told him of a link that, sort of, confirmed the matter, something in his man's past that would open Italian doors and guarantee co-operation of a sort. He knew what effect a kidnapping had on a family and an employer. There, but for God's grace. Because Dean Weymouth had called him, he was – damn near – obliged to get involved.

He lifted the telephone again and dialled the number given him by the one-time Royal Marine.

'Mrs Deacon? Hello. I'm Roddy Johnstone, but everyone calls me Duck. Dean Weymouth has just spoken to me, and explained your problem. Up front, Ground Force Security makes big money from governments, which sort of underwrites the costs when we deal with individuals. I want you to tell me what you know of your son's situation – all the names and locations – because I might have someone who can help you. If your fears are founded, time is always against us so we should push on. But it's your decision . . . Right, Mrs Deacon, begin at the beginning . . .'

Lukas ran. Just when the light had failed over the rooftops, he had come back to his apartment and unlocked the door. Dark in the hallway, and before he had switched on the ceiling light, he had seen the flashing red bulb on the telephone. He ran for the Solferino Métro station.

At the airport he would get downloads, but important now was speed and getting there. The bag, always packed with the few things he needed, was high on his shoulder. Pedestrians darted out of his path, as if realising that when a grown man ran at that speed he wouldn't swerve to avoid collision. He hurried because he didn't acknowledge complacency, and knew it travelled alongside failure. Lukas had been at Waco.

'Where the shit/the fuck/the hell is this place – Waco?' had been the chorus on the flight down from Andrews. They had half emptied the stores huts at the Bureau's place in Quantico, among the forests, where the HRTs sat and waited for the call. The beepers had gone and the Hostage Rescue Team had scrambled, and filled more than one C-141 could carry. They believed there – except for the few who had been at Ruby Ridge – that they were the 'invincibles' and were given missions beyond the capabilities of other SWAT groups. Seven weeks at Waco, endless books read, stuck behind a Barrett .5 calibre sniper rifle with 3000 feet per second muzzle velocity and a high hit probability at 1000 yards . . . and watching from a distance the fuck-up to end all fuck-ups, so many children killed in the fire, no medals, only inquests, and complacency stripped bare.

He went down the steps into the Métro station, and was still running.

Most had quit after Waco rather than face the interrogations, under subpoena, of the Office of Professional Responsibility. New snipers were brought into new teams. He would have quit if not for the creation of a Critical Incident Response Team, when the negotiators, profilers and Hostage Rescue heroes had to gather in the same room, even had to talk to each other. A new world and a new style of action, with a co-ordinator sitting at the end of a CIRT table. The job of the co-ordinator was to weigh the input of the negotiator, hear the profiler's analysis, listen to the fears and demands of the 'stormers', then make a decision and live with it. He liked the job. Only decent thing that had come out of Waco, the fire and the deaths was the creation of the job, its culture and the responsibility that went with it.

He forced his way on to a train as the doors closed.

He had had to break off. He had cursed when his mobile had rung. Always – Castrolami's belief – it rang at the least opportune moment. She was talking well. He would have kept her going all through the evening, changed tapes and not let her off the hook.

He took a call from Naples, from the palace, the personal assistant to the prosecutor.

Confused . . . a boy, English, aged twenty-seven, an adult-student English teacher, reported kidnapped, believed to be taken from via Forcella, named as Eddie Deacon. 'What has that to do with me?' Impatience shouldered out politeness.

An investigator from a private commercial security firm was flying tonight to Rome on behalf of the family, and would wish to see, at the start of the working day, Mario Castrolami.

'Tell him and whoever volunteered me to get lost. No possibility of me involving myself.'

The parents of the boy, Castrolami was told, had reported that their son had gone to Naples to find his girlfriend.

'I feel like my knees are weak, that I could throw up, because I know what you'll tell me. Let me have it. What's her name?'

He heard it.

'Mother of Jesu . . .' Castrolami told the assistant where he would be in the morning, at the start of the working day, and rang off. He murmured, to himself, 'What have I done to deserve that?'

He went back into the living room. He could mask reactions. It might have been his wife who had called with news of a new dress purchased in faraway Milan, or the administration department at the piazza Dante barracks with confirmation of his annual leave dates near to the Christmas holiday. He smiled thinly, switched the tape-recorder back on and prompted Immacolata Borelli on her father's involvement with City Hall. She started again, as if a tap had been turned on.

Why had he not believed she would lie to him? Why had she lied? He felt no sympathy for the boy, for her, and he let her talk without interruption about City Hall, then give the names of national politicians, the location of meetings, the dates. In the morning he would learn and then he would confront her. He took it badly that she had lied to him about a boy.

He was kicked in the face. That was first, then kicks to the chest and the small of his back. Eddie tried to curl himself into the foetal position for protection, and succeeded well enough for more kicks to find his upper arms and wrists where the handcuffs were, but not to reach the organs that would hurt more. His head was lifted, then punches were thrown at him. He realised the crime.

Feet had approached, the trapdoor had been lifted. Light had cascaded into the bunker but had not reached right into the corner recess next to the filled sacks. He had seen the man clearly, the same face as had been on the street, that of the man who had taken him. The man would have realised the hood was off and that he was stared at. Eddie hadn't really absorbed the face on the street, but now he'd had a good clean sight of him. It was when he was punched that he wet himself – all those bloody hours of lying on his side or sitting, clamping his muscles overtime and calling for will-power, wasted effort. When the punch went in he could hold back no longer. Could have cried then. He felt the heat of the urine and its stream on his leg, then the clamminess of his trousers. It was degradation, learned hard.

More blood in his mouth, swallowing it, unable to cough properly because of the sagging tape, and choking.

He felt a new emotion. Eddie Deacon, 'steady Eddie', easy-going and friend to almost everybody, little riled him and not much exhilarated him: he hated. He had, now, a true sense of loathing. Novel. He took in all the features of the face. Didn't think in terms of a police station line-up, or of having a crowbar in his hand, but reckoned he needed to get that face into his mind, acid-etch it there. He'd coughed and taken that blood down, and the heat was gone from the urine on his thighs. He could have just felt miserable and sorry for himself.

The hood was put on. He was back inside the small world, hemmed in by the material and the cuffs, the sodden trousers and his ankles were again roped and he was kicked some more. The kick went into the stomach. The force made him piss more. He didn't cry out.

No moan, no cry, no scream.

He wondered if the memory of faces, and the hope of a judicial process had kept those people alive in the camps – they'd done that at school, German extermination camps, and in Berlin he'd seen the plaque that marked where the railway station was from which the Jews were shipped, and he'd been on Prinz Albrechtstrasse where they had excavated the holding cells used by the Gestapo. He wouldn't forget that face.

Or the voice.

'I speak it, a little, English. You fuck the whore, Immacolata.

You come here to find Immacolata. Immacolata is with police. Immacolata is *infame*. Immacolata betrays her family. If she likes again to fuck with you, she will leave the police. To encourage her to leave the police, we send perhaps an ear, *orecchio*, perhaps a finger, *dito*, perhaps a hand, *mano*, perhaps we must send the *pene* – and she will recognise it as from you. Did you not know who was Immacolata, who was her family? Did you not know what she did? She will leave the police or we send the ear, the finger, the hand, the *pene*, then all of you but not breathing. I think I speak English very good. She will save you or she will kill you. It is her choice. Not another person will save you.'

He heard the man grunt as he levered his way up and out through the trapdoor, then it was closed. He heard the footsteps retreat. Bloody hell. What to think about? Sort of put pissing his pants in the background. He sensed all of them – his ear tingled, his finger scratched his palm and his penis was still wet, but shrunken.

He hated the man. He hoped the hate would give him strength.

Lukas walked out of the terminus where the airport bus had dumped him. The warm night air hit him after the cool of the vehicle, and he felt then the little lift in his step, the stretch of his stride, and reckoned the mission launched – always did feel good then. Afterwards was bad, when he had the name and face of a target, a threat level to assess. Then the hard times came. As yet, walking briskly, he was not burdened by the responsibility of a human life in his hand, but when he thought like that, Lukas either stubbed a toe on the kerb, spat, or kicked his ankle bone. He crossed a couple of dark streets, wove like a native through the traffic, was in the immigrant quarter – north African, west African, east African – predictable alongside a railway hub. He passed a telephone bar, where calls could be made to Mogadishu, Lagos or Algiers, and a café where guys sipped soft drinks and had at their feet the mountains of unsold handbags they'd try with again the next day. A trolley bus went up the street, rolled and rattled. There was a narrow door into the *pensione*. He was told by the guy behind the desk that a single room was booked for him, the bill open-dated and prepaid. He didn't bother with the lift and climbed two flights of stairs.

The room was fine: a television he didn't switch on, a mini-bar he didn't open, an air-conditioner going like a tank's engine and the noise of the street coming through a double-glazed window. It was the way Lukas liked it, the sort of place where he was comfortable. Why was he there? It confirmed he was still capable, not washed up, not yesterday's creature, that he wouldn't hesitate to accept an invitation to travel. It was why he was there, and it went unshared.

He hooked power into his laptop, wired into his mobile, and information cascaded through to him. He started out on the first steps of learning about Edmund 'Eddie' Deacon, and about a girl, and with each page passing on the screen, so the deadweight, the responsibility, settled heavier. Nothing ever changed. She looked a pretty girl, and he looked an ordinary boy – nothing was different from every other time – but the scorpion sting was at the end. Last page up was the sitrep profile on Immacolata Borelli – *who* she was, *what* she did, *where* she was. A Camorra-clan girl, a money-washer, now a traitor to her own, was what the kid had gone looking to find.

In his career, Lukas thought, there had been worse situations, but not many. He didn't know when he'd next get any rest, so he killed the laptop, stripped, and pretty soon was asleep.

9

The hatred was like the wire scouring pad that his mother had by the kitchen sink, and it cleaned Eddie's mind.

He needed it clean. He didn't think he could lie propped up against the sacks, hooded, handcuffed and bound, with wet trousers, his guts aching with hunger, his throat dry with thirst, the scars on his face itching incessantly and those inside his mouth shooting pain, and do nothing else. Hate had taken over his mind, and given him clarity of thought.

He had ditched the disbelief. He knew the reality, had had it confirmed. He thought he needed, more than anything, to regain a sense of control – with nothing to see, no leg movement, nothing to eat, no arm movement, he needed a sense of some input into his destiny, whatever it was. He had to find control. He had kicked off the process. Thoughts came, and jumped, raced, flitted. He must remember everything he had seen when the hood had been off, the trapdoor lifted and light had flooded in: the dimensions of the bunker, the colour of the plastic sacks and what was printed on them, face of the bastard he hated, the clothes he had worn, the markings on the trainers that had done the kicking, the Nike symbol – he had all that. He should keep a sense of time . . . How? He screwed his right fingers on to his left wrist and realised that his watch wasn't there – had to be somewhere on the floor, dislodged when he was beaten. They would bring him meals. Meals would be a routine. Told himself: no sentimentality and no self-pity.

Wait, heh . . . Wait, wait.

No self-pity? He'd picked up a girl in a park, hadn't even used a hoary old chat-up line. Apologies and stumbles and embarrassments and then, 'I don't understand this – "turn over". What is "turn over"?' He'd been picked up – might have been a thousand different girls but hadn't: had been her, Immacolata. Wouldn't tolerate self-pity, wouldn't entertain it . . . Would try not to tolerate and entertain self-pity.

No sentimentality? Didn't know who he could be sentimental about – not his mum and dad . . . Good enough people, on railway lines of predictability, not particularly loving and not particularly disapproving, much like everyone else's mum and dad. But worse things came into his mind and squeezed away the small matters, self-pity, control and sentimentality.

The man had spoken with a sing-song reciting voice, the sort of language he might have learned in a sixth-year classroom. He would have had a textbook open that showed a man's body, with arrows pointing to an ear, a finger and a hand – not to a penis. *She will leave the police . . . we send perhaps an ear . . . perhaps a finger . . . perhaps a hand . . . the* pene . . . *then all of you but not breathing* . . . He saw a knife and his gut squirmed in fear as the shock waves surged and the pains came hard.

Not easy – fuck, no – to plead the need for control.

Hardest to understand: they wanted nothing of him. He had no secret to hide or squeal, no ideology to cling to or renounce. He was not an agent in occupied Europe or a heretic in Tudor England: he was just a piece of garbage.

Would Immacolata, his Mac, leave the police – she would be in protective custody – and walk away to save him, his ear, finger and . . . ? Couldn't say. He had slept with her, loved her, sucked her juices, whispered with her, laughed with her – he didn't know.

Eddie thought he heard – indistinct – the moan of engine

noise. Cars, lorries, vans? Couldn't be sure. Might mean a new day had started. If he was right, noting that a new day was born was an act of control – pretty bloody small, pretty much all he was bloody capable of. He teetered then on the edge of self-pity – and righted himself. Another day.

Then teetered again, rocked, was near to capsizing. How big was Eddie Deacon in the emotions of Immacolata Borelli? Hard to say, admit, spit out that he didn't know. He knew where the birthmark was, deep brown at the top of her right buttock, and where the minute polyp was in her left armpit, but he didn't know her mind. Eddie had heard of prisoners in cells, or in interrogation rooms, who took a point on a wall or a ceiling and focused on it, or found a spider crawling and tracked it, but the hood didn't allow that.

Perhaps it hurt most, and made the worst fear, that he didn't know how Immacolata Borelli would react when she held his life in the palm of her hand and weighed its value.

'You lied to me. I take much from the shit people I work with – but lying disgusts me.'

She hung her head.

Castrolami seemed to tower over her. It was a theatrical, contrived attack. A knock at her door, a request that she come *now* into the living room. She wasn't dressed. Castrolami, Orecchia and Rossi were. No coffee had been made for her, no juice laid out, no rolls heated, but she had seen their plates on the draining-board in the kitchen. She thought they had ambushed her.

'You lied. We took you on trust. We diverted resources. All the time you lied.'

She hung her head because she didn't understand. She had talked of her father, her mother, her eldest brother. She had listed the names of men who laundered and bought for the clan, who handled transhipments. That day she had prepared herself to talk about Giovanni, the brother she loathed, and Silvio, who had depended and doted on her. She couldn't think, then, of anything she had said that was untrue. There was, Immacolata believed, genuine anger in Castrolami's accusation. His jaw wobbled and little froths of spittle were at the sides of his mouth.

'We were about to offer you the contract. You would have read the document, seen what we offered and what we required in return, and it would have been signed by the palace and by you. Now we find you've lied to us. I don't make deals with liars. I prosecute them, I send them to Poggioreale, but I don't sweet-talk with liars.'

She saw that he was holding a roll of papers, maybe ten sheets, and she noted a photograph among them. For emphasis, Castrolami hit his palm with it. Rossi was at the kitchen door, sober-faced and impassive. Orecchia was sitting in the hall and neither made eye-contact with her. She was the daughter of her father. She wouldn't bend the knee.

'I don't lie.'

Castrolami took a small tape-recorder from his pocket. He switched it on and held it out. There was the noise of the park – dogs barking, the kids screaming, the rain on the leaves, and his voice: *Can they find, hold and hurt, maybe murder, a lover?* She heard her own voice, dismissive: *No.* His voice again, seeking certainty: *In Naples there is no lover, no boy?* Her own voice again, giving the certainty: *No.* Castrolami pressed fast-forward briefly. She heard Castrolami first: *So there is a boy here . . . I have to know.* Her response: *Yes, but not significant.* Again, the fast-forward, Castrolami saying: *You go to bed. But you say it's not 'significant' . . . yes?* She said, crackling on the tape and distorted: *He's just a boy. We met in a park . . . It doesn't mean anything.* Querying her, testing her: *You won't pine for him?* Heard herself snort, then, *I'll forget him – maybe I have already.* 'I believe you had a passionate

affair in London, and that your protestation that the
relationship was meaningless was a lie.'

'I don't lie.'

'What was the boy's name?'

She didn't know where he was leading her. She saw the
tape-recorder dropped into Castrolami's pocket, as if its work
was done. She said, 'Eddie.'

Castrolami repeated the name, rolled it. 'Eddie . . .
Eddie . . . and he's not significant and fucking him meant
nothing?'

So, he was calling her a liar and a whore, implying she
slept around. 'I liked him.'

'Only *liked* him?'

'Yes, I liked him. There, I liked him. In London I liked him.
Is that a sin? Do I go to confessional and blubber it to a priest
who has his hand in his crotch? It was good in London. This
isn't London. People go on holiday, they fuck on holiday.
People go to work conferences, meet others and fuck. People
meet in cinemas in strange towns and fuck afterwards. It
doesn't mean anything, it's what happens and—'

She was cut short. The papers were allowed to unroll, the
photograph taken out and passed to her. She held it. Her
Eddie was leaning on a gate, arms resting on the top bar.
There were young cattle around him, nuzzling and nudging
him. She could almost hear his laughter. She hadn't seen
the photograph before. She thought it would have come
from an album at his parents' home.

Castrolami curled his lip. 'If I was the boy, and you were
in my bed, and I said I loved you and asked, with a caress,
how you felt about me, and you said I meant nothing to
you, I'd be disappointed.'

She saw a trap, a cul-de-sac, and thought she was led into
it. She handed back the photograph. 'Why did you show it
me?'

'Because you lied to me. That boy is huge in your life, as you are in his.'

'No.'

'The best boy you ever knew.'

'No.'

'Free to sleep with him, fuck him, without your mother criticising who you chose.'

'Not significant.'

'We shall see . . .' He dropped his voice, more theatre, and was casual, as in conversation. He smiled and held the photograph of Eddie in front of her face. 'We shall see, Signorina Immacolata, whether you lie or not. He, your insignificant, meaningless bed partner, was taken off the street in Forcella yesterday. Why should the boy have come to Naples if he's insignificant and meaningless? Why is he in Forcella? What is your response to him being taken?'

'He's not important. My evidence is.'

'Another lie – or the truth?'

'I'll stay the course.'

'A lie or the truth?'

'I'll go to court whatever—' Castrolami's big fingers made a small tear at the top of the photograph, above Eddie's head, and then, with a sort of formality, he handed her the photograph. She knew what was expected of her. She did it sharply, but looked away, through the window. The sun clipped the roofs, the water tanks and the satellite dishes, and was above the mountain range. She knew, and had judged it, that the rip would go through the middle of his face – his forehead, between his eyes and down the length of his nose. It would split his lips, his chin and his throat. She did it. She let the two pieces fall to the floor. She said, 'I'll go to court, whatever is set against me. I'll go in memory of Marianna Rossetti. Fuck you, Castrolami.'

He kicked away the two pieces of the photograph, and

Rossi came forward to pick them up and bin them. Castrolami said he had to go out. She thought he despised her, but he hadn't been in the cemetery at Nola.

She went and lay on her bed, heard the main door open, shut, and the key turn.

As he went into the via dei Condotti, Lukas understood why the piazza di Spagna had been chosen for the meeting. He came off the main drag and walked past the fashion houses. It was a good place to watch a man approach the steps, and to see whether he had a tail. He appreciated why they would be paranoid about security and didn't argue with it. He was later than he would have wanted but Duck Johnstone had been on the phone for more than half an hour and had fed him morsels of intelligence that hadn't been available last night. He reckoned Duck must have worked through most of it. It wasn't that Lukas admired dogged hard work, just that he couldn't abide the taking of short-cuts and easy opt-outs. He knew more about the boy, known now in the links as Echo – the girl was India – enough about him to have rated his journey to Naples as dumb-pig stupid, but Echo would still get his best effort – only effort he knew – to have him on a plane, and in a seat, not in the hold.

He came to the fountain. He knew that a description of his features had been sent ahead, for recognition. He didn't know whom he would meet, or have a code to exchange. The steps were a good place because he could be watched from more than four and up to seven angles. There were tourists fooling in the fountain at the foot, and locals were waiting to use the water spout for drinking. Lukas went past them, and the museum that was the Keats-Shelley house. He didn't do poetry – literature – or anything that was outside the confines of freeing poor bastards caught up, usually, in someone else's fight. Would have said it was full time and . . .

He started to climb the steps. Already the sun flared off the stonework and any shade was filled with sitting youngsters . . . Hostage rescue, hostage negotiation, hostage profiling and hostage co-ordination were big enough subject areas to swamp Lukas's mind.

He had been a sniper on the rescue team. He had once fired a live round to kill. He had carried the rifle and been in full kit on a live call-out close to a hundred times, including Ruby Ridge and Waco, but had fired only once. A death shot but not a clean one: the brains, skull fragments and blood of the robber trying to break a siege and bug out of a bank in Madison, Wisconsin, had spattered across the face and spectacles of the cashier he was using as a shield, and the mess had spoiled her dress. The Bureau's HRT had been called in because the target had crossed state lines. He'd had the cross-wires on the felon's head for upwards of thirty seconds and had fired a second after the guy's attention had gone to his right side and the handgun had been moved out from under the woman's chin. It was a hell of a shot, the rest of the team told him, but a shame about the dress. God only knew what the hairdresser would have found the next time the woman went. He had moved on, ditched the rifle and the big telescopic sight when the Bureau launched the Critical Incident Response Group.

Only one way, an old head had told him, to learn the skills of negotiation – and he had to know about negotiation if he was to command those people. 'Find the construction cranes,' the old head had said in a corner of the Quantico parkland, 'and some good high big-span bridges.'

Suicides went up crane ladders and out on the walkways of bridges. Lukas had taken two years of evenings, days off and holiday time to be on stand-by for a call from a duty officer. Nobody in town, county or state police was queuing to go up a crane to talk to a nutcase who wanted to jump.

Cranes and bridges were where 'teeth were cut', the old head had said. Couldn't fail with wannabe suicides and hope to make it in the big-time of terrorist sieges. The way to learn the soft, gentle, persuasive talk, and to calm a situation, was to be a hundred feet up a crane ladder with not much to see of the 'client' but the soles of his shoes fifteen further up. He'd met some interesting people and heard some interesting life stories, and had had to breed trust if men and women were to decide to face another day and climb down. He'd never liked heights, but had a top job as a co-ordinator, the negotiator rookies needed to get up high on exercises, and Lukas had had to take them. Leadership was shit. It was said, he heard later, that some jerks climbed and threatened and only wanted the star man to come up after them; he'd gotten a reputation round Quantico and into the suburbs of the capital.

The sciences of hostage rescue were squashed into Lukas's mind, which was why he didn't know about poetry, or about Keats and Shelley . . . He didn't look for the guy.

He reached the top. A big hotel faced him. Fellow Americans were spilling out of a taxi, and staff were bowing and scraping; others were having cases loaded into a limousine. From his crap room beside the station Lukas had come to the meeting by trolley bus, on the Métro and on foot. He didn't have to justify what some said was eccentricity and others called pathetic obstinacy. A man stepped forward. He would, too right, have watched Lukas traverse the via dei Condotti, climb the steps and wipe away some perspiration.

'You are Lukas?'

No warmth. A question put without enthusiasm, as if he was a stone in a shoe, a tick sucking blood on his leg, an irritation between the cheeks. He didn't do point-scoring, but he didn't do grovelling either.

'Yes.'

'I am here because I am instructed to be here.'

'Thank you for meeting me,' he said quietly, but briskly.

'I am Mario Castrolami of the ROS. Excuse me, that is the—'

'The special duties unit. I know what the ROS is.' He didn't spell out its full Italian name because that would have been to lord his knowledge – and get straight up the man's nose. He was an intruder.

Castrolami was heavy-set and overweight. Lukas read him as one of the workaholic guys who slaved through all the hours, and more, and who were the backbone of pretty much every law-enforcement outfit he had come across. They didn't get promotion, and they didn't care. And they were busy, had clear-cut priorities, and failed on small-talk.

'It is about Eddie Deacon?'

'It is, and Immacolata Borelli.' Lukas could have said it was about 'Juliet and her Romeo', because he had seen the movie on a flight out from JFK to Jakarta, a long time back, but neither of them wanted imbecile talk. He had to lead, but gently, as if the wind buffeted him when he was stuck up some God-awful crane and looking down wasn't an option. 'Can we go get a coffee? I'm told there's a *carabinieri* barracks behind the Parliament building – near here, I think – and that a very good *espresso* is served in the non-coms' mess. I imagine, Mr Castrolami, that you feel like you've stepped in a dog mess and that I'm the mess, but a coffee in the barracks might help to get the smell and the nuisance off your uppers. I suggest, though we'll be using up your valuable time, that we say no more until we've had the coffee.'

Duck Johnstone had all these things on the file, could hack into them and carry Lukas back six years, an easy ride in the nostalgia stakes. Had taken him there for a reason.

Of course, Lukas knew where the barracks was, off which

street on the far side of the via dei Corso, and how to get there quickest.

So, he led. It was a cheap trick, but he hadn't time for subtlety. They exchanged cigarettes, but kept off the talking.

Carmine Borelli fired. The stock of the sawn-off double-barrelled shotgun was hard against his shoulder. He squinted down the valley between the barrels and fired again. The recoil, twice, rippled through his chest and up his neck. The sensation, shuddering through him, was incredible, and he shed years. The cordite was in his nostrils – extraordinary. It was one thing to have used a pistol the day before and have the retort ripple up his arm, but the shotgun at his shoulder was just pure pleasure.

One man squealed, held tight to a lamp post for support, then began to hobble towards the car. It was down the street, the doors already open, its exhaust spitting fumes. The other man had ducked down on his knees, then twisted and tried to run but was bent double. He could hear a man in the car shouting for them both to hurry. Carmine Borelli ejected the cartridges, dipped into his pocket for two more and loaded them. He had three of his own foot-soldiers further along the street than the car, and two more behind him. Salvatore, his visor down, was astride the pillion of a scooter across the street. None of the foot-soldiers, or Salvatore, were to intervene unless the life of Carmine Borelli was at high risk. He saw why the man who tried to run was bent: a hand gripped his hip and the tan trousers were bloodstained. Two shots, at twenty metres, and two hits. The two men made the car and it roared away, wheels shrieking as it spun right. There were several hospitals nearby where the passengers could be dropped off, but the Incurabili on the via della Sapienza was the nearest. A good hospital, where his Pasquale had been born and where he had sent many men.

The street had been empty, now was filled. A woman stopped, set down her shopping bag on the pavement, crouched, picked up the two ejected cases and gave them to him. Briefly, he kissed her hand. She retrieved her bags and went on. A man filled the door of a bar and shouted, '*Viva Il Camionista!*' and there was applause behind him.

Carmine saw Salvatore ride off down the street. He knew that those who had been wounded would live now in mortal fear of Salvatore coming after them. The matter concerned the *pizzo* paid for protection by a shop on that street between the via Cesare Rosaroll and the via Carbonara which sold wedding dresses. Carmine Borelli understood that his granddaughter – no longer spoken of without a spit on the pavement – had fixed the *pizzo* at five hundred euros a month: chicken shit to the Borelli clan, small change. The previous evening, he had learned early that morning, men from the Misso clan or the Mazzarella clan – it was unclear – had told the shop's owner that they would take over protection, and the payment would be seven hundred and fifty euros a month. If he had weakened, if it was allowed to happen once, if it was seen that he couldn't fight to defend what he held, the Borelli clan was finished, dead and buried, forgotten. So he had taken the shotgun from the cache where it had lain hidden for more than twenty years, stripped off the damp-proof, oiled wrapping, loaded cartridges and found the old coat with the inner pocket where a shotgun could be secreted. He had been on the pavement when the men had come to collect seven hundred and fifty euros or to slop petrol over the shop's stock of gowns. He thought he had sent a second message.

Another shout: '*Forza Il Camionista.*' He acknowledged it, a slight wave. The scooter came back down the street. Salvatore would have circled the block to see if more men waited in more cars for orders to intervene – it was an old friend who had shouted – and the helmet shook. At this moment, there was no more danger. A gloved hand reached out, snatched the shotgun and the scooter was gone, lost in the traffic. The shop's owner was behind him, with the padlock that fastened the steel shutters to the loop in the pavement, but Carmine denied him permission to close for the day, demanded he stay open – his sent message would be reinforced by that gesture. He walked away.

They would now be arriving at the hospital, probably the Incurabili, and would be hustling for the Pronto Soccorso entrance, which was alongside General Surgery, where they were skilled in extracting bullets and pellets. It was near to Trauma – necessary if the wounds were serious – and the chapel was beside the *mortuaria* – a good design layout and convenient. The first professional man he had hired was from that hospital.

Sixty-six years earlier: the city starved, women picked dandelions and daisies to boil as soup, kids prised limpets off the seashore rocks and men hung nets to catch songbirds for plucking. Carmine and Anna Borelli made their first fortune from the brothels. Not all the women who went into the cubicles with American soldiers were married. They had to eat, so dropped knickers and opened thighs were the only currency they had, but the Americans had moved on. Carmine Borelli had hired a *professore* from the hospital, and for a fee per patient of ten thousand lire the eminent medical man restitched the virginity of the unmarried, and Carmine took fifteen per cent of the fee. That *professore* had delivered Pasquale safely into the world.

He would go first to the place where he could shower and change his clothing, then take more of the pain pills because he didn't want people in Forcella to see him hobble or limp. Clean, he would go home. He believed he had done well, believed also that he was on a treadmill, running, and didn't know how long, at that pace, he could last.

*

Once a week, regular as clockwork, Davide locked the door of his apartment, on the third floor of the Sail, and took a bus. It carried him from the architectural disaster zone that was Scampia into Naples, and there was a memorised sequence of meeting-places: the steep Funicolare climbing from the via Toledo, a gentleman's hairdressing salon on the corso Umberto, the *giardini pubblici* in front of the royal palace of the Bourbons, the open ramparts of the Castel dell'Ovo, or one of the distinguished coffee houses of the city. When he was in any of those places, with tapes and cassettes in the hidden pockets sewn at his trousers' waist, he was Delta465/Foxtrot.

He sat on the bus that morning.

He was not reckless, took no unnecessary risks in harbouring the secrecy of his double life, and felt no fear. In both his identities – Davide and Delta465/Foxtrot – he understood that the fate of an agent of the AISI, if uncovered, was death. Not negotiable. If it was discovered that a man from the Agenzia Informazioni e Sicurezza Interna was living in the Sail death was certain, with much pain beforehand. He lived with the threat. He had a compartmentalized mind, and could keep fear at arm's length. That ensured he was an agent of quality and valued by his handlers. He enjoyed meeting them in the funicular carriage, the barber's or in the gardens and would ask after their children and be told of their holidays – make-believe, of course, but it enabled him to feel he was inside a family, which was important to him. They had given him a number for the Apocalypse Call, but he doubted he would ever use it. He had no idea what his life might be outside the Sail and without the weekly meetings.

Nothing to report that week. Nothing that would interest the men and women who met him. They were interested only in material of high-grade importance. He had seen, through his obsessionally polished windows, nothing of that category. Neither did he believe there was anything on the tapes from the cameras in his living room or from the audio cassettes linked to the microphones buried in the outer wall. The position of his apartment, where a flight came up from level two and another down from level four, had not been chosen randomly: it was a meeting-place – men stopped, talked and took little notice of the cleaned windows, the blaring television and the old man slumped in a chair with his back to the walkway. He knew of nothing that week to intrigue his handlers.

She was no fool. Anna Borelli was as adept at losing a tail as any man half, a third or a quarter of her·age. She did back-doubles, shop windows, was last on to a trolley bus on the corso Umberto, and went into the church of San Lorenzo Maggiore by the main entrance and out by the narrow emergency door. Only when she was satisfied that she was not under surveillance, or had lost it, did she head for the meeting-place. She carried a filled plastic shopping bag.

She was another elderly lady, keeping death at bay for perhaps another year or only another month, and she wore black from stockings to scarf. She was unnoticed. She rang a bell. She was admitted through high gates. She crossed a yard of cannibalised vehicles and a door swung open when she prodded it with her toe. She was inside the building that had once been a car-repair business, but was now a place where stolen Mercedes, BMWs, Audis and the best models from the Alfa and Fiat factories were brought and dismantled. The parts would be shipped into Moldova or Ukraine, then moved further east. It had been an excellent business but was now slack and the yard was deserted, except for the scooter tucked against a side wall. The building seemed empty, but for the cigarette smoke that curled from beneath an inner door.

Then she was met.

She showed Salvatore what she had brought. There was bread, cheese, two slices of cheap processed ham, two apples, three small bottles of water, and the morning's edition of *Cronaca di Napoli* – on the front page a photograph of a man sprawled dead, half in a gutter, outside a bar. She had not read it. She thought that by now her husband would be home. She approved of what he planned to do, and she would appreciate that when he sat in his chair, with her beside him, he would be clean and not smell as was usual. Salvatore had a camera on the table, and the man who rode the scooter was stretched out on a sofa, asleep, with a pistol on the floor beside his head.

There was a corridor to the back, and a storeroom off it. A trapdoor was lifted and a torch shone down.

A stench came up through the hole's opening. She saw that the boy was hooded, bound, and that his arms were behind his back. She remembered him in her living room, his simplicity; remembered also when Immacolata, her husband's angel, had been in the same room, had sat in the same chair, drinking from the same set of cups and eating off the same set of plates. She remembered the boy, his almost shy smile, the flush of gratitude when he was told that a man was coming to take him to Immacolata. She felt no sympathy.

The torch showed the discolouration at his groin. She had not felt sympathy for the women in her brothels who had contracted syphilis from the American officers and had had to tell their husbands of the disease they carried. She had not felt sympathy for those widowed when she and her husband had climbed but others had been pushed aside, or for Gabriella when the births of Vincenzo and Giovanni were complex and brutally painful, or for Carmine when he was taken three times to Poggioreale. She did not even feel sympathy for herself.

She watched.

Salvatore rolled up the hood so that it cleared the mouth and nostrils but covered the eyes. He pulled off the binding tape and the young man, Eddie, cried out in pain because it had happened without warning, but then – so quickly – his face settled. Anna Borelli understood. Then Salvatore unlocked the handcuffs and allowed him, Eddie, to work his fingers over his wrists and bring back the circulation. She wondered if he was Edmondo or Eduardo. Then the hands were put together in front of his waist and the handcuffs went back on. Anna Borelli thought, from his face and the little gestures, that he was a fighter – it didn't matter to her.

She passed down a bucket and the newspaper she had brought.

She knew a little English from the Americans. Salvatore told the young man that he should use the bucket, that he could eat, that he was to put the hood back on his head each time he heard movement over the trapdoor. If he didn't he would be beaten. The bucket was stood in a corner. Salvatore had the camera. The newspaper front page facing the lens was placed in the young man's hands and held up. The torch was switched off. Anna Borelli thought then that Salvatore would snatch up the hood and immediately take the photograph. The flash lit the bunker, and the white face, the scars on it and the blood smears – easier to see in the flash than in the torch beam.

When the torch went back on, the hood was in place again.

The newspaper was left beside the bucket. The food was in the plastic bag beside the young man's knee. Anna Borelli saw the young man's ears and fingers, the stain at his crotch, and felt no sympathy. She accepted, however, that she didn't know how her granddaughter would react – what her response to the pressure would be when it built.

Salvatore climbed out, the trapdoor fell back into place and the bolt was pushed home.

With the tab from the camera lodged in her brassière, Anna Borelli set off for the office of the family's lawyer.

Castrolami watched. He thought it a performance for him and no others. He was sitting in the canteen area on the second floor of the barracks, the coffee in front of them with a plate of sweet biscuits. The swing door had been pushed open, and an officer – probably a *maresciallo* – had come in, looked around, seen the man, Lukas, and come to him, arms opening wide. Hugs, kisses – and Castrolami believed he saw tears. Not Lukas who wept, and not Lukas who kissed.

It was about the establishment of credentials. The officer had small scars on his face and walked heavily, as if his left leg carried an old injury. He would have been in his early forties, plump and pasty-faced. He clung to Lukas.

It was explained.

The officer was Marco. He had been in the detachment of *carabinieri* posted to the Iraqi city of Nasiriyah. He was asleep in quarters used by the detachment in the building that had once been the office of the local Chamber of Commerce. A suicide attack on it had involved a tanker truck rigged with explosives. Seventeen *carabinieri* had been killed, and more were injured. Marco suffered cut tendons in his right leg from shrapnel and his face was hit by glass shards. He had gone home, recovered, convalesced and demanded to be returned to his unit. He had come back to Nasiriyah . . . Castrolami heard the story and thought it told well and quietly. He waited to learn its purpose.

The canteen had filled. The short guy at Castrolami's side, now extricated from the hugs and kisses, seemed to Castrolami to find it a necessary nuisance, and was impassive.

'I went back, a dumb-fuck stupid thing to do – everyone told me so – but I was back. We had an outpost down the road and the day that those guys were supposed to get a week's rations there was also a search mission under way. Just one of those days when a schedule gets fouled up, and people think it doesn't matter. The consequence was a reduction in the size of the escort to take the rations. There were three of us, Italians, and two trucks. We got hit. They put an RPG through the engine of mine and blew us off the road. The driver, an Iraqi boy, was killed. The truck in front just kept going. I was taken.'

Castrolami didn't hear, in the packed room, that a throat was cleared, that a man's joints clicked as he moved his weight from one foot to the other, that a nose was blown, that a cup was put heavily on a saucer or that cutlery rattled. Lukas's face gave nothing away.

'I was taken off quickly – fast, immediate. Would have been well gone by the time a reaction force was back in there . . . I was held fourteen days. They didn't want a ransom, didn't want a truckload of dollars, didn't want a statement of intent to leave from our government. They told me they wanted prisoner exchange, people of theirs who were in Abu Ghraib under American jurisdiction. After fourteen days they got the message. No deal. They were ready to do me – would have been a knife job, decapitation. I thought they'd kill me that night. Those were fourteen long days – a different meaning to long than I've known before, like years and like hell. The guys who broke in were from Task Force 145, because we Italians didn't have that sort of group. They came out of the Anaconda Camp in the Balad base. This man – Mr Lukas – did the co-ordination. He married what the assets brought in with prisoner interrogation and reconnaissance, and did it right. I owe him my life. I'm supposed to be a rock-hard bastard but the sight of this little runt, and the knowledge of what he did for me, his skill, makes me want to fucking weep. I never had a chance to thank him there. We, the Italian contingent, didn't have such a man in Iraq. It was my great fortune that he was in country, with Defense Department, and allocated to my situation. Great fortune because he's the best. I saw him in the distance and then he was gone, but guys told me . . . What I'm saying, if he's in town, if some poor bastard goes through what I went through, then fuck the protocol and fucking listen to him.'

Applause spattered the canteen.

'Can we get out of here?' Lukas asked softly, close to Castrolami.

'It was your call to come,' Castrolami said.

'Someone thought it was a good idea. The chief honcho in the company I work for would have pulled him up on the files.'

'Maybe it wasn't and maybe it was – a good idea.'

He disengaged from the veteran – and Castrolami thought Marco now did some soft liaison job in Parliament but would never forget. Lukas endured one last, awkward embrace, then was pushing for the double doors, and the coffee hadn't been drunk. They went along corridors and down flights of stairs. They hit the street going fast, as if both men wanted to be shot of a place that was sugar-sweet on sentimentality.

'I suppose I should apologise, but it was reckoned a good, clean, fast way of establishing credentials – like fast-tracking them.'

'Could you do that sort of cabaret in other places, other cities?'

''Fraid so, quite a number. I do apologise – a stunt and a gimmick. Not my way but—'

'Give it me,' Castrolami demanded.

Lukas said, 'I don't horn in and play rank and pedigree.

Inside there was just about a CV, and to save you time, and somebody else's idea, if I'm invited I come in. If my advice is looked for, I offer it. There are no other strings, and no other agenda.'

'I warn you, we pull in different directions.'

Lukas was looking at his feet as they walked. 'When was it ever different?'

'I make no commitment to you, an outsider.'

'In your place, I doubt I would.'

The cell had no air and the heat was trapped in it. If she had been charged with shop-lifting, bag-snatching or aggravated assault, Gabriella Borelli would have shared a cell with five others, even nine. But she was special, had status, was awarded solitary confinement. She had been escorted back to the cell, and the heat had wafted at her as the door was unlocked, had wrapped round her as it was closed after her. The sun was climbing and played directly on the window. Distorted shadows were thrown over her from the light hitting the bars.

It had been a sour meeting with her lawyer, Umberto.

She had sensed his shock when he saw her with chains fastened to manacles at her wrists. He would have heard them rattling as she was led down the corridor and into the interview room, and she sensed he felt personal pain for her, and also that his worst nightmare would have been to wear those chains, to sleep in a cell like hers and not to walk on the Tribunali or the Duomo but in an exercise yard. He had dabbed a handkerchief dosed with cologne at his nose. They had taken the chains off her when she was ready to sit opposite him.

Did he believe that a case conference between accused and advocate was free of electronic audio surveillance? He did not.

Did she believe that a microphone was not wired into the room, its furniture, its walls, ceiling and electrical fittings? Most certainly she did not.

It had been a bizarre conference – she flopped on to the bunk bed on a raised concrete base. She kicked off the sandals which she had been issued with, loosened the blouse that had been torn when they'd felled her and unzipped the skirt that had ridden up when she was on the ground, but there was no relief from the heat. Umberto had produced a packet of cigarettes, cigarette papers for rolling but no loose tobacco, and two match books. The cigarettes were between them, and each had had a set of the matches. He had divided the papers so that they had half each. They had done the case conference.

He had asked her if she was well and she had told him she was.

He had written in an insect scrawl on a slip of the paper: *A boy, the lover of Immacolata, came from England to find her. Had an address of via Forcella. The priest sent him to Carmine and Anna.* He had pushed the slip towards her, and she had read it, then crumpled it and put it into the tinfoil ashtray between them.

She had written: *Was he stupid? Was he ignorant?* She had shown it to him, then crushed it and dropped it with the other.

They lit cigarettes, and allowed the lighted matches to burn the papers in the ashtray. A rhythm had developed.

Did she have complaints that he should take up with the authorities? She did not.

He knew nothing, had met Immacolata in London, loved her, knew nothing. *Carmine took control. He sent for help.*

What control? What help?

More paper burned in the ashtray.

Was the food satisfactory? It was.

It's control through leadership. It's to prevent secessionists and intrusion. He sent for Salvo.

To what purpose?

Smoke rose from the paper. More smoke curled up from the cigarettes.

Was she treated with respect? She was.

Carmine thinks the boy from England can be used as leverage on Immacolata. Salvo has taken the boy, holds him in Sanità. Bits of him will be sent to Immacolata if she doesn't retract her accusations.

I doubt the bitch will – but good to use the boy. Make pressure with him. More important, find the bitch, shoot her, stamp on her face.

In that note, she had allowed emotion to escape: her writing had been faster, larger, and the response had taken both sides of the paper.

He asked her what she needed. She had said clothing, a portable electric fan, a radio and some magazines.

What else?

Use the boy, with a knife. Kill the bitch.

What else did she want? She had not said that her love should be sent to her husband, to Vincenzo in London, to Giovanni or Silvio. She had not spoken of her parents-in-law or of Salvatore . . . She had said she needed a pair of her own shoes and more toothpaste. Together they had checked that all of the paper slips were burned to cinders, then had screwed out the cigarettes in the ash. He had stood, knocked on the door and the escort had come in. The manacles had gone back on her wrists. She had not thanked him for coming to the women's gaol at Posilippo: she paid him, and he was rich on the family's back.

She sat now in the cell.

She would, herself, have slit her daughter's throat.

She would, herself, have sliced off the ears, fingers and

nose of the English boy, her daughter's lover. What Gabriella
Borelli loathed most was the removal of power, the loss of
authority. She must play-act with cigarette papers across a
table. Anger welled in her, but was confined inside the walls,
three metres by two, of the cell. She could do none of it
herself. She was off the bed. In fury, Gabriella Borelli beat
her forehead against the wall, bruised and scratched herself
against the graffiti. She didn't care about clothes, an electric
fan or shoes. She wanted her daughter dead.

The old lady had been waiting for him. She was sitting in
his office amid the mountains of paper and files that were
Umberto's trade. When he came back from Posilippo – and
he had had coffee at the Café Gambrinus, where old friends,
the advocates of other clans, had greeted him – she was in
front of his desk. Extraordinary, but she didn't speak. She
handed him a small envelope, then stood, looked around as
if she was searching for a dead cat carcass, and was gone.
He tore open the envelope, retrieved the camera's memory
pad, then called for his clerk, Massimo. The young man was
his nephew, had his trust. He told Massimo to take money
from the petty-cash box and go to the camera shop on the
corso Vittorio Emanuele – a long bus ride but there was little
chance of his clerk being recognised there – buy a portable
printer and bring it back. If the clan fell, Umberto fell. So
hard for him to believe that the sweet pretty face of
Immacolata – always his favourite – might cause him to fall,
and fall far.

She had talked through the morning to the deputy prosecutor,
up from Naples. She had found, with each anecdote and
each item of evidence, that old loyalties had frayed,
disintegrated. A few days before she had hugged her brother,
Silvio, for driving out to Capodicino, collecting her, ferrying

her to Nola and back. That morning she listed all the occasions she knew, and would swear to it on oath, that Silvio had ridden on his scooter around the city distributing handguns and ammunition. She skewered him. She identified the weapons caches he had visited, the men from whom the weapons were collected and those to whom they were given. The tape spools had turned. She had seen, across the table, grim satisfaction on the face of the deputy prosecutor. She felt no more affection for her youngest brother than she did for the others, and none for her mother. She didn't think of her father. She kept in her mind, central, the image of her friend. She saw, as she condemned her family, the features of Marianna Rossetti. There was no other face in her mind. No other friendship was 'significant'. *I'll go to court, whatever.* She sensed, that morning, a growing relaxation in the apartment, as if a barrier had been broken down. She was not treated with the same suspicion – near hostility.

When they broke, the deputy prosecutor for coffee and she for juice, she had stood and stretched, sensing that her T-shirt rode up over her navel, then wandered towards Rossi. He was on the balcony, through the open doors, sitting in a rattan easy chair, browsing a newspaper. She could fight, as she did with Mario Castrolami, scratch. She could smile, too, flash her eyes and be docile. 'Please . . .'

'Yes?' Rossi looked up at her. 'What do you need?'

'Do you run – for exercise?'

'Yes.'

'Please . . . may I run? It's claustrophobic here. I'd like to run – if it's allowed but I don't have the clothes – I'd be so grateful if I could.'

'Can't see why not. Let me float it.'

'Thank you.'

Why did she want to run? Not for fitness. She didn't have a weight problem, she was young and healthy. She believed that if she could run along a pavement, as other women did, she would take another step towards changing her life. She drank the juice Orecchia brought her, sat again at the table and talked about Salvatore, Il Pistole, who had fancied her, had wanted to sleep with her and might have wanted to marry her. She stabbed him, too, with the stiletto, pushed it deep. Another tape was slotted into the recorder. She thought of nothing that was insignificant or meaningless.

There wasn't a dog in the household for Arthur Deacon to walk. Best he could do was borrow his immediate neighbour's, a cheerful golden retriever. He'd needed to get out of the house, stretch his legs and have someone – or something – to commune with who brought no complications. Betty had taken the day off work, and had warned them it might be the week. He'd felt hemmed in, as he had in the last months at the water-board office, and the dog was a sort of therapy against worrying – agonising – about Eddie. They hadn't slept, either of them, last night. Could have taken the dog round the loop of byways and bridlepaths all over again, but felt he should go home. He had dropped the dog off at the neighbour's, well short of Dean Weymouth's bungalow, and tramped the last hundred yards to his house. The back door, of course, because his dirty shoes lived in the utility room. He lived a pretty boring life, ordered, predictable and *boring*, so there was a place on a shelf for muddy shoes, and another place on another shelf for merely dirty shoes, and a cupboard spot for clean shoes – it was about as boring as it could get. He was about to sing out, 'Hello, it's me, I'm back,' but didn't. Who else might it be? The Queen? The Pope? Osama bin bloody Laden? He said nothing, but as he took off his shoes he heard his wife's voice, the accent she used for work, with all the vowels and consonants in place.

She said, 'I'm grateful, Mr Johnstone, more grateful than

I can say, and my husband . . . Yes, please do, please keep
in touch with us, any time of day or night . . . Can I ask you
one question, Mr Johnstone, only one? . . . Thank you . . .
Why, Mr Johnstone, are you doing this for us? . . . Perhaps
I do and perhaps I don't, but thank you.'

He heard the phone put down. He heard her choke, like
a sob, and couldn't remember when he had last heard or
seen his Betty in tears – wouldn't have believed it if he hadn't
heard the choke. He took off his shoes, put them on the
correct shelf, went inside and put his arm round her
shoulders. She was still standing by the hall table, facing the
silent phone.

She said, 'That was Mr Johnstone. He says his name's
Duck, but I'm not indulging him. He's building what he calls
a "profile" of Eddie.'

'Don't know that I could.'

'He says Eddie's been kidnapped and the likelihood is that
he's in the hands of an organised-crime group. This one,
called the Camorra, is in Naples. The likelihood is that the
girl Eddie spoke of, Immacolata Borelli, is from a criminal
family, a very successful one.'

'God, poor Eddie – an innocent abroad.'

'It gets blacker. The girl has turned herself in as a state
witness against her family. Eddie, our Eddie, barged in there
– supremely innocent but also supremely ignorant, I don't
know which is worse – and Mr Johnstone says they will try
to use his captivity to persuade the girl to withdraw her
evidence. He wanted to know how Eddie would withstand
extreme pressure and stress – he didn't say torture, but I
think that's what he meant – and the information will help
in building the profile. I said he was just ordinary, a bit lazy
and a bit stubborn.'

'Usually aware, kind, not very ambitious.'

'Without malice. I said that. It was almost like I was doing his obituary for the *Western Daily Press*. I said he was a nice boy, decent, and steady, but hadn't too much imagination. His own mother, selling him short.'

She did a brief sniffle, blinked, and the weakness of tears was gone. Arthur Deacon held her tight. Her eyes were still on the phone.

'A man's flown to Rome. I wasn't told his name. He's called a co-ordinator, and he works on a freelance basis for Mr Johnstone's company. He has FBI experience and has been in Iraq for the American military. He's an expert on hostage rescue, whether by negotiation or use of force. It's all because of Dean. Dean spoke well of Eddie. I'm in areas I don't understand but I think it's a sort of family – Dean Weymouth, the people who work for this company at whatever level of importance, and the man who's going to Naples. It's like a brotherhood of mutual support because of the awful places they operate in. The expert – he's as good at his work as anyone in the world, Mr Johnstone says.'

'We have to be strong, and pray Eddie is.'

'What Mr Johnstone also says, we must hope, we must believe, and we must understand the desperate nature of the situation Eddie's in. And Mr Johnstone says we mustn't feel angry with him. That's the natural emotion, extreme anger, for having caused our misery. Eddie may not be the brightest star but he's done nothing wrong, has nothing to be ashamed of. This expert, the co-ordinator, is used to going where governments get entangled in bureaucracy and pomposity and guarding territory, Mr Johnstone says, and side-stepping them all. But he doesn't flannel.'

'You live nearly a lifetime, then into your cosy world come people you didn't know existed. I'm not trying to be profound, but now we share space with them.'

'He says Eddie's position is "difficult". He's going to ring us twice a day, and he promised that all the questions he'll ask are relevant for the profile. I asked him why. He said that people climb mountains because they're there, cross deserts because they're there, get involved in problems because they're there. He didn't mention anything about money . . . I'm frightened for Eddie.'

Arthur held her, couldn't do it tighter.

'Which is more important? That the girl gives her evidence or our Eddie's life? I'm not asking you for an answer.'

They had walked without speaking, had had a coffee and walked some more, not spoken, and drunk a second coffee. Lukas knew that the exhibition in the canteen had left a sour taste in Castrolami's mouth, but it was easier done that way than having to explain himself.

Near the end of the second coffee, at a bar that overlooked the big square, piazza Venezia, where the coffee cost more than a meal, Castrolami put his gripe: 'Mr Lukas, it was dishonest.'

'If you want it to be.'

'Implication – you win them all.'

'I win a lot.'

'Not all.'

'I could have had you put on an Alitalia big bird and you'd be mid-Atlantic now, and I could take you to a trailer camp in Arkansas or Alabama, and I could wheel out the family of a marine or a ranger or a military truck driver not past his nineteenth birthday who was lifted and killed because I didn't save him. I could do that, if it would help you.'

'You don't win them all.'

'I lose people, yes. I try to win. I don't ask for a shoehorn. I'm there if I can help, and I try to win.'

'What keeps you in the game?'

Lukas said, 'It's what I know – about all I know.'

A hand reached out, slapped Lukas's face – quite hard

but not malevolent, and not playful. Lukas supposed he had said the right words, the right thing at the right time, but that, too, was a skill of his. One day, if time allowed, he would work at sincerity – what was real and what was not.

Castrolami said, 'We should go and see her. Then maybe you can judge better what happens to the boy.'

He had eaten, used the bucket and ditched the hood. The focus in his mind was the hatred, and the need for control, and Eddie held it. With the darkness around him there was the silence.

Self-pity, which would not have been control, cursed that he had stepped on to a flight when he'd thought he was 'lucky', cursed that he had made it on to a train going south, cursed that he had found a priest in a great church who, distracted and seeming not to care, had told him where to find his Mac's family – and cursed that he had lingered over cake while the man was sent for. Any cursing was self-pity. He would not have turned his back on Immacolata – would not and could not. Mixed it up in his mind – the face that was the source of hatred, and the face of Immacolata, and she was laughing, sharing her happiness with him. He mixed the two, but the hatred was of greater importance . . . He mustn't lose control.

He couldn't stand in the bunker, couldn't pace, couldn't lose the smell of the bucket, couldn't allow his head to drop.

A new decision faced Eddie. A week before, it would have been whether to do Shakespeare or Agatha Christie with his class, drink British bitter or Czech lager, eat pasta or Oriental, sleep the night with Immacolata or send her home, put the whites in the washing-machine or the woollens. Big decisions, but all in the past.

How to get a pair of locked handcuffs off his wrists, in near total darkness, was the problem that needed a decision.

He doubted there would be an anaesthetic – maybe, at best, alcohol or iodine to keep the cut clean. It might be a medical student, a man who cut up chicken for his family's evening meal – a butcher – or any bastard off the street. He had been told that his ears, his fingers, his hand and his penis would be chips in the negotiation stakes, which seemed a good enough reason to work on the locked handcuffs. Do nothing? Not a bloody option.

How to do it? He didn't know.

He had searched the floor space for wire, then gone over each wall, hoping to find a nail hammered in. He had crouched under the ceiling and smoothed the surface with his hands, but there had been no nails, hooks or wire. They had done the Holocaust at school. There were pictures, downloaded from the net, of day-in-the-life scenes at Auschwitz-Birkenau, Belsen and Treblinka. It had seemed a long way from a sixth-form college in north-west Wiltshire, until an old man had been brought in on a wet Tuesday afternoon in February

1998. He had been in the camps as a child and had survived, and was – a half-century later – a witness. He had the tattooed number to prove it and had rolled up his sleeve to show it. The class had seen the photographs of the crowds shuffling in lines, with suitcases and bundles, holding their children's hands, towards the gas chambers. The Jew had talked about death, its certainty. A boy, Robinson – cocky little sod – had asked the Jew: 'Why did they all just accept it? Why didn't they fight it? They were dead anyway, so why didn't they give it a thrash?' The class teacher had told Robinson that the question was offensive, but the Jew had waved him down and said, 'A few did, a very few, not enough. The state of Israel today still has a sense of shame at what is seen as the inability to fight, the lying-down, the docility. Israel will defend itself now with the utmost robustness, but then we had come from ghettos, we were exhausted, starved, degraded of dignity. We did not have the strength, physical and mental, to combat the inevitable. It was a good question.' They'd talked about it afterwards, in the canteen, the school corridors, and had all said – Robinson at the helm – that they wouldn't have gone like sheep. Easy to say at a school in north-west Wiltshire. Eddie Deacon had not come from a walled-in ghetto, was tired from lack of sleep but not exhausted, was hungry but not starved, and his dignity was fired by hate. How best to regain the freedom of his hands?

He told himself that they would cut off his ears, fingers and penis. Maybe it had been his failure to react fast enough on the pavement, in the moment after the fish-seller had given the glance, but it was all an unwalked road for him.

Fighting was about films, about stories. Heroes did fighting with scumbags. He didn't know heroes or lowlife. He had to learn how to fight. First lesson: shed the handcuffs.

Eddie found one place on the flooring where the concrete had a rough edge. Might have been where one load had gone down as liquid against the previous load that had almost set hard. The ridge was about half a centimetre high and sharp. The handcuffs were not the bar variety that the police were issued with when they came into Kingsland Road, but the old sort with a short chain linking the manacles. Eddie knelt. He planted his elbows, crouched, then had the chain against the ridge, made it taut and started to scratch, working the chain over the ridge. It hurt like fuck in his elbows but he kept on at it, and when he had rubbed smooth one short section of the ridge he edged further along to a new position. Dust came up and was in his nostrils.

Better to be beaten – face the knife – and have given it a thrash.

'It's about windows – the best opportunity for escape by the potential hostage – right at the start. Chaos, confusion, maximum tension for the hostage-taker. You can count it on the seconds of one hand, the sight of a window. That's when the hostage is most likely to get clear, but an attempt to escape is when the hostage is most likely to be killed. It's a hell of a risk and—'

Castrolami interrupted: 'You go in there?'

Lukas saw the façade, behind high, heavy railings, of the building, the flag drifting limp, and the barricades to keep the truck bombs away from the embassy walls. There had been a time when he would have been welcomed, open arms, at any US embassy. He wondered how it was for them, living in a fortress, bringing the Baghdad Green Zone to the via Vittorio Veneto. 'I'd go in there if I'd lost my documents, assuming I was travelling on American papers. Get it straight, I don't belong to governments.'

They kept walking. It was hot, the sun high. Lukas thought the city not yet back from holiday and the temperature too great for the comfort of tourists. He was not told why they walked in the heat, or why Castrolami checked his watch, as if that would make the hands go faster. Castrolami said, 'Sorry I interrupted. Don't think I'm not interested.'

Lukas asked, blunt, 'Are you fooling with me?'

'No.'

They left the flag, no wind to make it proud, behind them. Lukas said, 'After that first open window, there's less likelihood of another. We used to advise, at those seminars the state put on and the private security companies host for big bucks, that once taken, a hostage shouldn't try to escape. Then along came Iraq. Remember the Brit? Doesn't matter how, but he managed a runner, barefoot and in darkness. He was actually within three hundred paces of an American checkpoint when they caught him. Maybe he was already condemned but the escape confirmed it. His throat was cut. Would we now advise people to hang about and see what the sun brings up? We're a bit humbler with advice. What we do say: to escape and fail is a death sentence. These people here, do they have qualms about killing? Is it a big deal for them?'

'Like changing their underpants or brushing their teeth,' Castrolami said. 'In Naples, life doesn't count. They would go for an *espresso* afterwards and talk football.'

The dust in his eyes didn't matter because he couldn't use them. What came up his nose was an irritant and several times he sneezed uncontrollably, then froze to listen. He heard nothing – no engines, no music, no voices. He kept on scraping the chain against the ridge of concrete. He didn't – wouldn't – feel the chain to see whether the effort he made was winning a degree, however small, of success. He didn't run a thumb or a finger, the sensitive part, against it to learn whether he had made a fraction of an indentation in the link – too scared of finding there was no difference. Then it would be hopelessness, he would slump, join the line that had shuffled towards the gas chamber, that hadn't needed whipping or the prod of bayonets to keep it moving. How long had he been scraping? An hour? Might take a day, or three days. Might take a week.

The bucket smelled worse. That was a new worry. Better to have the worry about the bucket than about the knife homing in on his ears, or his fingers, or of them pulling aside his trousers. He went on scraping the chain against the concrete, and the smell was lodged in his nose. He worked on the chain manically. A new worry: what if the scraping dulled his ears? What if the footsteps came to the trapdoor and he didn't bloody hear them? What if they knew he was busy with escape in his mind? New worries, old worries – hardly fucking mattered which danced in him.

'We tend to suggest that the hostage looks hard for opportunities to escape, but we can't say where they might be. Every case is different and—'

Castrolami grunted, 'Do you go there?'

The Union flag flew, had no more life in it than the American one. The British place was sixties modern with a water feature at the front. There was a police jeep outside and a uniformed guy lounged with his legs draped out through the open door, a submachine-gun across his thighs. In the square just beyond, a fine statue of a Bersaglieri soldier, double life size, stood high on a plinth. Lukas said, 'Today I travel on a French passport – sort of a return for favours rendered. I work all right with UK Special Forces, and with spooks, but the diplomats tend to see me as street dirt. So, I'd go there for a glass of water if I was thirsty . . . I saw those troops in Iraq. I liked the feathers in the hat. You like useless information? Tough shit if you don't. The feathers are from the capercaillie bird, and the gate behind is the

Porta Pia through which they came to complete the unification
of your God-forsaken country and give the Holy Father the
boot.'

He was punched, a hard, short-arm blow with a clenched
fist, and Lukas rode it and rated it a compliment. They went
through the gate – he thought there were bits of ancient
Roman brickwork in the walls. 'We're nearly there,' Castrolami
said.

'Where I was . . . We can lay down guidelines. We know
how we *think* guys should behave but we cannot be arrogant
enough to dictate . . . and this boy has never been to a seminar,
nor on a chief executive's course, or probably ever read a
newspaper, a magazine, anything with hostage-survival
guidelines. He'll know nothing – which might be a bonus or
might be fatal. I can't say.'

Castrolami said, straight face, without expression, 'What
a pity he cannot hear your encouraging words.'

Still, he had the discipline. Still, Eddie worked, and didn't
move his thumb or forefinger over the chain's link. But with
two hours gone he found the first evidence of progress. The
chain seemed to lock more easily on to the ridge.

Then feet.

It would be such an opportunity – in a day, three days
or a week, if the chain was broken and his legs untied: wait
till the bastard came down the hole, belt him on the back
of the head with the sharp edge of a manacle, knee him in
the crotch and leave him stunned, be up and out, dropping
the trapdoor, bolting it and running . . . Running where?
Running anywhere. The scene played endlessly, as if it was
on a loop in his mind, as he worked on the link, an image
of action and response that pleased him. The image removed
the fear, gave him the sense that he was not a fatted bloody
calf tethered in a shed awaiting the stun-gun. But this was

not the time. The opportunity did not exist. He blew hard on the floor, hoped he'd dispersed the dust he'd created, and edged himself back against a side wall. He groped to find the hood, arranged it on his head and let the rim cover his eyes. He waited, and didn't know what would happen – didn't know if the footsteps heralded the knife – and squeezed his thighs together so that his penis was protected, pinned back his ears and clenched his fists to hide his fingers.

The bolt was drawn back. The torchbeam flared into the bunker and caught the hood. Pimples of light pierced the material. Could he, at that moment in time, rip off the hood, stand, grab a leg or a foot, drag the weight down, do damage with the handcuffs on? Eddie hesitated. Could he take the decision, allow the man to come down into the pit, rip off the hood, stand up? He heard the impact of the plastic bag. The light went off. The trapdoor closed and the bolt was pushed through.

There was food in the bag – more bread and cheese, one apple and water in a bottle. His bucket was not emptied. He ate a piece of the bread and a nugget of cheese, rinsed some of the dryness out of his mouth, then went back to scraping the chain on the rough ridge of the concrete. The heat in the bunker built on him and sweat drenched him.

Castrolami said that the parkland was the Villa Borghese gardens, that it dated back four hundred years, that it covered eighty hectares. Lukas said he didn't care to know the history of the park and its significance: his feet hurt from walking and his throat was parched. Castrolami looked at his watch, might have been the tenth or twelfth time, and must have reckoned then that a schedule was on course. He supposed that the walk to the park was of similar importance to his own visit to the *carabinieri* barracks. He showed no impatience. Lukas knew people – at the Bagram base outside Kabul and at Anaconda camp inside the Balad air base – who would have demanded dedicated space, computers wired in, maps on walls, secure communications, iced water, iced coffee, iced tea, and maybe their name on a card at the front of the desk. Lukas could be patient because he sensed Castrolami – a hulk, heavy and clumsy – to be a man of substance, a guy with whom business could be done. He thought it would be rude – and tactical shit – to chivvy for detail. He didn't require action to enhance his role. He saw two boys, rucksacks off their backs, half stripped and washing in a pool into which water fell from three levels. To him, the sculpture of rampant horses that supported the fountain was art. Set among huge mature pines, which gave wide shade, the massive statue of a man in fancy-dress uniform sat astride a warhorse, and Castrolami murmured that it was King Umberto I. There were mock Roman pillars, designed as ruins, and in an amphitheatre the workmen were setting up scaffolding for a concert's sound systems. He saw men with dogs, women with buggies, and tourists who digested their lunch with a stroll, not a siesta. He saw everything, and let his eyes follow where Castrolami's gaze went.

He saw her.

Had to be her.

There was a wide avenue lined with the high pines, sparse grass in the shadows. She led. A young man, good stride and arm movement, relaxed, was a metre behind her but close to her shoulder. Her T-shirt was damp-streaked and the shorts were baggy, too large – Lukas reckoned she'd begged or borrowed them from the young man. She ran well, but it was harder for her than him, and he thought she was not as conditioned as he was. Twenty metres behind them an older man rode a bicycle, the awkward sort with high handlebars that were hired out in parks, wherever. She didn't look up, to left or right. He saw her face clearly, full and in profile. Gazed at the thrust of her chin and chest. He rated her as the type of girl who would collapse on her knees in serious exhaustion before she allowed the young man to go past her. Dust spurted from under their sneakers. He sensed the privilege he was given. He could make judgements from the sight of her, a few seconds of watching her. 'Tough, hard and committed. Not a quitter,' he said.

Castrolami was grim-faced. 'We would have turned her out on to the street if we had thought she was.'

Lukas shook his head, 'Why . . . why? Tell me, why does a decent nonentity boy get his arms and legs around that one – why?'

'She is the daughter of her father. All her life she has what she wants. When she is finished with it, no longer wants it, it is discarded. There is something new she wants, and she takes it. It is the culture of the criminal clan.'

Lukas watched her draw away from him, and her escort. The bicycle squealed, needing oil. He almost enjoyed the wiggle of her butt, noted the drive in her arms and that she kept her head up and still.

'A pity for the boy, our Eddie, that she once wanted him.' Lukas saw her pass the kids washing in the fountain. She didn't deign to glance at them, and he lost her.

She had made her own world and stayed inside it. She didn't need panted conversation with Alessandro Rossi, wouldn't stop, slump and have Giacomo Orecchia give her water. Sweat soaked her.

It was a city of betrayal, hers. Had been throughout the centuries of its history, and she thought herself a mere footnote. Betrayal was the ultimate weapon of the clans. It meant nothing, went against no culture. She took a text, an episode of the city's history, better to remember betrayal.

She stretched her stride and couldn't hear panting in

Alessandro Rossi, but she could in Giacomo Orecchia and his wheeze went with the shriller wail of his bicycle wheels. She had learned the text as a child at school. In the year of 1486, a day in August, when Naples was further forward in architectural standards, sophistication and wealth than anywhere else in Europe, King Ferrante I of Aragon, the ruler, invited the aristocracy, who, he believed, were plotting his overthrow, to the Castel Nuovo on the shore to witness the marriage of his granddaughter to the heir of the Coppola family. They came. After the marriage service they attended a banquet in the great hall. Near the end of the feast, the king's lord chamberlain read out the names on the arrest warrants: all of the nobility's names were heard. The Royal Guard came in and took them into custody. That day they were tried and – before sunset – they met the king's executioner in the yard below the castle's ramparts. They would have betrayed the king, so the king betrayed them. It was a good story, and one from the history of her city.

She ran well.

Immacolata could not have held that pace, and kept the length of her stride, without the escort behind her. She thought herself liberated. Nothing nagged in her mind. London was behind her, and the boy, and there was a new intoxication – the betrayal. She didn't concern herself with Eddie Deacon. She hadn't asked him to travel, hadn't summoned him. She thought her hair flew behind her, and still there was the wail of the bicycle wheels, and she thought that, for the first time, Rossi struggled. Those betrayed were fools to have trusted; those who betrayed were tacticians and without guilt.

She ran until *they* called the halt.

'In your experience, how does it play?' Castrolami asked him.

'They will have moved him first to a holding location,

then will shift him to something more permanent. That completed, they make the contact. They have something they consider of value and wish to trade. There has to be dialogue. I'm grateful for the opportunity to see her.'

'You want to walk some more?'

'To my room, to pack, then to the train station. They have to make the contact.'

The prosecutor took a call. He knew the lawyer well. For all of the prosecutor's years in the city – in the offices of the Castel Capuana, now deserted and derelict, and in the new tower to which the Palace of Justice had moved – this man had handled the legal affairs of the Borelli family. He had contempt for him. He believed him bereft of integrity. He thought him a symbol of the corruption alive in the city. He had first met the lawyer when he had tried to prepare a case against Carmine Borelli, himself a young official, his target a man of substance, and had failed. He had met him again after the arrest of Pasquale Borelli, had negotiated a way through the court-imposed minefields and now had that clan leader locked away in Novara. He would doubtless meet the lawyer frequently now, with the arrest of Gabriella Borelli, Giovanni Borelli and Silvio Borelli, and after the extradition of Vincenzo Borelli. He heard honeyed words.

The prosecutor was asked if he was available in his office to meet with the lawyer the following day, at any time in the afternoon that was convenient. He was called 'Professore'. He was not a professor of any form of jurisprudence – or of street-sweeping, or of the cultivation of tomatoes under glass. He did not address the lawyer by any title that might flatter him, but he could not refuse the request. He named the time and rang off.

He worked in a fortified enclave. Below his office, in the basement, were the courts in which his accused were judged.

In those courts, the accused would sit on benches inside barred cages. The prosecutor was prey to a personal fear that he had not shared with a living soul: would those men and women in the cage contaminate him? They probed, all of them, for weakness. It might be through intimidation, bribery, the honey-trap and a Ukrainian prostitute, or a business opportunity that seemed legitimate and offered rich returns. The prosecutor's wife worked in a school as an administrator and was vulnerable there, and his son was a teenager and could not have been protected without dislocation of his entire life. He himself had only a state pension to look forward to, and cash payments could be made easily into offshore accounts. He was away from home often, for meetings in Rome at the ministry, then slept in hotels and sometimes was lonely. He had enough cash in hand for a relatively frugal existence – his one indulgence his love of opera – but taxes were high and the cost of living had soared. There were many ways in which he might have been contaminated. They had such wealth, so many resources, those who sat in the cages, and he had been – so far – one of the few men regarded as incorruptible. His fear, nurtured in privacy, was that he would stumble at some hurdle. He went to conferences in Berlin, Frankfurt and London. In those cities, of course, there was criminality, organised and serious. In those cities, also, senior policemen and jurists regarded him – he was aware of it – with hands-off suspicion: he came from that city where the clan gangs ran out of control, where murder, violence and extortion were embedded, where integrity was long corroded. He did not have the respect of outsiders. For a few more years he would endure the pressure of prosecuting the clans, then retirement, home in a village in the northern mountains and . . . Alone, the fear was always with him.

He made a note in his diary. The lawyer to visit in person, no agenda set, the following day in mid-afternoon.

He believed events would play out predictably. He thought a boy's life was threatened . . . and he would, in the next hours, prepare himself to make judgements on the value of that life.

He held his wrists as far apart as the pain would permit. Using the ridge of concrete and its serrated edge as a saw's blade, Eddie worked on the chain. Now – yes – he was prepared to let the tip of his finger feel the scraped line on the chain's link, and he was prepared to believe he had made a weakness. His mind roved as he scratched on the line . . . The time he had once grabbed a man: he had crossed a street to a far pavement where a man and a woman struggled and the man had hit the woman across the side of her face. He had intervened, had dragged the man back with some force. He had been kicked and punched – not with the ferocity of the beating in the bunker – and had been on the pavement. His eyes had misted, but he had seen the man and the woman walk away without a backward glance, and the woman had put her hand on the man's arm, then he had dropped it across her shoulders . . . Scraping at the chain, feeling a line made by the concrete, switched his focus. *If* he succeeded and parted the chain, *if* he was free to fight, *if* it was the guy who had taken him off the street, *if* . . . What damn chance did he have?

Better than no chance. Big, brave thought. He kept on with the scraping.

He ate fit to bust, and the gastrics put the gas in his gut. Twice he had noisily released it, but Carmine Borelli had to eat a little of everything that was offered, and much was pushed at him. Most recently, he had had a piece of orange and ricotta cake, *sfogliata*, and a good slice of pizza Margherita, with a deep coating of mozzarella, and before that more ricotta cake, but the *riccia* version, with twisted pastry, and he had drunk tiny quantities of Stock brandy, *sambuca* and *grappa*, all of which should be consumed after the evening meal but would have come from handily available bottles. He must eat, drink and be seen.

He should not have drunk on the pills. Without the painkillers he could not have made his long walk around the territory he had claimed, so many years before, for his clan. The street urchins, the *scugnizzi*, followed him. Young men and women watched him from the pavements or from the seats of their scooters and seemed uncertain, as if they did not believe that he, Carmine Borelli, could deliver opportunity, money and the calm required for decent trafficking. It was the old who pushed cake and pizza on him, and the little glasses. Some, he thought, had known him all of those years since the power base had been formed and the men took off their caps for him and the women rose from their street chairs to touch, with a degree of reverence, his arm, his mottled gaunt hands, or to pinch a grip on his coat. The old had known him since he had made Forcella his own.

Trade in the brothels had declined and the troops had moved north towards Cassino. Heavier competition existed for the dispersal of American aid, stolen and available on the street stalls, and then God had smiled on him – a day in March 1944. Carmine looked on it as the most significant of his life. Vesuvio had erupted. A great cloud had risen from the crater in daylight, and the beginning of the molten flow was visible when night fell. Villages were consumed, roads blocked. A military airfield and its planes were enveloped in the caking, heavy dust. Food warehouses collapsed – disaster for many, a triumphant moment for a few. Carmine Borelli was Il Camionista. He owned a small fleet of lorries. The shortage of transport was desperate. He was given a lucrative contract by the military government. He prospered. He bought more lorries and was able to profit mightily from post-war reconstruction, then speedboats to pick up contraband cigarettes, heavy plant for digging the foundations of industrial sites as Rome's government ladled money at the disaffected city. But it had all begun when he had mobilised a small fleet of lorries on the morning after Vesuvio had erupted. It was said that only firearms and ammunition, of all the items brought to Naples' docks by the Americans, were not available on the stalls of the via Forcella the morning after they were unloaded. The men who now pressed close to him had driven those lorries and unloaded them, and the women who touched him had sold from the stalls.

Carmine toured his streets. He tried to demonstrate his authority. He was not fooled. This was the city of the *lazzaroni*. The mob had taken its name from the patron saint of lepers. It wanted, to be satisfied, the three F words: *farina, forca e festini*. It was necessary to give the *lazzaroni* sufficient flour, a scaffold to gather round and public festivals of entertainment. Twice in the last forty-eight hours he had given them a whiff of the scaffold, and his progress up the street was similar to a celebration.

All threatened, though, by his granddaughter. The mob could turn, owed no loyalty. If necessary, he himself would kill Immacolata's boy. He could see, craning his neck, when he was at the top of via Forcella, near the church, the summit and cone of Vesuvio. The mountain had made him. He waved, and thought himself a king. How could she have betrayed him?

He knew. It was a germ in the family, in their blood – she had been so pretty, and he had loved her with an old man's passion. Now he would happily slaughter her, and feel no more than if she was a sheep in the *mattatoio*, kill her with a knife as they did the sheep in the abattoir. He wove again, and the old men and women applauded.

*

Her clothes were in a loose heap. She heard the immersion heater going, as it did when someone was taking a shower. There was an en-suite bathroom off Immacolata's room. She went into it, collected her towel from the rail, and wound it round herself, turned her back on the T-shirt, shorts, pants and bra, the socks stained with sweat from the run.

Maybe she was what they called her, a whore . . .

The towel covered her, except her shoulders and her legs below the knees. She went out of her room. The older one, who had bicycled, had his back to her but sat where he could see the front door to the apartment through the hallway, and did not look up as she glided, almost, over the marble veneer. She could hear the cascade of the water and went to that bathroom, which was off the corridor past the kitchen – the master bedroom was for her, the secondary two bedrooms were for them. Orecchia had not reacted as she went behind him.

She headed for the water. Immacolata thought that Rossi had toyed with her on the run in the gardens, could have passed her, gone ahead, drawn away from her, speeded up till she had sagged – and had not. He had kept his station behind her, had finally called to suggest that enough was enough, but had not succeeded in disguising his superiority, his strength. So fucking patronising. She went through the room and saw the neat pile of clothes, sweat-streaked like hers but folded and laid carefully on the floor beside the bed, which was immaculately made with perfect corners. The holster with the pistol was on the table. She went into the bathroom. This one was half the size of the en-suite attached to her bedroom. She opened the door. She could see his outline behind the screen. Did she want – at that moment – to be what they thought her, a whore?

Two movements, but simultaneous. She tugged back the plastic shower screen, and loosed the knot holding up her towel.

He gawped at her. Water, steaming, cascaded over his forehead, down his face and through the hair on his chest to the tangle of his lower stomach, and she saw the size of him, and the thick thighs. She expected him to blush, but he did not – expected him to jerk up with an erection, but he did not. The gawp had lasted only a moment. She stood naked and the towel was on her feet. It was what she would have done in the terraced house in Dalston, but only when Eddie was in the shower – God, not when any of the other boys was there. Eddie always blushed and always went . . . His shock was brief. He reached past her. His right arm brushed the curve of her left breast. His hand came back with a towel. He put it round him, and water spilled down it. She didn't move, make room for him. He had to work his way past her, and when he did, his hip was against her stomach and his chest was against hers. She looked into his eyes, and he into hers. Then he was gone, behind her.

He said quietly, 'I'm sorry your shower isn't working, Signorina. We'll get a plumber in to repair it.'

She stood and regret bloomed.

'Please, Signorina, feel free to use ours.'

She stepped into the shower, felt the heat of the water, then dragged the screen across. She didn't know then whether he watched her silhouette. She thought she had, indeed, made a whore of herself.

He said, and she could see the shadow movements as he dried, matter-of-fact, 'In our training for induction into the Servizio Centrale Protezione, we do role-plays to cover many situations. One concerns the *pentita* from Naples, Carmela Palazzo, known as Cerasclla. She was barely literate, pregnant at twelve, and active in the Spanish Quarter. With the family men in gaol, she controlled their speedball industry, drugs – heroin and cocaine. At a meeting inside the Poggioreale prison visiting room, the men blamed her for huge debts arising from her incompetent dealing in narcotics. She screamed abuse and was slapped across the face. In her humiliation, she went to the *carabinieri*, offered herself for collaboration. She was taken to a safe-house, had protection. But she was beyond control. Our role-plays involved walking with a woman collaborator on a street of shops. She puts an arm through the guard's, which is forbidden, pretends he is her lover, her husband. How can she be protected if she holds his hand or links his arm? She goes into stores that sell underwear. She waves items of intimate clothing at the guard – 'How do you like this, my sweetheart?' – and the guard is embarrassed. She runs away. She is brought back. She accuses, falsely, a guard of raping her. We did many role-plays, Signorina, that were based on the actions of Cerasella. Yes, she helped in the destruction of the Mariano clan. No, the protection didn't last. We threw her out, cut her adrift, and she was regarded as a sad, inadequate person, fit only to sell narcotics. In the role-play we're taught how to respond to erratic personality, as when a collaborator behaves with the modesty of a prostitute. Enjoy your shower.'

The shadow was gone. Water fell. She scrubbed herself with soap. She had heard, of course, of Carmela 'Cerasella' Palazzo, had never met her or seen her from a distance.

She switched off the shower, towelled herself. She had wanted to show power over him.

When she came back into the living room, Rossi was dressed and sitting beside Orecchia. Nothing was said, which increased her humiliation.

She wanted arms round her, to be held, to be saved from the shame . . . Who could have held her? She saw his face – had gloried in betrayal – and knew who would have held her, forgiven her.

*

In the darkness, Eddie scratched at the chain. He reckoned he had now smoothed some two feet of the rough concrete that made the ridge, but had at least six more to work on.

New thoughts, new attitudes swam in his mind. He must cope with isolation and the fear it induced, and he believed that sawing at the chain, grinding at it obsessionally, focused him away from misery . . . which led to the next necessity: must try to stay *positive*. 'Positive', to Eddie, had meant advertisements to be sniggered at in which companies quoted some unheard-of American electric-shaver sales guru who would teach – for a fat fee – how to acquire confidence. His mother was a positive thinker – always regarded the glass as half full and ditched the empty bit – and his father had chided him for not having the ambition to go to the furthest limits of ability. There had been so much crap to Eddie Deacon – not any longer. And, because it was a *positive* reaction, he started to play a word game – took a word, stripped it, jumbled it, found new words. He would have derided it in the staffroom, and the guys in the house would have hooted at him if he'd suggested it as an exercise in mental agility . . . but he had stored it as an entertainment, with mental arithmetic, meaningless figures . . . and further down the line there would be physical exercise – maybe he would try squats, press-ups, or lying on his back and lifting his legs three or four inches. Eddie thought that being *positive* was important, and thought that *if* he ever broke the chain and freed his hands the agility – physical or mental – would save him . . . Had to think that.

Once he heard a voice, a whistle of some tune, and footsteps, but they didn't approach the trapdoor. Once he heard an engine, faint and muffled, as if a car had come close, and then a radio had been switched on and off. The sounds didn't make a pattern . . . That was another thing: a *pattern* was to be observed, noted, analysed, clung to in case the chain broke and . . . He worked hard, and the sweat was in his eyes, making them smart. The bucket stank worse.

He thought he wanted the bucket taken and emptied more than he wanted fresh food, more even than he wanted water.

Eddie was certain of it now. The link in the chain had a clear indentation. Not wishful thinking, more than mere *positive* thinking, there was a line in the steel of the chain's link that his nail could settle in. He went at the work harder, and didn't care to think of the consequence *if* he were to break open the chain link and free his hands.

Time drifted – and he created word games, arithmetic games that were more complicated, taxing, and the dust of the smoothed concrete was thicker in his nostrils, caking the outer skin of his lips. He had to do it for himself. No other bastard would.

'How will he be?'

'Scared,' Lukas said. 'Scared and alone, feeling that the world, already, has given up on him. Probably in darkness, probably trussed up, likely to be hooded.'

Castrolami drove. 'We have kidnapping in the south, in the toecap of the boot. It is an industry, and when payment is slow there is the possibility of a knife taking off an ear or a finger and the item consigned to the postal services. But not here. I do not have the experience of it.'

Lukas thought Castrolami drove well. They went fast, had come off the *autostrada* and were now on a dual-carriageway. Ahead, there was a wide panoramic vista of lights, different intensity but constant, then a short, curved horizon and beyond it almost total darkness. But the Gulf of Naples was broken up by oases of lights and Lukas thought one would be the island of Capri, but didn't know which. He could keep most layers of excitement well suppressed, but always a faint buzz-glow grew in him when he saw, the first time, his place of operations. Might have been from the hatch window of a Cessna light aircraft coming in to a jungle strip up in the mountains and far from Bogotá, or from the porthole of a C-130 as it corkscrewed down towards the Bagram runway outside Kabul, or from a Black Hawk's open hatch and over the shoulder of the machine-gunner anywhere in Shia or Sunni Iraq. If he didn't have the buzz-glow, if he'd gotten too cynical for it, it would probably be past time for him to call it a day, go quit. It was all, sort of, routine and he had played this game so many times, and he didn't expect to be surprised. He still had, and was grateful, the focus. They hadn't talked much on the journey. Lukas reckoned that Castrolami was poor with chatter: they had done a little – Castrolami had a wife and children up in Milan, and they'd gone there because the job was shit and they never saw him; and he had a friend who painted, and most times he took her out he was asleep at the table by the time the meat was served; and he was forty-six, and bullets had come through the post in little padded bags . . . Lukas had given some: had done the FBI's unit for Hostage Rescue, had been on the sidelines at the 'big' events, Ruby Ridge and Waco, did co-ordination now, and was a year older at forty-seven. His mother had brought him up in a trailer camp and had cleaned offices to get him through college; she was American-Italian and his father was pretty much a shit and long gone. There was a wife, Martha, and a boy, Dougie – had only mentioned his son's name, but Lukas had said nothing else of him. They all lived together now, mother and wife and son, in the trailer park, adjacent to each other, and the cut-off didn't seem to bother him . . . They had talked a bit about things that didn't matter and didn't affect why they rode in a car down a hill and into the city of Naples . . . Seemed they'd each talked enough about themselves.

Lukas said, 'Very few hostages taken have an expectation

of the risk. They come to the situation with an experience bank equal to that of a newborn child.'

'We talk the language of "leverage"?'

'That would be an appropriate word. "Leverage" is where we're at.'

'And negotiation is not an appropriate word?'

'When we have an open line of communication, we talk a fair amount about negotiation. But it's talk. I accept that. Talk buys time . . . The time is used for assets of intelligence, surveillance, informers, for just plain old-fashioned luck to chip in – I don't come from a world where hostage-takers get rewarded. Maybe, up front, I've been party to them being paid for a freedom exchange, but then they get hunted down, shot or hanged, or they disappear off the face of the earth. I understand the reality.'

'In this case, Immacolata Borelli, if we paid we would destroy an anti-kidnap strategy applicable in domestic Italy for more than thirty years.'

'I said I understood,' Lukas murmured.

'And if we permitted Immacolata Borelli to withdraw her evidence in return for the boy keeping his ears, fingers, eyes – whatever else of his body that can be cut off – the programme we have of collaborators with justice is finished. The postal service would be filled with the stink of decaying flesh.'

'Again, I understand.'

Castrolami said, 'Close to the *autostrada*, where we left it, was the territory of the Nuvoletta clan. We have bypassed the zone of Scampia, which is the base of di Lauro. Now we cross the suburb of the city called Secondigliano and it is under the control of the Licciardi clan and the Contini clan. As we drive towards the old city we pass the territory of Mallardo, Misso and Mazzarella. They are the principal families of the Camorra. Then there is another level – Lo

Russo, Sarno, de Luca, Caldarelli, Picirillo – and the clan of Borelli, then another level of perhaps as many as eighty clans. The first level we cannot destroy. We can make arrests – occasionally, when we find a principal – and we can disrupt, but little more. The second level is where we find the Borelli clan. With a collaborator it is possible – I used it with care, but *possible* – to take the conspiracy apart to the extent that it ceases to exist. The opportunity does not come every week or month, it might come once in a year, but I would believe that is optimistic. Every two years or three . . .'

Lukas asked, 'She has that capability, Immacolata Borelli?'

'We believe so. We remove a clan's leadership. It is a ship that has no crew. More important it has no rudder. It sinks. Warfare breaks out as the void is filled, but many opportunities then come our way. In the scramble for the empty territory, other clans – ruthless in what they will do, the risks they will take, the numbers they will kill – make mistakes. Mistakes are fertile ground for us.'

'She has that importance?' A gently posed question. The tower blocks of great housing estates, lights climbing into the darkened skies, were gone. The streets were filled now with cars and they had slowed. Off the route, Lukas could see narrow little openings. Noise – engines, horns, music, shouting – came through the windows.

'Immacolata Borelli can deliver us the clan – her mother, her brothers, the hitman and the enforcers, the buyers and the bankers. It is a chance for us to win. Do you know what it is, Lukas, not to win?'

'Keep it for another day – winning and losing,' Lukas said.

'Some days, in life, it is necessary to win.'

'Another day we talk about winning – and we decide if we can win twice . . . with the girl, with the boy.'

'I don't bargain with you – it is not for discussion. We

have to win with the evidence of Immacolata Borelli. It is primary. If, afterwards, we save the boy – Eddie Deacon, the idiot and the imbecile, now forgotten – then we may drink some *spumante*. It is made at vineyards near the town of Asti, in the region of Piedmont. They use the *moscato bianco* grape. It is very popular in Italy. It is drunk on a celebratory occasion. I like . . .'

Lukas said, drily, 'I think you don't often get to taste *spumante*, my friend.'

'It is my regret that, true, I drink it rarely.'

Lukas gave him the winter smile – no love, no life, no humour. The car was stopped against the kerb. Lukas was given directions – how far he needed to walk, how long it would take him, and was told to watch his back and put his watch in his pocket, out of sight. Castrolami told him he was going to his office, his workplace in the barracks, and would set up, discreetly, a crisis-control desk. He took from his wallet a card that bore just his name on one side, no logo, wrote his mobile number on it and gave it to Castrolami. Then he reached to the back seat and pulled the laptop out of his rucksack – needed a contortion but he achieved it – and asked that the computer be lodged at the desk overnight. They shook hands perfunctorily, like an afterthought.

He closed the door and slung the rucksack straps over his shoulders. He saw the car veer away, then lost it in traffic, but he didn't think Castrolami had swung in his seat and waved. The sort of man Lukas was – and his judgement of Castrolami – did not take time out for relationships with professionals. A sharp punch, a quick handshake was a good par on that course. He had asked to be dropped near to the piazza Garibaldi, had not been asked why, or where he had booked a room. He recalled what he had been told, peeled off his watch and pocketed it.

The streetlights were low, the headlights blinding, and it

seemed that around him the city was vibrant, alive. It flourished. Lukas couldn't walk along a street in Baghdad or Basra, Kabul or Kandahar, Bogotá or Cali. He saw backpackers in front of him, guys and girls who were half his age, would have come off a train and now trekked from the main-line station to whatever fleapit they could afford. His clothes were, of course, clean – laundered but not pressed – and he was shaven but not closely, and his short cropped hair was not brushed or combed. He lit a cigarette, dragged on it, and tobacco smoke mingled with what he breathed out. He felt good here. He pondered: Castrolami and himself, were they on opposite sides of a chequered board? A girl who was needed as a state witness was one queen, and a boy who had done 'wrong place at wrong time' was the other, and if the game was played to conventional rules only one could be left standing. He would have to act, if they were to claim a victory, on maverick rules. But, he had been told, it was not a city that threw up victories. He went by the cafés, the bars, the little restaurants and pizza houses, past the stalls where clothing was slung, and past tall west Africans who had laid on the paving handbags with fancy labels.

Not good for a man in Lukas's trade to stand up and cheer if the hostage walked free, or to crumple and sag if the hostage came out zipped into a body-bag. Could do his best, nothing more. After success came another day, and after failure there was one more day to be met. He thought, though, and this hurt, that the priorities were not with the boy, and it would be a difficult road to walk . . . He saw the sign, lit, hardly welcoming . . . One more backpacker in town, older and more wizened, but unexceptional. He smiled wanly at the small group of men who stood by the step up into the *pensione*, and worked his way past them. None seemed to notice him.

He was greeted at the desk. He thought himself a welcome diversion from the Australian kids who had come into the lobby complaining that the toilet was blocked and wouldn't flush. He murmured a name – the one that had been used on the reservation, which was on a passport he now offered, Canadian – then asked the guy whether he was Giuseppe. He wasn't: Giuseppe was the day manager, worked from seven in the morning until seven in the evening. Lukas lied, said a friend had been here, had spoken well of the *pensione* and of Giuseppe. He was given his key.

Slowly, tired, he started up the stairs. He did not know yet which had been the floor where Eddie Deacon had taken a room. He was tired, a little hungry, and the room allocated to Lukas would, inevitably, be shit, and his situation would, inevitably, be about a thousand times better than Eddie Deacon's. He unlocked a door, went in, kicked it shut.

He said quietly, 'You get my best effort, kid, can't say more – and can't say it will be enough.'

11

As did his wife, Carmine Borelli possessed the cunning of the elderly and the wiliness of a veteran.

He didn't understand the technicalities of the most modern surveillance systems employed in the piazza Dante barracks or inside the Questura, but he had grasped the need for total vigilance . . . His jacket collar was turned up, a loose cotton scarf covered much of his lower face and he wore a cap with a peak to hide his nose and eyes from elevated cameras. He had walked more than two kilometres, done back-doubles and alleyways, before he was satisfied. Then he had been picked up in a small repair garage in which he had a commanding financial stake. An old friend had driven him.

The car in which he had travelled to the north of the city was not a Mercedes, a BMW 7 series or an Audi, not a vehicle of status. It was a humble mass-produced Fiat, churned out by the Turin factories, anonymous. He would have confessed, climbing stiffly from the passenger seat and stepping into the sunshine, to a flutter of apprehension. It was hostile territory, and he was inside it. Mobile phones would have logged each metre the Fiat had brought him deeper into the complex of towers. He saw the scooter accelerate towards him, then brake and swerve.

He was happier to have Salvatore at his back.

When Carmine Borelli had taken charge of the Forcella district of the old city, where the streets followed the old layout of foundations put down by Roman builders, the district of Scampia had been scrub, fields and smallholdings. There was now a population of some seventy thousand. It was outside the area of his experience, and a new breed of clan leader was found here. They did not frighten him, but were a cause of anxiety. He had created wealth that was exceptional by the stricken standards of the Forcella people, and Pasquale had built on it, hugely increasing it. Vincenzo – if he was ever freed – would take it further.

Salvatore had removed the helmet and tucked it under his arm. Carmine Borelli took a cue from the hitman and doffed his cap. He unwound his cotton scarf and smoothed the collar of his jacket. It was, almost, an act of submission. It was a sign that they accepted they walked now under the protection of a more powerful man's authority.

The families, supreme in Scampia, had wealth on different strata from that of the Borellis. They were, here, among the richest in the entire Italian state.

Those families also employed violence on a scale that could almost turn Carmine Borelli's stomach. They fought, pursued vendettas, tortured, amputated, burned alive. He came with a request. The difficulty of asking the more powerful for favours was that a high price could be exacted. Desperate times meant desperate measures were employed.

They were checked in at a pavement-level entrance. Men spoke on mobile phones, men searched him with aggressive, disrespectful hands, men took the firearm from Salvatore's belt, men eyed them as if they were lesser creatures. Carmine Borelli could accept the reduced status, but thought it harder for Salvatore to bow the knee. He imagined, in Salvatore, that pride burgeoned. It had to. It could not be otherwise. They were led up a flight of stairs – filth had accumulated in the well – past scattered syringes. He would not have tolerated the heroin addicts' needles left as litter in Forcella, but the drug trade and its trafficking had come after his time of ascendancy. He was brought to an iron-barred gate across the first-level walkway.

It was unlocked by more men.

They went through, heard it clang shut, then the rattle of a heavy chain. Carmine knew little of ironwork but would have been an imbecile not to have realised that the fire brigade would need sophisticated oxyacetylene cutting gear to get through it, and it would be slow work. They walked some more, then went through another gate, similar, and climbed another staircase.

Little in life could frighten Carmine Borelli – but later he would admit to Anna, if the Virgin smiled on him and he was clear of this fuck-place, that he was uncertain, unhappy, with his experience on the lower floors of the great Sail tower in Scampia. When they were on the third level, there was another pause at another barred gate, and he breathed hard, sucking air into his lungs – and cursed a lifetime's cigarettes. His hip ached sharply. It was good that Salvatore, disarmed, was with him. He thought, by now, they must be close. More men waited here, more mobiles were used, and he heard little jabbers of code talk. He thought the numbers were a show of strength, of power. He must acknowledge it.

What would he say? How would he say it? And why?

He would say – and it had been rehearsed in his wife's presence, with her making suggestions, and when he had walked, avoiding possible surveillance and the gaze of cameras, and when he was in the car, being driven north to Scampia: 'I value this meeting. I appreciate that you have given me your time. I am grateful for this opportunity. To the point. These are difficult times in Forcella. My son, Pasquale, is in Novara, and I believe your cousin and your nephew are also in Novara. My eldest grandson, Vincenzo – a fine boy – is held in London, and my younger grandsons, Giovanni and Silvio, are in Poggioreale. My beloved daughter-in-law, Gabriella, also is arrested. These are very severe times for my organisation, built with my blood and sweat for half a century and more. The threat to us now is from our own. I could tear out my tongue for speaking her name. My granddaughter, my Immacolata, has prostituted herself and taken the money of the government. She destroys all I have built. We identify a weakness. A boy from England followed her here, is stupid, is ignorant, and loves her. We hope the whore loves him. We hold him, but not where we can keep him. We need a secure place. I ask for a secure place – a week, no more – under your protection. I ask also for my son's most able associate, Salvatore, to be allowed free access. We will put as great a burden of pressure on my granddaughter – to retract and withdraw – as is possible. Here, under your control, is the most secure place in Naples. I would, of course, pay well for such a service.' That was what he would say.

There were more men on the walkway, at either side and in front of a door.

The door was rapped, opened.

He saw then that Salvatore was blindfolded with a cloth, perhaps one for drying dishes, but he himself was not. He prayed to the Virgin that Salvatore would accept the indignity, not curse and rip it off. He was rewarded, but he saw the heave in Salvatore's chest. The people in Scampia could recruit Salvatore or shoot him and leave him sprawled on a pavement. He thought, himself, he was safe – too old to be butchered. Too feeble. Too insignificant. He was shown in. Salvatore was guided after him.

He was taken to the kitchen.

A man sat there, dapper, with rounded shoulders and a cigarette, lit, between his fingers. A packet of Marlboro Light lay on the table. He had good hair, well styled, and clothes that looked expensive but not luxury wear. Beside the cigarettes there was a pocket calculator and scrap paper with scrawled figures in columns. Pasquale had known this man. There were no alliances in Naples, as there were in Calabria or in Palermo, but there were arrangements. He played his part. He ducked his head, showed respect. He knew, if the request for help, co-operation, was granted that a high price would be exacted. There was no alternative. He was fascinated by the face of the man, his features. A photograph of him appeared regularly in the newspapers, but was more than twenty years old. No more recent image existed, and the newspapers said the police had never succeeded with a telephone intercept in recording his voice.

Salvatore had made the links, arranged the meeting. He had done well.

Carmine Borelli was waved to a seat. If his request was granted, the boy would be moved to the most secure suburb of the city, would be beyond reach.

He began, 'I value this meeting. I appreciate that . . .'

He sawed at the chain. It was not a dream, not any longer. Eddie Deacon could ease his thumbnail into the growing slit in the link.

He worked harder, frantic.

He had his jacket off, hitched on his shoulder. Without the sticks that were offered at the café, Castrolami would not have reached halfway up the steep path.

It was still early morning, but already the haze was building and the dawn clarity was wiped out. The city was far away and distanced further by the skim of cloud that sat over it. When he stopped and turned, he could make out the runway at Capodicino, the high-rise blocks of Scampia, the cranes at the docks, the curved line of the via Francesco Caracciolo, the Castel San Elmo squat on the hill, and the Castel dell'Ovo

that jutted out into the sea. He could not see his own district,
let alone his block, or the block of the artist.

He had started this trek on the south-west side of the
mountain for the view. It was so many years since he had
attempted anything as childishly idiotic as a climb to the
crater rim of Vesuvio – maybe ten. Perhaps, then, it had been
in February or November, not in the heat of a September
morning. The sweat spilled off him and the dust lay on his
face.

It was annoying to Castrolami that the American – well,
American, but claiming some Italian, maybe some German,
a possibility of some British ancestry, and the certainty of
being a gypsy, a mongrel that was a *bastardo* – walked well
and kept just behind but did not heave, pant and gasp. His
annoyance was increased by the refusal of the *bastardo* to
ask, at any time, the purpose of the journey. They had left
the barracks at piazza Dante, climbed into Castrolami's car,
driven away from the city and parked in the yard by the
station at Scavi Pompeii. They took the bus up the hill, past
the old fortifications that overlooked the sea, the ever-
thinning scrub. When the bus came to the park, they were
left with a final three hundred metres on foot to the rim.
It would have been good to hear, 'What the fuck are we
here for?'

He had not thought to bring water. Sweat discoloured his
shirt. Each time he stopped, to calm his breathing and pretend
to examine the view, a steady column of tourists passed him,
going up and coming down. He alone wore suit trousers and
carried a jacket. It could have been that Lukas found
amusement in the climb, in Castrolami's discomfort. They
hit the last metres.

The path of caked, stamped-on dust cut through a lunar
landscape. Almost nothing grew here. The stones and rocks
were angular, punishing, a dull, lifeless grey. There was a

first viewpoint where a fence kept the tourists a metre or more back from the rim and the cliff beyond it. There were Japanese, in large numbers, so Castrolami pushed on and headed for a white metal and plastic contraption, a couple of metres high and fastened with wire stays. He thought it would do for his purpose. He leaned on a rail. Lukas came alongside him, gave him nothing, waited and kept silence. Not being asked *why* took the gloss from Castrolami's moment.

His calm broke, almost a snarl of anger: 'Do you want to know why you are here or do you not want to know?'

He was not certain but he thought he felt a weakness.

Could have been mistaken, didn't believe so. Eddie Deacon worked at the link, running it on the rough concrete ridge. What was certain, the pit where his nail went was always deeper.

Lukas said, 'Do you want any smart shit talk from me about what volcanoes I've visited, where I've picked up hunks of lava? I can do that talk if it's necessary. I don't think it is. The view is non-existent. Comfort is non-existent. Shade is non-existent. We're the only two cretins in this place too dumb to bring water. You have, friend, my undivided attention.'

He saw Castrolami's lips purse, reckoned the anger was at the edge of control. He thought the morning wasted. Lukas said, 'Say what you want to say.'

There was a harshness about the crater's rim, and the sun came up from the stones of lava fields to reflect back into his eyes. He looked down, could see far into the hole, and found himself straining to see better. A hawk soared on the east side. The drop of the cliffs from the rim to the core was uneven, ragged. Faint curls of thin smoke or steam emerged from the rocks and dissipated. Lukas supposed there was some relevance to it . . . and was patient. He was rewarded.

Castrolami said, defiant, 'I should bring here everybody who visits the city to meet me. I should use it as a theatre set to explain the reality of Naples. Anyway, you are ready?'

Lukas didn't often do snide and smartass, thought the rewards short-lived. He would need the big, sweaty, armpit-stinking *carabinieri* guy. He said, 'I am.'

Castrolami flung out a hand theatrically, waved at the hole. 'It is one thousand nine hundred and thirty years, less one month, since the eruption that destroyed Pompeii and Ercolano. There was an eruption in the year 1631, three more in the eighteenth century, four in the nineteenth century. There have been two in the last century, 1929 and 1944. Look down. You see nothing that is threatening. It is at peace, something dead. That it exploded is in history, not actual. You cannot look down and see anything that is a maximum danger. Maybe it is only the newspapers that speak of the danger. Look at it, see nothing, and be blind.'

Lukas permitted himself to be led. Did not interrupt. He assumed that Castrolami had flogged his body through the ordeal of the climb for a good reason, and waited for it.

'The scientists call it, in English language, the "plug". For us it is the *tappo*. The plug holds down the lava underneath. The plug hides the reality of what is there. The plug, to keep the vision of harmless peace, is some ten kilometres deep. Below the plug is the burning liquid mass, the lava, and you have to imagine an enormous cavern in which it boils, bubbles and is unseen, and that cavern may have a diameter of up to two hundred kilometres. If the plug breaks the cavern is emptied and pours upwards. The volcano is the city of Naples. At peace and tranquil, with fine churches and wonderful galleries and good food and wine, a triumph of sophistication, and safe. It is an illusion maintained by the strength of the plug. Out of sight and beyond your gaze there are powerful destructive forces. I brought you here to explain about Naples, the real danger and the false calm. We can go now.'

Lukas did not chide, did not complain. He thought, actually, it had been a good image and he doubted he would soon lose the sight of the scree slopes, the rockfall debris, the rough lava pieces and the smoke wisps that were all of the great forces at play he could see. He must imagine.

He started out again on the path, and dust slithered under his soles. The tourists came by him, gasping, struggling, and the sun was higher, hotter. He paused and looked down, not into the pit and on to the plug but at the city. He saw nothing that threatened, only the mist. He saw no danger in the faint hazed buildings that were toy-sized. Hard for him to understand that a poison was down there, hedged in by the blue of the sea. 'I have it, thank you. Yes, let's go.'

He thought of the boy – not good for him to feel emotional involvement. About the same age as the son who lived with his mother in the trailer camp, and didn't write. He had heard from the London office that the boy's parents spoke well of their son, and with love, and were on their knees with anxiety. He thought his own son, placed where the boy was, would have lost any will to fight after about ten minutes of capture, maybe less. He liked the face of the boy from the picture sent to him, and thought his own son nondescript, perhaps ugly. But Lukas didn't do soap-opera sentiment. It wasn't about the son he wished he'd had. Anyone, lame and halt or fit and fresh, would have his utmost endeavour. He had killed the thought of his own detached family, but not his mind image of the boy. They went down together. He thought Eddie Deacon would be existing in a living hell. Maybe the city itself lived under a plug but could destroy.

'It is a good place, you agree?'

'Do you want me to flatter you or kick you?'

'Nothing in Naples is as it seems.'

'Wrong,' Lukas said. 'The boy is kidnapped. That "is as it seems". I enjoyed the walk, and this is not about tectonic plates, it's about criminality. Don't give it excuses. And I'll buy you lunch.'

He thought it would break in another hour if he could increase the pressure on the link where it ran on the concrete. It seemed to bend, fractionally, in his hands.

When he had broken the link, and the chains hung from the two manacles, what would he do?

Couldn't face that. Couldn't think about it while the chain still held. Christ, why did nobody come? Why no sirens? Why no help? Why did nobody care? Could have screamed it – didn't. Eddie went on sawing at the link.

'Very grave times, Professore. Grave and unhappy.'

'Please, distinguished *avvocato*, explain your request for our meeting.' The prosecutor had not done the lawyer the favour of meeting him in his personal office – had he done so, he would then have had to abandon it while fumigation and scrubbing were carried out. He was able to be civil to and understanding of the principal criminals he met after their arrest, always found them polite and correct, of good intelligence and, in a few cases, exceptional intellect. He found some well read in modern classics and some in poetry, and with a few he had discussed with passion his love of opera. He was not sworn at, neither did he feel his home and family were threatened. The professionals – the lice on the criminals' backs – disgusted him.

'You understand, Professore, that material comes, unsolicited and without prior notification, through the post to my office.'

'I understand.'

'Material that is sent anonymously, no cover note of explanation. In this case a single sheet featuring a photograph and a written demand. Upon receiving it, I immediately telephoned your office, Professore, and you were gracious enough to permit this meeting.'

Everyone called the lawyer by his given name, Umberto. He gloried in that familiarity. Even members of the judiciary were known to use it in court. The prosecutor would not. The professional men were, the prosecutor's belief, essential crutches for criminality. They cared for the legal matters that were the inevitable cost of a career in organised crime: they opened the bank accounts and transferred the laundered monies; they placed investments and advised on what stock should be bought or sold; they were the politicians paid handsomely for access to contracts. Sometimes, if he walked alone and unknown in the darkness and thought deeply, the prosecutor considered that the professionals might indeed be the ones who pulled the strings and the clan leaders were mere marionettes. This lawyer disgusted him, but was clever. Many man-hours had been devoted in the Palace of Justice to bringing him before the courts. As yet they had failed.

'What do you have for me?'

'I must say also – I was this morning stopped in the street by a stranger. A message was given to me. I have this . . .'

From a frayed and scratched briefcase – a symbol of experience and also of humble poverty – a transparent sheath was taken. Not 'poverty'. The lawyer would be worth, for his work with the Borelli clan, many tens of millions of euros – paid well because he served well. The meeting was in an interview room. There was a table, with an ashtray and, four chairs. Three walls were bare and one carried a framed portrait of the President of the Republic; it was minimalist and intended to offer no comfort. The sheath was passed across the table. He saw a photograph printed on the top half of the page, and under it was the handwritten message:

> *If Immacolata Borelli does not make, within one week, a statement that she has left the custody of the palace and will not give testimony now, or ever, against persons known to her, this man will be killed.*

The prosecutor had enjoyed a varied career but remembered best the time – four years – he had spent in Reggio Calabria; there had been similar photographs then. Staring eyes trapped in a moment of fear by the brightness of the camera flash, the filth on the shirt, or blouse or dress, the thickening stubble on a man's face and the tangle of uncombed hair if it was a girl. Usually they held a newspaper. Usually, also, they seemed to demonstrate the desperation of the damned, as if they didn't believe help existed, or that they were anything more than supine participants. In this photograph, the boy had a pleasant face.

'The man who stopped me in the street – I assure you, Professore, he is unknown to me – he said that the boy taken would lose an ear after four days, a finger after five, his penis after six, then would die if Immacolata Borelli's statement was not passed to me. I don't know why me.'

The prosecutor remarked briskly, 'Because you represent Pasquale Borelli and all his tribe.'

'I'm just a messenger.'

'Of course.'

'I would deny that my clients, the family I have the privilege to represent, and who are hard-working, honourable people, are linked to this sad, difficult situation.' Then he asked, innocence creasing his face, 'Do you know who this young man is, Professore? Do you know his connection with Immacolata Borelli?'

'No.'

'It would be a tragic distortion of reality if the position of this young man was to weigh against the family, my clients.'

'Of course.'

'I'm only the messenger.'

'Again, of course. You don't have the envelope in which this communication was sent to you? For forensic studies?'

'I regret that it had been shredded before its contents' significance was noted.'

'Could you give a description of the "stranger" who accosted you?'

'He was behind me. I never saw his face.'

'Of course.'

There were four directions in which the future career path of the prosecutor could go. He might write the letter, give the notice of termination, go to walk in the beloved Dolomites, quit. He might be transferred to the anti-terrorism force and posted anywhere. There was the chance of promotion to Rome and the chair of command over the three primary prosecutors in Palermo, Reggio Calabria and Naples. He might just soldier on, maintain his office at the palace, beaver away at his work and log seventy hours a week. The last option had a saving grace. One day or night, he would nail this shit bastard and see him dragged away in handcuffs, unable to shield his face, past the lines of flashbulbs, and know that he was headed for the remand cells of the Poggioreale gaol and a chance to share life with pimps, thieves and pushers, the scum of the city. He never lost his temper in public. He did at home – he would pace his living room, his child shut in a bedroom and his wife gone to the kitchen, and howl at the unfairness of life. He stood up.

The lawyer rose awkwardly from his chair. The advantage of the interview room was that it did not have air-conditioning, and was therefore uncomfortable: sweat streaked him. 'Should

I be telephoned, should I be accosted again, is there a response I can give, something that will save this unfortunate from mutilation or death?'

'No, there is not.'

The lawyer said, a cut in his voice, 'You play, Professore, with a life.'

'Do you speak as a link in a chain of negotiation, and therefore as part of a criminal conspiracy, or as the mere messenger?'

He did not expect a reply. The guard outside the door would escort the shit bastard from the building.

How hard was she, the girl? The prosecutor took a lift high up the tower, to look for coffee. Who could read her, and know her break-point? He carried the sheath that protected the paper with the photograph of the staring eyes, the white cheeks under the stubble, colour burned from them by the flash, the tousled hair and the dried blood on the skin. To destroy the Borelli clan would be a triumph but would carry a price. It was indeed, beneath the wide-eyed fear, a pleasant face.

He sawed, and felt the chain link weaken. He hadn't imagined it – he knew it. He began to think of it, fighting. Began to stiffen with the stress of it – a dream or a nightmare – but kept sawing. The dust was thick on his face and his eyes hurt. He thought of everyone he knew, and wondered if any among them would believe that Eddie Deacon – in a hole with no water and a shit bucket – could break out of handcuffs and fight. His Mac, would she? Couldn't answer that.

The shower hadn't been mentioned, or her strip in front of Alessandro Rossi. She was subdued. Immacolata talked of her mother. The tape-recorder was controlled by Rossi and Orecchia prompted. It was general, not the detail required by Castrolami, the prosecutor or his deputy. She scratched in her mind for memories and tried to offer up the minutiae of detail. And between what she had to offer, Orecchia would speak or Rossi, as though events elsewhere had taken centre stage, and the safe-house apartment on the Collina Fleming was no longer of pivotal importance.

Orecchia had said, 'The position of women in Naples is unique. In Naples a woman can rise higher, faster, than in the south or in Sicily. It was the legislation of 1991, all the collaborators provided for, all the arrests that followed, that took away the glass ceiling, and women flourished. If there's a problem, what do they do? They call for the women.'

Rossi had said, 'The women have less loyalty than the men. Pupetta Maresca, first lady of Nola, knows that her son is dead, knows that her son is in the tower supporting a flyover bridge, knows that a cocaine importer killed him, and she moves in with that man and has twins with him. She was a star – not as clever as your mother, but colder.'

She talked of her mother with detachment, as if she was speaking of a stranger she had met casually and briefly.

From Orecchia, 'The men in the family will usually follow the orders of their father but always the orders of their mother. Another, from near Naples, Anna Mazza from Afragola. Her husband is shot so she sends her thirteen-year-old son to kill the assassin. He fails. All the men in her family are enlisted, and they go to war. Her order, the family of the killer is exterminated, and another family. One of Anna Mazza's hitmen is killed. The revenge? That killer is taken within a day, tortured with electricity, then crucified against a door – because a woman wanted it.'

From Rossi, 'We say of the women that they're clever, they're ignorant, they can't read and write, they're coarse or vulgar, but they're respected and feared. All of those are true of your mother, except that she's neither illiterate nor innumerate. She's clever and she's feared.'

She talked of her mother holding a meeting in the house, rare, and discussing a pending shipment from Venezuela, and seemed to acknowledge no blood ties, no family.

'The woman at the clan's heart enjoys the privilege given her – if she leaves it, she has nothing. Maybe it's more important to the women than it is to the men.'

'They say escape is impossible from Poggioreale, but Patrizia Ferriero succeeded in taking out her husband. The scam: she complained he had a severe kidney problem. She was the supreme fixer. She went to a hospital, bought the blood of a kidney patient, then arranged for it to be fed into a dialysis machine brought into Poggioreale to monitor his condition. She was allowed to transfer him to a hospital and he served his sentence in luxury. And she bought the policemen on guard duty with cocaine. Then, one day, he rose, and the police did not look, and he walked out of the hospital. Her driver and bodyguard was a former *carabiniere*. She was very intelligent.'

She talked in the flat tone about the mother who had not kissed, hugged or praised her.

'We think women are more capable at criminality, but less visible.'

'We believe that few women will stand against the lust, an orgasmic attraction, of power.'

'You owe your mother nothing.'

'An accident of birth does not have the right to demand loyalty.'

Immacolata said she would go to the kitchen and make lunch. Salad, fruit and cheese. She had not asked if she could run again in the gardens at the Villa Borghese.

Through his cleaned window, using the small mirror that he kept between his knee and the arm of his chair, Davide watched, saw the movement on the walkway and the bustle, and his head did not seem to waver or his eyes to move off the big-screen television. It was not usual for there to be so much movement, so many men, so early in the day. He thought he had seen, also, a clan leader, hustled along the walkway among guards towards the barred gate on level three. But his pay-masters were not concerned with the day-to-day, night-to-night dross life of the Sail. He watched everything. In his memory he noted everything. But he had witnessed nothing that would break his routine of meetings.

Eddie reckoned that in five more minutes he would have broken the chain's link. He worked feverishly, had pain in his arms and shoulders, more dust on his face and in his eyes, more sweat and—

The footsteps came.

With them there was music, louder, as if doors had been opened and not closed, and the music flowed closer with the footsteps. Not one pair – might be three. They had differing rhythms and weights. Eddie didn't know whether to use the last moment, as the footsteps came nearer, to try to break the link, or to leave the goddamn thing. Could have fought one, couldn't fight three. Low voices were above him. They would examine the handcuffs, see the scratch line, the sawed indentation, and know what he'd done. Wouldn't kill him, no. Might beat him. He heard the bolt pulled back, had the hood on his head and peeled down the hem, and the fraction of light from between the trapdoor's planks was gone. Darkness enclosed him.

What was the best that could happen? That the bucket was taken out. What was the worst? Eddie shivered. The sweat on him had no heat. He realised it was a tremble. A dog in a farmyard knows it has done wrong, is called and goes forward on its belly. He had seen that on the farm where the

heifers were, near his parents' place. Wanted still to hate the
man who had taken him off the street, wanted more to hear
him laugh and know he was not to be beaten. The trapdoor
was opened, the hinges groaning. The torch shone down and
light seeped below the hood. Hands grabbed him.

He could smell the breath – chilli, maybe, but onion and
nicotine too. He was pulled up. As he was dragged out through
the hatch there were hands under his arms. There were no
grunts, no wheezes – big men, powerful. His feet scraped
the edge of the hatch and he was swung clear. His hands
were dragged forward and he felt the pressure as a key was
inserted into the handcuffs' lock. They were removed. He
had enough freedom to run his hands over his wrists and
felt the smoothness of the welt he had made as he scraped.
Then the laughter broke round him, and the chain of the
handcuffs rattled – as if one manacle was held and the other
danced beneath it. He heard, then, the snap as the link was
prised apart. The laughter was more raucous. He waited for
the blow. He tried to duck his head and to have his hands
in front of his crotch, waited and— His arms were pulled
behind him and a plastic tie bit into the skin where it was
raw. He thought – and was bitter – they should be fucking
grateful to him for giving them a fucking laugh by trying to
break the fucking chain. All the hours he'd done, sawing and
scraping for nothing, had given them a laugh.

Eddie could have wept.

He was held. He heard one go down into the pit, and
there was the noise of the bucket swinging – whining – as
its handle took the weight, then an oath. Some of his urine
or faeces might have spilled out as it was hoisted. He heard,
also, the rustle of the plastic bag in which his food had been.
The rope at his ankles was untied. He was taken forward,
and the trapdoor dropped behind him.

New fear played with him, mocked him.

Was it now they would take his penis, his finger or his ear?

He had only her picture to cling to. He had the blown-up photograph on his wall, the smile, and was so far from it and . . .

He kicked out his foot, took a good step. He had verged towards self-pity: forbidden. Had edged into the area of regret – that he should never have come: forbidden. He tried to walk tall, upright.

He was led out of a building and his feet crunched on broken glass. A vehicle door opened, and he was pitched forward. He knew from the smells that it was the same van as before. He didn't think, now, that they would bring the knife to him. A rug or a blanket and maybe an old carpet were heaped on him and a boot pushed him against the bulkhead.

They went out of a yard on to a potholed track, then a tarmacked road.

Where was he going? Why was he being moved? What was the immediate future? It didn't fucking matter. Eddie lay on the floor of the van and rode with its motion. He didn't know of anybody out there who cared, so it didn't fucking matter. He was near to weeping, but held off.

It was Massimo, the lawyer's nephew and clerk, who met Anna Borelli, a legitimate meeting, not one that could have aroused suspicion. He met the aged lady on the broken pavement, among the cheap little clothing stalls on the piazza Nazionale, and they walked slowly together, her dictating the pace, towards the Poggioreale gaol. It was natural that Anna Borelli should wish to visit her two grandsons in the prison, and natural that a lawyer's clerk should attend with her – it was an opportunity to feed the prosecutor's reaction to the family.

The clerk didn't chivvy her to move faster. He was well paid, already owned a car and had bought a good apartment in the high complex of offices, hotels and accommodation close to the prison and the Palace of Justice. He had done better than any of his colleagues at the university in the Faculty of Law. He would, he realised, gradually take over greater responsibility for the legal affairs of the Borelli family – the Borelli clan. He was sucked in, pulled towards a vortex. How to step aside? Difficult. How to forsake the material rewards? More difficult. He believed, with the certainty of night following day, that his future would be eked out on the far side of the high wall, which had watchtowers, guards with guns, attack dogs, searchlights and cameras. He thought it had been only the brilliance of his uncle Umberto that had kept the old man from the cells in the blocks beyond the wall. He went slowly because he hated going inside the place. It had been built ninety years before. Massimo knew the statistics. It had statutory accommodation for eleven hundred inmates and actual accommodation for two and a half thousand. There was tuberculosis in the goal, hepatitis and HIV. A nine-hundred-metre subterranean tunnel linked the cell blocks to the Palace of Justice. It was a place of hell, but it was glorified in the folklore of the city: there, clan leaders had enjoyed carpeted cells, had had personal chefs and had drunk champagne. There, murders were commonplace, alliances forged. It was where he would go, and his uncle Umberto, into sardine-tin cells, into dirt and violence, if he did not break the link . . . But he had a high-performance car and a fine apartment with a balcony view of the mountain.

He told Anna Borelli of his uncle's meeting with the prosecutor. She did not reply immediately, but instead coughed, hard and grating, then spat phlegm ahead of her and let her laced shoe step in it.

They were near to the gate now. There, they would face banks of cameras and metal detectors, and they would go to cubicles for body searches. He was struck, always, by the quiet. With staff, some three thousand souls were inside the walls of rough-carved basalt from Vesuvio, but there was almost silence. Like many in the city, Massimo, the clerk, enjoyed the rewards of association and could not *quite* bring himself to break the link. Her voice was harsh in his ear. 'We should have drowned the bitch at birth. Now we should slice up that boy, use a bacon cutter on him, and send her the pieces.'

Massimo knew the old woman had made coffee for the boy, had brought him a slice of cake, and would have smiled and simpered at him while her husband went for the man, Salvatore. He had, in truth but unspoken, admired Immacolata Borelli. She was four years older than him, and had hardly seemed to notice him, but he had often thought of her – and his uncle would have approved.

'She has to be broken. Only when he is in pieces will she break. Tell the fat fool that – tell your uncle. Salvatore will understand.'

The smells hit him. He couldn't have said which was stronger, the urine, the sweat or the disinfectant. They went through the side gate.

Salvatore rode the pillion. The problem revolved in his mind. Would he use a sharpened short-bladed knife, a chopping knife or a knife with a line of tooth points? A knife for an ear, and a different one for a finger? And which one for a penis? It was what he thought of as he rode and his chest was tight against Fangio's back. They wove through the traffic, went fast, and the pistol barrel was hard in his groin. The problem, and the wind on his shirt, ripping at his shoulders, gave him a sense of power. They had gone through

Secondigliano, were now far away from his own territory, Sanità and Forcella. They were high above the bay and crossed the ground of the Licciardi and Contini clans. That part of Secondigliano was called by everyone, maybe even a postman, Terzo Mundo. If Secondigliano was the third world – another problem – what was Scampia? It was the war ground. He was used by Pasquale or Gabriella Borelli to enforce authority perhaps once a month and no more than twice. On these streets, and in Scampia, there were bodies on the pavements most nights. They had come off the Quadrivio di Secondigliano, gone past the low-security prison, the towers were to their left and they were on via Roma Verso Scampia. He had read a week ago, before the idiocy had started, in *Il Mattino*, that a sociologist had said: 'If you live in Scampia you have no hope of anything ever being better. You cannot have optimism. You have nothing and no possibility of legal work or anything that is psychologically rewarding. It is a prison. The boy growing up here as a teenager might as well be locked in the cells of a goal.' He had read that because it was on the same page as the story about himself, named, with a photograph. He had thought it a shit article about a shit place. He lived in safe-houses scattered through Forcella and Sanità, he was optimistic, his picture was on the screen of kids' phones, and he was rewarded. One day, *one day*, he would drive a Ferrari on the seafront at Nice and stay in a hotel, where a movie star would have stayed, and it would not be Gabriella Borelli in his bed – one day.

He saw the Sail again.

Fangio took him towards the great weather-stained mountain of concrete. He supported Carmine Borelli's decision to bring the boy here for safe-keeping, but he thought the old man had given too much in return: too much of a percentage of a shipment coming to the Naples docks in three weeks, too much of a share in a contract for the rebuilding of a sewage system on the north side of Sanità. He thought them peasants, *contadini*, here, but he had masked his anger when the weapon was taken from him and he was blindfolded.

They were on the via Baku. Salvatore did not know where Baku was, in what country, or why a street in Scampia was named after it.

They were waved down. He said who he and Fangio were, where he went and by whose authority, and he gave the registration of the van, its maker and colour, and then he was allowed to go through.

There had been that knot of men, another at the outer end of via Baku and more at the junction of the viale della Resistenza, otherwise near emptiness . . . He knew that, from every angle, he was watched.

He laughed.

The scooter swerved – Fangio had twisted. He laughed because he had remembered the scratched line in the manacles. He laughed at the effort, wasted.

He thought escape from here, from the Sail in Scampia, was impossible – as impossible as from the maximum-security wing at Novara, or the one for Sicilians at Rebibia. *Impossible*. He had not resolved which knife he would use, which blade.

He was jolted. The braking of the van, no warning, threw Eddie forward and his shoulder cannoned against the bulkhead. The back door was opened. No ceremony. A blanket was draped over him. He was moved fast. No voices.

Eddie thought it had been four or five paces from the van and into a building. He couldn't see, but he could smell – all the human smells but, above all, decay. They had hustled him inside but it seemed they were happy to slow and go at their own pace now, wherever they were. He was taken up a staircase. He didn't know whether it was enclosed or open, but there was no wind on his hands, and no sun's warmth, and the rest of his body was covered with the blanket.

He was not hit.

Small mercy. He was thankful.

Another flight of stairs – he'd tried to count. To count was to be positive. Reckoned, as best he could, that he was on a third floor, then went along some sort of corridor – it was wide because men were alongside him, to his left and his right, and they had his arms at the elbows. Not a word spoken. Would have said he went a clear hundred paces along the walkway.

Heard a knock, heard a door open in an instant response. Was jostled through the gap, narrow because one man led, he followed and another man had to wait to come behind. Now he heard a television set blaring, but not near. Bolts were drawn back, and another door opened. He was pushed and pulled inside a room, and knew the space was small and that there was no open window because he was hit by clammy warmth, suffocating.

A chain was put on Eddie's ankle – he felt its weight, tight against the bone. The blanket was pulled off, and the plastic strip that had gouged his wrists was cut.

The door closed, was bolted.

The sound of the television was gone, and silence crushed him. He did not start to learn his new prison, its dimensions. He slumped – stood against a wall, bent his knees and let his weight take him to his haunches, then toppled over. The chain tightened and he lay on his side. He had not bothered to remove the hood.

He wondered if he was beaten.

Lukas walked. It was good for him to feel the air of the city, to breathe it and learn from it. It might be the last chance he had to indulge himself, and he was mean with his time, did not willingly waste it. He soaked up what was around him.

He called it a 'tipping point', and had identified it from what Castrolami had told him. A mobile call, the Italian's phone clamped to his ear, the frown deepening, the gasps on the cigarette faster and deeper, the phone shut down. They had been close to the barracks at piazza Dante. He had been told of the meeting at which an official at the Palace of Justice had met the corrupt lawyer, one of those who always ran with bad guys, a photograph and a demand. He had asked them if he could walk, feel the small streets.

They crowded close to him. Hanging washing made an arch over him. Cooking scents fed him. Lukas went to a chapel, paid to go past the door, stood in awe and stared at Sammartino's *Veiled Christ*, so lifelike, marble made into flesh and cloth, and was in the majesty of the place for three minutes, no more, had learned and had pondered on the tipping point.

Not original. A lecturer at Quantico had spoken of a tipping point, had offered an analogy of the final gram going on to the scales and toppling the equilibrium. A legal assistant, drawing up the separation agreement in Charlotte, had talked of the tipping point as the moment when a failing relationship became irretrievable. A sociologist doing demography out of the Green Zone, in safe, comfortable Baghdad, had done the study on Sunni and Shia mixed neighbourhoods, but when one side began to leave – Shia or Sunni – the tipping point was reached when goddam ethnic cleansing was on its way, the flight started, and what had been mixed was now either Shia or Sunni. A tipping point was reached when what had meandered took on a new momentum.

It had.

A photograph and a demand changed the game. It increased the pressure on Castrolami and his people to keep the girl in line, and on Lukas to get the boy out. It increased the pressure on the girl he had seen running, and on the people who held the boy. Heavy pressure now – all different.

He did not have a map in his pocket. He was in an old city, on streets where shoes, sandals and boots had strolled, walked and trekked for two millennia. He did not know, could not have said, whether he was close or far distant from where Eddie Deacon was held, but Lukas seemed to flare his nostrils. He gazed at faces, at windows and at shadows. He was a fighter. It was his preparation once a tipping point had been reached.

He went to work, walked faster.

12

Three men brought food. Two filled the doorway, and the third came in. There was light behind them, above their heads and shoulders, and it flooded inside. He was still sitting, hadn't moved, cramped and stiff, but he pushed himself up. The man who came in was the guy who had snatched him off the street; the eyes were clear, cold and blue-grey. The fingers were long, delicate, almost a musician's. The lips were thin, without the life that blood brought, perhaps cruel. Eddie barely looked at the face, only the eyes and lips, then the fingers.

In the fingers there was a lightweight plastic plate, with slices of sausage and a portion of cheese. There was a plastic water bottle on its side. The plate was laid on the floor, but beyond Eddie's reach. A trainer toe edged it across the floor. The movement shook it and a piece of bread fell off on to the worn, grimy linoleum. It could not have been washed in months, maybe years – there was a tackiness to it that could have come from dried urine or spilled food. Eddie looked into the eyes: had it been an accident or done purposely? Nothing showed.

It was no matter to the guy that the bread had gone on the floor. The lips didn't move and no expression crossed his face. Eddie took the opportunity. He'd heard once that it was called 'peripheral vision', and he tried to keep his head static but to use his eyes to rake across the space. About eight feet square. About seven feet high. A window at the

top of one wall, but covered with heavy-duty hardboard –
he could see the pattern of the nails fastening it. There was
a metal bucket. There was a ring attached to the wall to
which the chain was fastened. There was graffiti on the walls,
which had once been whitewashed, but he couldn't read
what had been written. The door had steel sheeting on the
inside. All those things he absorbed and stored, and his head
didn't move. Why did he absorb, store?

It was his refrain. No self-pity, but acceptance of reality.
No one was coming for him. His life was in his own hands,
that sort of crap . . . Heavy, heavy stuff. He saw ants on the
floor, little beggars scurrying. The piece of bread off the
plate was in their line of march.

A voice: 'You are OK?'

Eddie gagged. Why did the bastard care? He didn't know
how he should reply to the hesitant question in accented
English.

'Well, there's a fucking chain on my—'

He was kicked. The trainer swung over the plate and the
toecap caught him a little above his right knee, hard. When
the foot swung back, the heel clipped the plastic plate, and
all the bread was on the floor, with the cheese and the sausage.
The water bottle rolled away. He wasn't kicked again but
the door was shut, locked and bolted, then nothing.

He would initiate a short debate. Better to say, in answer
to the question 'You are OK?', that he was fine, grateful for
the kindness and room service? Better to say that he was
not OK because he had a 'fucking chain' on his ankle? Better
to be passive, or better to earn a kicking? No decision taken.
No consensus of opinion. Better to crawl to the bastard, or
better to fight? Didn't know. How could he? They hadn't
done survival training at the sixth-form college in Wiltshire,
or at the university. At the language school there were no
extra-curricular classes in it. The kick had hit the bone above

the knee, and the bruising hurt, but he felt better for bawling out the bastard.

He wondered how far the ants had reached. Wondered if they had found his food on the floor. He squatted down, gave the chain a pull but merely jarred his wrists, then reached out, blind, to collect the bread, the sausage and the cheese. He had thought, when he had been able to see the food, that there might have been blue mould on the bread crust. Better when there was no light, and when he couldn't see the ant column.

Eddie ate his food. He didn't taste mould but had grit from the linoleum in his mouth, and didn't know if he had swallowed a platoon of ants. He ate part of the food left for him, then went to work.

He stood up. Stretching, leaving his weight on the manacled foot, he could touch the wall where the window was set. It would be his first target. He tried to get his fingernails into the space between the wall at the edge of the hardboard, but could not. He tried until the nail of his right forefinger cracked far down. The pain was sharp and he winced, then sagged back – maybe half a minute, no more. Stood again, stretched again – and again could get no leverage on the window. He realised more. His head was against the hardboard, his ear to it, but he couldn't hear anything: no music, no television, no kids, no laughter or shouting. What he did not hear told Eddie that there was soundproofing beyond the hardboard, which meant additional layers, and he couldn't shift the first layer, and he couldn't reach the door, and he couldn't shift the ring that held the chain – and he couldn't stop the pain in his finger from the broken nail. He'd once read something an academic had said on *courage*: 'The important thing when you're going to do something brave is to have someone on hand to witness it.' And he'd read something an American had said on *heroes*:

'We can't all be heroes because somebody has to sit on the kerb and clap as they go by.' Might have been both, might have been one – didn't know which – but he laughed. Good to laugh, bloody good. Not a big laugh, a belly laugh, a gut-shaker, but a pleasant enough chuckle.

New experiences walked with Eddie Deacon. On his hands and knees, on linoleum and in the crack where the edge met the base of the wall, he searched, wondering whether he was close to the ants' camp from which they came out to forage on his bread, cheese and sausage. While he searched he didn't think of the knife, which blade they would use. His hands pushed and probed. He didn't know what he was looking for, but he searched.

The game-show on television was new – one of the Milan-based independent channels – and the girls in the show went topless. It was the third week that Davide had watched it. He would have said, if asked for a true response, that he believed the girls on display were hopelessly anorexic . . . He didn't have that level of conversation in the Sail.

Ostensibly, in his chair in front of the television, it appeared to any man on the walkway peering through the cleaned, polished window, that Davide – the idiot, harmless – gazed longingly at the slack breasts that bounced on gaunt, lined ribcages. But the agent had the mirror wedged between his thigh and the side of the chair. He had seen much movement that day, more than was usual, and personalities.

He was an agent, a watcher, and had been sent on a crash course to gain the skills, was knowledgeable on the workings of electricity. Nobody, of course, who lived in the great Sail paid the state company for electricity. Nobody ever had to face final demands delivered by postal officials. Nobody was ever cut off for non-payment. Davide, as he was known, was not required to run cables from the main supply into the apartments on level three, but he was useful when a fusebox blew and when new plugs were needed. Then he was sent for. That was good. The poor, the derelicts and the addicts did not have the electrical appliances that blew out fuses. Men high in the chain of command did. That was good for his handlers.

Four months before, he had been to an apartment nineteen doors further along the walkway, and had wired in four new power sockets, had noted the carpeting and furniture, the shrine to the Virgin and a copy of Dostoevsky's *The Possessed*, in translation, on a table. So, Delta465/Foxtrot had identified the safe-house used by a principal clan leader on the third level of the Sail. He had seen the man, the reader of a Russian classic, that day. That man – who, the agent's handlers said, was among the four most influential and powerful crime players in the city – had walked past the polished windows surrounded by his guards. He had gone towards the apartment, and an old man, limping, with another man, had been escorted after him. Then the big player had come again past Davide's window, and a hooded man had been dragged by. His handlers would be interested only in information relating to that principal. His handlers were not policemen: they were interested only in the most senior men. Everything the agent saw he remembered, and to back his elephantine memory there were tapes.

His handlers had placed him in the Sail four years before. He was a crusader. He was there because he wished to make a difference. A son buried, and the heroin microbe gone in his veins to the grave. A wife had walked out on him, unable to weather the strain of an addict youth. At the time of the death and the walk-out, he had worked in a bank in a resort town on the Adriatic. He had volunteered himself, had not been accepted, had come to live in a neighbouring tower on the far side of the viale della Resistenza, had made the second approach, had been accepted, given a code name and a cover history that checked, had been found the apartment, number 374. Once every week he took the bus into town, reported and delivered tapes. Once, also, every week he went to the mini-mart and bought the basics of sustenance. The rest of his waking hours he spent watching the walkway, or sat behind a lace curtain in his bedroom, observing the street below.

He knew every pulsebeat of the Sail.

Knew the times that the buses came from the railway station down the hill on piazza Garibaldi. Scampia, with the Sail at its heart, was the narcotics supermarket of Italy, even of Europe. Both users and dealers took trains to come here from all over Italy, from Frankfurt and Berlin, Paris and Marseille, London, Birmingham, Manchester, Madrid and Barcelona. The regular bus service waited for them at the station, and if the police stopped the buses there were taxis. A watcher on a street corner, a teenage youth, was paid two hundred euros a day, and there were twenty *piazze*, each administered by a *capopiazza*. They were the locations where cocaine, heroin and ecstasy were sold in Scampia. All needed watchers, and watchers were employed in three shifts. An army had been recruited to watch the bus passengers coming in, and those driving their own cars, and to warn of the approach of the police. The boy who went from the customer to the dealer could make eight thousand euros a month – and eight hundred if he was, extraordinarily, to get a job in a factory. Each *piazza*, his handlers had told Davide, generated an income of fifty thousand euros a week, so the trade for this abandoned urban slumland brought in a guaranteed minimum of fifty million euros a year. Just what was sold on the streets of one suburb of the city. The figure, they emphasised, was a minimum. A young buck, if ruthless, if charismatic enough to find blind followers, can head a clan by the age of thirty – can be worth a billion euros. It was a fighting ground. In the late evenings, when his television was turned off, Davide would sit in his darkened bedroom and rely on the few streetlights still working for necessary illumination to watch trading and killing, linked. Clans clashed: assassins went after a man, couldn't find him, took his woman, tortured her for information on his whereabouts. She wouldn't tell so she was trussed and put into a car, which was torched: in Scampia. A man was beheaded with a butcher's axe: in Scampia. The assassins came to take a man from his mother's home – he had already fled; his mother, in her nightdress, was shot on her step and bled to death: in Scampia.

He watched, every day and every night, and knew the vagaries of the pulsebeat of the Sail . . . and a short bus ride from the stop on via Baku was the old city, patronised by the tourists, the lovers of fine arts and the gourmets, who did not know about Scampia.

His eyes flitted between the mirror against his thigh and the game-show. He knew that, in the depths of this monstrous building, a drama played around a hooded man.

'Don't ask me any questions. If you ask it will be wasted breath, yours, wasted time, mine. All I can say, what you tell me is of critical importance to the well-being of your friend, of Eddie.'

He had marched them down to the pub. Roddy 'Duck' Johnstone had taken a corner table, then gone to the bar, had been given a tray by the barmaid and had come back with two pints for each of the three lads – one missing, still at work – and a single Scotch for himself, six packets of crisps and six of peanuts.

His question: 'Tough or weak, determined or vacuous, hard or soft, serious or kid-like? Which is Eddie?'

He didn't need names, hadn't a tape-recorder and no need of a notepad.

From the club waiter, who would be late at work: 'He'd like you to think he's just a lazy tosser, that nothing matters to him, that he's a push-over. Maybe he was, but not any more. He's changed. Actually, he's quite tough. I think he's pretty determined.'

The PhD student's contribution: 'The role he acts is that he's weak and soft – just a prat, really. Maybe he was. Everything's altered, though, hasn't it? A new man, our Eddie. Quite funny to watch it.'

Hunched forward, the Revenue and Customs clerk said, 'He wanted to seem a kid still, never going to grow up – like the thing he'd run a mile from fast was responsibility. That's in the past. Gone to the recycle bin. Different guy – and maybe carrying us with him. Tough? Probably, and getting tougher. Determined? Wouldn't have jacked the job and done what he has if he wasn't. Hard and serious, I suppose so – but it's like I said, and *us* too.'

He listened. He let them tell their anecdotes, put more pints in front of them and didn't speak until he felt he'd drained them.

Late, Duck asked, 'What was different? How had he changed? What was new?'

Like a chorus, spoken together: 'It was Mac. She turned up. That is one fantastic person. Immacolata was what was different. She changed him, maybe us. Immacolata was the new thing. Sorry and all that if we don't express it well. Immacolata was brilliant. Any guy would be crazy not to go after her. Are you going to tell us what this is all about? What's of critical importance?'

He bought a last round, more crisps, and left them.

He drove back to his office, went inside. He started to type and tried to express what three pretty inarticulate guys, decent enough, second-rate enough, had said about their friend and about the girl – and didn't know whether he did a good job or a poor one, and whether he had painted a fair enough portrait of her.

Could she go into the Borghese and run?

Rossi said she couldn't.

Why not?

'Because Castrolami has to give permission, and he's in Naples.'

Why was he in Naples?

'I think you know, Signorina. Try to remember, please, the lie you told.'

The tape-recorder had been put away. Of course it was foolish to imagine they would allow her to run in the darkness. She worked towards the challenge.

Could they go that evening to a restaurant?

Orecchia said they could not.

Why was it not possible to eat in a restaurant?

'It requires the permission of the investigating agent, Castrolami, or of the prosecutor. Both are in Naples, and I won't call them for this. There is food in the kitchen.'

Why were they in Naples?

Orecchia did not look up from his magazine. 'I think you know very well, Signorina, what business they have in Naples. If you hadn't lied it would have been different, but you did. You aren't going to run or to a restaurant.'

She stood then, legs a little apart, pelvis forward, head back, chin jutted, and built on the challenge. 'Am I difficult? Are many collaborators "difficult"? Will you write a report on me as difficult?'

Rossi said, 'A few aren't particularly helpful.'

Orecchia said, 'Some, not many, go on believing, Signorina, that they're still on the pedestal they enjoyed while their family was Cosa Nostra or 'Ndrangheta or Camorra. Some, until they have disabused themselves, are "difficult". We believe they're frightened of the reality of their situation – which they created of their own free will. You can flounce, pout, stamp, throw plates and slam doors, shout or wave your boobs and fanny at Alessandro, but nothing will change.'

She sucked in her breath, prepared to bare her spirit.

'I should tell you that Alessandro's wife is exceptionally attractive. Very much more attractive, mentally and physically, than you.'

She spat the question: 'What's happened to him?'

They looked at her dumbly. Perhaps they'd practised their expressions of incomprehension. Orecchia had returned to his magazine, as if he didn't understand who 'him' was. Rossi had not reacted to the description of his wife. Orecchia's tone had been harsh and unforgiving, as if he had spoken to a child in a school room – not that such a volley of insults had ever been directed at Immacolata Borelli at school. Her mother had brought her on the first day to the Forcella infants' classroom. The head teacher and the year teacher had been lined up as if she was heiress to the Bourbon dynasty. A seat had been found for her at the front of the room, and the staff had bowed and scraped because she was the daughter of the Borelli clan. Her father had taken her on the first day to the middle school, had materialised from his life as a fugitive, and slipped an envelope stuffed with banknotes into the hand of the head teacher, murmuring about new electronic equipment. It had been pocketed, with discretion. Her eldest brother, Vincenzo, had escorted her to the senior school, and had oozed power as he walked alongside her into the building. At every level of school she had attended, her marks in examinations had been exceptional, her reports remarkable. She was the daughter of the Borelli family, and no teacher would have been stupid enough to mark her down or criticise her. Only at the accountancy and book-keeping college had she been treated, almost, as another kid – and there she had met her friend, Marianna Rossetti, and . . . Orecchia and Rossi spoke to her as if she was any other child, one who was not given the seat of privilege at the front.

She repeated it, more shrilly: 'What has happened to him? What has happened to Eddie?'

Their eyes met. Unspoken acceptance that something must be said, something minimal.

Orecchia said, 'The boy you indicated was unimportant to you? Yes? We don't know what has "happened" to him.'

Rossi said, 'Signorina, we are very junior links in a very long chain. We would not be told the latest intelligence. We don't know.'

'Castrolami would tell you if he knew anything, or the prosecutor.'

'We are merely functionaries. They don't share that sort of information with people at our level.'

Doubt clouded her. 'You know nothing?'

'Nothing.'

'Nothing of substance.'

She went to her room, didn't bang the door but closed it carefully. She stood at the window and gazed out over the roofs, and myriad lights stretched away from her. None was in the home of a friend, or lit the street of a friend, or was driven on a road by a friend. She had no friend in this city. She stripped, let her clothes fall, and stared out of the window at the expanse of lights. The air chilled her skin. It hurt that she didn't know what had happened to him – hurt that she had made a play in her mind of ignorance.

She knew what happened to members of the family of a collaborator, to their friends and lovers. Ignorance was not a screen behind which she could hide.

She thought it was Orecchia's voice she could hear, and imagined he had telephoned Naples to tell Castrolami of her hysteria – but had not rated it a problem.

Off the operations room at the piazza Dante barracks there was a square annexe space, four metres by three, no more. Into it had been crowded a work surface, six computer screens and keyboards, the same number of chairs and scattered telephones and, at the edge, more chairs. There was no window, and cigarette smoke fogged the air.

He knew the names of the two men who shared the work surface with him, but Lukas did not make conversation, had no wish to or need to; neither did he think it would be welcomed. One was the *carabinieri* unit's *psicologia*, the other was the unit's intelligence collator. He bided his time because experience had taught him that the psychologist and the collator had to be won over, would not respond to being battered into submission. Lounging against the annexe walls there were sometimes three, sometimes four, of the fast-reaction team – Lukas knew about the Raggruppamento Operativo Speciale – their kit scattered at their feet: flak-vests, caps, windcheaters, boots and radios. Down a corridor there were more of them. He was an intruder, tolerated only because word would have come from Rome that he had saved the life of a colleague: it allowed him to be accepted but not welcomed. That would come later, *if* he could insinuate himself without breeding hostility. They talked Italian round him and he gave no sign of understanding a word they said. He had good Italian but, as with other European languages, he favoured often disguising the fact.

A concession: he had been brought coffee, with a ham-and salad-filled roll.

He learned that every informant in the city, used by the Squadra Mobile of the police and by the *carabinieri*'s serious crime squad, had been alerted to the kidnap of the English boy. Learned also that teams scoured CCTV tapes for evidence of the abduction and the movement of a hostage. Learned as well that the grandparents of Immacolata Borelli were now under twenty-four-hour surveillance, as was their lawyer, as were all known associates, and that the watchers and tailers had been stripped from high-profile targets. Learned that one of the clans' most effective and feared assassins, the Borelli family's man, was loose on the streets, location unknown. Learned that an ear, a finger or a penis was expected in the post, soon.

And Lukas learned that the informants had produced nothing. Learned that the CCTV tapes had given up nothing, or the surveillance operation. He would have said that the faces around him were not cut by disappointment: he sensed fatalism, the inevitability of failure. Too early in the relationship with the annexe for him to chivvy, far too early to press a point. Did time exist for the niceties and the protocols? It had to. An alternative did not.

Lukas would know when he was accepted by the psychologist and the collator, the guys from the ROS, the storm squad, when they took his cigarettes and offered him their own . . . Not yet. They smoked theirs and he smoked his, but the coffee and the roll were a start.

As a kid from the trailer park, he had found virtue in waiting and patience. Any kid from a trailer home – a father who was part-Brit, part-Polish, and gone in search of better-carat gold-paved streets, a mother who was part-American, part-Italian, who cleaned offices, no money sloshing in pockets – knew that waiting and patience paid dividends. He would wait with patience until his opinion was asked and advice requested. Already he sensed a poor outcome was anticipated.

Could have been worse. There was an icon story about hostage negotiation, had to be true, too precious not to be.

Some said the icon was a British guy, having a real black day, climbing a crane ladder to a jerk sitting on a spar above him, squealing that he was about to go fly and that he'd not be talked out of it, mind-made-up crap. The icon had shouted back: 'Way I'm feeling this morning, friend, way my missus is carrying on, do you mind if I come up there and join you? We can bloody jump, fly, together.' The story was that the Brit guy meant it – would have. The story also was that the jerk didn't want to share and came straight down. There was always somewhere that it was worse for someone.

It was getting late, and there was room in the ashtray, on the table between Lukas, the psychologist and the collator, for maybe six more butts. He'd stay that long . . . It was always about intelligence. The psychologist could feed in opinions, but intelligence gave facts – and nothing came.

Late that evening, he walked with the prosecutor. It was difficult for either man to say that he was subjected to a greater or lesser emotion – or no emotion – than usual when they knew a wretch was beyond reach. Both the prosecutor and Castrolami relished the cool of the air, almost a chill on the face, drying the day's sweat. They were outside the palace and traversed the wide piazza, with the towers of the financial district, the Holiday Inn and sought-after apartments ahead. On what they earned as servants of the state, Castrolami and the prosecutor had no chance of purchasing or renting a place in one of those blocks. Neither did they need the services of the financial institutions lodged there, but to their right was a church, a better place. Lights beamed from it, and Castrolami could see the figures inside. He thought it a rehearsal for a wedding.

There were bodyguards behind them, the prosecutor's, a pair of men. The church drew them as they talked.

The desk at piazza Dante reported nothing.

Rome reported a crisis point.

What to do?

The church was modern, finished in 1990, and the concrete of its slim pyramid shape, and the narrowing twin towers that supported the bell, was not yet weather-stained. It was named after a saint, Carlo Borromeo – died 1584, aged forty-six, in Milan of a fever from the plague sweeping the city; he had helped the sick at great personal risk and paid for it with his life. It was a dramatic building, a feature of the *centro direzionale*, and the prosecutor was a familiar figure there. He led Castrolami inside.

The bride was not beautiful and the groom was not handsome; she wore a skirt about three centimetres too short and the other faded jeans. They pledged their future, and had good voices.

Castrolami said, 'I had felt her to be strong. Now I sense weakness.'

The prosecutor's voice was soft, would have been inaudible to the couple, their supporters, the priest, and the woman who worked the portable CD player for their music. 'I always look for a priority.'

'Her evidence statement, taken with full legal cover, her appearance in person in court as a witness.'

'I look for a priority, then for accommodation of it.'

'There is no accommodation – excuse me. There cannot be.'

'We cling, then, to the priority.'

'The statement, then the appearance. There can be no manoeuvre.' Castrolami shrugged. Perhaps then he thought of his own marriage. His wife, severe-faced, wrapped in sheets of white material, and himself in a full-dress uniform, a serious dispute within a week over the date of her mother's first overnight stay at their one-bedroom apartment: his mother-in-law and his wife would share the marriage bed, and he would sleep in the living room on a pump-up – no accommodation, no compromise, no manoeuvre. Extraordinarily, he had stayed long enough with his wife to produce three children. He visited each year, stayed a few days, drank too much, then piled, with relief, on to the fast train from Milan to the south. He was – his own words – pathetic, sad *and* a committed, dedicated, single-minded, focused investigator. He supposed that – in an inexplicable fashion – he represented the hopes of the girl with the short skirt and the boy in old jeans. 'The priority alone is worthy of consideration. She goes to court, she gives evidence. There is no question of stepping aside from the priority.'

'The boy came of his own free will. He was not volunteered. We'll do what we can for him.'

'He doesn't intrude on the priority.'

'Even if we condemn him.'

'I want to bring her back to the city.'

They watched the taking of the mock vows, heard the moment of laughter filtering through the high building as the couple were invited to kiss, and did so with rare passion. Castrolami told the prosecutor what he wanted, why and when, and it was agreed.

'And the boy? Attractive, intelligent, interesting?'

'It doesn't matter,' Castrolami said. 'We've decided on the priority. He is in second place.'

The prosecutor bowed towards the altar where the couple talked small detail with the priest, crossed himself, then turned for the door. He was reflective. 'In the world war, there were occasions when a ship was torpedoed and sunk, and sailors were in the water, injured and choking on oil, but because the enemy's submarine wasn't located ships didn't dare to stop and pick up the survivors. They sailed past and through them. It was a question of priorities. I think they weigh heavily.'

'We'll do what we can,' Castrolami said flatly. 'Priorities rule us. A great truth can't be ignored.'

'Good night. Pray for him.'

They parted, turned their backs on the church.

Nobody could refuse her. Nobody could dare to leave a shuttered window, a locked door and a darkened interior for her.

With a slow, crabbed step, Anna Borelli – in her eighty-eighth year – came late that evening along the via Duomo. She had already been the length of the via Carbonara, up the slope on the right and down on the left, and before she was finished she would have traversed the via dei Tribunali, the west side. Some boys walked with her. They had been ordered to stay outside the shops and bars she visited, but they were seen and they carried hand weapons – axe handles, a baseball bat, a claw hammer – and they had mobile phones linked to an outer ring of watchers. It was not necessary for her to intimidate. All paid the *pizzo*. It was not inside the perimeters of reality to avoid payment.

She was a small crow of a woman.

She stepped among filth and rubbish because those streets were not on the tourist routes. There was a corner, a junction, where Carmine had shot a rival more than a half-century before; had fired two shots and one had missed the target, the rival's head; there was still the mark in the stone by the bar's entrance where the bullet had struck. There was a bar, now under the clan's control, in which five shots had been fired into the ceiling before Carmine had been accepted as protector. There was a vehicle-repair yard where a body – a man killed by Carmine, manual strangulation – had been kept for five days before it had been safe to move it to the pits of a factory's foundations into which concrete was poured. She walked well, and felt the control that power gave, and fear. People on those streets begged for her cracked smile and blessed her when she gave it.

She called on those shopkeepers, small businesses, cafés and bars, and all were there though it was now late in the evening. She was admitted and shown the books. She discussed profit margins and heard dismal explanations of the pressures from global, national and local economic recession.

Unmoved, Anna Borelli told them what they should – in the future – be paying. In very few of the premises did she offer a reduction or no change in the amount paid monthly in the *pizzo*. She raised the protection fee, and in so doing she gave the impression that her daughter-in-law had allowed slackness to creep into the affairs of the clan. Those for whom the price was hiked did not complain, bluster, argue. There had been a woman, four years ago, who owned a paint store in the San Giovanni district: she had refused payment, and also to cash a cheque made out for a hundred thousand euros. Men had been imprisoned and the woman had been in the newspapers; and even in *Time* magazine. There had been demonstrations in support of her, but nothing had changed and people still paid as they had before. The woman lived under police guard now and made no money. An empty gesture, Anna Borelli thought.

With some, she gossiped about their children. With some she talked about her husband – a bladder problem and difficulty in the hips. With a few she recounted the situation in the Poggioreale that faced her grandsons, the misunderstood, persecuted Giovanni, the innocent, gentle Silvio. With others she discussed the circumstances of the incarceration in the north of her only son, Pasquale, and the brutality of the prison officers. All of them, she knew, would have liked to talk about the *infame*, the treachery of her granddaughter, Immacolata. None did. None dared. The majority had had their *pizzo* fixed by Immacolata and confirmed by Gabriella Borelli. All knew the girl. She was not spoken of.

The old woman knew that when she left each of the premises, and the door was locked, the shutters dropped, the lights turned off, it would be Immacolata – the whore – whose name flitted on the lips, and there would be sniggers. The bitch was dead. A grandmother had decreed it. The whore, the traitor, the *infame* was condemned.

Her secret: she knew also what leverage could be exerted on the girl who was damned – as a lemon was squeezed until the pips burst through the rind.

He searched. He crawled on the floor, went as far as the chain permitted him: there was no concrete ridge on this floor and the chain links were double the thickness of those in the bunker. That opportunity would not be repeated. He started again, and searched.

Couldn't find a thick woollen red sock under the bed or the easy chair or in a corner of his room in Dalston. And couldn't find a shoe in his room at his parents' home in Wiltshire. Couldn't find the big bright-coloured folders with his teaching notes that he'd left lying in the staff room at the college. The idea of Eddie Deacon on his hands and knees in darkness, relying on touch to a methodical, careful, painstaking search would have appeared ludicrous to the guys in the house, or his mum and dad, or to the other lecturers. They would have had him down as a 'shambles' in personal organisation, 'untidy' to a degree, simply 'chaotic'. The chain rattled, responding to each movement of his trailing leg.

He wasn't hungry or thirsty, but it seemed an age since he had eaten the food brought him.

He had lost track of the times when it was necessary to eat

and drink. Get up in the morning, in Dalston, wash, shave, do his teeth and use the toilet, then down the stairs and *must* have a slice of toast from old bread past its date, *must* have with it a smear of margarine and jam, *must* have coffee to wash it down. A break for lunch at work. Bells ringing, lecture rooms emptying, and sandwiches, rolls or instant soup in the staff room, *must* have something or all known forms of life would end. A microwave meal in the evening, or a trip to a cheap Italian, a curry house or the Afghan was a *must*-do, and the familiar corner seat afterwards in the pub and some pints. Down to his mother and father's at a weekend and *must* have a piece of beef, pork or a leg of lamb for lunch – life couldn't go on without it. Eddie had no watch, no sense of hours passing, no knowledge of when darkness would come beyond the boarded-up window, no hunger and no thirst.

What did he look for? He didn't know.

Why did he look for something? There was no acceptable alternative. It wasn't acceptable to lie back and wait for them to come with the knife.

He did the floor and the walls, smoothed them with his fingertips and used the sensitivity of his palms. Didn't find anything. Found nothing that was of use. Only the clank of the chain kept him company. He had gone round the floor, up the walls and round the blocked window, but had found nothing.

He began again.

He made a change. He took the image of Immacolata out of his mind, as if it was a transparency slide and slotted in a projector, and replaced it with the image of his captor – the man he hated – and kept it in his mind. Like a new day starting. Was he delirious? Was he hallucinating? Was the face a fantasy? It had its use: it concentrated him.

He worked at the search, and had a refrain: he must save himself because no one else would.

★

The streets around the *pensione* were raucous, crowded, exploding with noise and movement. Lukas came through the door, which swung shut behind him. Inside there was stillness.

He was handed his key by a small man, dapper and neat. Lukas thanked him. 'You're Giuseppe?'

'I am, sir.'

'You're the day manager?' Lukas wore his best smile. 'And it's night. I thought I'd see you in the morning.'

'Better at night . . . and my friend's baby has a colic so . . .' The man shrugged. Lukas recognised the conspiracy. He had asked, on leaving that morning and handing over his key – briefly but not furtively – to meet the next day. He hadn't expected the duty rosters to be juggled. The man flashed his eyes across the darkened hall, looked briefly, but fast and comprehensively, for an eavesdropper, but the bar was empty, the breakfast room deserted and in shadow. 'I took my friend's shift. You are, sir?'

Lukas did a droll grin. 'I am who my passport says I am.'

'Of course, sir.'

Truth was, end of a long day, Lukas could not have remembered with certainty which passport he had used when he checked in. It wasn't that he was difficult, secretive, covert – he just couldn't remember which goddam passport he'd had, and thought that age crept up on him, stabbed him in the back.

'It was a Canadian passport, sir,' the day manager said, impassive.

From under the reception desk, a bottle was produced, with a couple of plastic beakers, and measures were poured. Lukas saw the shake in the day manager's hand. He didn't offer money. Might, but later. The best intelligence, in Lukas's experience, was not bought.

'It's about the boy.'

'Yes, sir.'

'I would have talked to you this morning, but you had breakfasts, check-outs, the Dutch complaining about the hot water . . .'

Still dry: 'I had the New Zealanders who wanted a reservation in Sorrento for two nights and the Greek couple had fucked – excuse me, sir – till four in the morning, my friend told me, and broke the bed. They want a replacement not repair.'

'It's about the boy.'

'I understood that, sir. Forgive me, sir. The world comes across my lobby, dresses in many ways and has many ages, many disguises. You're not a tourist. You have no map and no book, and do not ask directions to the Palazzo Reale, the Castel dell'Ovo or the Teatro San Carlo, and no businessman stays here. I understand, sir.'

'We have to trust each other.'

'I expected you – someone. I made a telephone call. Perhaps I regret it. I realised afterwards there would be consequences. Someone would come. It is a city where humble people – myself – do not seek attention. I have to trust you . . . or I walk off the beach and into the sea.'

'You have my word,' Lukas said. His right hand took the day manager's, his left lifted the beaker and brushed it against the other's. He held the hand while he sipped bad brandy. He respected informants – many did not. The Brits, he knew, had put up bureaucratic barricades to block entry to Iraqi collaborators. They were lonely and unloved by most handlers, seldom thanked for the risk taken. He knew it from the FBI days. Lukas would have thought that a few hundred euros palmed across the desk would have insulted the integrity of the day manager. He did good sincerity when he guaranteed his word – and meant it. Many he had known, attached to Task Force 145 out at Anaconda in the Balad base, who did a year's Iraq duty, had handled agents, milked their udders dry, then cut them adrift. Lukas had little sentiment, but he appreciated that agents who volunteered help were vulnerable – like the day manager. 'My word is good.'

'I telephoned the family of Eddie Deacon.'

'That's why I'm here.'

'It is not yet in the newspapers, his capture.'

'They're trying to keep it suppressed. Can't do that for many more days.'

'I did not see him taken.'

'Tell me.'

'I was brought a piece of card. It is what we give to guests, our address and phone, and we write on it his room number. It was dropped in the street.'

'And picked up and brought to you?'

'Yes.'

'By a witness?'

'Yes.'

'Who was the witness?' Lukas saw the squirm on the day manager's features. One thing to have involved himself, another to involve his informant. Lukas understood, in this culture and in this city, what would be an informer's reward: death would come like mercy. Twice the day manager seemed to rehearse a statement but nothing was said, then . . . Lukas could have sworn, did not. An Australian couple, young, handsome, bronzed and near to collapse, came through the door. His eye was already closing and the bruise had started to swell, while below the hem of her shorts the knees were grazed. He backed away. Heard the babble about her handbag, the snatch from the motor scooter. Her dragged along the gutter. Him catching the shoulder of the snatcher who rode pillion and being lashed clear by the driver's elbow. In the bag were passports, plastic and some cash and – Christ, did they think they were in bloody Woolagong on

the Bondi? Christ, didn't they know they were in Naples,
Italy? He knew about Woolagong from a Special Forces guy
who had a girl there and they'd spent long hours waiting
for the assets to turn in something of value. Lukas thought
he had lost his man.

He hadn't.

The brandy was produced again. More beakers were found.
The Australians were given alcohol, were sat down. The day
manager said he was going to telephone the police, but as
he lifted the phone he murmured into Lukas's ear: 'In via
Forcella, at the bottom, is the home of Carmine and Anna
Borelli, old people. He came out from their home and was
taken. There is a stall for fish beside the outer door. He is
Tomasso. He will have returned from the market at dawn.
He saw it. Have I killed myself? Have I killed him?'

'I gave you my word. The key, please.'

The day manager dialled, 112, then started to shout. He
did well. He stood in the corner of the robbed couple and
demanded an appointment for them the following morning.
Lukas thought it all bullshit, but the Australians would have
been pleased with his vigour. While he shouted, he handed
Lukas his own room key and a second. He thought the
Greeks had had their bed repaired or a new one had been
moved into their second-floor room. He went on up, climbed
a further flight.

There was police tape on the door.

He broke it, used the key and went inside. He experienced
the feeling that a law-enforcement man never lost on going
into private space with entire legitimacy but as a trespasser.
The room had been searched, but he reckoned the check
had been perfunctory, done without interest or enthusiasm.

Later he would sit on the bed, think and contemplate. He
believed in the value of association, with a suitcase, clothes
or just where there had been a presence. So little of Eddie

Deacon was there. The bag, clothes on the floor, including the previous day's socks and boxers. There was a passport, a wallet with a few euros. Lukas thought the boy had left behind as much as possible before venturing out. In the wallet was the photograph. The picture brought alive the girl he had seen run in the gardens; more important, it brought alive the boy. He had been, perhaps, a hundred yards from her in the villa Borghese gardens; here he was close and could touch her, could almost smell her, and hear the laughter that seemed to ring from the picture, infectious. He saw the prettiness, the vitality and the youth, not matched in Rome seen at a distance. He knew, holding the photograph under the ceiling light, why Eddie Deacon had crossed the continent to bring back the girl. In his trade, he was not supposed to feel emotion and relate to victims – it was thought dangerous for involvement to feature. He knew about hostage rescue, hostage negotiation and the co-ordinator's job of evaluating talk against force, and his whole life was the work . . . Lukas had never loved.

The work made do as his family. Could have been inside the broad family of the Bureau, or in the gargantuan family of the military, or in the close, tight-knit family of Ground Force Security. Love was now, had been in the past, absent from Lukas. He had admired his mother. He had felt affection for his wife, Martha, at first. He had not reacted to his son's birth on a date after the divorce was finalised. He looked a long time at the face of the girl.

Then, he had seen enough.

He left everything as he had found it, except the photograph from the wallet. He laid the picture with care in the breast pocket of his shirt, careful neither to bend nor mark it. It was the photograph that screwed Lukas's intention to deny any emotional involvement. He looked around him for a last time, switched off the light, closed the door, locked it, then resealed the jamb with the adhesive police tape. He went off down the corridor and down the stairs, and the Greeks were still at it. He felt, as if it was a weight on him, the picture in his pocket, saw the smile and heard the laugh.

Good if it had been possible to make promises.

'Can't do it, kid,' he murmured. 'It's not a business where promises are possible. Sorry, but you have to appreciate that.'

His own room would be so empty, and without a photograph to light it.

13

He didn't know how long he had slept but, blessed relief, it had been dreamless, without nightmares. He had rubbed his eyes hard, stretched, scratched and had started again to search.

He talked quietly to himself, a whisper or a murmur – seemed to take the guys in the Dalston house as an audience. 'What's strangest is that I can't hear anything from outside this place and I can't see anything inside it. I have no light, and there's no noise, other than my breathing and the chain. I've just slept on linoleum with no blanket under or over me. Where my mum lives, if a dog had to sleep on linoleum without bedding then someone, sure as hell, would be complaining to the animal-rights people.'

The routine of the search hadn't changed from before he'd slept. He did sections of the floor and the walls, on his hands and knees, on his knees, crouched and standing.

'I don't know what I'm looking for, but I'm going round again until I find it. Off my trolley, right? Might be, and I won't argue with you. What sort of clears the mind, though, is the thought of that knife – ears, fingers and privates. Get me? Makes for good encouragement.'

Had to answer that, didn't he? Had to face it. Couldn't simply squat on his backside and wait for whatever the world threw at him. There was a knife on call. It was laborious, conscientious and repetitive but – too right – the thought of the knife kept boredom at bay.

'I wouldn't have thought it possible to exist without sound

or light. It is. I have to find something. I have to believe there's something to be found.'

It was the last sector of floor and the last area of wall, and he had gone over them, fingertips and palms, five or six times. When he had completed the sector, he would start again at the beginning where the chain was fastened. A success: the discovery of the crevice through which the ants went back and forth. Before he'd brushed them clear they'd countered the obstruction of his hand by crawling over it. There was dust at the angle where the linoleum met the wall's base. Sometimes he forced it away from the wall, at others he didn't. Sometimes there was compacted dirt at the angle and he would run his fingertip into it, excavate it, and at others not. He had lost track, had been round so many times in the search, of where he had prised up the flooring and where he had scraped at the mess caught in the join . . . but this time he felt something hard, and almost squealed. 'Guys, it's there. I have it.'

Hard and sharp, long and thin, buried and wedged. He must, each time before, have thought its slight shape was a flaw in the wall or a bulge in the linoleum. It came away. It had been deep in the dirt. Perhaps, on the previous searches, he had dislodged some of its covering or shifted it fractionally. He held a nail, and euphoria swept through him. It was a strong nail, a little bent in the middle, but otherwise flawless.

'Can't see, no eyes, have to do it all by touch. The nail's about four inches long. I'd run my fingers along that place so many times, and now it's there and I have it. Not thinking at my best – sorry and all that – and not being logical. It's the window, the boarding across it, which was nailed and the nail heads recessed. Always, isn't there, one nail that bends, jumps back and falls, and who has the patience to get down and find it? It's no damn use anyway because it's bent – but it's a nail and I have it.'

He would have found one like it in the cardboard boxes his father kept in the shed, built as a lean-to at the far end of the garage. He had nails and screws of every size, calibre, length, and always said they should be kept because it was 'a certainty of life that if you don't have them all then the one you want will be the one you don't have'.

'Do any of you guys know what to do with a nail? Do they hand out nails in that toffs' club or at Revenue and Customs or on a campus for PhD students or in the ticket hall of a main-line station? I doubt it. What I'm thinking is that a four-inch nail, even a bent one, is either a multi-task tool or a multi-task weapon. Can I have your thoughts, guys?'

His mind had begun to race: it could be used as a chisel, turned into a bar for leverage, could be a screw-driver, a stabbing knife – used against a soft stomach, an eye, a throat.

'You disappoint me, you know that? Are you still in bed? Washed and shaved yet, in the bathroom queue? Not gone to work? Don't know what time it is. Is it a tool or a weapon? You're useless sods.'

They wouldn't have known – how could they? – the value of a nail that was probably rusted, certainly blunt, and bent halfway up its length. He hadn't been so clever either: he'd found the nail directly under the window hatch, which was boarded with heavy-duty plywood. The nail heads that held it in place, immovable, were recessed down. It was the obvious place to have searched and searched again. It was now his most important possession. Eddie doubted there was anything in the Dalston house, belonging to any of them, that competed with the importance of a single nail. And nothing in his parents' home – prints from numbered editions, wide-screen TV, DVD player, jewellery that only came out of the wall safe for special occasions – was as important as the nail.

'They're useless, Mac. Couldn't kick their way out of a

paper bag, tossers. Mac, help me. There has to be a use for it. Do me a favour, Mac, and tell me what I can do with it.'

Couldn't see it, could only touch it. Eddie started to think.

A dog barked at her from its high balcony. A maid, muffled against the morning cold, shuffled past her on flip-flops and went to work – she would have been Somali born, and taught already not to stare into the faces of Italians. A dustcart came round a corner. A porter, without his tie on, his collar unbuttoned, stood in front of the lobby of a block and coughed on his first cigarette of the day. Dawn was a smear, far away and grey on the mountains.

Immacolata walked down the street, past the long-stay parked cars with Saharan sand on their bonnets and roofs. A few lights were on above her, but most of the apartments were still dark. It had been easier than she could have believed.

She hadn't showered and risked the noise of the apartment's plumbing, but she had washed quietly. She had dressed simply, trousers and T-shirt, a hooded sweatshirt of Rossi's, and trainers. They took turns to watch over her. Rossi had been in his room and she had heard his soft snore. The older man was in a chair in the living room and, had he been awake, would have had a clear view of the main doorway in the hall – but he had not. Half dressed, Orecchia had been sprawled on a settee, mouth open, eyes closed. A mug of coffee stood beside him, untouched, and a cigarette had burned out in the ashtray. The strapping holding the holster in place was across his open shirt, and the weapon – she recognised the types of pistol on offer and this was a Beretta – was loaded. She had skirted the room, slipped behind Orecchia and crossed the hall. She had slipped back the bolt, turned a key, gone out, closed the door gently. She had gone down the main staircase, not used the lift, and had seen no one. Half of the residents of the lower floors were still on the dreg days of their summer holiday. Had she met any she wouldn't have spoken – wouldn't have shown them what they would have recognised as a proletariat accent from Naples. The hill where they had housed her was among the most select neighbourhoods in the capital, and there would have been immediate protests at the thought of a collaborator harboured among them. She had gone out, and the chill had been on her skin.

She carried her handbag, nothing else.

She went past the clinic, past the tennis and swimming club, where sprinklers already played on the grass, past shops in the piazza where the steel shutters were down and nothing moved, except one scurrying cat.

It was a brisk walk. She wouldn't run: that would draw attention to her, but she needed to be clear of the *covo*, and off the hill, before the sun rose over the mountains that formed the spine of Italy. She stepped out, and the pace she took helped to warm her. She went down the hill, was under the canopy of pine branches, then beneath the big highway, the via Flaminia, and walked along the river, but hugged the trees and tried to stay in the shadows.

Ahead of her was the piazzale di Ponte Milvio, where the early-morning buses were parked, and a long taxi line where drivers waited for the day's first fares.

She knew where she was going, and why.

And in the square there were shops and bars. It was too early for her, but if she hadn't gone before dawn, before Rossi's alarm went on his wrist, before Orecchia shook himself, yawned and stirred, she wouldn't have been able to slip away.

Sunlight speared her, caught her face, and her hair fell back as she tossed her head. Her shoulders were squared and her chin was thrust forward.

She cared nothing for the chaos she would have created
when the alarm sounded and Orecchia woke.

He had gone from the *pensione* in the half-light. The day
manager, behind the desk, had glanced at him with bare
recognition, then resumed his reading of the newspaper, and
Lukas had dropped the two keys on the counter.

No small-talk, and nothing serious had been said – as if
a conversation had not taken place the previous evening.

In London, or in a northern German city, or in that engine
house of the Italian economy, Milan, people would already
be on the move, office workers, shop managers, certainly
the street cleaners and rubbish collectors. Not in Naples. A
few moved, lost souls. There was a girl ahead of him, and
Lukas thought she wore a party frock and that the buttons
were not in kilter; her hair was a mess and her shoulders
hunched: she had that look, her back did, of a girl who
wished she'd been in her own bed half a dozen hours earlier.
He followed her, playing his mind game, making associations
for her, a life story, as he did with the individuals, randomly
selected, who came to the Musée d' Orsay and paused in
front of the elephant and the rhinoceros – and his mind
flitted. The daughter-in-law of the artist who did the river
in crayon, the Notre Dame and the Louvre, had she had
her baby? The waiter in the bar on the Bellechasse, had the
laser for his eyes gone well? And Monique, who came once
a month to clean the apartment – unnecessary because of
the pristine state in which he kept it – and wash his clothes
and iron them, had her cat survived the kidney infection? It
was indulgent of Lukas to allow himself such fancies. He
saw the sign high on the building at the top of the street.

He went briskly down the slight hill that was via Forcella.
A church door, on his right, opened and he saw a young
priest, but their eyes did not meet. The girl was no longer

in front of him, and the artist's grandchild, an operation and a cat's ailment were ditched from his mind. He was focused. There had been kids at the top of the street and he had seen them stare at him, comatose. It was why he had come at that time, before the street's awakening.

He imagined how it had been. Eddie Deacon would have come down the street, walked on the hard cobblestones, but later in the morning, kids would have followed him. He wouldn't have known where he was going, would have stood out as a stranger. He saw the fish stall.

There was a door, the paint flaking off, and immediately beyond it a man was laying out plastic trays and polystyrene boxes, then shovelling ice from a big rubbish bin. There was a van behind him with the rear doors open. Lukas slowed. Not difficult to anticipate the sequence. The ice went on to the trays and into the boxes. The fish were brought from the back of the van and laid out without order, and a car hooted for the van to move. Impatience built. A brief argument followed, the two drivers. All predictable. The van driver slammed his rear doors, gave a finger to the car driver, then pulled away. The man on the stall began to place his fish in the correct trays and boxes. Lukas went forward.

'Excuse me . . . it is important for me to meet you. You're Tomasso?' When he needed it, he had good enough Italian.

A nod of agreement. A wild look past Lukas's shoulders, suspicion and anxiety. Sour: 'If I am?'

'Please, keep working, and I'm examining your fish. It's natural. The swordfish is magnificent.'

Wary of an outsider: 'It was caught yesterday, brought in today. I think it is thirty kilos.'

'I'll take it. Tomasso, please listen to me. I am here now, I'll leave with the fish. I won't be back. I have come to you to save a man's life . . .'

He saw Tomasso flinch. He had nowhere to go. He would

have realised that setting out his catch, brought from the market, and preparing for a day's trading was explicable and that an early-bird customer – even a stranger – was also explicable. He couldn't run, shout or protest without attracting attention.

'I'll have the swordfish, but show me the mullet too. You tried to help the boy, Tomasso. You reported what you'd seen. You'll never see me again, I promise. When I go, your involvement ceases. All I work for is the safety of the boy and his freedom. Tell me.'

A low voice, guttural, perhaps coarsened by years of nicotine: 'He saw Carmine and Anna Borelli. He was English, an outsider. I do not know why.'

'To find Immacolata.'

'They call her the whore. Everybody in via Forcella now calls her the whore. Before, they called her Signorina Immacolata and she could have anything, everything. I do not know why he came.'

'To find her.'

'They would kill me.'

'It's to save his life.'

'I, too, have a family.'

'Tell me, and I'm gone. I'll never come back.'

The trays were filled, the fish sorted, the water spray turned on, the scales were set up and the cash tin was opened. The man, Tomasso, looked Lukas straight in the eye. 'The price for the swordfish is a hundred and fifty euros. The boy stayed upstairs in the Borelli apartment, with the old bitch who is Anna. Carmine came down and sent a message and then he went back. I saw him at the window several times. I regret, sir, that I cannot do a better price for the fish. It is rare. The van arrived and the driver waited, and Salvatore came here, to where you stand. Salvatore is called Il Pistole and he is the assassin of the clan Borelli. Do you follow me?'

'I do.'

'You pay me a hundred and fifty euros for the fish, and the old bitch takes fifty euros. They screw me in the market and on the stall. I apologise for the price. I tried to warn the boy with my eyes. He did not react quickly. You say he came to Naples to find Immacolata?'

'Yes.'

'He must have believed he was going to her. He looked very happy. Perhaps that is why, when I warned him with my eyes, he was slow. Salvatore put him in the vehicle. Salvatore is the killer, has killed more than he has years. Salvatore took him.'

'Thank you.'

'Salvatore would kill me, and would kill the person at the *pensione*, would kill anyone. It cooks well, the fish. He looked a nice boy.'

Lukas paid him for the fish, and it was wrapped in newspaper and plastic. Blood oozed from where it had been gutted and from the gills. The tail stuck out behind Lukas, the sword in front of him. His promise to Tomasso, a fish-seller and frightened, with reason to fear, was meaningless, so the guarantees had been sculpted with care. Those pledges of anonymity, handed out with the carelessness of jelly babies and chewing-gum, had no value.

He carried the fish out of the street, hoisted on his shoulder, and never looked back. Lukas thought the day had started well.

Rossi's alarm woke him. He blundered towards the bathroom, showered, shaved and dressed fast. He came into the living room. It was a few minutes past seven and the sunlight stormed through the blinds. He opened them, illuminating Orecchia, and started to whistle a tune popular in the far south, then went to Orecchia and slapped his face gently.

Orecchia jerked up, and groped for the holster under his arm, then saw the grinning Rossi.

Rossi went to the kitchen, switched on the electric kettle and took a carton of juice from the refrigerator. What they had in common, the two men from the Servizio Centrale Protezione, was a love of tea, exported in tins from England; they started each day with a mug, but Rossi also had juice. He called from the kitchen, with the mock-respect of a courtier, and asked if *she*, the important one, had yet made an appearance. How could Orecchia have known? He'd been asleep. He hadn't heard her, or been woken by the water system. It was agreed that she was not yet up.

Rossi said, as the kettle boiled, 'She's usually washed and dressed by now.'

Perhaps because he was irritated at having been discovered asleep on his watch, Orecchia snapped, 'Today she isn't. Today she sleeps.'

'I only said it was unusual.'

Rossi went down to the ground-floor hall, collected the newspaper from the front gate and came back up. He heard Orecchia in the bathroom, poured the tea, took him a mug, put the rolls into the oven and switched on the television for the breakfast news: more killings in Iraq, a bigger bomb in Afghanistan, instability in the currency markets, defections from the ruling coalition . . . Time passed.

Orecchia was dressed and smelled good, had used the Hugo Boss stuff. Rossi made a show of recognising it and teased his colleague. They had worked together many times. They had been on a detail that had done a Cosa Nostra killer, and twice had done the escort and security on an 'Ndrangheta bagman. They had been with the collaborator from the Misso clan in Naples, and with a Triad from the Chinese community in Genoa. They knew each other, were regarded by their superiors as of exceptional competence and . . . Together they had the thought. Rossi, extraordinary for a man who had been with the Guardia di Finanza before transferring to the SCP, could call upon almost poetic imagery. He thought of a wave on its way from the horizon, not yet seen, then closer and noticed for its ripple. Closer still, it seemed to cry that catastrophe approached, broke upon them and swallowed them. They were choking. He was in the spume and under the green darkness of the water, Orecchia too.

There were no sounds from behind the door. No grumbles from the plumbing. It was long past the time she would normally have risen. The sense of disaster caught them. Not a word was exchanged.

They didn't knock. They didn't pause respectfully after calling her name. Orecchia went in first, Rossi at his heels. Perhaps from the door the shape in the bed might have confused them, but it was obvious that a pillow substituted for a body. Rossi heard the sharp intake of Orecchia's breath.

They were not recruits. They had valued experience. They did not scream, curse, shriek or blaspheme. Rossi felt a chill settle on the hackles at his neck and shivered. Orecchia was breathing fast, gasping. Orecchia did the bathroom, went inside as if there was no chance of finding her on the toilet. They scoured the apartment, each room, each cupboard, each wardrobe.

Rossi knew – was thankful for it – that Orecchia was senior and would have to make the telephone call. They went down to the ground floor and checked there, then to the subterranean garage, which they didn't use, and looked there. They were supposed to have a roster whereby one slept and the other was alert, but both had been asleep. In older times, in history, to be asleep on duty was to invite a meeting with a firing squad. Today it would be a return to the uniform of the Guardia di Finanza, and they would be checking VAT statements in Bari or Brindisi. Maybe for Orecchia it would be dismissal.

Rossi asked, 'Are you satisfied?'

'That she is not here, yes.'

'What has she taken?'

'Her handbag – she has some money.'

'Has she taken any clothes?'

'She has hardly any to take, and no case to put them in.'

'Could she have gone to the piazza to buy bread or a magazine?'

'Could pigs fly to the moon? I think not.'

Rossi saw that Orecchia's mobile was in his hand. He was scrolling through the directory. He felt aggression towards the girl, their 'Signorina Immacolata', and might have exploded, let the fury rip, but he turned away and took the deep breaths counselled by the anger-management people. He could see the rooftops, then the hills and part of the city, the haze and gold light on the mountains. Where could she be? How long had she been gone? How far?

Orecchia gave him a wintry smile and pressed the call button.

She sat on a bench by a bus stop, a weed- and litter-filled flowerbed behind her. The bushes were oleander. She knew them from Naples. Their flowers were soft pink and pretty, well formed. As a child she had walked with her mother in the garden between the sea and the riviera di Chiaia, and had picked a sprig of those flowers and put it in the top buttonhole of her blouse. Her mother had seen it, snatched it, thrown it away and smacked her, open hand and hard, on her bare thigh above the knee. She had said that the flower of the oleander was the most dangerous in the city, could cause grave illness, even death; the sap was a compound of strychnine, a poison of the same strength. It had been so pretty, so delicate. Nothing was as it seemed, and she had learned the lesson. The shop she wanted was across the street, and she was waiting for the man to come and the shutter to be raised.

Nothing was as it seemed, and nobody – except Eddie Deacon – those days, those nights and that time.

Mario Castrolami was not a man of crude temper. He took the call, he listened in silence, he cut the call.

In his mentality there was a practised survival routine in the event of what many would describe as 'disaster'. He began it. He lifted down his jacket from the hook, shrugged into it. He slipped out of the annexe and into a toilet where he dribbled out some urine. Then he went to the canteen, bought coffee and chocolate and took them out past the desk at the front. He circled the piazza as he drank the coffee and ate the chocolate. The wrapper went into a bin and the plastic cup followed it after the next circuit. He did the disaster routine when news came through from the palace at the *centro direzionale* that the judiciary had thrown out a case that might have taken three years to prepare, had involved dedication and massive man-hours, because of a supposed 'technicality', or because a politician had interfered in the process, or a file had walked from a supposedly secure archive. Others went to bars and drank, or dug with manic intensity into new files. Some went home and took their women to bed, or walked by the sea and gazed at the water. He plodded round the piazza, with coffee and chocolate, and pretended that a new day was starting when he eased into his chair. Judges were not known for patience when a collaborator's testimony was withdrawn.

His friend, the artist, would have said, if asked, that he needed a holiday, but she would not be asked.

His wife in Milan would have said, if asked, that there

was work in the private sector – in that city's banking industry – for a man of his experience and that he should take the plane north, but she would not be asked.

There was, of course, a check-list of actions that followed the disappearance of a collaborator. A watch on the railway station in Rome, on the principal coach station and the airports of Fiumicino and Ciampino – and she might have been gone for two hours, or four. Orecchia, a good man, had spoken woodenly on the phone and Castrolami had put the question: how long had she been gone? Had put another question: how long had he slept? And the final question: how long between the time she was found to be missing and the time of reporting it? She might have been, he reflected, through and out of the airport, at the other end of the country, holed up in Rome – might be dead with a bullet in her head.

He came back into the annexe. Both the men at the table, the psychologist and the collator, looked away, and the hard men of the ROS group shuffled in their seats and made room for him to get past. As if a black cloud hung over them, the cloud of failure. He could give instructions. They waited on his leadership. He didn't often feel, or sense, the burden of aloneness, but it was his shout, his right to activate whatever procedures he thought appropriate. There were none. She was gone, was clear, lost. Castrolami let his head fall into his hands and his elbows on the table took the weight. He had hoped for a small victory and had thought it within his grasp – and the fate of a young man, held somewhere, was erased as of no importance. He stared at the surface of the table. There was silence around him, except for the breaking open of the cellophane round a cigarette packet, then the click of a lighter, and he felt a rare, isolated misery, then heard rippling laughter. First nervous and quiet, then growing, gaining confidence, then playing on the walls and bouncing on the table, driving into Castrolami's ears. He looked up.

The fish could not be fitted through the door. Either the tail stuck or the sword did. The body, with the tail, would have been more than a metre long and the sword the same. The beast was two metres in total and death had left it rigid. It could not be bent or folded. It wedged. Lukas held it. Castrolami recognised it as *pesce spade*, and knew it as the most expensive fish on any market stall. It was the size that would be bought for the celebration of an extended family. No one helped Lukas.

He didn't seem to want help. He had another go, but the sword caught the table and jarred it and the laughter was louder. He turned round and led with the tail, squeezed and heaved. The flank of the beast caught in the lock of the open door – and then it was through. Laughter chorused the success. Lukas dumped it on the table, and the annexe was filled with its smell. Only Castrolami did not laugh.

Lukas said, droll, 'If there's a restaurant the guys use, maybe they'd do us the favour of cooking it. My news is useful. I look at you, friend, and say to myself that yours is between disaster and catastrophe. Get it over with.'

'We have lost the girl.'

He saw the grin wiped off Lukas's face. 'What did she take?'

'Her bag, money, her ID. She went early and—'

'What clothes?' He used Italian now, as if the pretended ignorance of the language was no longer important.

Castrolami said he didn't know of any.

'Did she take knickers and a spare bra?'

Castrolami said he didn't know.

'Just an opinion, and humbly put. I know very little of women, enough to fill the back of a postage stamp, but I doubt they travel far without next-to-the-skin necessities.

Think about it. Each item you've spoken of, however small, it'll be there – usually is. I make, of course, only a suggestion. It might be worth thinking about the little things.'

Castrolami looked sharply at him, wondered if he was mocked – realised he wasn't. He thought he saw honesty in Lukas's face. He couldn't criticise a man who had confessed to failure with women. After all, he had no medals in relationships. He turned behind him, poked a finger at the chest of a man from the ROS, perhaps his favourite in the unit. The guy had unevenly cut hair that fell to his shoulders, and his cheeks, jaw and upper lip were painted with stubble. He told the man to take the fish, and its spike, to Donato at the restaurant on the piazza Gesù Nuovo, book a table for a dozen that evening, or whenever cause for rejoicing was justified, and ask for the beast to be prepared for cooking. The big man heaved it off the table and carried it out, but the stink stayed.

'What was your news, Lukas?'

He was told, and instructed the collator on action, if any. He didn't rate what he'd learned against the importance of the girl having gone, but he took the suggestion given him, and went back outside to pace, think and scratch at his memory. It had started as a bad day and Castrolami thought it had the potential to get worse.

Twin celebrations grew in pitch. A senior police officer took a call in his car and was heard by his driver to say, 'They've lost her? Tell me again . . . Incredible . . . If they've lost her, can they hold the mother, the brothers? Will the case against the Borelli clan collapse? . . . Incredible . . .'

The driver, an elderly policeman with little in his life to create excitement, and little to augment his status, told a colleague that Immacolata Borelli was loose on the streets. The colleague told a cousin who ran a quality furniture chain. The cousin, meeting a young man who sought to bring in a comprehensive contract for the refurnishing of an apartment in the bank section of the city, repeated the story – and the young man was Massimo, nephew of the flamboyant Umberto. Word rushed along certain selected channels that Immacolata Borelli had fled protective custody. From the lawyer's office, news of it was inside the gates of Poggioreale within an hour, and within an hour and a half it would be behind the walls of the Posilippo gaol at the far end of the Gulf. At both prisons the foot-soldiers offered congratulations, which were received by Gabriella Borelli, and by Giovanni and Silvio Borelli. Within two hours, the message had infiltrated the top-security prison on the eastern outskirts of London, HMP Belmarsh. Men and women crowded around the mother and her sons. It was felt that power had been restored, an old order retained.

Davide, the agent who was Delta465/Foxtrot, saw more movement on the walkway that early morning, and recognised the clothing as that worn by a blindfolded man. He noted the presence, and his memory would be backed by the tapes. He did not himself sift and evaluate what he saw. It was for his handlers to make definitions of priority.

Salvatore held the torch. He alone went into the chamber. Two men, neither known to him, held back and guarded the door. More were on the walkway. He couldn't complain of the number of men allocated, but had thought, still thought, the price to be exacted from Carmine Borelli was cruel. The door was left ajar behind him. He was good, the boy, disciplined. He had the hood over his upper face and eyes, and seemed grateful when told food had been brought. It was fruit, some cold pasta, coffee in a plastic cup, more cheese and water. He bent and took the boy's ankle in his hands. The leg kicked clear, but he stayed at the task and checked that the chain did not cut deep. He thought it a gesture of kindness: he was not familiar with compassion, could not have explained why he showed it, here, now. The boy had his head ducked down and did not respond. He let his hand brush the boy's arm, only a slight touch, and the boy shrank from him, his fist clenched.

Since he had been eleven or twelve, people had recoiled from close contact with him – other children, women, old men and men in their prime had backed away. His reputation now was that of a killer – no conscience, no mercy, no love. Salvatore needed that reputation to survive in Naples – but he did not think it important that a foreigner, an outsider, a stranger, should have that fear of him – but he would still, of course, cut off the boy's ear, finger or penis. There were confusions in the mind of Il Pistole. He did not love and did not attract it. The nearest he knew of ecstasy was not in laughter with a friend, or in the penetration of a girl. It was when he looked deep into the eyes of a man he would kill and saw the spreading terror. It was the greatest thrill in Salvatore's life. He didn't know how he would go to his own death, but swore to anybody who needed to be told that he would not be taken alive, locked away and left to rot in Novara, Ascoli or Rebibbia: he would not be captured, arrested, and if there was a hallucinating nightmare in his life, it was the moment of failure, capture, and the parade past the camera flashes, and of being merely a number on a landing of a cell block. He did not hate the boy. What was more difficult for Salvatore: he wasn't indifferent to him either. Confusing.

'What is your name?'

'My name is Eddie.'

'What is that, Eddie?'

'It's not Eduardo. It's Edmondo, but I'm called Eddie. That's my name.'

The hood masked most of the face, but the mouth was good, hair grew clumsily around it and the skin was clear. Salvatore despised men who had acne and pimples. The replies were hesitant, soft-spoken. He saw that the bucket had not been used, and that only part of the food was eaten.

'You have not finished the food.'

'No.'

'I brought food for you.'

'Thank you.'

'But you do not eat it.'

'I apologise that I did not eat the food you very kindly brought me.'

'All right – I have brought more food and more water.'

'Thank you.'

Was the gratitude sincere? Always, Salvatore craved to know what people thought of his character, his actions. So difficult to know with certainty . . . Was he generous? Was he intelligent? Was he handsome? Was he the best company, the best in bed, the best enforcer in all Naples? He didn't know who could tell him. He had been thanked for the food and had received an apology, but he couldn't judge sincerity from a dropped, hooded head. He had killed men, had shot or strangled them, because they had not offered him respect.

'You are from London.'

'Yes.'

'What do you do in London?'

'I am a teacher, a language teacher.'

'I speak English very good.'

'Very good.'

Was that respect? He had gone into a bar in Sanità and a man had spat on the floor, just in front of his feet, a metre from Salvatore's shoes. That was not respect. A man, who had known his face and identity, had parked a saloon car on a street in the piazza Mercato so that Fangio's scooter was blocked in, then had told Fangio to 'go fuck your mother' but his eyes had been on Salvatore. That was not respect.

'In London you met Immacolata?'

'I did.'

'It was bad for you that you did.'

'I love Immacolata. So I came to find her.'

'She is dead.' The boy, Eddie, cringed away from him, huddled against the wall. His shoulders trembled and his arms shook. 'Not yet – she will be. She is condemned. She is living but dead. Better that you had not met her and loved her.'

'When . . . when do you . . . ?'

'I understand you well. Tomorrow. They have until tomorrow. If we do not have heard by tomorrow, we send . . . our word is *dono* – you say "gift", yes? Or do you say "present"? You ask . . . It is tomorrow. I think my English is good, Eddie.'

'Who are you?'

'It does not matter to you.'

He thought the boy, Eddie, might have cursed and tried to kick him, or to plead with him. Some swore or screamed when he came at them with the knife or the handgun, and there were others who wet themselves or soiled their trousers, who knelt and clutched his legs, begging for their lives and moaning their children's names. The boy had not sworn or begged – and he loved Immacolata Borelli, and she had ignored him as scum.

He kicked the boy. Did it hard, in the shin, saw the pain that spiralled up the leg, the jerk of the hood and heard the gasp. He went out, shut the door and bolted it. He was escorted away. He felt unsettled, and the confusion nagged in him.

He left by the same walkway, and saw an old man low in a chair watching the television, could see the back of the head clearly because the window was well cleaned.

When the pain in his leg died and aching took over, Eddie put the nail to work. His fingertips told him that the chain's links were slid into a loop at the end of an iron pin concreted into the outer wall. He used the point of the nail to drive down, two or three millimetres at first, into the minute gap between the concrete and the pin's flank. He couldn't hit the nail with the bucket because the noise would have reverberated, but he could use the heel of his trainer for want of a heavy-duty claw hammer. Eddie reckoned he'd done well, that the day had already given him something positive. He tapped with the shoe, felt the nail driving down, but every few millimetres he would extract it, then reinsert it, wiggle it, and feel the gap, the hole, widening. He thought he had, in probability, twelve hours before the man came with the knife. Time to be used. He had also learned a little of the routine. Two men at the door, only one entering the cell. Knew it was two because one had coughed and the other had lit a cigarette, and he had been able to separate the sounds.

He would not go quietly.

Denied the use of his eyes, left with the power of his ears, Eddie reckoned the man had lost certainty. Reckoned, also, that the loss had taken him on to unfamiliar ground. Downside: he didn't know what was beyond the inner door, didn't know what weapons the two men carried, didn't know whether at the key critical moment he would be able to use the nail to stab, didn't know whether he was capable of it. He'd have to learn the answer to that. It would have been so easy to roll over on his side, lie limp and wallow, give free rein to the self-pity and the unfairness – maybe they'd use alcohol on his skin before they made the cut, maybe they'd gag him or stick a wad in his mouth for him to bite on – but that wasn't an option.

The concrete round the pin was of poor quality: it cracked easily, and little pieces crumbled. Then, using the nail as a lever, he could work the gap wider.

He thought it had been an hour, but it might have been two, before he could use his full strength, tug on the pin and feel it rock – but it wasn't yet loose. Would be soon.

Carmine was under surveillance. Anna was not.

'I promise you that the contract will be honoured, payments will be to the accounts you have nominated, nothing is different.'

Carmine, with his escort – he had life-long experience in recognising when he was tracked – went to a café in the square opposite the old entrance to the Castel Capuana, where he had done his first sentence of penal servitude a half-century before. He took coffee and, with old friends, played a game, twenty-ones, with cards and looked for the watchers. He had pleasure in identifying six, and two cars. Anna, with no tail, talked business.

'For how long will I be making decisions that affect our contract? As long as is necessary. Depend on it. I have the authority to speak for my family, for my daughter-in-law, for my son, and you have my hand.'

Anna Borelli, who was less than 1.60 metres in height and less than forty-five kilos in weight, peered across a table at a Venezuelan, an Ecuadorian and an Irishman who together made up the cartel that would oversee the shipment from the Colombian port of Cartagena, via west Africa and transhipment at Dakar, into the port of Naples, of a tonne of cocaine. And she could haggle.

'You have my guarantee, and I tell you that predictions

of the collapse of my family are exaggerated, lies spread by envious rivals. You are wise to trust me.'

In front of her was an old calculator she had not used for more than twenty years. Her first stop that morning had been at a corner shop for batteries. What concerned her was the drop in the street price of cocaine, and she showed keen determination not to commit herself to an excessive front price when the market rate had deteriorated through saturation. A bony forefinger alternately rapped rhythms on the table and pointed at the men for emphasis. When her small hand was wrapped successively in the fists of the two South Americans and the Irishman, they would each feel the strength of her claw grip.

'It's a pleasure to do business with gentlemen,' she said. Behind her, the clan's treasurer beamed.

She was asked then – natural and inevitable – for news of her daughter-in-law, Gabriella.

'I expect her home very soon, and my grandsons. We had a sweet granddaughter, wonderful as a child, but now suffering a mental collapse, a fugitive from those who tricked and deceived her. It's cruel what they will do to turn the head of a naïve and simple young person . . . It's a good deal. Please don't forget that my hand is my bond.'

She stood, tiny. They towered over her. She revelled in the deference offered her. She would have stood in line to slit the throat of Immacolata, 'naïve' and 'simple', who had been 'tricked and deceived', and would happily have used a blunt knife.

She walked out of the shop, the sun beat down on her and the early-morning traffic built. Its fumes were in her nose, horn blasts in her ears, as she carried the bag they had given her.

She knew the stories of betrayal in her home city. She

had learned them at school. Betrayal was in the culture of
Naples, bedded in its stonework.

One story she had always enjoyed was that of Belisarius.
The sixth century after the birth of Christ had been,
Immacolata's teacher had declared, a time of catastrophe.
The city had fallen to Odoacre, king of the Ostrogoths,
Roman rule had disintegrated, the network of lucrative trading
routes had collapsed, malaria was rampant. A dark age had
begun.

It was a story that still lived with her, carried forward
from the classroom.

But in the year of our Lord 537 deliverance advanced.
The Byzantine emperor, Justinian, sent his finest general,
Belisarius, to win back the city. He came to Naples, saw the
height and strength of the city walls, and despaired of
capturing and sacking it. Then he found a traitor.

Immacolata could remember the hush of the children, the
sucked-in breath of those around her, and the teacher spoke
of an *infame,* a collaborator, a *pentito.*

And the traitor guided the general to a broken, disused
aqueduct that had carried water to the city in the great days
of the Empire. Led by the traitor, the soldiers of Belisarius
entered the city through the forgotten tunnel, moved in silence
in the quiet of the night – and sacked the city, butchering
the Ostrogoths.

No child in Immacolata's class had raised a squeal of
indignation against the act of treachery. It was the Neapolitan
way.

She walked towards the river.

Around the table in the annexe, there had been no criticism
of Castrolami's long absence from his chair. Reports were
brought to the collator who beavered at them, opened
computer cross-files, pushed paper at the others. The

psychologist drew a word profile of Salvatore, enforcer to the Borelli clan, and painted a psychopath's portrait. Lukas put bricks in place, built contact: he murmured, never allowing his voice to intrude, to both men the hopes he harboured for the hostage's behaviour, how Eddie Deacon should be.

Should be . . . combating the sense of disbelief that 'this is actually happening, and to me', confronting fear and holding on, however grimly, to a sense of control. He should establish a routine for himself, and learn the routine of his captors. Regrets and sentimentality should be ruled out, unacceptable. Talk with his guards should be kept to a minimum and attempts to ingratiate himself with them would usually be doomed; they 'don't like a crawler or a whiner', Lukas had said, or a guy who hit back and antagonised; 'he's best staying quiet' and should never complain. He should not be uncooperative or short-tempered, and should not compromise his integrity. Always he should be remote from the cause of the hostage-taker. When a phone rang, or more paper was brought, Lukas would back off.

'And escape?' the psychologist had asked. 'Does he work towards an escape attempt?'

'Should he, shouldn't he?' the collator demanded, and the men behind – the storm squad – murmured support for an answer, an opinion.

Lukas said, 'Eddie Deacon's a nice guy, a second-rate guy, a teacher. He's in a bunker, a cell, probably in darkness, likely hooded. Assuming he breaks clear of restraints, chains, gets through a door, a trap, he will have no knowledge of what's beyond. Again, assuming he gets out of the building, he doesn't know where he is, on hostile ground. Who will help him? Escape is the measure of desperation at a last resort. Almost inevitably it will fail.'

'You paint a black picture,' the psychologist said.

'His situation is black.'

'He depends on us,' the collator said.

'A failed attempt arouses a reaction of extreme brutality.'

He heard footsteps stamping along a corridor, then across the operations room.

'Usually, then, they kill.' Lukas saw Castrolami's entry. He questioned with his eyes, spoke the name of the girl, and the collator – as if it was his personal cross to bear – shook his head.

Castrolami lifted a phone, dialled. Lukas heard him tell a minder in Rome that he had walked twenty-four times round the piazza Dante, and had thought. Then he told the minder where to find Immacolata Borelli, bit his lip and rang off. The breath sang through his teeth, like dice rolled but not yet settled.

14

He had crossed the space, the chain dragging behind him.

He was against the door, standing, and when he pressed an ear to the crack below the upper hinge he could make out, very faint, voices and music. He couldn't understand what was said or by whom, or distinguish what music was played.

Once the pin had come clear of the wall and the chain was free, Eddie had not stopped to consider, step by step, his actions. He had gripped the nail tighter in his fist and had crawled across the space, groping in the darkness until he reached the door. He had moved his fingers up the smooth metal sheeting nailed to the wood, then listened. He would have worried if the sounds had been more distinct.

He didn't think he would be heard.

A glass is half full: the nail would enable him to break out, flee for freedom. A glass is half empty: he would fail, be mutilated, butchered, buried in secrecy and some day, *some time*, someone would find this place and read his name. He scratched with the nail tip in the blackness and trusted that he had fashioned the capital characters: EDDIE. Didn't do a message, or an epistle, didn't do an approximation of a date, didn't make a heart and arrow and gouge 'Immacolata', just did his name and thought that if, *some time*, it was read and files were turned up, it might just be that the bastard who had him there would face some sort of retribution. He didn't believe that to have done his name with the nail was

the same as admitting defeat, accepting ultimate failure. He
didn't know whether it could be deciphered.

Eddie began to work on the lower hinge, sank down to
his knees. He knew what he had to do. His dad, back in
Wiltshire, had given over the inside end of the garage to
shelves and boxes. Neat as a hardware-shop display, he had
about every tool a man could ever want and plenty more.
His mum shrugged about it, and Eddie had sort of sneered,
but his dad had the tools to get the hinge off in about two
minutes flat. Now Eddie didn't sneer. He used the nail, first
off, to try to open a fraction of a gap between the hinge and
the metal sheet – and didn't like to think again about a glass
being half empty.

And didn't like to think about whether his name could
be read or was just the scratching of an imbecile.

Minutiae dominated Eddie Deacon's existence. Top of the
list was the depth that the nail tip could go down behind
the hinge bar, starting at two millimetres, estimate, and
needing to open right out so that it could go down more
than ten, and likely twenty. Then there were the screws to
be loosened, and he had no screwdriver. Any time before
he had been 'lucky' and had caught that flight, 'lucky' again
and had caught the train from Rome, Eddie Deacon would
have said, 'Fuck it,' or 'No can do,' and walked away from
the problem. Would have said, before, that Eddie Deacon
did not take off hinges, the lower one first, without the
necessary tools. He would have said that it was *impossible* to
dislodge two old hinges, both held in with likely rusted screws,
without a cordless or powered drill – and he had only a
single nail that was slightly bent halfway up.

He did not acknowledge 'impossible'.

Through the focus came small solutions. He had the pin
extracted from the wall as a lightweight hammer. He had a
handkerchief in his pocket, dirty and disgusting, and could

fold the corner and use it as a wad across the nail head to dull the hammer sound. He had the bucket – and he had the thought of the knife: he could feel, on his head, on his hands and in his privates, what the knife would cut.

He had no way of judging time.

Eddie hit the nail three or four times, then stopped, listened, let the quiet cling round him, and the darkness, then repeated, listened again, and had the nail behind the hinge bar by – his estimate – five millimetres. Double that insertion, then utilise the bucket, and he reckoned he made progress, did well and—

Voices, louder music, as if an internal door were opened. He scurried, hands and knees again, back towards the far wall, used his fingers to find the hole where the pin had been, jammed it home, stuffed the handkerchief back into his pocket, put the nail into his right trainer against his instep. He had his back against the wall, had found the hood and slipped it on, and his knees were drawn up, his head dropped and resting on them. He waited.

Seemed a damned eternity.

Couldn't be certain, but Eddie thought that men had come close to the door and had started a bloody conversation. He resented that, was pissed off that he'd heard them, had backed away from his work and now sat idle, wasting time and— The bolt opened – which told him, because now he listened hard for everything, that it was lightweight, and a key turned. A heavy key. The door was opened.

Through the hood he realised a torch powered against his body.

The voice was the same as before, the bastard's voice: 'You did not eat. Why did you not eat?'

Didn't eat because he'd been too busy – got that, bastard? 'I wasn't hungry.'

'If I bring you food you should eat it.'

'I wasn't hungry.'

'Did you drink?'

He'd needed the water – hot work, dragging out a pin, in the stifling space with flaked concrete making a dustcake in his throat, and heavy work, trying to ram a nail tip behind a hinge bar. 'Thank you, yes.'

'You have used the bucket?'

'I have – the minimum. There is no paper and if I use the bucket and have no paper I will stink worse than I do already. Thank you.'

'I bring you food, Eddie, and water, and I change your bucket. Am I kind, Eddie, or not?'

'Kind. Thank you.'

'I leave food for you, and water, and a new bucket.'

'Thank you.'

'I hope, Eddie, that we hear something today of Immacolata. We give them until tomorrow. For you, I hope we hear today.'

He heard the food, in a bag, dropped, a water bottle, plastic, roll, and the clatter of a new galvanised bucket.

'Thank you for the food and water, and the bucket.'

Then wistful, softer: 'I think she is very beautiful, Immacolata . . .'

Eddie anticipated. He was kicked.

He used his legs to protect his stomach and groin, and his arms were over his hooded head. Not a single kick but a flurry of them. Eddie understood it. He understood that the bastard regarded him as a rival – not just as a bargaining chip but as a rival for Immacolata Borelli's affection. Could have laughed while the kicks came. Maybe she hadn't done it with him, the bastard, maybe she'd turned him down. He heard the bucket, the one he'd used, knocked over. The kicking stopped.

He heard the rhythm of it. Door opened, voices, door

closed, faint voices. Door locked and door bolted. Silence. Only his groans . . . She had been his, not the bastard's. He saw her face, then crawled awkwardly through the mess from the upturned bucket, which wet his hands and knees. He saw her face clearly, and began again to work with the nail.

The river level was down. The Tiber's flow was erratic and followed channels between sandbanks.

She was on the bridge.

She lifted the lock from the bag. It had plastic wrapping round it, and she used her teeth to break it open. There was another couple on the bridge, their arms locked, and the girl was kissing the man. Immacolata pulled the padlock clear of the packaging, and the keys fell to the paving. She bent to retrieve them. There was, immediately below her, a current moving in the water, a free flow between two banks. The river had been low long enough for scrub to have taken hold on the banks. Great dead boughs and trunks were scattered in it, old trees that had been swept downstream by the early spring's flood rip.

All she knew of the bridge was what Castrolami had told her – not the crap about its history, but about the lamp post that had threatened to collapse and the replacement of low metal posts with a chain running between them that the city mayor had ordered to be erected. The padlock she had bought was heavy-duty, would have been a struggle to break through even with large bolt-cutters. It had two good keys that shone in the morning sunshine. The man in the hardware shop had wanted to sell her a padlock with combination numbers. She had refused and he had persisted until she had flared at him that it was not his business what sort of padlock she purchased. Then he had understood, and the smile had crossed his face, a patronising tolerance of the young, and he had offered her a cheap, shiny model, made in China;

the implication was that a good padlock would be wasted when fastened to the column. Castrolami had said that young people in love came to the bridge with padlocks – like the couple who stood along the rail from her and kissed. She had told the shopkeeper she wanted the best, and that she was prepared to pay thirty-five euros for a lock with keys. Only when she had paid did he tell her slyly that it was possible to buy the padlocks from an Albanian trader on the bridge, but not of quality. She could see the one the couple had. Together they hooked it on to the chain, and she thought it would have cost ten euros at most. For them it was a joke, a diversion, and a chance to kiss again. There was a long line of padlocks on that section of chain, enough to make it sag. Names had been written in indelible ink on some.

Immacolata did not have a pen with indelible ink: if she had, she would not have used it.

She threw the packaging over the bridge's stone rail, watched it flutter down, fall into the flow and float away, like a boat. The couple had broken in their embrace and now eyed her with hostility. She gave them the look of contempt of a daughter of the Borelli clan, and must have intimidated them because they hurried on with their business on the bridge. She might, perhaps, in that gesture of throwing away the plastic and cardboard, have unsettled them; they would have seen her face – her chin and eyes – and been nervous of intervening to chastise her. Their moment of declared love had, maybe, been lessened by their fear of her. She watched them go south, and towards the road sign for the Lungotevere. They didn't turn, kept their backs to her, and held close to each other.

Immacolata thought that placing the padlock on the chain on the bridge was about as relevant as laying fresh bouquets beside a road where there had been a fatality in a traffic accident. Irrelevant, but she thought it worthwhile.

She wondered then if he saw her, pictured her. She had the image of him: grubby jeans, socks that usually had a hole at the heel or the toe, yesterday's shirt, his hair unbrushed, the smile and the laughter that walked with him, the flatness of his stomach, the delicacy of his fingers, the thin thighs and . . . She seemed, inside herself, to arch and press and be closer so that he went deeper. She remembered Eddie. She knew what they would do to him. She was of the Borelli family, and she knew how pain and fear were used as regular weapons of choice. She did not have him there to kiss.

She kissed the padlock face: it was cold, remote. She let her lips linger on it.

The chain was rusted, lower than the rail, and festooned with the padlocks of lovers. She hesitated. She heard a little squeal of mirth, mocking, and the Albanian who sold the padlocks on the bridge was staring at her and would have been wondering why she had come alone, and why she paused. Could she not make up her fucking mind? He might have thought that. The water was dull, dirty and wound between the banks. There was nothing attractive about the view upstream, nothing of majesty.

She made her commitment. Immacolata took three steps, four, to the chain, then looked for a section that was not already crowded and found one. She didn't kneel because that would have been an act of sentimentality. She crouched, used a key to open the padlock, then secured it to a link in the chain and snapped it shut. It hung there, and for a moment the sun was on it.

She stepped back, held the keys between her fingers and remembered what Castrolami had told her, and what she had seen the lovers do hurriedly after they had scowled at her for letting the packaging drop. They would have taken longer over it but she had destroyed their moment . . . Not important to her. The sun was over the next bridge, still low enough to dazzle her. It was indeed her commitment. There were three keys on the ring, little bright trinkets of her mood. Not diamonds, not jewels, not flowers, but three keys from a Chinese factory. She raised her arm, saw his face, threw them, watched them fall, irretrievable, saw the splash and the fast-forming ripples, then only the swirl of the current.

'The old *mendicante* was right. I'm surprised,' Rossi said.

'The old beggar's usually right,' Orecchia said.

'Is she going to jump in after them?'

'I don't think so.'

'Do we go for her now?'

Orecchia said, 'As we would for a mourner beside a family grave. Half a minute for contemplation, then we go.'

They had been there a quarter of an hour. They had been sitting on a low railing in the shade of the trees, with the scent of the market's fruit stalls behind them, and they had waited to see if Castrolami's judgement was sure or whether it leaked. They had seen her come, with that haughty stride, as if she was of God's chosen few, on to the bridge – as Castrolami had said she would – and each man had let out an involuntary sigh of relief.

'Would we have been fired?'

'Probably "returned to unit", probably on a trash heap. I think he told very few. It's contained.'

'Would you do that? Buy a padlock, waste it, throw away the key?'

'I know too little about romance.' A faint grin broke on Orecchia's face. 'Come on.'

They stood.

'How do we treat her?'

'Like an old friend. How else?'

Orecchia led. They skipped through the traffic, crossed the far pavement and walked out on to the bridge.

Rossi asked, 'Do we go gently or kick hell out of her?'

Orecchia answered, side of his mouth, 'I lead, Alessandro, an uncomplicated life. I have a wife who tolerates me, a kid who accepts my usefulness to him as a milch-cow, I have a cat who ignores me but doesn't scratch. I have an apartment I can afford, I have a cheque in the bank on the first day of each month and an attractive pension fund. I don't live with a perpetual crisis at my shoulder. *They* do, the collaborators. *She* does. I would say, Alessandro, that betrayal brings a heavy burden. It would be attractive to kick her for what she has done to *us* today, but our anxieties are small in comparison with her agony.'

'Sensitively put. It does you credit.' Rossi grinned wryly. 'But has she capitulated? Is that what this crap, the padlock and the key, is about?'

'I think not,' Orecchia said.

She looked proud, the older of the two thought, and seemed in no hurry to leave the bridge. She would have seen them coming from the edge of her vision but made no move. Orecchia had seen the flash of light on the keys but not where they went into the water. Almost magnificent – better than proud, he thought, as she stared up the river. Beside him, Rossi was alert, on the balls of his feet, ready for pursuit. Orecchia was beside her, close but not intruding on her mood.

He said, 'I think, Signorina, that it is time for us to go back up the hill and continue with our work. Are you ready, or would you like a few moments longer?'

She shook her head.

'You're ready?'

She nodded.

He was at her shoulder as they came off the bridge, Rossi behind them. They walked briskly at his pace, and she matched it. She told him she'd paid thirty-five euros for the padlock, and seemed to expect a comment.

Orecchia quoted a frequent remark of his child, usually offered when the father attempted to limit expenditure: 'I think in this world, Signorina, you get what you pay for. I imagine that for thirty-five euros you have a very fine padlock.'

He wondered if she would be weeping, eyes glistening, but she was not.

Fangio drove him. Salvatore was pillion. The clan that had offered help to Carmine Borelli had asked for a great deal in return – narcotics, an investment portfolio and Salvatore's services. It might have been that there was a genuine requirement for a stranger's face among the towers of Scampia, or a need to demonstrate power and humiliate the old man from Forcella. He had been given a photograph of a face and a map that showed a wide street and a cut-through leading off it. Then a bar was marked, built into the ground floor of a fifteen-storey block. Rare for Fangio – the most skilled scooter driver Salvatore knew – to demonstrate apprehension. On the pillion, knees clamped on the padding and one hand in the deep pocket of his leather jacket, Salvatore sensed the older man's nerves. He, Salvatore, would never grow old. His friend, Fangio, had a less fatalistic mentality and did not look to die that morning. It was not their territory, and others back at the Sail building played with them.

Fangio had studied the map drawn for them, memorised it, did not need directions from Salvatore. In silence, of course, they rode on the high-performance scooter, couldn't have spoken through the visored helmets. Salvatore leaned with the cant of the machine as they came off the via Arcangelo Ghisleri, and the alley was ahead. They were seen. Watchers tracked them. In unison, Salvatore and Fangio lifted their smoked visors. Without showing their faces they would not have reached the far end of the narrow cut-through. Little enough space but Fangio had to weave between heaps of rubbish bags, most broken open with refuse spilling out. Once he swerved hard and missed, by a tail's length, a large scurrying grey rat. They went into an enclosed piazza and the bar was under the end of the block. It seemed squashed under the weight of stained concrete above, and weeds sprouted outside. When Salvatore swung his leg off the pillion he walked on a carpet of discarded cigarette tips.

The doors were open. They had little paint and the glass was cracked. It was dark inside except for the glimmer thrown by candles on the carved-wood Madonna. He saw three men sitting at a flimsy table, Formica top on steel tube legs. There were empty cups in front of them and they played cards. The one who faced Salvatore most directly wore a short-sleeved green shirt, was bald and had a goatee-style beard. It was the description he had been given at the Sail. He realised then the extent of the pain in his leg as he limped to the door. Why did his foot hurt? How had he injured it? A kick. Repeated kicks. The big toe of his right foot had been the strike-point when he had kicked the boy. The boy had loved Immacolata, maybe Immacolata had loved the boy. Twice he had thudded his foot against the pelvic bone, which was hard, reinforced. Immacolata had not loved Salvatore, had seemed not to notice him – as if he was merely a paid servant of the clan. So he limped into the bar, and felt a fucking idiot because he couldn't walk casually, as if he was in control.

He took the pistol from his pocket. Around him chairs scraped and table legs screeched as they were pushed back; the television in the corner seemed louder and dinned into his ears. He fired. Always two shots, and for the head. Salvatore didn't know the name of the man who pitched forward, whose head fell without the protection of his arms on to the table surface. Blood spilled, the cups jumped, the ashtray flew sideways and emptied, and the cards scattered. He didn't

know the man's name, or why he had been killed. What
hadn't he done?

He turned. He saw Fangio astride the scooter, gunning
the engine; he had lowered his helmet's visor. A bottle was
thrown at him – Sprite, Fanta or Coke. It came from behind
the bar and he saw it in flight, then the figure ducked. He
was hit full in the face and the bottle broke – his helmet or
his nose – he couldn't see and felt the moisture. A hand
clawed at him, another. He fired once more – into the ceiling.
He was freed. Couldn't run so he limped out.

Fangio snatched at him, pulled him clumsily on to the
pillion and was gone, and Salvatore realised then that what
he had not done was lower his visor as he had gone into the
bar. He wiped a sleeve across the bridge of his nose and
there was blood on the leather. They went back up the alley
and now he had the visor down. He had shown the world
his face. Blood was in his nostrils, already caking, and when
he snorted to clear it there was a spray on the visor's screen.

Fangio drove him away.

It was the clumsiest killing Salvatore had done, without
finesse, and the first in which he had not known a man's
name or what he was accused of. Because he had kicked the
boy, because he had limped, it was the worst of his killings.

The bucket was crucial to Eddie. The nail eased the hinge
bar a few more millimetres from the steel surface of the
door, at last enough for the rim of the bucket. There was
insufficient leverage from the nail for the heavy effort of
shifting the screws. The bucket did the job.

The first hinge, the lower one, was loosened. One more
heave, the big effort, all the muscles in use, and it would
come apart. Eddie didn't finish it off. He didn't know when
the bastard would come back. Couldn't take off one hinge,
then start to free the other: he had to do the break-out when

both hinges were ready – a few moments of heaving – to come away. When he had used the galvanised-steel bucket, which stank, the noise of the screws moving, the scraping against the steel and the splintering of the wood had seemed to shriek in the black space . . . But no one had come.

He had heard nothing, not even the faint voices and the murmur of music.

One last time he had the bucket rim behind the hinge bar and dragged it back, the sound screaming at him. The sweat ran on his shirt, and his knees were still damp from crawling in the urine, but he felt a glow of triumph.

The kicking hadn't hurt, couldn't compete with the elation. He was Eddie Deacon, 'steady Eddie'. Many said that nothing flapped or fazed him. He didn't do football and hadn't the tribal loyalties of those who howled and yelled when a goal went in or didn't. A woman from Algeria, in a class taken by Eddie Deacon, had gone into labour, and he had cleared the room, except for a woman who could help, then called the ambulance and had taken his coffee in the staff room, as if it wasn't a big event. There had been a— Didn't matter what else there had been because everything in Eddie's old life had been to the shredder. He clenched his fist, didn't punch in the air, but allowed it to shake as if that was good enough.

Nobody would have recognised him now. All who had been in his life would have recoiled at the sight and smell of him, wouldn't have understood the ecstasy of moving a hinge bar with the rim of a galvanised bucket.

He started again.

He was up on his toes to give himself the fraction of height that helped, and had the nail tip on the angle where the upper hinge's bar was flush against the steel plate, had the filthy handkerchief folded as a cushion on the nail head. He beat down on it with the pin from the chain.

There was a little give and he thought the nail tip was down by a millimetre or two, but it might have been wishful thinking – or even bloody fantasy. Nothing before in his life that was measured in a couple of millimetres had been important to Eddie Deacon.

It was late morning in the annexe off the operations room. The ROS men were back on their chairs, legs splayed out in front of them, and a couple snored quietly. One used a multiple-blade knife to clean the dirt from beneath his fingernails, and another read a magazine called *Fur, Feather and Fin*, seeming interested in waterproof socks. A fifth chewed gum and had a list in front of him of what was included in a personal survival kit, available in a mail-order offer; he elbowed Pietro, distracting him from the socks, and told him that this PSK had two non-lubricated condoms for water-carrying. He was Luigi.

The collator often worked alongside the ROS men. They seemed good at taking rest where it was offered, on a hard-backed chair, a floor or in a car. In fact, they seemed to rest more than anything else and had the weird magazines, everything about the kit they wore and how to improve it. But the collator knew that, when the location surfaced, they would be running, awake and alert. Pietro did not speak to him. Neither did Luigi. He was not regarded as having a useful opinion on condom water-carriers or water-resistant socks. It was nothing personal – the psychiatrist was similarly ignored. Both men would have agreed that they found the personnel of the storm team extraordinary: could face amazing crises, could hibernate mentally in lists, and could be mawkishly sentimental, cold-blooded or uncaring, and juvenile in their humour. Both men had a deep, sincere respect for them.

Castrolami was not in the annexe, but was on the end of a mobile signal. The man, Lukas, was with him.

They talked. A question and an answer, a pause for maybe five minutes, then some more talk.

It took time to get round to the psychiatrist's big question: 'This American – whatever he is – is he good? Is he the best? Is he a man who talks well? Does he deliver?'

Then the collator's big answer: 'He has the pedigree of a prize-winning mastiff. Can he deliver? Tell me the circumstances.'

'Some would say it's an insult to our professionalism that he's here.'

'Some, also, would say his presence was not asked for.'

'If he succeeds, and delivers the English boy, *our* reputations are denigrated.'

The collator grinned, flashed his teeth, showed mischief. 'Have faith in our city. Naples doesn't bow the knee to foreigners.'

The ROS man interrupted their murmurs, hit Pietro again with his elbow and told him that this personal survival kit, top-of-the-range in America, had a brass snare wire, a length of fishing-line, six hooks with four weights, and a leader trace with an integrated swivel. Both men – as if at a signal – laughed, were close to collapse and held each other. They wondered whether the PSK was designed for the third world of Secondigliano or the via Baku of Scampia, and whether two condoms would be enough. The collator and the psychologist returned to their screens.

A phone rang. The collator answered, listened, put down the receiver. 'They have the Borelli girl.'

'What's she going to do? Stay or quit?'

'Do we have her or not?'

Castrolami was told. He showed no enthusiasm, no excitement.

'Do you believe her?'

Lukas hovered. He didn't crowd Castrolami.

Castrolami took a big breath, as if that was necessary
when a decision of importance was taken, and let the air
whistle out again between his teeth. He said, 'Bring her down
to us. She's not hidden now. If she runs on these streets she's
committing suicide. That will end the shit. Bring her.'

They walked.

'Things you have to understand, Lukas.'

'What things?'

A square stretched out in front of them, with big churches
on two of the four sides; on a third there was a view of the
sea's horizon. They were near to a fountain with statues at
the four corners; no water flowed and the basins where the
water might have been were filled with cardboard, plastic
and other junk. The statues were of crouched lions but each
had been decapitated, and the centre of the square was
populated with kids' bikes, plastic tractors and tricycles, and
plastic garden furniture. It should be a fine place, Lukas
thought. In Paris it would have been a fine place. Castrolami
told him it was the old *mercato*.

'Do I get a lecture in history?' Lukas asked quietly, and
the smile flickered.

'It was the last year of the eighteenth century. The English
navy restored a Bourbon tyrant to the throne. The piazza
dei Mercato was the execution site, it was where those who
had sided, erroneously, with the Napoleonic revolutionaries,
were brought for hanging. Many thousands died here over
several months, kicking the air, to the drunken jeers of the
lazzaroni, the street thugs. One hangman was a dwarf and
it pleased the crowd when he climbed, like a monkey, on to
the shoulders of the condemned, putting more weight on
the strangulation. Women were hanged here and abused –
it was a true terror. It satisfied the mob – it was their narcotic.
It has not died in Naples. On the streets they like a good

killing and a display of horror. Nothing has changed, Lukas. If we deny them the ears, fingers or penis of the boy coming through the post, or hand-delivered, they will be angry. Certainly, they will not help us. It is a lesson of Naples I learned many years ago, and learned well: the mob enjoys death.'

Lukas looked around him. It was a place of decay. He did not like to imagine but he felt the presence of the baying drunken crowd, a lynch mob, and saw a gallows of rough wood and used, well-stretched ropes. The sun blistered his forehead and he had to squint. There seemed no takers for the toys and the plastic furniture.

His gaze had gone beyond the church in front of him and past the broken statues. He saw the mountain, huge, grand and hazed. Cloud sat on it, a white cushion.

Castrolami said, 'In the rest of Italy there is no love for this city. It does not concern the citizens because they have each other's love. You know Narcissus? Of course you do. He could be the patron saint of Naples. The society is fashioned by the mountain. The mountain dominates. Tomorrow it may blow, or next week, or next year. The mountain creates fatalism. If it blows it will be fast and there will be no escape – perhaps half a million people will die, most sitting in their cars and hooting in a traffic jam as the ash comes down. There is resignation and acceptance of death. They used to be in this square to watch the death dance at the hangings. Today they gather, crowded close and pressing forward, to see the spasms of a man bleeding on the pavement after being shot. I hate this city, my home, and I hate its absence of morality, its acceptance of corruption, its compromising of honesty. They are total in the city. I have to tell you, Lukas, that Immacolata Borelli swears she will testify. She will not back down.'

'Then find him – find him quick, before the bits are sent to you,' Lukas said.

They turned their backs on the piazza and the mountain.

He had already bought the shirt, inexpensive and manufactured in China, wrapped in cellophane, when he met his handler. It was one of Davide's routines that he bought a cheap shirt when he took the bus down the hill to the old town. Then he had something to bring back to the Sail and talk about if anyone wanted to know why he went so far.

That day he didn't know the name of his handler. There were men and women, and some he thought were senior, and others little more than clerks. Neither did he know from what building in the city they worked. He had, that day, requested an extraordinary meeting and broken the schedule.

A man in a hood, handcuffed, had been hustled along a walkway. There was a view, fleeting, of the *capo* of the clan that had control of the Sail and half of the rest of Scampia, who, with his family, was a billionaire in euros and had been a fugitive for twelve years. There had now been four sightings of a man who was a stranger on that floor, not seen before, escorted. An old man, unable to disguise arthritis or rheumatism, had been brought past the agent's apartment window. He told it all. He was not expected to interpret or analyse. He said that the activity was of greater intensity than he could remember and he thought the presence of the outsiders, and the hooded man, of sufficient interest to be reported.

He passed to the handler two small cassettes. He was given two replacement spools.

He received no encouragement, no praise. Neither was he criticised for requesting the extra rendezvous.

He left the handler at the table, also routine. He knew

that when he had gone, the handler would leave. Using his pass, which showed him as disabled, he took a bus to the railway station, then another back up the long hill. It would drop him – with the rest of the flotsam and the addicts who came each day to buy – in Scampia near his block.

He had seen the shape of the hips, known it was a young man, – but his handler had shown no humanity, was unconcerned. Perhaps he had cared more for the cake on his plate.

Umberto, the lawyer, used his open hands to demonstrate helplessness. 'I don't seek to be an intermediary. What am I to do? A note is left at my office, and an answer demanded. I do my best, and attempt to save the life of an unfortunate.'

The prosecutor had the note in front of him. They were in the same room as they had met in before and, again, no dignity was offered to the clan's advocate. He considered his answer. He had learned much that morning. Castrolami had come to him and brought news that Immacolata Borelli was back with her minders, that Operation Partenope proceeded and her support was guaranteed. Excellent news. Less excellent – in fact, dismal: a further communication via the *lumaca*, the lawyer he regarded as a slug crawling in slime, and an ultimatum that had hardened. Time was running fast, fine sand between fingers.

With Castrolami there had been a short, slight man, who looked unfed and carried no spare weight, whose clothes were clean but unironed, and who had pepper-speckled hair that was cut short – as if by using scissors harshly the need for brushing was removed. He wore a short-sleeved checked sports shirt – not the collar and tie that the prosecutor and Castrolami habitually put on. The man had on jeans, not suit trousers, trainers, not polished leather shoes. His accent was a little American, had something of French, intimations

of English, the language he used. The expression on his face
was of humility. The prosecutor would likely have dismissed
him as an indulgence that wasted precious time but for two
factors: Mario Castrolami had brought him and would not
have done so lightly, and the man had eyes that pierced, in
which a light burned and demanded attention. He used only
one name: Lukas.

The prosecutor, formulating his answer, recalled what he
had been told by the soft voice with many accents. The man,
Lukas, had said they were now in the 'stand-off' time, that
they needed to get to the next stage, the 'negotiation phase',
and there followed only 'termination'. Right now – with a
tenuous line of communication open – they should be stalling,
playing the game towards deadline extension. He should not
be negative, should not refuse, but should delay while always
reassuring that a solution of mutual benefit could be found . . .
And when nothing is negotiable? The man, Lukas, had said
with simplicity and candour: 'You swallow the truth and lie.'
It stuck, like a mullet's bone, in the prosecutor's throat. He
had been told how he should begin the dialogue and wanted,
almost, to throw up.

He smiled sickly. 'What you must remember all the time,
Umberto, is that I want to help.'

Nothing was negotiable. Immacolata Borelli would testify.
She would denounce her mother and brothers. Her evidence
would send her blood relatives to harsh gaols for the greater
part of their lives. There was no slack, no elasticity in the
rope he now played out. He had, in his desk drawer, a
photograph of the boy. A decent photograph, one that had
been used for a passport. It was a photograph of an ordinary
boy, and nothing was negotiable. The boy's freedom could
not be bought. It would be duplicity that saved the boy, not
honesty – which did not sit easily with the prosecutor. He
had talked of it that morning with his wife, who had remarked,

predictably, 'His parents, how awful for them . . .' The parents, of course, were another burden for shouldering. Often, when faced with the gravest problems, he would talk to his wife and listen to her, then decide on the course to be followed. He would go to his office in the palace tower and listen to none of his closest aides. His wife had said, 'But you cannot *buy*, dear one, the life of the boy.' He valued what she told him, and could be strengthened by her opinion. What would change when he was gone, retired? What would be different on the streets of Naples when Castrolami was gone, and all the men and women who worked in that trusted loop round him? Would anything have altered? Was a great victory possible before the day that he, his wife and child turned their back on the place? He smiled again, looked across the table at the lawyer and felt the purity of hatred. 'I need you to know, Umberto, that I want to help resolve this matter in any way I can. My help is on the table.'

She didn't talk about her mother. The tape-recorder was not produced. She didn't speak of Vincenzo in the British prison, Belmarsh, or of Giovanni and Silvio, in the Poggioreale gaol. She made no more accusations against her father, locked in a solitary cell of the maximum-security block in Novara.

Her plastic bag was filled.

She had cooked an omelette, with cheese and diced ham, had mixed a dressing and tossed a salad, and had about emptied the refrigerator of bread and fruit. She had drunk a glass of water from the tap, as they had, and she had cleared the table. They had offered to help and been curtly refused.

Immacolata washed up the plates and bowls and the frying-pan, the knives and forks.

They were behind her, still at the table.

She could have asked if there was news of Eddie Deacon.

She did not. They hadn't spoken of anything significant, major or minor, of the purchase of the padlock and it being left to rust on a chain on the Ponte Milvio, a place of history. She used scalding water and no plastic gloves. The pain flushed her skin and she didn't know whether they approved of what she was doing or thought her a cold, heartless, treacherous bitch. Knives and forks clattered on to the draining-board.

Immacolata had not asked for information on what was being done to save Eddie Deacon's life. She knew she wouldn't be answered. They would have shrugged, pleaded their junior rank, and she would have demeaned herself. The salad bowl and the frying pan dripped on the draining-board, and she attacked the plates.

Her problem – why she washed up and would then mop the floors and wipe the surfaces – chewed inside her. A junction reached, two turnings for choice. To take one betrayed the death agonies of Marianna Rossetti, to take the other condemned Eddie Deacon. There was no middle road. A plate broke. Maybe it had already been cracked, or she had put it down too forcefully on the draining-board. Without thinking, she collected the pieces, laid them out and looked to see if the damage could be repaired. Only for a moment. She picked the pieces up, marched across the floor to the bin, dumped them and let the lid slam.

She was finishing. Orecchia came from the table, gestured that he would help to dry up, but she waved him away. She wondered, briefly, who would be here next – a *pentito* from the Camorra, from the far south or Sicily? She had thought once that the hill, with its views, its fences, its guard dogs and its money, could be a home. She would never come back here. She saw a future of cars with privacy windows, false identities, and apartments that displayed nothing personal. No friends. She supposed, one day, they would give her a number to ring if she had difficulties. She would not, after a few more days or weeks, see Orecchia or Rossi again. There would be no friends. She would not love.

It hurt too much to think of Eddie Deacon.

She cleared the draining-board, made the correct piles on the shelves – and wondered if, for a department of the ministry that dealt with housing collaborators, she should write a confessional note reporting the broken plate. Then she went to the cupboard and brought out the mop. All the rooms would be cleaned. Orecchia and Rossi would understand that she needed to purge the place of her presence. She was a memory that would be erased, as if she had never been there. But she would have left something. She bit her lower lip hard, felt no pain but the warmth of blood. Without what she left, Immacolata would be a changed person.

She would not know how, again, to love.

The prosecutor's car had brought him to the city hall. He did not see the mayor or any elected politician, but an official in the Interior section of the city's bureaucracy. 'We believe the successful prosecution of the entire Borelli family is a matter of great importance to the administration of Naples.'

In his own world, at the Palace of Justice, the prosecutor was a king, an emperor, and had – almost – the authority of a Bourbon.

'We are concerned that the image of the city is fractured, that national leaders from the north regard us as a nest of anarchy and criminality, and that the city is ungovernable.'

He was not in his own world. Power, absolute, resided in this building, and when he was summoned, the prosecutor came.

'Without a mark of success, we face the very grave dangers of attacks on the city's budget as supplied by central government – it would be reflected in police and *carabinieri* budgets. There is the expression, "throwing good money after bad", and it is used frequently in reference to our society. We have to succeed. The election, also, looms.'

A small mountain of paper was on his desk, with foothills of files on the carpet around it, but in acknowledgement of that power he must show dutiful attention.

'There can be no question of a bargain being done. We deal, Dottore, with justice and we are not in a souk. Justice comes first, always. The case against the Borelli family will be prosecuted with full rigour. The mayor, or a principal in his administration, wishes – very soon – to give a media conference at which the iron-fisted determination of the city hall will be shown as resolute against organised criminality.'

The prosecutor nodded, seemed to show what was required of him: respect.

'If the young man dies – and no negotiation will be deployed – it is believed that such a tragedy can be turned to advantage as a clear indication of the barbarity of the clans, their ruthlessness. *If* . . . We demand there is no weakening.'

He was dismissed. He had stood throughout and had not been given coffee. What angered the prosecutor most: he had been dragged across the city, brought here, lectured, and he agreed with each sentiment voiced. Nothing was negotiable. He left through the ornate double doors. He wondered how high a level of deceit was required to save the boy, and whether the man, Lukas, who had been in his office was capable of lying to that level.

A priest said, in brisk Italian, 'Yes, he came here. He came to my church of San Giorgio Maggiore. I'm told he waited a long time for me. Before, he had been the length of via Forcella and back, and had asked where he could find Immacolata Borelli. Her last home was with her grandparents. He was a stranger and no one would tell him. If a stranger asks for the directions to the home of an old clan leader and his wife, no one will tell him . . . except me. I told him. I realise now that I should not have, but I did. And the boy has "disappeared", a way of saying he has been kidnapped, and will be used to pressurise the granddaughter, Immacolata. I know Immacolata. If she had stayed, if she had taken a young man from her own class, from another family, I would have been asked to marry her in my church, and I doubt I would have refused. It would have been a grand wedding, followed by an obscenely lavish party, and horrible amounts would have been spent on the principals' clothing. A heap of banknotes would have been given me for the repair of the church roof and most of those notes would have tested positive for recent cocaine exposure. A predecessor of mine refused, and he was not supported by the hierarchy, and his condemnation of the killing of a child in a gun battle was not backed. For a few days after the girl died there were demonstrations of hostility towards the clan. The anger was a wind that blew out very soon, and the priest was isolated, under threat. When the TV cameras had gone, and their lights, he was alone. He is now in Rome, and when he comes back to visit his mother and father he has an explosion-proof car to travel in and armed bodyguards to escort him. Our cloth and our collar do not protect us. There are bullet marks by the main door and you passed them. It is not easy to stand against such a force. You wish me to ask in my pulpit on Sunday for information to be given to the police concerning the boy. I would be wasting my breath. They are the state, not you, Dottore Castrolami. They have complete power, complete authority. Even inside this house of God I feel the fear. It is always with us. It shames me, but it's there. Fear is in the fabric of this street, this church, this congregation, this priest. A priest stood out against the Casalesi clan and was shot dead. You say you have few hours left, and you have no idea where the boy is held. I'm grateful for the trust you place in me that you can give me information so sensitive, and I can suggest only that you pray for good fortune and that the sun will shine on your endeavour. It is Naples. We are all, believe me, friend, powerless in the face of this force of evil. We lack the strength to stand against it. But I tell you, friend, if it is one or the other – the force of justice exerted against the family of Forcella or the boy's life – I choose justice. I feel inadequate, a failed man, not only today but every day I serve here. I will pray for the boy, but privately. The Church has little use for another hero, less for another martyr.'

Castrolami shook his hand, then Lukas. They left him in the quiet, cool, empty cavern of his church, and went back out into the sunshine. Lukas was not a man, *ever*, to criticise the actions, the self-preservation and the priorities of a victim skewered on dilemmas. They went for coffee.

Did he want it?

Eddie shivered.

The enormity of what he had achieved struck him, a hammer blow. He was shivering, his legs were trembling spasmodically and his hands shook.

He had two hinges loose.

He could now, using the galvanised bucket for leverage and the head of the nail as a screw-driver, free the hinges from the door.

At any moment, on his decision, with a five-minute window to shift the screws, he could open the door, forcing the bolt from its slot, and go through it. He would have the nail as a weapon, with the end of the chain and its pin.

He didn't know what was beyond the door.

He could get through one, might find another that was locked, bolted and barricaded . . . might find that the handle turned and it opened. He might confront, beyond it, three men with knives, guns and coshes, or he might find it empty, or one man asleep. He might be too high up to go out through a window – or there might be a flat roof for him to drop down on.

He didn't know.

If he opened the door that took him beyond the chance to turn back – he'd be going for broke. If they caught him they'd hurt him, then kill him.

Choices faced Eddie Deacon, almost crushed him.

15

It was as if Eddie pressed on a coiled spring. His breathing was hard, uncontrolled. His leg muscles had tightened and his hands were clumsy, insensitive. Tension built in him.

He did it.

Eddie had the galvanised bucket under the lower hinge bar. The upper was already detached and had swung away from the steel-sheeted door. He let the spring go; his energy danced free. All of his strength now was directed on to the bucket and his fingers were gripping it. He pulled, tugged, forced back the bucket and the two screws screeched. He had been more careful, had worked slower, on the upper hinge and it had made less noise. Now the lower hinge made a cat-fight sound. No going back. A sound – proverbial – to wake the dead. Enough to wake any guy on sentry duty, drowsy in a chair. He did the last heave, and was hurled back across the space as the hinge bar came away and one of the screws exploded into his face, like gunfire. The bolt fittings loosed. The door sagged and fell away.

A strip of light came into the space. Eddie could see where he had been – walls that were graffiti-marked, and his own name a scrawl across other writing, the boarded window, the turned-over bucket and the plastic bag in which the food had been, the bottle on its side, the crevice of broken concrete from which the chain's pin had been dislodged, and the hood. He could see all of that. Then he scooped up the length of chain, might have been five feet of it, the nail in his right hand, and he put his body into the gap, using his hips and shoulders to force the opening wider. He was snagged – he struggled, writhed . . . and broke out.

He didn't know how much time he'd used since the screech of the screws – seemed an age, might have been a few seconds. Time, then, was most precious to him.

Eddie crouched. He had two weapons and readied them. He had the nail held like a knife for stabbing downwards, and the chain with the pin on it which he could swing as a flail. The room was small, empty. No chairs, no table, no cupboards or chests, but there were sacks against one wall, three, opened, and in them were stacked packages in sealed oiled paper – like it was their warehouse. There was wallpaper, peeled and damp-stained, with mould by the skirting and a loud flower pattern, and there was a window, daylight.

Going fast, crab-like, Eddie reached it. Light poured through it and stung his eyes. He blinked and they watered. He didn't know how long he had been in darkness or with the hood over his face. He realised, peering through the grime on the glass, that he was high in a block. He could see below an empty road, then a path on which dogs fought, snarling and posturing, and a woman pushed a buggy. Beyond, kids kicked a football and the shadows were small, the sun high. He saw also that a man urinated in the bushes, his back to the block, and further down the road a couple, young, looked behind them furtively, then went into the cover. He knew he could have waved at that window, screamed, jumped up and down and yelled some more but no one would hear, see or care about him – not even the bloody dogs. But he pulled at the window latches. They were rotten and broke, and he had the window wide. Eddie had to close his eyes to protect them from the glare. He stood vulnerable – thought it pathetic – rooted and blind. He had to open his eyes, take the pain. He did.

He put his head out of the window. He saw a cruising police car, but only the tail, then it was gone – and a scooter coming up the street. The driver and his pillion wore black helmets with darkened visors.

What was he looking for? Perhaps he hoped to find, under that window, a drainpipe or a balcony, a hand reaching up from a window below, or a builder's ladder, the convenience of a fire escape. He craned forward, lost sight of the dogs and the kids, the woman with the buggy and the man who had now zipped up and was walking. The scooter had gone and the road was empty again. There was nothing. Maybe a film stuntman could have done something, or a Special Forces soldier, a guy from a comic – not Eddie Deacon. There was no hand or foot grip, and the pavement was fifty, sixty feet below, the drop sheer.

He heard, behind him, the door open, then an oath.

Turning, he faced the man. Young, muscled, not focused but confused, T-shirt and jeans, hair slicked with gel and a chain on his neck with a crucifix hanging. Eddie saw every feature of him. The sun spot on his temple and the mole on his chin, his T-shirt inside the belt on the jean waist. Not more than two seconds, and Eddie had absorbed that the man had no weapon.

He charged him. Hit him hard, clenched fist holding the nail, hit him in the chest where the ribcage gives way to soft stomach skin. Didn't know who he was, why he was there. Eddie felt he'd punctured him. Hadn't seen him before. Hit him, wounded and hurt him, because he was in the doorway. The man grunted and doubled. Eddie didn't know whether it was a flesh wound or a fatal injury to an organ. He pushed him aside. As the man went down, Eddie went through the doorway.

He was in another room. The men's hands loosened, the cards fell haphazardly to the table and dropped on to the banknotes they played for. Chairs were pushed back and the table rocked as knees caught its underside. Three more men, all matching the other's confusion, disbelief. But the door out of the room was beyond them. A hand clutched his shoulder from behind.

He was brought to the Sail by Fangio. His nose was a dull pain that throbbed. Blood was in his nostrils, and he had sucked some into his mouth and swallowed a little.

The anger burned in him. Salvatore had had to return to the Sail to report to the clan men who had sent him out, given him the photograph of an opponent to be killed and the map for the location of a killing. It had been demanded that he report back in person. Already a witness would have called a cut-out number, which would have phoned into the Sail. He was not bringing news of a killing – like when he was ten, before he was full time on the streets, and standing before a goddam teacher, his goddam writing commented on – 'Poor, needs more practice. Improvement required', but it was a part of the price Carmine Borelli had paid. They would know already that a bottle had hit his face, and that the execution had not shown calm, casual power.

When he lifted off his helmet, the visor spattered, the blood had been dammed by the padding and made a ring below his lower lip and on his cheeks. He was Salvatore, the idol of kids who had his photograph on their mobiles. He was Il Pistole. He was the enforcer of the Borelli clan. He could have screwed Gabriella Borelli, should have screwed Immacolata Borelli. He was a man of consequence in Forcella and Sanità, but in the Sail he was a servant and had been sent with a P38 on an errand. The blood on his face was as humiliating as if, a kid, he had soiled his pants.

He went up the stairs fast and hoped to find a washroom

before he saw the principals. As he took the steps – two in each stride – the pain caught him.

The car was a high-performance Alfa 166, a three-litre engine. Orecchia drove and the seat beside him was empty, except for a machine pistol, gas canisters and a protective vest.

She had Rossi with her in the back. It might have been Orecchia's sense of humour that he had insisted on driving and put her with Rossi, who had seen her naked as she had seen him. They sat at the far extremities of the black-leather bench seat, and there was another machine pistol between them, more gas and vests. She thought the car was low on its wheels and presumed it was armoured. Rossi, now, ignored her. It was as if, she thought – her signature on the 'contract', the agreement that she would collaborate and give evidence guaranteed – they were about to pass her on and therefore had no need to humour, flatter, cajole or dominate her. She was to them used goods.

Their eyes did not meet. Their hands stayed far apart, and their knees. She was behind Orecchia and stared out of the left side window. Rossi's attention was locked on the right.

They went fast on the *autostrada*, kept a place in the overtaking lane. Traffic in front veered out of their path and blue lights flashed behind the radiator grille. They had been escorted out of the Roman suburbs by a marked car and would be met again when they approached the southern city. They were now south of Frosinone, north of Cassino, and cruised at an average of 145 kilometres an hour. Orecchia had music on, light opera, and there was no conversation. The radio filled the void.

She wore the best of her few clothes, had done her makeup and brushed her hair before leaving. She had seen residents on the balconies of the block on the hill and had walked

straight-backed to the car. It would have been obvious from
their body language that the men with her were a protection
detail. She thought there would have been sneers from those
balconies and it would have been obvious that she was a
collaborator – she had protection but not the clothing of a
person of status. By now she would be gossiped over. Like
dogs with old bones, they would be exchanging anecdotes
of sightings of her. Not one, she was certain, of the residents
on the hill would have admired what she had done.

They had gone out to the *autostrada* by the north-east
route. She had had only one glimpse of the river. The old
bridge, built originally by a Roman-era architect, and carrying
now a padlock sold that morning for thirty-five euros, was
far behind her.

Immacolata Borelli was going home.

One man had a lacerated face, a ribbon of blood, from the
chain swung against it.

Another had run and was gone down a corridor, a door
slammed after him and a bolt pushed back.

Another was dazed from the collision of his head with
Eddie's and doubled from the impact of Eddie's knee in his
groin.

The man who had been stabbed with the nail and had
grabbed Eddie's shoulder, now moaned on the floor and
held his throat. There were welts on it where the chain had
wrapped round it, and he had almost choked with the
constriction of his windpipe.

There were two doors, closed, ahead of Eddie.

The moment would not last, could not. They were in
shock, and shock would clear.

Eddie opened the left-hand door. He saw a lavatory seat
and a basin. He came out, twisted and dragged on the second
door. He was in a hall. An artist's conception of Christ hung

on the wall, a candle under it, not lit. Eddie understood that
adrenalin coursed through him. When it was used up, he
would weaken. His pace would slacken, while their shock
and confusion ebbed. There were more sacks in the hall and
another door, with a steel-barred gate, and beyond it a steel
sheet on wood. But the lock on the gate was unfastened and
he could wrench it back. In the local paper, the one that did
Dalston and Hackney, there had been a piece about crack
houses that had been busted into by the police, with
photographs and the crack houses had had those barred
gates for security. Heavy keys were in the door. He didn't
know what was beyond it. He pulled it open.

An alarm wailed. He couldn't have known the door was
alarmed – had seen no key pad. Eddie reeled out on to a
walkway. He could have gone right but he went left. In either
direction there was only a long corridor of concrete with
chest-high walls and wires running across it, looped to
overhead bars, with washing slung on them – he had to duck
his head below shirts, sheets and skirts, cotton trousers,
lightweight towels and underwear. He ran, and heard the
pursuit.

Because of the washing his head was down, and it was
awkward running with the shackle on his ankle – bloody
excuses, Eddie. He looked up. He saw, ahead of him, a gate.
It was as if the air was vacuumed from his lungs. It was like
when hope died. There was no way off the walkway and it
was lined with doors – closed, blocked to him. There was a
staircase, perhaps fifty paces ahead – might have been a mile
or five. He slowed. There was a knot of men at the head of
the staircase and between them and him the gate. He saw
it so clearly. He could see five vertical and three horizontal
bars, and it was topped with a loose coil of barbed wire.
The pandemonium behind him came nearer. He had almost
stopped. He saw the man, with caked blood on his face,

approach the gate and talk to the guards there, and attention was distracted.

Eddie was level with a window. Some on the walkway had been broken and repaired with cardboard, others had old sheets or towels draped across them for privacy, or were too filthy to see through. He caught the eyes of an old guy slumped in a chair but who had turned, twisted, then was on his feet.

The door beside the window opened. It must have been in Eddie's face: two big words – *per favore*. He heard a key turn. The door wasn't opened. For him to do it.

Eddie understood the survival instinct. Refuge given, but for him to open the door, and for him to determine whether it brought the dogs of hell into the old guy's room. Nowhere else to go. He went inside.

Old blood on Salvatore's face. New blood on the men confronting him. He had been slowed at the gate, they had been slowed by the washing slung across. Some items had been torn down when the cloth was across their faces. Women screamed and were in the walkway, collecting up what had been torn down. For dirtying washing, foot-soldiers of the clan could be abused, not for murder, not for selling narcotics or for intimidation, but for washing that had been dragged off the pegs and would have to be washed again.

Salvatore was allowed through the barred gate. He could have been let through immediately, but that was not the way power was exercised in Scampia. He was kept waiting on the pretence that an answer to a mobile was needed – bullshit. And amusing, too, the blood on his face. He saw men coming towards him. He recognised three of the four, knew where they had been and what their work was.

Incoherent ramblings greeted him. Then clarity.

Salvatore screamed.

His man was lost. Where? Above the scream, close to where he stood, a television was turned up loud and blasted out of a closed window. He had to scream to be heard above it: 'Knock down every fucking door. Find him.'

The handler of Delta465/Foxtrot had enjoyed his cake and coffee, had put the tapes given him into his briefcase and had wandered back to the office used by the service, a block in the Mussolini tradition that was behind the Posta e Telegrafi building and backed on to the piazza Carita.

He had wound fast through the picture images, had seen a clan leader whose image was perpetually on the database. He had seen a close-up of Carmine Borelli and his hood, Salvatore, both thrown up by computer recognition, and the three still frames that showed a hooded prisoner being frogmarched along the walkway – a front frame, a side frame, a back frame.

He had typed his report.

He had gone down a corridor and had knocked with due respect on the door of his line manager. He had been admitted. He had explained what matters the agent – Delta465/Foxtrot – had felt sufficiently important to warrant an extraordinary meeting. He had shown the images.

The concerns of the agent were logged.

His line manager said, 'We operate, Beppe, in a world of priorities. We're not policemen, not detectives of the Guardia di Finanze, or investigators of the *carabinieri*. We are defenders of the state in matters of national security. This is mere criminality. We do not, for any short-term position, endanger the safety of a long-term asset. If the police or other units were to act on this information it would hazard his safety – our agent. It should be filed. Thank you. Please, excuse me, I have a meeting. The usual file and without specific flagging.'

*

The search had started. In the warren of concrete that was the Sail, on its third floor, where the walkway had the numbers of the three hundreds, odd and even, doors were hammered on for entry. Like a pack of hunting dogs, hurt and demanding blood, men went about the task of tracking down a fugitive.

It had been the washing suspended from the wires criss-crossing above the walkway that had permitted the escaper to lose his pursuers. The washing was gone now, and the women had retreated.

It was a methodical search, down two sides, and every apartment was scoured. All those who hunted or watched waited for the triumphant shout that would tell them of success. There was no love for strangers here.

News travelled fast in Naples and its environs. It might as well have been carried on the hourly bulletins of the independent radio stations or on the RAI network. It burrowed through prison walls, over the barbed-wire defences, into the great heat-stifled blocks, where the cells were, and into the wire-roofed exercise yards.

At Posilippo, north of the city, Gabriella Borelli heard a whisper through her door that her daughter was back in the custody of the Servizio Centrale Protezione and would testify. She sat on her bunk and the sweat streamed off her. She thought of the boy, the one lever left, and wished him dead, his corpse dumped at her daughter's feet. She was near to tears.

At Poggioreale, south of the city, Giovanni Borelli strutted in a yard and Silvio Borelli slouched around the circuit, and it was murmured to them that their sister had returned to the protection of the state and had guaranteed her willingness to give evidence. The older swore, cursed and blasphemed, his cheeks reddened, and his brother heard him say, 'The whore, the fucking whore – she should have her boy, have him dead.' The younger shook his head, didn't understand the scale of his sister's hatred or why it was directed against himself. He would have seen the boy butchered if it would open the Poggioreale gate for him.

Umberto, the lawyer, heard – brought to him by the grapevine his nephew, Massimo, listened to. He thought: then the boy is condemned. And his building had cameras aimed at it, his phones were listened to. If he walked to a bar for coffee and a pastry he was followed on foot, and if he drove to the launderette to deliver or collect his cottons a car came after him. 'The boy is condemned and has little time. Sad but inevitable . . . little time.'

Eddie Deacon had no bloodlust, would have said he did not practise cruelty to the defenceless. He had memories. He could hear – through doors, walls, above the volume of the television – the search coming closer . . . doors breaking, shouting, always closer.

A memory of fishing for pike in the Avon as a child, with other children. A small roach or a juvenile perch, maybe three inches long, was impaled alive on treble hooks, then thrown into still water in the ebb of a weir and near a reed bed, and a float would bob around as the fish swam for safety from the predator. It would try to reach the cover of the reeds and find shelter there from the pike's jaws, and the children would yank the line and pull it away from the reeds so that it would swim where the big beast could see it. Always the live bait went for the most tangled reeds to hide.

The apartment was a trap, and its teeth had closed round him.

A memory of the kids who lived on farms – and the child, Eddie, went to their homes at weekends and headed off with them across the fields – and had set snares. They were put in place on a Friday afternoon, inspected on Saturday and Sunday morning. Sometimes the rabbit was already dead, sometimes there was just blood and fur and a fox would have taken it but occasionally the rabbit had crouched, so still, and seemed to know its fate and merely waited for the killing blow. Always, with its final strength, it had tried to get into what deep cover the snare's restraint allowed.

There was a front room in which an old man sat and watched the television. It was a dirty, smelly, hot room, and the man had gone back to his chair after turning the key and hadn't looked at Eddie. He had watched a film, technicolour, cowboys – it could have been Robert Mitchum, half a century old, and had not caught Eddie's eye. What alternative? A pack running behind him. A closed gate in front. No steps off to the sides, up or down. The door had been unlocked for him to open and close. A front room with a window that was exceptional for its cleanliness. He had gone inside. A corridor ran from the living room, and there was no air-conditioner, no electric fan, and the heat caught inside was a blanket in his face. There was a kitchen space off the corridor with a small cooker and a fridge, both from a museum, and small cupboard units. It wasn't a place where a man – five foot ten, twelve stone six – could hide. No chance. There was a bedroom and a double bed, and under the mattress there were fixed drawers, a wardrobe that looked ready to fall apart and a chest with more drawers. Again there was no hiding place.

A memory of the ferrets that most of the farmers' kids had. Little sharp-nosed, sharp-eyed, sharp-toothed killing machines. Nets put across the burrows, the ferrets slipped in, then the listening, the pounding of a rabbit running and a net bulging. This child had not enjoyed the spectacle but had gone so as not to lose face – bloody important at nine or ten. He had often thought of a rabbit going deeper and further into the far extremity of the burrow and all the time hearing the scurrying brush of the little bastard's clawed pads, and having nowhere further to run.

The bathroom was the only room remaining off the corridor. The hunters were in the next apartment. The walls were thin, little more than partitions. He thought of it as a bathroom, but it had no bath. There was a basin, a lavatory without a seat, a shower unit with a curtain drawn half across and sagging for lack of support. There was a small cupboard, and a window.

The memories were of the defenceless ones who had tried to reach thick reeds, bramble cover and the last extremity of the burrow.

Not much went through Eddie's mind as he looked at the window, heard the banging and shouting through the wall. She wasn't in his mind. He didn't think of love, of getting his leg over, of growing old in her company and owning a bloody cottage with roses growing. Eddie thought of survival. There was a man who had blood on his chest from a rusted nail's wound, and another with slash marks on his face from a chain, and a third who had doubled when a knee had crunched his testicles. He thought they were all coming, they and plenty more, and where he was would be next for the search.

He had the window open.

The breeze through it, slight, riffled the plastic curtains. He couldn't think of anywhere else to go that offered the possibility of survival.

Then the door down the corridor and beyond the living room was hit. He saw the men, in his mind, pouring inside, the blood on their clothing and skin.

Eddie went out through the window. He stood on the rim of the lavatory bowl and swung a leg out, then the other, and his weight was taken on his shin, which was across the sharp metal of the window frame. He looked down. Once was enough. There was the road, and long, sun-scorched grass. There were bushes and rubbish trolleys, long filled to overflowing, and there was concrete. What had he thought when he was looking out of the window in the holding place, his cell? That the drop was fifty or sixty feet. Seemed fucking further now. A pipe jutted out of the concrete a little to his left – an overflow pipe for the lavatory, maybe – diameter of about half an inch, protruding maybe six. He thought, from what he heard, that they were now in the bedroom or the kitchen. The nail went into his pocket. Again, Eddie took a deep breath. It was about survival. If he was taken now he stood no chance. He didn't think of her, or his father and mother – didn't see the childhood home or the house in Dalston. Saw a bastard drop, a pipe from which water dripped, the edge of the window frame and the flutter of the curtain.

Eddie went over, and the chain cascaded down. He let his chest and stomach scrape down the iron window fitting, then against the old concrete of the building. His feet kicked. His fists, clenched to give his fingers the strength needed and gripping the bottom of the window frame, took his weight. Then a trainer found the pipe and a fraction of the weight was shed. But, he did not know how long the pipe would carry its share of the weight, and the chain swayed beneath him. He hung.

He played the idiot, a deaf idiot, well. They swarmed through Davide's living room, shrieking questions at him, and he grinned but barely turned his head from the big screen in front of him where a gunfight blazed. He didn't answer and left them to think he was afflicted by deafness as well as idiocy. The agent was not deaf and was not an idiot. His years of living the lie in the Sail had required of him the

acutest sense of self-preservation. It was irrelevant at that
moment whether his hearing was good or impaired: his sanity
was on the line. He could not have articulated why he had
risen from his chair, gone fast across the worn carpet through
the polystyrene takeaway trays and unlocked his door. Their
eyes had met. He had looked back through the window, had
seen the face and the desperation, the stains on the clothing,
the nail in the fist with the dark stain at the tip, and the
chain, and he had known that a fugitive ran. Had seen that
shirt below a hood, had seen that dark shade of jeans when
a prisoner was brought along the walkway. He saw so much
of human misery, the arrogance of the clan *capo*s and the
swagger of the foot-soldiers, and he performed his duty and
reported to his handlers. He had never before intervened.
Not much of an intervention, the unlocking of a door, but
a first time. Now he was ignored. Four men at least flowed
through his apartment and doors banged but he did not
hear the whoop. There was no place of refuge if a search,
barely a thorough one, was made but they came out of the
corridor. He muttered a short prayer. He dedicated it to
Matteo, the patron saint of bank workers and book-keepers
– as he had been. He said the prayer again, silently but never
allowed his eyes to leave the screen where revolver shots
were exchanged in front of a timbered saloon. He could not
imagine where the boy had hidden. They were all gone, but
one stood in the open door and lit a cigarette.

It seemed that his arms were slowly being wrenched from
their sockets. He didn't know for how much longer he could
keep it up. Cramp had set into his fingers, which gripped
the base of the iron window frame. What sustained him was
the diminishing voices. They had been right above him. The
voices and the clatter of movement had come so close, within
spitting range, but his hands – what little of them would

have been visible above the window frame – had been behind the flutter of the curtain. It would have been just a glance, a moment's check, and they would have seen no place where an adult could hide. Maybe they had then been in twenty apartments, maybe they had ten more to go through, maybe they had gotten careless . . . and the voices had drifted. Maybe another half-minute and then, God willing, he would begin the attempt to regain the window.

The first stone missed him, was well wide.

The second, thrown harder, more expertly, a better missile, hit the concrete level with his head, around a yard from him.

He swung momentarily, as if he had tried to swat the grit its impact spat at him, on one hand, then clawed the other back into position, and the extra weight had shifted the overflow pipe on which there was room for one foot. Little voices were far below, shrill.

He looked down. Had to tuck his head almost into his right armpit and his view went past flush window sills, to the paving, the rubbish bags, the bushes and the kids . . . Fucking kids. The chain swung languidly below his foot. Not the kids. Nothing half-hearted about the little bastards. Four of them down there. The smallest had a catapult. Three slung stones up at him, which made a random shower, but the smallest kid had the range, had damn near hit Eddie's head, and had another stone loaded. Eddie looked back up at the window. Couldn't look down any more. He heard their shouts – voices that were choirboys' – and imagined they were all pointing up. Wrong. All except the sod with the catapult. He was hit in the shoulder-blade. Imagined one man looking down from a window and seeing them pointing. The next stone from the catapult hit the back of Eddie's leg, where it was soft, just above the left knee.

He tried to lift himself. It would have taken the ultimate of his concentration – real focus – to find that strength,

channel it and get himself up high enough so that his elbows
could go over the window frame. A stone hit the concrete
a foot from his eye and level with it. He couldn't turn his
head away – wouldn't dare destabilise himself. Eddie knew
his strength was going, and with it the heart.

The drop was below him, and the kids bayed, and more
had come, and it was a chorus below his feet and the chain
with the pin attached. Too much pain in his fingers.

Where it all ended. Some God-fuck-forsaken awful housing
estate somewhere out of Naples.

Get it over with. Get it done. He had only to loosen his
grip and it was over, done. The pain would be gone from
his hands and he would have peace and . . . would hit the
paving, a potato sack. Eddie felt tears welling.

His wrist was grasped.

He couldn't look up. First one hand had taken his left
wrist, then a second. He thought of the old man in the chair
and sobbed, in silence, thanks to him. He didn't doubt that
the grip on his arm was strong and wouldn't fail him. He'd
hug him, kiss him. His foot was off the pipe and his hands
had lost their hold on the window frame. He was reliant.
When did he know?

A truth came to Eddie Deacon when a third hand and a
fourth, then a fifth had a grip on him. Two hands on his
left wrist, two more on his right and a fifth had a fistful of
his shirt. He was lifted. He saw the faces. There was blood
on one, and blood on another man's T-shirt. And there was
the man who had put him in the van on via Forcella, whose
eyes seemed to dance with laughter.

He was pulled up, lifted through the window, then thrown
down on to the floor. The tears came.

As the investigator in charge of the case, Marco Castrolami
had the prime place at the end of the table. It was rare for

this committee to be called together, but he thought it worth the effort. There were few other places he could go. The meeting had lasted twenty-four minutes, on the wall clock behind his chair, and its usefulness was exhausted.

Around the table were the head of the *carabinieri* criminal-intelligence section for the province of Campania, the officer who headed intelligence-gathering for the Naples police, the senior intelligence co-ordinator of the Guardia di Finanza, and a dapper, slight man who seemed to offer no name and was set apart from the rest.

Castrolami said, 'I repeat, for the final time, that only a few hours are now available to save the life of this British boy, Eddie Deacon. I repeat that all surveillance of principals has failed to find – as best I know – a pattern of movements or intercepts that can locate him. I hope you will all examine your memories with due diligence. Whatever else you have in on-running investigations, I request your help. So, I repeat, has anyone even the smallest information on where the Borelli clan is holding this boy? Please.'

His eyes travelled round the table: to his colleague, to the police officer he had known for a dozen years of late-night drinking, bitching, complaining and laughing, to the fiscal policeman who was new in the city. They had all shaken their heads or used their hands to gesture ignorance. Last, his glance rested on the official from the secret service, who was doodling on a sheet of paper. He looked up and Castrolami lip-read his quiet answer: 'Nothing.' But it was not said aloud.

He stood. He had no more to offer.

They came off the *autostrada*, through the toll booth, and on to the slip-road. Below, far to the west, were the city and the sea, its beauty and its magnificence.

In the glove box, Orecchia had found a lightweight raincoat, flimsy, but sufficient for what he needed. If it hadn't been there he would have used a newspaper. He covered the machine pistol with it, then switched off the flashing light behind the radiator grille.

Now Rossi caught her eye, accepted the contact. There was a query in his expression and she nodded decisively. She was prepared for the last stage of the journey, into Naples.

And memories swept her. Immacolata knew the features and signs of the road. She knew the filling station, owned by the Mauriello clan, and the garden centre that seemed to have hectares of rattan furniture on display and was owned by the Nuvoletta clan. There was the restaurant beside the dual-carriageway where her father had taken her and she had met the Lo Russo family – she had been seventeen and had taken an instant dislike to the boy whose company she was supposed to enjoy. It would have been a good alliance, and her father had laughed all the way back into the city at the scale of the failure. There was the truckyard where the long-distance lorries were kept, maintained and repaired; it was owned by the Licciardi clan, and the fleet could be hired by her father or her brother for the empty run north, under the terms of a sub-contract, and the return laden with chemical waste for the Moccia or the Alfieri clan. It was excellent commercial co-operation. They came past the great angled towers of the Scampia district, and on through Secondigliano and into the territory of the Contini clan. She saw cafés where men had been killed, and bars where men had been killed, and pavements where men had been killed, and she had come home.

Immacolata was adult. She was intelligent. She knew what happened in her home city, and the history of its streets. She knew where the envelopes of five-hundred-euro notes, tight in elastic bands, had been slipped into the smart, expensive leather briefcases of politicians, national and local; she knew where civil servants who prepared recommendations on contract choice of cement manufacturers were entertained by Romanian or Belarussian girls; she knew where the men who led the clans housed their mistresses – and where there had been a concrete-lined hole in a yard that had been the home for eight months of a clan leader's eldest son, his heir. The police had needed reinforcements before they could remove the twenty-six-year-old and had fired gas at a screaming crowd. They had lost two patrol cars, torched, before order was restored for long enough to make the retreat. She knew where. It was her city.

She could see the Sail building, and knew that her father – in an earlier prison term – had been in an adjacent cell and had shared exercise with the clan leader's cousin. Now it had drifted away from her view, with the other towers, and she saw the signs to Capodicino airport.

The car went fast. She saw now that Orecchia spoke – outside her hearing – into a button microphone that hung loose from an attachment. She had not noticed him put an earpiece in place.

They were near to the bottom of the last long hill, on the via Carbonara, going past the high walls of the Castel Capuano. Rossi had stiffened in his seat and had undone his seatbelt, as if he felt the need for greater freedom. His hand was on the stock of the machine pistol, and a car – unmarked – was in front of them, with another behind. It was not the direct route. She sensed they were playing with her, testing her, or steeling her.

Immacolata saw, very clearly, the lower end of the via Forcella. There was the bar where her grandfather went for coffee and brandy, to play cards or dominoes with old friends. There was the vegetable stall where her grandmother bought broccoli and spinach, tomatoes and spring onions. There was the narrow entrance to the shallow arcade where Silvio played the machines, and the hairdresser Giovanni used was beyond it. Momentarily, she had a view of the façade of the block where her grandfather and grandmother lived, then the three cars – in unison – had swung left.

She could see, fleetingly, the shops, businesses, outlets from which, as a teenager, she had collected the *pizzo*, and those to which, older, with the benefit of her newly learned book-keeping, she had gone to revalue their contributions. She could recall her ice-cool responses when she was told that such sums were not possible. They always were. They crossed the big square in front of the railway station, and it was from there – only a few times – that she had taken the train, anonymous and unidentified, to the town of Nola to visit her friend. On down a crowded, log-jammed street. Then the siren started. They had gone the wrong way in the traffic chaos and the sun had been blocked by the height of the Poggioreale walls, where Giovanni and Silvio were held. She saw the church, modern and magnificent, and the triple towers of the Palace of Justice.

They went down a subway entrance and a barrier was raised.

She had never been there before, descending into the greyness of the tunnel under the palace. She had been through the main public entrance, off the pedestrian area, through which the families of the accused were admitted, but not this route. In Naples there were the Castel Capuano, the Castel Nuovo, the Castel dell'Ovo and the Castel San Elmo, all great historic monuments, but the palace was another castle, as formidable, the home of what had been for every one of her aware years the 'enemy', the *nemico*. One thing to meet the enemy in a park in north-east London, and to travel with the enemy from London to Rome, then to be in a safe-house on a hill with exquisite views of the capital. It was another to be taken, under the protection of guns, into the enemy's castle.

She was in an underground car park, dimly lit, and there was the stench of petrol fumes.

Immacolata did not look into Rossi's face as he stood beside the opened door of the Alfa. She climbed out, making light of the awkwardness in slipping her legs from the low seat, and stretched. She followed Orecchia towards a lift shaft where more men waited. She was ringed with guns. Theatre? Or real and present danger? The men had hard faces and she didn't think they play-acted.

In the lift, she was hemmed in, and Rossi's machine-pistol magazine dug into her arm.

She could not have said when on the journey she had last thought of Eddie Deacon. She wasn't certain if she'd thought of him since she'd fastened the padlock and thrown the key into the river, where it meandered among sandbanks.

Salvatore came out through the door. The man with the face wound, now caked and dried, had taken his place. The door was closed, a poor fit since the power drill had replaced the hinges and gouged new screw holes. He went to the sink and started to wash the blood off his fists and the sweat from his body.

A man came up behind him. 'The door is always locked by any person who lives on any floor of any walkway in the Sail.'

He didn't understand. It was more important to him that his fists hurt and the knuckles were scraped. Much more important: the boy had not yelled.

The man said, 'Every door is locked. How did he get in? Was the door left open? Was there a plan? I think not. Was the door opened for him? I think it was.'

If the boy had screamed, begged, it would have given

Salvatore more satisfaction. He could hear now the thudding blows he had inflicted. There would be more blood from the eyes, the lips, inside the mouth and the nose. There would be much more when the man with the nail wound in his chest took his turn, and the man who still walked badly because of the knee and the bruising.

'What are you saying?'

'They found many new shirts in the cupboard, still wrapped, never worn. He's Davide. He goes to the city each week and buys a new shirt. Why? Why does he need new shirts that he never wears? He's an idiot. Is that the behaviour of an idiot? Why did he unlock the door for a fugitive? No one would.'

Salvatore's upper teeth closed on his lower lip and bit hard. He was a stranger here, isolated. He had loyalties: to Gabriella Borelli, whom he had not protected, to Carmine and Anna Borelli, whom he revered, to himself, paramount. He wondered where Fangio was, what he was doing, how he was treated down there among the shit, not allowed to come up to the third level. He sensed alarm. Two men waited, each with different wounds, to beat more hell out of the boy. He said they should not take the boy's life. He dried his face. He said the idiot, Davide, could wait. He went to find Fangio. He walked along the walkway and past the apartment and noted, for the first time, the cleanliness of the window and the old man watching television inside.

'He wants to know when.'

There was surveillance throughout the city. Each of the forces, the *carabinieri*, the Squadra Mobile and the Guardia di Finanza, would have loved to be able to claim plaudits. For recognised faces – Umberto, Carmine Borelli, Salvatore, Il Pistole, named foot-soldiers of the clan – there was foot surveillance, camera surveillance, audio surveillance and telephone surveillance. Almost – not quite literally – the men and women of the three law-and-order agencies jostled each other.

'When is he to kill him?'

Fangio walked in a cemetery with Massimo, the lawyer's nephew, beside him. Neither had any idea of the identity of the corpse in the coffin, the sex or the age. They took a position near the tail of the cortège as it wound towards a high wall and the line of small *capelle* in front of it. Within the last four months, over a meal in the evening heat at a *ristorante* on the west slopes of Vesuvio, Gabriella Borelli and Salvatore had chosen this as a method of avoiding watchers and cameras. Salvatore had activated it now, a plan decided on after the whore's departure to London.

'And where, for best effect, is he to leave the body?'

Massimo cultivated a north-European pallor, but he fancied his face had gone bloodless. He was, could not avoid the implication, now at the heart of a conspiracy of murder; might before have avoided that conclusion by playing at semantics – no longer could deflect his own guilt.

They had reached the *capella* in which that day's body would be placed. By happy coincidence another funeral had ended. A column of mourners – men loosening their ties, women dabbing their necks with cologne and using the order-of-service cards as fans – came past them and headed for the gate that would lead into the Sanità district. They switched.

'When? Where?'

They didn't leave together. Fangio was far down the via Foria and accelerating through slow traffic by the time Massimo had telephoned Anna Borelli, had apologised profusely for disturbing her siesta and begged permission to collect clean underwear for her grandsons and take the items with him on his visit the following day to Poggioreale gaol.

It did not surprise him that Anna, the crow in her perpetual uniform of black, would make such a decision: when a young man would die and where his carcass would be dumped. But he was hooked and could not step back.

He sat on great smoothed stones. They were at the foundations of the narrow metalled track leading to the main entrance of the castle that jutted into the bay. A wedding party hung back, but the girl bride and her fresh-faced new husband had come off the road and over the low wall, had stepped on to the stones, a photographer with them, and posed close to where Lukas sat.

He should not have been there. He should have been in the annexe off the operations room. If he had been there he would have been able to soak in the collator's surly acceptance of his presence, and the psychologist's sneered hostility. The ROS men, who would have made up any assault team that might be mounted, would have sat around him, yawned, broken wind and belched, as such men did, as he had when he was a member of a hostage rescue team. And, if he had been there, he would have been close to Castrolami who seemed to him now a man of split priorities: the life of the boy, the testimony of the girl. And the scales, as Castrolami demonstrated them, slipped fast towards the girl as his priority. He watched the bride pose in front of the towering castle walls and hold out her train so that the afternoon breeze caught it and made a sail of it. He saw the adoration in the groom's face. It had not happened in Lukas's life.

It was good for him to see real people and share what they offered, not to be incarcerated in an annexe with a gallows-humour crowd.

There should, of course, have been intelligence coming in from the assets, but the way Castrolami had told it there were the usual, inevitable, divisions and rivalries. If it was a *carabinieri*-instigated investigation, would the police crime squad or the fiscal police help? Small chance. And there had been, at their meeting, the domestic security service. They wouldn't. No chance. In the States, it might have been the Agency, the Bureau and Alcohol, Tobacco and Firearms, might have been Counter-Terrorist, Intelligence and the Junglas, Colombia's supposed élite, the Agency, the Bureau, Task Force 145 and the local warlords in Iraq – might have been in any goddam place where a life hung by a thread and the big boys disputed territory. The wedding party lined the road to the castle entrance, shouted approval, and the groom had come to hold her. Lukas liked the image.

He thought that unless luck was served up in buckets he had lost the boy: no assets quoted, no intelligence offered, just silence in close-set walls around him. He could lose a hostage, climb on to a flight, get himself back to Paris and not feel that the world had fallen in. He didn't understand why this boy had gotten to him.

He let out a long, slow sigh, which was pretty damn self-indulgent. Nothing to do with his own boy – with whom contact was severed – not a piece of 'replacement' psychology that the shrinks would have enjoyed talking up. He didn't know why this boy had burrowed, like a worm, under his skin. He had gone through the routines of hostage negotiation so many times and not felt that anything was personal. Maybe it was the goddam photograph he'd been shown, or the sight of the girl running in the park. Maybe their romance had fuelled that worm, and little of romance had crossed his tracks. Perhaps he was just damn jealous. He hailed a taxi and gave it piazza Dante as a destination. All his instincts told him that a body would soon be in a ditch, or in a car, or in an alley, and he felt shredded of power.

16

It was not mercy that stopped the beatings, but their exhaustion. He was a punch-bag, a kicked football, a bleeding, bruised mess.

Eddie lay on the floor of the same space where he had removed the chain's pin from the wall and the door's hinges. He had no longer any sense of time, or of hunger, but his throat burned with thirst. He thought he'd swallowed some of the blood, and mucus, and the sweat that poured in rivers off his head. He didn't know whether his ribs were broken, only that the pain there came in sharp spasms if he moved an inch to right or left. He thought his forearm wasn't broken, but it might have been: it had protected his kidneys and had probably screened his liver.

He was on his side.

His wrists were fastened together behind his back, held with a plastic stay that had been pulled tight and cut into the skin, but with so much pain elsewhere that was a small matter and he ignored it. His ankles had new manacles. He was on his side and had been since they had dumped him. He had been able to lift his knees into his stomach, twist his shoulder and chest towards them, drop his head and shorten his neck, and he had kept his eyes tight shut. Eddie knew he was condemned. They had not hooded him. It seemed unimportant to them that he saw their faces. One was contorted in rage and had new scars across one cheek. He had kicked and punched hard. One had laughed each time he had kicked and punched, and had the blood on his T-shirt. Eddie knew a name. He had heard the one whose testicles he had kneed call another Salvatore. Again, it had not seemed important to them that a name had been used within his earshot. It was confirmation that he was condemned. The one they called Salvatore was the man who had taken him in the via Forcella, who had kicked him before, who seemed to have a slack, irresolute mouth and vacant, distant eyes.

Between the first beating and the second – the one from Salvatore and the one from the man with the scarred face – he had almost called out to Immacolata to end it for him, back off, quit, refuse. He had slid into weakness, but he had ditched it in the gap between the second and third beatings. He had thought of little between the third and fourth, nothing coherent. After the fourth, now, he had no thought of anything beyond survival for the next five or ten minutes.

He did not have a noble, romantic or heroic thought. All gone. He existed in a vacuum, no hope and no despair, where no intellect was admitted. He was the animal in the snare or the burrow, or the treble-hooked fish unable to reach the reed bed. He did not consider a greater picture, the rule of law over the supremacy of criminality, that might govern Immacolata. Eddie thought of nothing beyond lying still and managing the pain in his ribs and the pain in his forearm, which might be broken, and the pain in his lip, which was bloody and swollen, and the pain in his eyes where the bruising had spread. His vision was through tear-wet slits. He didn't think of his class filling a room, or the guys in the house, didn't think any longer of Immacolata. They had nothing to do with his possible survival for the next five or ten minutes.

They hadn't closed the door on him. He could see, through the open door, the shoes, trainers, that had kicked him and they were propped on other chairs, and he could see the fists that had punched him, which cradled cigarettes – one was wrapped in a handkerchief and the blood showed through.

The inspiration of escape was behind him.

He could see a spider. It was in the angle between the wall and the ceiling. A monster of a spider, with a fortress of close mesh around it and a food store. It moved lethargically. Eddie wondered how long it took a spider to weave a web of that extent. It was his first thought – other than survival – since the fourth beating. Who was the enemy of the spider? Who threatened it? His mind turned, cranked, on the queries and . . .

Salvatore had gone, was no longer in the room with the others, but the one with the shirt wound, blood in the chest from the nail, came to the door and stood there, tobacco smoke playing across his face. He was a grown man, might have been thirty. Eddie didn't understand how a man of thirty could be as savage as a cat with a victim as helpless as a winged songbird. He didn't have the clarity to think it through. The man watched him. Was it work for a man? The man was older than Eddie. He guarded prisoners, kicked and punched them. Maybe he might just get to kill one. Eddie shivered. Did it fucking matter whether the man had a wife he went home to sleep beside, or small children to play with at the end of a long, hard day of smoking, kicking and punching? Did he talk about kicking, punching and guarding over supper with his wife and kids? Eddie knew nothing. Did the man say to his woman that it had been a good day at work?

To think, to imagine, was all the independence left to him. Better off without them. He turned, which hurt his ribs and tried to get on to his other side so that his back was to the man, but the pain was too bad. He managed only to flop on to his back, which left him more vulnerable: his privates were unprotected. He rolled back. He was where he'd started. Better to have stayed put, better not to think and not to imagine.

There had been the one chance. He'd given it his best shot, but it hadn't succeeded. And he was condemned, which was what Immacolata had done for him, and the certainty of it gave him a sort of peace.

Were the foot-soldiers of the Borelli clan inside the Palace of Justice?

Immacolata had been given a soft drink, iced, and now was brought down a corridor, guns in front of and behind her.

Did Salvatore, Il Pistole, have access here?

She could smell the gun oil, the chilli on their breath and the scent from their armpits.

A door was knocked at respectfully. A pause. Then it was opened and a smartly dressed woman, who might have been as old as her mother, gazed at her with the expression that was devoid of approval or criticism, then stepped aside. She was walked through an outer office. She realised now that the guns were gone. So this was the sanctum into which her father's foot-soldiers and even Salvatore were thought unable to penetrate. An inner door was rapped on. Another pause, long enough to indicate that work must be completed, then a call: 'Enter.' Of course the prosecutor had not looked up. His head was low over carpets of papers that were rumpled across the desk.

She was not asked to sit.

She realised then that this was deliberate – a casualness meant to implant in her the certainty that she was not extraordinary. There were many files on the floor and she wondered if they had been laid out to a purpose: they carried the names in heavy indelible ink of Lo Russo, Contini, Mazzarella, de Lauro, Misso and Caldarelli. It might have been done to demonstrate to Immacolata that she was a small fish, that she swam in a big sea, but she didn't know.

He asked, 'A good journey, Signorina?'

'I sat in a car. It was satisfactory.'

'I'm told your mind is made up.'

'I said so.'

'You will give evidence?'

'I said I would so I will.'

'I regret that your decision may cost the life of Eddie Deacon. I regret that.'

'I will give evidence.'

'And you will not, Signorina, be surprised if I seek to stiffen your resolve.'

She was told where she would be taken. She turned on her heel. It was a grander exit than had been her entry. She knew they did not trust her word.

Salvatore stood by a broken wardrobe. Under its plywood sides, back and doors there were dozens of cellophane-wrapped shirts. None of the packaging had been opened, none of the shirts used.

The man sat in his chair. The television played. He seemed oblivious to the movement around him.

The apartment was filled with men.

The truth came slowly to them all – to Salvatore and to the men of the Sail clan. He was Davide. He was an electrician and could be relied upon to fix a broken fusebox, to route power round a meter box and bypass it. He would come at any time, was so helpful. He was a man of routine and went to the city centre, down the long hill, on the bus every week and would mutter to any who listened that he thought, that week, he needed a new shirt. He was a man who polished the window behind his chair, which fronted on to the walkway. When he had been ordered to stand, there had been a secreted mirror in his chair, like a woman kept in her handbag to check her eye makeup or lipstick. He was almost unique in the great block in that he had allowed a fugitive to enter his apartment. Either his main door had been unlocked, or he had seen the fugitive and decided to aid him. Nothing fitted. Only suspicion meshed.

With the suspicion, the adding of the parts, came realisation of a truth.

The apartment was searched, stripped bare.

The camera was found.

The cables from the camera led to the recording box.

The recording box and its loaded tapes were lifted from the hidden recess.

The wire that ran from the recording box to the audio microphone, the pinhead type fitted to the outside wall, was ripped clear.

And he stood. None of the men, the clan foot-soldiers or Salvatore, seemed aware of him as he left his chair and the television. He took a last glimpse at the screen. It was afternoon scheduling, too late for the midday film and too early for the girls to be topless; they wore flimsy one-piece swimming costumes and pranced cheerfully. He did not, of course, bolt for the front door. He went down the corridor.

He did not know what he had achieved in his recent life.

Could not know to what use the handlers had put the information he had supplied.

He understood that the men who swarmed in his apartment were, almost, in shock at what they had found, and that time was short for him. Soon enough heads would clear and thoughts would focus. He went down the corridor towards his bathroom.

★

'Duck here. Can you speak?'

'Wait one—'

Lukas was in the corridor, had passed the main desk, where his ID was checked, had been through the metal detector, and turned. It raised eyebrows that he went back through the doors and on to the street, then into the square. He made for a central point, and it didn't concern him that he had intruded into the middle of a soccer game. The kids buzzed round him.

'Shoot.'

'It's like you've been on the dark side of the earth.'

'Nothing to report. Didn't report because I had nothing.'

'I'm not nagging.'

'I didn't report because I had nothing to report. One-syllable stuff.' The ball came by him and he hoofed it away. The kids clapped. 'There's no intelligence. There are no assets that anyone will share. Every agency here is fighting a breezy turf war. The contact, my door-opener, thinks the spooks are less than frank. Duck, how many times we heard that? But it's just his reading of body language. I have nothing to do. I can't advise on negotiation because we haven't reached that status. I can't suggest how a rescue might be launched because we don't have a location. There's no role for a co-ordinator if no negotiation's in place, and there's nowhere for a storm team to assault. Sorry and all that, Duck. That's pretty goddam obvious. It's frustrating.'

'You want to hear about something?' The voice rasped in Lukas's ear.

'What is it?'

'Could I try you with a snatch off the Niger Delta, about sixty klicks into the Gulf, an oil-flow platform? Yanks, Canadians and three Brits. What makes it different is that local workers were killed when the hostage-takers came on board the rig so they can't simply be paid off. The temperature's hot. Chevron have the rig and their security people asked for you. I'm merely passing it on.'

'You could tell them I'm spoken for, regrets and all that.'

'Any idea how much longer?'

'It'll move fast.'

'Too fast for you?'

'Maybe.'

He liked Roddy 'Duck' Johnstone, trusted him and was appreciated, and he thought the call didn't yet have purpose. It was peculiar for the boss not to needle in on a point without preamble – without crap.

'I'm just throwing past you the second call on your time. The German Red Cross have contacted us. They have people in western Afghanistan, round Herat, and they've lost a field worker. Well, not actually lost him, just don't know which warlord has him, and if he goes into the hands of the AQ . . . Well, they asked for you.'

'Like the man said to Chevron,' Lukas answered.

'That you're spoken for?'

'That I'm spoken for. I feel kind of obligated to stay with this, let it run its course.'

'Not getting soft and sentimental in your old age?'

He heard a brief grim chuckle. No one who knew him would ever accuse him in seriousness of either.

'Hope not.' Lukas bridled, and the ball was back at his feet. The kids stayed off him and he did a shimmy, kicked for goal. Wide. Lukas thought hostage co-ordination was easier than kicking footballs.

'Don't take this as impertinence, but can you see yourself making a contribution of value?'

'Hope to. Will try to.'

'A good kid?'

'I didn't do the legwork. You did,' he said softly. Lukas wouldn't put down his boss. No one had ever labelled him sarcastic . . . and he thought of those he had searched out, the close-up witnesses: the hotel manager, the fish-seller, a priest with a knapsack of guilt.

'It'd be nice to bring him out.'

'Yes. I have a desk to get back to.'

'I'll tell them you've work in hand – not available for the Niger Delta. Tell them you've things stacking up, not available for Herat. Damn you, Lukas, because you never give me anything. He's an ordinary kid with an ordinary background, yet I think he's special. It's what people say and—'

'The desk calls.' Lukas rang off. He understood why the company boss, the God almighty of Ground Force Security, should waffle on about a 'good kid' and 'nice to bring him out'. In the company there were people from differing law-enforcement and military backgrounds, and personal involvement was regarded as suitable for the fairies, not for them. But the matter in hand involved the fate of a kidnap victim, not pipeline security, not close protection for an ambassador, not convoy escort up a road blighted with culvert bombs. Kidnapping was different. It had a particular status with the people of this company, all levels, and of every other company in the same trade. He understood why his boss had put saccharine on the assignment, would have known there was no possibility of Lukas pulling out from Naples and taking a flight to Lagos or heading to Kabul. Almost the boss had pleaded with him for a best effort. He'd never done that before. He'd trawled the boy's background, had done the parents, the guys who lived in the east London house and maybe some people the boy worked with. Most important, the boss had been lined up by a guy, one-time Special Forces, who did close protection for the company in the dark corners where the money was earned and where the risk of getting lifted was greatest. They were all, in this trade, bound together like blood relatives. All that made sense to Lukas, but there was something more – as if his boss had been well hooked . . . Funny thing, the emotion business: he could feel emotional about a complete stranger. Lukas didn't do emotion – if he did, he could be slashed, minced. Great to feel good when the hostage walked to a helicopter or an armoured Humvee, a luxury of indulgence. And when the hostage didn't walk, but stank from the sun, the flies swarmed, and was carried away in a black bag, emotion would wreck him. He needed the protection of apparent indifference . . . but it had gotten harder to play-act.

He had seen bad things in his time, and been party to them, and a tear had not fallen from his eye. Might be time to quit when it did. Should have felt calm, but didn't. Should have felt on top of his game, the acknowledged expert in the field, but didn't.

He went back inside, walked through the operations room and took his chair in the annexe. Quiet and respectful, he asked what was new, and was told that nothing was.

Two rats came close. They didn't approach the body but blood had spurted from the mouth on impact.

Salvatore saw the rats when he craned out of the bathroom window. They had realised Davide had gone through the window a full half-hour before, and from three floors up each of the men who had looked at the man lying with his head at such an angle had pronounced death. They had gone on with the search. More had arrived. There was a *capodecine*, bustling with urgency, there to see at first hand the scale of an intelligence failure in the midst of the Sail, a *comando piazza*, who traded off that walkway, came to check on the parameters of that failure, and two *magazzinieri* who warehoused on the third level. There was an *aquirento*, the principal buyer for the clan. All came, from the walkway, to try to measure the limits of a small disaster. They had gone.

Salvatore watched the rats from the window and saw them lap the blood of an old man who had played at being an idiot, like cats with milk.

The body lay on the concrete paving, with a crown of weeds for the shattered head, the feet between two overflowing rubbish bins.

Immacolata stepped out of the Alfa, Orecchia and Rossi on either side of her. Two more men had peeled from the police car outside the gate. The front door was open and she saw more men in the hallway. She wore dark glasses that covered most of her cheeks, with a headscarf over her hair: it was a crude disguise, would have fooled few. A man, with no intention of backing off in the face of force, the guns and the threat, watered a flowerbed in the middle of his front garden. She had been told she shouldn't hesitate on the pavement or the path. Across the street, a couple watched the show – little else would match the arrival of an armed convoy. Orecchia had taken her arm.

She had been to the house before but it seemed an age since she had last walked up that path and gone through the front door to be greeted with the hug and the kiss of the closest friend she had known.

It was because they didn't trust her that she had been brought here. There had been no consultation. She was a gift-wrapped parcel on a conveyor-belt. She had not spoken in the car but her mind had turned over the previous time she had been on that road out of Naples and across the flat inland plain that stretched to Nola. Then Silvio had driven. Then there had not been a machine pistol on the seat, gas grenades and a vest. She could not have said, tracing that same route, how many days, hours, nights it had been since Silvio had driven her to Nola. The days and nights since had concertinaed, and the spread of time no longer had meaning for her. She couldn't have said how long it had been since she had run from the basilica, how long since she had paid fifty euros for a ten-euro posy, how long since the heel of her shoe had broken, her clothes had been torn and she had lain on the ground, assaulted and abused. She didn't know.

She followed Orecchia into the hall. Castrolami was there. He seemed to tower in the place, to minimise it. On the floor, near to his feet, there were two neat piles of female clothing at hip height. Across the hallway there were three black plastic sacks, filled and knotted at the neck. She realised her visit had interrupted a schedule. One of the two piles was of clothes for early spring, late autumn and winter, and she recognised the anorak Marianna had worn on a January day, down on the via Partenope, when they had walked and done the farewells. The next day Immacolata had gone to London. The other pile was of late-spring clothes, which would have lasted through summer and early autumn, and at the top of the heap lay the faded T-shirt with the image of Che that had been a favourite of Marianna. She had arrived, which meant the disposal of her friend's clothes was delayed. She assumed the plastic bags would go to a rubbish tip, and that the heaps had been sorted carefully and would be taken to a charity – perhaps one overseen by the nuns at the basilica. She could remember her friend in the yellow anorak with the black underarm panels and the North Face logo, and in the guerrilla T-shirt.

Castrolami said, not dropping his voice, seeming not to care if he was overheard, 'At the palace the decision was taken to provide security for the family as soon as rumour would have reported your collaboration, Signorina. It was thought that the parents of your friend were at risk when you came into our custody, as leverage. Then the boy, your one-time lover, made himself available to them and the threat against the parents was – briefly – reduced. We anticipate that the boy will be murdered. You have not made a public announcement that you are withdrawing your potential testimony and the deadline expires in a few hours. If we had a good line into the kidnap situation we would be able to delay and protract the process. We do not. We cannot rescue him because we don't know where he is held. He will be murdered very soon, we anticipate tomorrow, unless we can stall and deceive. Then *they* – the Borelli family – will need more leverage. Possibly they will come here for it. The lives of these people are doubly ruined, Signorina. They have lost their daughter, poisoned by toxic greed, and they should – if they have any sense – pack up, sell their home, leave their employment and move away. They would then have left behind the grave of their daughter, and to visit it they would require an armed escort.'

'Will they run?' she asked.

'For them to answer,' was his curt response. 'There is a consequence for your actions. You should know that. If they were to stay, we couldn't commit the resources for a permanent guard. They would be alone. The support of their neighbours would be temporary and soon they would be alone. Every day they must look over their shoulders and try to spot the killer stalking them. Quite soon, at their places of work, Human Resources will say, "It's not personal but you bring danger to your colleagues, and it's with great regret that we must ask you to leave. We must think of the company's welfare, the school's, the safety of colleagues and pupils." If they stay they won't be forgotten. They're marked. They're a permanent way of hurting you. It's the world in which we live.'

'Why do I have to see them?'

'So that you can never say you didn't know the consequences of your actions. And when the boy is dead and we're given the body, I'll drive you to the mortuary – perhaps the small one at the Incurables – so that you can look into his face and see what they've done to him. You'll never be allowed to say you didn't know.'

She stepped out. She pushed past him. She knew the layout of the house and went right, through a door that bypassed the kitchen entrance, then out through the room where the computer was that Luigi Rossetti used to prepare the modules of his classes for his pupils, and where Marianna had done work she brought home from her college course. The doors were wide open and there was a patio outside, with chairs and a table, and wire mesh on which a vine grew, throwing shade.

Beside that door there was a large cardboard box, whose top flaps had not been folded down so she could see textbooks – the same she had used – and ring binders. She thought they had eradicated their daughter from the home. How long was it? She had kept no track of time, but it might have been a week.

They were sitting down. The garden stretched away, neat and small, and a policeman stood at the far end with a machine pistol slung on his neck from a webbing strap. She saw the hands that had snatched at her clothing, the feet that had kicked her and the mouths that had torn away her dignity. Neither stood and neither waved her to a chair. Nothing, Immacolata thought, is forgiven.

Marianna's father, Luigi, said, 'We didn't want you to come, but they insisted. There is no welcome.'

Marianna's mother, Maria, said, 'There is a boy, nineteen, admitted this week to the *ospedale*. He has followed Marianna to the Santa Maria della Pietà. He may now be in the same bed, but certainly in the same ward, and he has the same symptoms. I don't know the family but Luigi taught him for a year. It's said he'll die the day after tomorrow.'

Luigi said, 'We haven't visited the family – we didn't want to intrude on the crisis afflicting them.'

Maria said, 'There were others before Marianna. There will be others after the boy.'

'Will you go?' she blurted.

'Go where?' A frown knitted the father's forehead.

'Will you leave?'

'And take Marianna with us, break her peace? Or leave her behind? Can you imagine us doing either?' The mother's shaking head expressed her incredulity.

'I wondered if—'

'We shall stay. If they kill us we'll join her. We're not frightened of them. There's nothing else they can take from us,' they said in chorus.

'You know what I'm doing?'

'We were told,' the father said.

'We respect it . . . but we do not forgive and we do not forget,' the mother said. 'Also, we were told of a boy who loves you, and that they'll kill him. But you won't weaken – it is what we were told.'

'I'll testify against my family.'

She had said it, 'I'll testify against my family,' and at that moment the scales tipped and she had made her commitment. They turned away from her. It was as if she was of no further use to them. She was ignored, vulnerable. Did Castrolami rescue her? He did not. She fidgeted and shuffled her feet. She wondered if, one day, she would be somewhere in England, in the countryside, green, near cows, and she would be with the father and the mother of Eddie Deacon, explaining to them what choices had been made and the consequences.

She spun on her heel.

She faced Castrolami who lounged at the door. Immacolata said, 'Let's get the fuck out of here.'

A smile widened at his mouth, his arms unfolded and he took her elbow. At that moment, she believed, she had his respect.

She walked past the box of books, the files, and past the bags that would go to a tip, and past the two heaps of Marianna's clothing. Orecchia came out of the kitchen, Rossi following him, and they readied their weapons.

They went out into the sunlight and the brightness dazzled her.

They headed back towards the dual-carriageway and Naples, driving past fields that had been harvested and groves of apple trees, and crossed a stream that was almost dry. She didn't know where the poisons had been dumped or where Marianna Rossetti had played, or whether that was the stream she had paddled or swum in. The car was silent.

Nothing more to be said. She had made her pledge and could not turn back if she wanted ever again to walk with a pinch of pride. She had killed the boy – might, herself, have held a knife or a pistol.

She broke the quiet: 'Am I a circus freak?'

She wasn't answered.

'Do I have the right to know where I am to be exhibited next?'

No reply.

It couldn't be challenged. A lawyer's clerk had the right to escort the mother-in-law of an accused woman, not yet convicted and entitled to legal presumption of innocence, to see the daughter-in-law, and take her toiletries, clothing and fruit.

Massimo escorted Anna Borelli, drove his car and listened.

'Too much time is lost, and no message is sent.'

He wished he hadn't heard.

'It should be done in the morning.'

His own grandmother had a baggy stomach, wide hips, an excessive bosom, a twinkling eye and a smiling mouth. She teased him about the marriage invitation that hadn't been sent to her, the lack of babies to drool over. This woman, the hag, was sheer contrast: not a gram of spare flesh, no fullness in her chest, a dulled deathlight in her eyes and thin lips. She seemed to find no pleasure in her world. His own grandmother, on his mother's side, living in comfort in Merghellina, north along the coast and only a few kilometres from the city's centre, couldn't have spoken those whipped words.

'Or done in the night, then dumped in the morning.'

He crossed the piazza Sannazzaro, then cut down to the via Francesco Caracciolo. Soon they would be close to his grandmother's apartment. At this time of the day, she would be watering the plants on her balcony, or maybe she would have started to mix a pesto for Massimo's uncle, a bachelor of fifty-three who hadn't yet left home. His grandmother's life was ordered and regulated. His other uncle, Umberto, the lawyer, was on his father's side and his character was harsher and colder. Umberto would have been at ease with this woman – a *strega* – in his car and would have listened unfazed as she discussed, without passion, the killing of a young man.

'I have thought of where the cadaver should be left.'

His own grandmother was nervous of small spiders and wouldn't even swat a fly on a window-pane. Massimo wondered as he drove – near to his grandmother's now – how many men and women had lost their lives on the witch's say-so. He could imagine those fingers, with the wrinkled skin and the pared nails, wrapped tight round a man's throat – he swerved and nearly hit a taxi.

'The cadaver should be where the impact is greatest.'

They were past Merghellina and the marina where the

launches rolled on the gentle waves in the shelter of the breakwater. At one more set of traffic-lights they were beyond the franchise area of the Piccirillo clan, and were entering the territory of the Troncone and Grasso families. That information might have been given on an advertising hoarding or a frontier control point. A man who answered to the Piccirillo would not cross that street beyond the traffic-lights and go north to trade narcotics or to extract protection dues; neither would a man employed by the Troncone or the Grasso come south. Very ordered. He would be at the gaol in ten minutes.

She said, 'The cadaver should be left at the main door to the Palace of Justice, but not before nine in the morning.'

He didn't ask how a vehicle would bring a dead body across a wide piazza that was a pedestrian-only zone. How could it be tipped on to the patterned paving, under the sign that read, 'Palazzo di Giustizia' and the flag, when there was always a *carabinieri* vehicle parked there, with two armed men inside it from the protection unit? How? He did not ask.

'I have spoken to Carmine. I told him what I thought and then I told him what he thought. It was the same.' He thought, incredibly, that a suspicion of a smile hovered briefly at her lips. 'You, Massimo, will take my instructions to Salvo. There is no time for a rendezvous. You take them to him. Kill him early in the morning and leave his body for when they arrive at work.'

His hand shook. The direction of his car wobbled. He would not have dared to contradict Anna Borelli. They drove in silence the last kilometres to the parking area outside the walls, fences and watchtowers of the women's gaol where the daughter-in-law was held.

What did guys do? They had last visits, sent messages and wrote final letters. Eddie would have no visit, did not expect an opportunity to send a message, and could hardly write a last bloody letter with his hands trussed behind his back.

What else did guys do? They put their affairs in order. Problem was that Eddie had no 'affairs' worthy of the name, none that were tidy or chaotic. He had no money beyond a current account and a Post Office savings book that had somehow been forgotten while he was at college or it would have been stripped bare. He had other things to exercise him than worrying about whether he had paid his tax, and whether the last pension contribution had gone out of his account, and that he hadn't made a will.

Was that actually what guys did?

He thought that his father's and mother's affairs would be in order – last letters sealed, with a second-class stamp on them, legal things up to date, all relevant tax settled.

It was because Eddie had become, after a fashion, comfortable and because his body hurt less that his mind had allowed that door to open. He was better off when the pain was rich and *thinking* didn't intrude.

Next thing would be – going through that door. How would they do it?

Had to squirm. Had a flash in his mind of the hood going over his head, but seeing a pistol before his eyes were covered, or a knife, or being taken to a high floor and feeling the air on his skin and knowing he was beside an open window. Quite deliberately, Eddie turned on to his right side so that his weight crushed his ribs. The pain might have made him squeal, but he welcomed it, which seemed to slam that door. When 'How would they do it?' was gone, he rolled back. The exertion sent the pain into his head and feet, legs and arms, chest and stomach, but the mind was cleared.

More philosophical.

Quite a jab on the nose, actually. A reality check. Eddie Deacon's life didn't count when it was set against a principle.

Pretty bloody heavy stuff.

He chewed on it. Who had made the decision? Who had sat on the judgement bench? Had they applied logic and intellect to the process? Or tossed a bloody coin?

If it was logic and intellect, would they go to a chapel, lower themselves on to a hassock and say a smug little prayer? If a coin had been tossed, would they have headed off to the pub and sunk a few, raising a glass to him – 'Sorry and all that, Eddie, nothing personal'?

Would have been nice if it was all faceless people. Big policemen in fancy uniforms, with medal ribbons in bright lines, politicians waiting for the limousine to pull up, escorts to open the door, and judges in robes – easier for Eddie if it was men who did not have faces.

It was her.

It was his Mac who had said that the 'principle' won out.

His Immacolata . . . He was curled on his side, the pressure off his ribcage, and the pain had subsided. It might have been, from what Eddie remembered, three weeks after he had met her, maybe four, and they had been in the pub with the boys from the house. He'd only been on the second pint and his glass wasn't even half empty, but she had pushed the table, reached out her hand and taken his, then yanked him up and led him out. They had gone back to the house and she had set the pace, going ever quicker, had run the length of the street to the steps and the front door. It had not been a slow seduction undressing, but a strip-off – and she had beaten him to it, naked when he still had his socks on. They had made love fast, then again, slower, and hadn't stopped when the boys had come back from the pub. They had done it again when the house was quiet and the boys' late film was finished. He'd probably only ever said it to her once, whispered it in her ear with wonderment: 'I love you, Immacolata, and will love you till . . . ' She hadn't let him finish. He thought, remembering the declaration, that it had been after the first time and before the second. The third time, bloody near knackered, she had brought him on hard and deep, and he had damn near broken the bed. He had meant it, every word, every syllable – ' . . . will love you till . . . ' She hadn't let him say how long he would love her, and her mouth had closed over his, and her tongue had stilled his, and her body had brought warm sweat to his and he had squirmed under her. 'I love you, Immacolata . . . ' He had said it, she had not. There was a cough at the door.

Salvatore was there.

His Immacolata . . . Only once had they shared a sour exchange. He'd drunk too much, she was sober. He'd wanted horseplay, she'd wanted to read a textbook. He'd had a normal, undemanding day tomorrow, she'd had an exam.

Salvatore leaned on the door jamb and watched him, was huge above him.

His Immacolata . . . He had told her, boisterous, to 'lighten up', she had told him he was wasting his talent, could do more and go further, that he could make a difference – and he had flounced out, gone for a leak, and it had never been mentioned again and there had been no suggestion as to how he could 'make a difference'.

Salvatore studied him, as if he was an enigma. Mindful that he was open to another kicking, Eddie glimpsed the face looming over him, and thought it vulnerable – bloody bizarre.

Returned to the core theme. The principle had won, breasted the tape, for Immacolata's prize. He had not won, bloody hadn't. Principle coming before his survival didn't make him angry: it stifled his feelings.

Salvatore had a cigarette in his mouth. Smoke came up from it and went towards the web where the big spider was.

Abruptly, he moved a hand – Eddie, trussed, unable to shift, didn't feel threatened – which went into his pocket and took out a pack of Marlboro Lights. He pulled out a cigarette and bent to slip the filter into Eddie's mouth, where the lips felt triple-size swollen, and lit it. He didn't say anything, and Eddie didn't thank him.

Three times the ash broke off and scattered on Eddie's chest, then Salvatore retrieved the stub and trod it out under his trainer. He didn't leave, but stayed in the doorway and stared down.

He did not know if it had been, for Immacolata, a big or small decision to go with the principle rather than his life . . . He didn't think he'd ever get to know.

There was a sliver of window that Eddie could see, past Salvatore's shoulder, and he realised that the day had died and the light had failed, that dusk closed on the buildings. He didn't know if he would see the dawn – because he was second to the principle.

A body lay on the paving at the base of the giant block that was the Sail where in excess of ten thousand souls lived, and it was unreported. Many who lived in the disparate towers of Scampia, with a population of seventy thousand souls, walked close to it as the shadows lengthened, but were careful not to see it . . . The rats had drained the pool of blood. Later, with darkness, they might start on the cheeks or the throat.

Few of the residents of the third level of the Sail knew of the first movements along the walkway. It was a precaution. Heavy sacks, filled with packages sealed in oiled, water-resistant paper, were carried away. And – an additional precaution – the locks on the barred gates were checked and heavier chains used to fasten them. Merely as a precaution, the clan *capo* who controlled that sector moved out, slipped away, went unnoticed.

Massimo had waited more than fifteen minutes at the chaotic road junction at piazza Nicola Amore, one of the pods for tunnelling the new metro system, when he was flashed by a scooter.

He was given a helmet. Awkwardly, he climbed astride the pillion and had barely achieved a grip on the man's heavy leather coat when it surged away. Massimo knew the statutes of the law – he could have quoted the article that listed Accessory to Murder. The scooter wove though rush-hour traffic. He didn't know whether he could control the feeling of acute sickness or whether he would fill the interior of the helmet with vomit.

Castrolami came into the annexe.

Lukas raised his head, queried with his eyes.

Castrolami said, 'She's strong, she's fine. I have other surprises for her, but she's good. What do we have here?'

The collator used his hands for the gesture. The psychologist murmured, '*Niente di nuovo*,' and shrugged, seeming to squirm a little at 'Nothing new', and the ROS men kept their heads down, as if they declined to be part of the failure.

Lukas said, to himself, to Castrolami, to anyone with nothing better to do than strain and listen to the gentle lilt of his voice, the soft accent when he spoke in Italian, 'It's what we do, isn't it? We sit around and we wait. We live off sandwiches and fries and high-dosage coffee, and we tell ourselves that the break will come. Don't know from where and don't know how but we have to believe it will. Smoke too much, eat too much, drink too much caffeine, but be ready to go, because we're not the people out with the kids at a parents' staff meeting, and we're not at the goddam cinema, and we're not doing a fishing weekend up-country, so we wait, and we believe it'll come . . . And if we get the break, and *if* we get up front and we have audio contacts, maybe even an eyeball contact, it may get played out for a week or be settled in a half-minute – a few words that foul up or do the business. We hit the break running, and we can't say we're tired or that we're coming off shift, or that we're going into a meal stoppage, and because of all that we're the privileged few. What's best – my small, insignificant opinion – is that we're not in armies and we don't have a big picture to fulfil, or generals breathing on our shoulders. We're anonymous and unsung, and we don't get to stand in a line for a regulation quota of medals. We live in the dirt, we operate in dark corners, we're accountable only to success or failure. We smell and don't get back home or to a hotel room for changes of underwear and socks, but there's no place I'd rather be, and there are no people here that I wouldn't want to be with. I hope we get the boy back. That about wraps up the bullshit stakes – apologies and all that.'

One of the ROS guys muttered, 'Bravo,' and repeated himself. Another slapped the stock of a weapon he was cleaning. Lukas had not, in his adult and working life, made a remotely similar declaration. It was as if the boy, the victim, had released something trapped deep in his soul, reached where no others had. Someone else folded his magazine tight and hit Bravo's head with it in simulated applause. And he recognised that a sense of growing apprehension, new and unlearned, had driven him to make the speech. And there was a short rippled clap from the collator and the psychologist. Apprehension? He cut it. Before it blazed, he doused it.

Castrolami, dry, asked, 'You do that talk most days?'

'Every morning in front of the shaving mirror.'

The quip, bogus, was ignored. 'Are you quitting, win or lose?'

'Doubt I've anything else to do. Suppose not.'

'Why did you say that stuff?'

'Seemed a good idea.' Lukas grinned. 'You wait for the break – what's the puzzle? You don't know where it's coming from, but the chance is that it comes.'

17

He was asked by a voice, now detached, the face in shadow, did he want food? It hurt Eddie to speak. It meant he had to suck air into his lungs, which expanded his ribcage and the bones that might be cracked. His throat was dry, his lips grotesquely misshapen. His voice was a croak. 'I don't . . . Thank you. No.'

There was no reaction: no indication of softening and a degree of kindness, or offence that the offer was refused. Eddie couldn't read the face high above him. He was unable to judge whether the chance of food meant that his hope of survival was greater or less. Did they bloody bond? Was it a last meal being ordered? He couldn't control the rambling of his thoughts, which bounced, pinballs in a machine: home, Immacolata, work, the guys in the house, *her* again, pains in his chest and head, curry in the Afghan, the knife or the pistol, Immacolata. Some of the thoughts, jumbled and without process, were comforting; others wounded.

He didn't understand why the man, Salvatore, stood over him, watched him.

Should he have accepted the food?

Did refusing it diminish his lifespan by a day, an hour, five minutes, or did it make no difference?

He had said he didn't want food because he wasn't hungry – seemed a good enough reason to turn it down. His throat itched, seemed rubbed raw.

Eddie wheezed, 'Please, I'd like water.'

'You would like water?'

'Please . . . yes . . . please.' Did it play well if he grovelled?
Should he not stand upright for himself? Eddie didn't know
whether he should be cowed or whether he should goddam
show some fight – there was no one to tell him. He thought
he needed to earn respect and wouldn't if he bowed, scraped,
slithered. 'I want some water.'

'You want water?'

'Bring me water.'

Would he be kicked? Was there any more shit left in him
to be kicked out? He saw the shadow turn and it was gone
from the doorway. The darkness was falling. A light came
on down a corridor and he heard running water. Well, Eddie
had a target, a new aim. Might not live, might not hang on
and cling to the pulsebeat, but he was looking to achieve
respect. What a man wanted. The tap was turned off. A light
was switched off. The feet came back down the corridor and
across the room, then the shadow shape filled the doorway.

Eddie looked up at the shadow. 'Thank you . . .' He
coughed. ' . . . for bringing me water. Thank you.'

The shadow moved. A bucket swung. The water came in
a wall, slapped hard into Eddie's face and drenched him. It
was in his eyes, his ears, up his nostrils and down his throat.
His lips smarted and he feel sharp stubs of pain from the
grazes on his face. The water puddled on the floor round
him. He expected, then, to be kicked and tried to curl himself
up so that the soft parts of his body were better protected
– but no kick came. He thought he would hear the maniacal
laughter of a man demented. There was none.

More movement in the doorway.

Eddie dared to look.

The man, Salvatore, bent his knees, slid his back down
the door jamb, then pushed his legs out. His trainers buffeted
Eddie's knees, but it wasn't a kicking.

Salvatore sat with him.

A second cigarette was offered, held up in front of his eyes, and Eddie nodded. It was put between his lips. There was a brief flash from the lighter and Eddie sucked. He could hear distant, occasional traffic and a cacophony of barking dogs. The smoke climbed. His thoughts were sharp now, as if they'd been tempered on stone, and the moments when he had bounced them, juggled them, were gone. He had learned a truth: a man had total physical control over him, could snuff out his life as easily as he would let go of the little lever that kept the cigarette lighter alive, yet the man was vulnerable. Eddie reckoned that the water thrown over him, and the cigarette between his swelled lips were signs of earned respect.

'If you want to talk,' Eddie said, 'I'll listen.'

There was only silence and he could hear the rhythm of Salvatore's breathing.

And Eddie heard, also, the dogs bark again, raucous, as if a pack hunted.

They had frightened away the rats, which scurried to holes. The dogs circled the body.

The rats and dogs fed well round the rubbish bins at the base of the Sail. The rats had made a meal of the blood, and the dogs, soon, would use the body as a toy.

A mastiff-cross was the pack leader. Had that dog been a pedigree, a pure Neapolitan mastiff – the symbol of the most fanatical *tifosi* following the city's Serie A football team in the glory days when Diego Maradona had lit it – it would have been pampered, not running free among the rubbish bags of Naples's most deprived *rione*. It would not have gone close to the corpse, sniffed it, then worried at its clothing and taken a leg in its jaws. This animal, though born to a mongrel bitch, retained many of the mastiff characteristics.

It weighed in excess of seventy kilos, and lifted the man with ease. The beasts in its pack attempted to join in, tugging at the other leg, the arms, the head and strips of clothing.

The struggle for possession moved away from the refuse bins and the body was carried through scrub towards the viale della Resistenza, the dogs howling, barking, whining, yapping and dragging what their teeth held.

The mastiff-cross couldn't lose his pack. The game progressed. It didn't wish to chew the man's flesh, but it was sport to have smaller dogs compete for possession. Bones were broken, joints dislocated but the sinew, gristle and muscle held the body together.

They were in the middle of the road.

The big dog still had the leg and ten others had a grip on the arms and the clothing. The body seemed suspended a metre or so from the tarmacadam. They tugged, growled, snarled and . . . A cruising police patrol car swerved to a halt.

The observer said, 'I can't fucking believe what I'm seeing.'

The driver said, 'If you want to throw up, do it out of the car.'

They watched for a full minute. The noise grew as the mastiff-cross was unable to assert its authority over the pack, and the game was played out noisily. Traffic was backing up behind the police vehicle. The ambulance, called on their radio, would be there within minutes – not that a paramedic was going to be of any help to the poor bastard being pulled apart. Back-up was coming too.

The observer said, 'The big one, that's a mastiff.'

'On the leg.'

'It was used as a fighting hound in Roman times, against lions. It's a guard dog now, possessive, obstinate – it's fucking big.'

'What are you telling me?'

'Are you going to put the man and the dog in the ambulance? Or are you planning to tell the dog to let go of the man?'

'Shoot it.'

'Shoot a mastiff? That's like shooting Maradona himself? Shoot it with a handgun?'

'Shoot the fucking thing.'

The observer used his Beretta 93R to fire four 9mm rounds into the dog's head before its grip on the body's left leg loosened. The others had slunk away.

An ambulance came, and the body was removed.

From the pillion seat, over the shoulder, Massimo watched the ambulance pull away and the headlights caught an animal's carcass spread out on the road. Beyond it, in deeper shadows, a group of dogs had gathered and Massimo could have sworn they were whining. The road was still blocked.

The scooter jolted as it mounted the kerbstones and ploughed through the oleander that grew wild there, then again when it came down on to the road at the far side of the dog's body.

The township of Scampia had been built immediately after the earthquake of 23 November 1980 that had killed more than 2900 people, injured some ten thousand and destroyed the homes of three hundred thousand. Money wasn't a consideration. The finest architects available were employed on creating a heaven for the dispossessed. Scampia rose from wasteground. Massimo had been born the year that the first blocks were laid. He had been twelve before he was driven past the great complex and shown the ludicrous size of the Sail. He had been back twice since then, once with a school party on a field trip to examine modern demography, once because a pretty shop girl lived there. His last journey to the jungle of concrete and heroin had been seven years ago. He was – and couldn't have hidden it – terrified to be on the viale della Resistenza.

The scooter braked. The engine was cut. Shadows moved. He thought himself encircled and the streetlights close to him were dark – he presumed they had been broken so that trading was easier. A finger jabbed at his chest, then his helmet. He lifted it off and it was taken from him. The finger pointed, and he made out an ebony black opening in a grey wall. He was told how many floors up he was going, and given the number, that he should use the name of Salvatore to get through the inner gates. The beat of Massimo, working for his uncle, was between Umberto's office and the Palace of Justice, and there were excursions to visit clients in the gaols of Poggioreale and Posilippo. Twice there had been visits to the head of the Borelli clan, which had taken him and Umberto to Novara; they had stayed two nights in a decent *pensione*. He had not, till that day, had to make the big decisions in life: to go right or go left, *destra o sinistra*. He had been able to hide behind the enablement of justice – every man and woman's right to professional representation. Now, facing the black pit of the opening, he was at the road's fork.

It was, of course, about fear.

What was he afraid of? Going into the crowded stinking hell that was the Poggioreale gaol.

Who was he afraid of? The old woman, dressed only in black, with the wizened face and throat, the bony hands, the sun's cancer scars on the skin.

What was he most frightened of?

Her.

He couldn't quantify it. It existed. The glance and brilliance of the eyes denying age, the withering contempt in her voice, the touch of her fingers and their rap upon his skin when she gestured. He wouldn't have told another human being about it, not Umberto or his grandmother. The fear lived. He could remember each word she had said, at what time it should be done and how the body should be disposed of. During every trial when a member of the Borelli clan was before a court, Massimo walked from his apartment across the pedestrian piazza with a capuccino in his hand and a sweet pastry, a *sfogliatella*, and he would cross the patterned paving where the witch had said the body should be left. He carried the sentence of death that would put the body there, and guilt made him shiver. He headed for the darkness.

He left behind the scooter and its rider.

A man loomed out and blocked his path. Massimo stammered the name. He wore his suit. Every day that he went to work he wore a suit, sometimes silk, sometimes cotton, sometimes mohair, and a shirt with a tie and good lace-up shoes. He didn't think he possessed any clothing that would have made him feel unnoticed here.

He was let through, and a mobile call was made. He thought he stepped on a syringe and held a handkerchief over his face against the smell . . . but he had more fear of her, and went on up the steps and remembered – word perfect – the message she had given.

'It's a very grave situation, Dottore.'

'Any situation involving criminality and a threat to an innocent's life is grave.'

Umberto, the lawyer, pursed his lips, seemed to feel genuine pain. 'Again these wretches are using me as a conduit. I follow the paths of the law, and do my best to save a life. I seek no personal advantage. I'm above suspicion, with no guilt in this matter. Dottore, the wretches who are using me predict that the English boy will be killed tomorrow. Is Immacolata Borelli's testimony so important?'

The prosecutor didn't answer. An answer was not yet required. He revolved a pencil in his hand and waited for the speech to continue. A sip of water was taken. The pause was allowed to continue for a beat or two.

'As the messenger, I want only to help. Is the testimony of the Borelli girl so valuable? I hear many things in confidence as a legal practitioner. I'm told she's disturbed, has psychological difficulties. She has an incomprehensible hostility towards her mother and siblings. I see an unreliable witness, a troubled woman with a misplaced sense of grievance against her relatives. I also see an innocent in desperate circumstances whose life may have only hours to run. If, Dottore, you could see a way to issuing some public statement to the media, stating without equivocation that Immacolata Borelli will *not* give evidence against her family, and that those members of the family recently arrested are to be released without charge, I believe I can save this young man's life – as a messenger, you understand.'

The prosecutor had taken no notes. He was aware, of course, of the need to prevaricate, delay and not to deny, but the lawyer would be as well versed as he was in the tactics of obfuscation and diversion. He thought a dance was played out, elaborate and choreographed, but a doomed dance for all that. His thoughts drifted. He remembered the dance his wife had seen, the Dying Swan, set to a cello solo by Camille Saint-Saëns, inspired by the poem of that name by the English milord, Tennyson, and designed first for Anna Pavlova to perform a century before. It was a good image – the Dying Swan.

'Dottore, we are professional opponents, but we are also defenders of justice. You, as much as I, must have serious misgivings about the process of collaboration. Too often the evidence is unreliable and self-serving. Immacolata Borelli no doubt believes she can escape scrutiny of her own actions by concocting lies about her family. Perhaps, also, greed drives her – the more lurid her accusations, the greater the rewards that the state will drop into her bag. Collaboration makes for bad law. I have one thing further to say, Dottore, and it involves the image of the city we love and cherish. If Gabriella Borelli and her sons do not go to court it will not be noticed beyond the circulation area of *Mattino* and *Cronaca*. If the English boy dies, reports of his death will go round the world and our city will be denounced as a dangerous hell-hole. Is there something, Dottore, that I can take back to those who use me as a conduit of information?'

The prosecutor laid his pencil neatly beside the blank sheet of paper. His hands went across his mouth, as if for prayer. He reflected. Had his career not taken a path towards making judgements on which freedoms depended, what might he have done with his life? He could have gone for well-paid management of the electricity-supply company, safe and honourable employers. He could have practised corporate law in Milan or Venice, civilised places. He could have forsworn responsibility and owned, with his wife, a hotel in the mountains. He could have been valueless. He thought he had respect for himself, and prized that achievement. To him it was of paramount importance. He said quietly, and with equally false sincerity, 'We are all grateful, my friend, for the efforts you're making on behalf of the innocent. I want you to know that I shall reflect on the substantive points you've laid before me, and I hope you'll have an opportunity to urge those in contact with you to avoid precipitate action. I do not rule out an accommodation – it's difficult but not impossible. I appreciate what you're doing. If necessary, I'll go to Rome next week to raise questions of priority with the minister. Thank you, my friend.'

When the bastard had been shown out and escorted from

the building, the prosecutor stayed by his phone. Dusk turned to evening, and it didn't ring.

Salvatore stood over the boy. There was no light and he could see only the outline of the body, but he could hear the breathing and smell the boy.

He broke the silence that had been long, lonely. There were other men outside the main door on the walkway but none inside. Those who had been hurt and who had taken revenge were gone . . . He needed to talk.

'What do they call you? At your home, in your family, how do they call you?'

Salvatore didn't know anything about the season of spring, had not noticed its start six months ago, or the blooming of small flowers. Without a sense of romance or fantasy, he would not have seen that question – 'What do they call you . . . how do they call you?' – as a mood change, as if he had come from the darkness of winter. Why should he wish to know such a thing about a boy he was shortly to slaughter? In Forcella he wouldn't have asked or in Sanità. He wouldn't have asked if Fangio had been with him, or if he had come from Gabriella Borelli. And flowers played no part in the life of Salvatore, Il Pistole, and he had never in his life picked or bought any to give to a girl. If he had given a bouquet to Gabriella Borelli she would have laughed in his face and maybe slapped it. He didn't know whether his own parents were still alive, or had been buried and had needed flowers. Maybe there would be flowers at his own funeral, because he would not be taken alive to rot in a cell – and maybe kids would throw flowers at the hearse as it passed. He didn't see that asking such questions weakened his resolve to kill and, if he had been told, he would not have believed it.

'They call me Eddie.'

'Just that?'

'It's what they call me. Eddie.'

'Where is the home of Eddie?'

Many thousands of people lived inside the Sail, and many tens of thousands in the other towers around it, but quiet had fallen, which heightened his isolation. The need to talk was an itch that had to be scratched.

'In the country.'

'What is in the country?'

'Fields – green fields – villages built of stone, with churches, and a river through the fields, and cows.'

'We do not have fields, green, because it is too warm, and everything is built in concrete, and we do not have cows but we have buffalo – and we have to kill many.'

'Why are the buffalo killed?'

'They have poison.'

He heard surprise, a smear of confusion, from the shape on the floor. 'How do they have poison?'

'It happens. There is poison.'

'Ridiculous – where is the poison? Why are the buffalo killed?'

'The buffalo make the milk for the mozzarella cheese, and they have poison so the cheese cannot be eaten and they are killed. Enough.'

'Where is the poison from?'

'Too many questions.'

'Why is there poison for the buffalo to eat?'

'You ask too much. It is enough.'

He kicked out. He caught the boy on the hip, and the jolt went up through Salvatore's ankle and his knee and right to the joint in his pelvis. The boy did not shout or whimper, but seemed to wriggle further from him. Salvatore thought he had shown weakness by kicking Eddie, but he was angry: he had wanted to talk, he had asked in innocence where the boy came from, and had said in innocence – without thought

– that buffalo were killed because the cheese made from their milk was poisoned, and he had been questioned. Salvatore, Il Pistole, was not questioned by any man. He could not have said, 'They are poisoned because *we*, the clans, have killed the ground with toxic material from which great disposal profits are made, and the ground is poisoned for generations to come, and the poison is now in the blood of the buffalo and the milk for the mozzarella is contaminated. *We* spread the poison so that *we* could make money.' He could not say it. Instead he kicked. Again, he heard the quiet and felt the aloneness.

'It is a good place, the village, Eddie?'

The handler, Beppe, was told by his line manager to bring to his office the recent package from the agent, Delta465/Foxtrot. He retrieved it from his safe and carried it along the high, echoing corridors of the building, knocked and was admitted.

The line manager said, 'Whether he was taken to the window and thrown out, therefore murdered, whether he was in flight and crawled out in an escape attempt and fell, whether he has determined to take his own life to avoid capture and the rigour of interrogation, I don't know. Whatever, he's in the mortuary of the hospital in Secondigliano, and in due course we'll find some women to claim him and show suitable grief. This evening, we have no more use for him. We don't admit to ownership or knowledge of him. Because we don't need to safeguard that intelligence source, his past film can be sent to the relevant officials. There is a *carabinieri* officer, Marco Castrolami, at piazza Dante. He should be given the films and told that the camera was sourced at apartment 374 on the third level of the Sail. He should be assured that this material reached us only this evening and has been transferred to him directly, without delay. We will answer no other questions about the film. Beppe, the death of an agent, whether by murder, accident or suicide, is sad. It leaves emptiness and creates humility, tomorrow is another day. Take it. Thank you.'

He put it into his leather bag, hitched it on his shoulder, and went off down the wide, high corridor, symbol of an age of power. He didn't know that a life depended on the package in the bag that swung against his hip.

The priest had told her she was sitting in the seat Eddie Deacon had taken when he had come to the church of San Giorgio Maggiore. She didn't know the priest well, had seldom confessed to him before she had gone to London. She had known better the one who had fled under armed guard to Rome, who had despised her and her family. Two of Castrolami's men were on the door, one inside and one out, and another was at the side entrance to the sacristy. Two women were at the altar, arranging the flowers, and they would have seen her come in, but hadn't acknowledged her, their backs to her: know nothing, see nothing, hear nothing. Immacolata thought Castrolami, three rows behind her, was playing with her.

The priest said, 'If you've come to me for the Church's praise of what you're doing you'll leave with empty pockets. I, the Church, have little interest in your conversion to legality. Society in this city embraces criminality, which feeds half of our population, provides work and opportunity, is enjoyed. I hazard the opinion that the majority of Neapolitans take pleasure and pride from the reputation of their home as the centre of the western world's most successful criminal conspiracy. The reason for your conversion, after so many years of benefiting from illegality, is not important to me. You denounce your family. You seek to imprison your mother and brothers, to earn their enmity for the rest of the days you will all breathe God's air, and reconciliation will be denied you even on a death-bed. Your family is destroyed, but that doesn't mean Forcella is freed from its criminal burden. Outsiders will use these streets as a battleground while they fight for supremacy over insiders who believe they are the natural successors to your family. Equilibrium is broken and I will be called upon for many funerals. It will be a time of great danger for the old and young who live here. Your actions will create no respite . . . and you will have on your shoulders, until the day God calls you, the weight of responsibility for the life of the boy who came, with his love, to find you. All you will have as solace is a principle. Those are the complications you face, the potholes in the road you have taken, but I admire your determination to walk along it. The example you set cannot be countered by sneers or contempt, and cannot be ignored. Immacolata, may God go with you.'

They prayed together, hunched down, for a bare half-minute. Then she stood up, straightened her skirt, tugged down her blouse, and pushed her hair back from her forehead. She did not look again into the priest's face, and did not shake his hand. Facing the altar, she crossed herself, then turned.

At the door, Castrolami asked, 'Do you want to do it?'

No answer, but a firm nod, her hair bouncing on her neck.

He said, 'I can't predict the reaction.'

She gave him a cold smile, showing him her authority. He wondered then – at that moment, and as the evening settled on the via Forcella – how Eddie Deacon had thought of love when he had stood with her.

'Right. We'll get this fucking circus on the road. If I grab you, don't fight me. If I run, run with me.'

They came down the steps of the church, past the twin

chips where the bullets had nicked the stone pillars. They turned to their right. Two of the men, those from the front entrance, walked ahead of her, each with his right hand hidden under his jacket; the one who had watched the sacristy door was behind. She didn't know whether he would have his pistol exposed or secreted. Castrolami was half a pace behind her, at her right shoulder.

Immacolata allowed her bag to swing with the rhythm of her hips.

It was as she remembered it. Nothing had changed.

She saw the barber's shop, the hardware shop and the shop where cheese and fresh milk were sold; she knew what *pizzo* each paid because she had determined the amount. She saw the shop where the wedding gowns were sold and the suits for grooms and principal guests, then the bakery. No one inside – shopkeepers and customers – caught her eye and no one called to her, abuse, support or a greeting. A scooter came towards her, bouncing on the basalt blocks. The rider's visor was up and she recognised a young man who had been at school with her, whose father had been killed by hers. It swerved past her. Men played a last card game in the light thrown from a bar's window but did not look up.

It would have been easier if insults had been shouted, eggs or tomatoes thrown. It would have been a triumph if there had been a shout of support.

What she was doing was not acknowledged. She did not exist as a living human. She passed many she had known since childhood. None cheered and none spat at her. She assumed that the mobile phones were in contact and a network of messages rippled the length of the street and off into the side alleys, that a foot-soldier had been called out, a handgun sent for, lifted from a cache, unwrapped and stripped of its protective cover, a magazine hurriedly loaded.

She saw a man hosing down the cobbles where his stall had stood, and through the open door of a van boxes of unsold fish lay among melting ice. She had often bought octopus, mullet and bass from him, but he didn't see her. She saw lights at the front windows of her grandparents' home. She assumed, by now, they knew of her walk down via Forcella, but they didn't show themselves on the balcony.

The cars waited. Walking briskly – not running, as if afraid, but not dawdling with a fool's conceit – they had covered some hundred and fifty metres in two minutes. Castrolami pushed her without dignity through a back door and had barely slammed it before the vehicle had pulled away. It wove down the street, headlights flashing to clear a way, and skirted the square in front of the Castel Capuano, then went fast on to the via Carbonara. In three minutes there might have been a gun and a marksman, in five there would have been. She thought she had sent a message of her resolve, and that she had killed Eddie Deacon.

The boy wouldn't speak – and had been kicked again – so Salvatore did.

'I am from the city, from the old city. I do not know about fields or a village or where there is a river that is not a sewer ditch. I do not know about cows, and I have never been into the country and towards the mountains where they keep buffalo. I do not know it here. I am here because it was decided to bring you to this place. I hate it. My home is the old city. It is where people follow me . . . Many people follow me and give me respect.

'I lived on the street, Eddie. I worked the street, the via Duomo and the via Carbonara. It was best on the via Duomo because tourists came to the cathedral, and fewer were on the via Carbonara because the Castel Capuana does not have many tourists. I start at nine years. I finish the school at nine years. I am a spotter at nine years. I spot for tourists who have a bag loosely held, or a Nikon camera that is on a shoulder strap, or a Rolex watch. At nine years old I am not strong enough to get a watch or a bag or a camera, but I am the best at spotting. At ten years old, I am the leader. Boys with more years do what I say. I am commander, and I sell on what we take from the tourists.

'At eleven years old, I am taken by Pasquale Borelli, the father of Immacolata. He chose me. He could have had a thousand kids, our word is *scugnizzi*, but he chose me. I owe everything to him. I can read and I can write and that is because of Pasquale Borelli. I am not a kid from the gutter and that is because of Pasquale Borelli. I am a person of standing in Forcella and in Sanità, and that is because of Pasquale Borelli. I think that after his eldest son, who is Vincenzo, I am the most important. I have more respect from him than Giovanni and Silvio. I am the favourite of Gabriella Borelli and she is among the most admired women in the clans in the city. Everybody has respect for me.

'If I had wanted to, I could have been married with Immacolata. You understand that? Both Pasquale and Gabriella Borelli have sufficient respect for me to give to me Immacolata if I had wished it. Did I want her? I think she is not good in bed and I think she has poor skin on her face. I did not want her. I am trusted by them, and I am trusted by Carmine and Anna Borelli, the old people. They do nothing if they have not talked first with me. Do you know that the kids in Forcella have my picture on the screen of their mobile phones? I am a person of importance. All the police hunt me, and all the *carabinieri* special teams, and the prosecutor. I am, in Naples, in the list of the ten most wanted – I have that status, and that respect. I have a place in the ten with a Russo and a Licciardi and a Contini. There are many days when I am in the newspaper. In the newspaper is my photograph. The journalists write about me.

'I read everything that is written about me in the newspaper. They call me Il Pistole in the newspaper. Many times I have been on the front page of *Cronaca* and of *Mattino*, and they talk about me on the news from RAI. I am a celebrity in this city. I am more famous than a film star, or a singer, or a footballer. They say I am the *assassino* – you understand that? – who has no fear and who does not give mercy, we say *senza misericordia*. I have killed more than forty men. I do not know exactly how many men because it is not important to me. I am the killer, the expert at killing, and I do not have hesitation in killing.

'When I have the instruction I will kill you, Eddie. It is not personal. It is not because you sleep with Immacolata Borelli who has fat ankles and bad skin. I will kill you when it is ordered by the clan. I will not kill you because I hate you, but because it is ordered. I will not hurt you. I am not your enemy, but if I was ordered to kill you and did not I would lose respect. I must have respect.'

He heard the voices at the door, then heard it opened. Salvatore turned away from the figure bound on the floor, lying in the darkness.

It had been a nightmare. Massimo thought himself in the corridors of hell, with no end to their length. They were a labyrinth. It had taken him an hour, might have been more, to travel the extent of a walkway set between reinforced doors, barred windows, dull-lit corners, refuse heaps, washing that was draped, and still stank, across his route. He did not think the nightmare complete, or half consumed. He had climbed the staircase and at the top had been searched. Fingers had prised into every pocket. Then he had been stripped almost bare and those fingers had gone inside the orifices of his body. Then he had been allowed to dress and had had to scrabble in the near darkness at his feet to collect what had been taken from his pockets, examined and dropped. He had gone through the first barred gate.

There had been three more searches, as if no message had been passed ahead on the mobile phones. Three more times he had been questioned, then strip-searched. Then the fingers had been in his mouth and in the anal passage, and lights had been shone into his ears and up his nose and the sac under his penis had been lifted. There had been more delays at more barred gates. He thought contempt was shown him.

He was left with little that preserved dignity.

Each time he was allowed to progress he had taken time over dressing, knotting his tie and shoe laces.

He feared for his life.

He saw the silhouette of Salvatore's head. He had seen the man several times before, always a half-stride behind Gabriella Borelli. Massimo had thought the man who hovered at Gabriella Borelli's shoulder to be a psychopath, probably medically certifiable. He thought his own feet, in the expensive handmade shoes of soft leather, were on a treadmill, that the motor went ever faster and struggled to keep up the momentum. If he did not he would fall, and he didn't know how to jump clear of the treadmill.

He saw the body on the ground, strained his eyes and detected cuts on the face.

'What did they say?' Salvatore murmured – the voice of a dreamer, a sleepwalker.

He remembered the equation of fear: the cells of Poggioreale, or the anger and retribution of the old witch.

Massimo did not lie, did not dare to. He stuttered through the message he had been given by Anna Borelli, now in her eighty-eighth year, and realised that what he had said was understood by Salvatore and by the figure bound on the floor near his feet. Salvatore nodded, as if the matter did not concern him, but the figure twitched and he heard the intake of breath. Massimo thought himself damned. He said where the body should be dumped.

Damned. He had a law degree, he owned an apartment in the most select district of the city, he drove a high-performance car, and already could count his assets in hundreds of thousands of euros, yet he was reduced to ferrying instructions, was the boy sent from a reception desk at the Excelsior Hotel on the via Partenope. Damned for ever.

He ran.

He wasn't stopped.

He ran as fast as he could and the barred gates seemed to open ahead of him. He was not searched, questioned, delayed or hindered by men with mobile telephones. He careered down the staircase, syringes and glass shards crunching under his shoes, and broke out into the night.

The scooter took him only to the edge of Scampia. He was dropped where the via Baku made a junction with the via Roma Verso Scampia. He was left at a bus stop.

The evening air played on his face, and he waited for a bus, alone, and believed he had killed a man.

They clustered round the screen. Those who worked the annexe had prime positions, but others from the operations room peered over shoulders for a glimpse of what the video showed. He had thought it a tipping point when a contact had been made, but had been wrong. This was.

The collator gave the commentary, Lukas hunched beside him. 'That is the Great Nose – to everyone except him and his face. That's him. We have one photograph of him in ten years and that was with dark glasses. It's excellent. He has that territory of the Sail. He has been a fugitive for more years than the photograph has existed . . . Incredible.'

The image on the screen was monochrome and the walkway poorly lit. The figure of the man identified as Il Grosso Naso came from under hanging washing slung across the walkway and was clear for a matter of seconds in profile, then was gone under more draped sheets.

'Typical of those bastards, the spies. They won't share. They have a camera on him. Another visitor, far from his home ground. It is Il Camionista, the old man of Forcella, and his rheumatism is bad again. So, the Grosso Naso and the Camionista do business. Carmine Borelli is off territory. He will be nervous, he will not be there with a position of strength and he will have come to ask a great favour, for which he will pay.'

Lukas reckoned that in other company the old man would have used a stick but not there: a stick was weakness and frailty. A younger man walked two, three paces behind him, but he was led, a cloth tight round his upper face, blindfolding him.

'No trust. They're strangers in the Sail. I cannot see all his face but I know from the walk, from the mouth, from the shoulders and the hips, that Carmine is escorted by his son's killer – it is the hitman, it is Il Pistole, Salvatore. There is a file, fat, on him. When he goes to prison – if he is not shot dead by us, by another clan – he is locked up for the rest of his life. He is to be *condanna all'ergastolo*. He will never again feel grass under his feet, hear birds sing or swim in the sea. They were all here but the spies wouldn't tell us until their man was dead and we couldn't blunder into their precious world. The file, the fat one, says there are many murders proven to Salvatore, usually with the Beretta P38, usually with a man on a scooter to take him to the target and away, and there are many more homicides with him as first suspect. He has no parents, no family, no woman. He has only the pistol and his dependence on the family of Borelli. He would want to be killed, and that is the only reason not to kill him.'

Lukas craned forward. Far beyond that point, the tipping done. He understood that he saw an opponent. He did not use, verbally or in his mind, a word such as 'enemy'. In his world emotion and rancour were put aside. He saw an opponent brought under the draped washing, shuffling past the lens, then taken under more washing. They went on through the films and did fast view for the departure of Big Nose, the Lorry Driver and the Pistol. The collator muttered more names, but without enthusiasm, as if they had no part to play. Many images went at jerky old-movie speed across the screen, cigarettes were lit, more coffee was downed.

Their attention, again, was jolted, and silence fell. Lukas could smell the sweat of many bodies, and his own, of socks and underclothing not changed, and his own. Men came down the walkway and gestured dismissively, women went indoors abruptly and kids fled. It was as if a route was cleared of obstruction and witnesses. Lukas saw Salvatore again, and the boy. He was within touching distance. Lukas could have reached out and let his finger brush the screen. The boy went slowly, as if exhausted and hurt. His feet did not have good traction on the walkway and he was mostly dragged; his shoulders were down. Lukas knew him because he had spoken with the man at the hotel, and with the man who sold fish. The fish, yes, the fish presented to the annexe at piazza Dante, the swordfish, was in a freezer tray in the kitchen area of a local restaurant. It would be thawed and cooked if there was a successful outcome, and would go on a rubbish heap if there was not – fuck the fish. He had spoken to both men and knew what clothes the boy had worn when he left the *pensione* in the morning and when he

had met the eye of the fish-seller. Lukas had demanded of
them what shirt, trousers and trainers the boy had worn. He
saw them in the black-and-white image on the screen, and
the hood. Lukas had only once been hooded – in his time
as an instructor at Quantico, after he'd come off the Hostage
Rescue Team and before he'd got himself lodged with the
new Critical Incident Response Group. He had been one of
the FBI instructors doing close-quarters battle training: in
simulating the storming of a building, they had needed a
'tame' prisoner and it hadn't seemed fair to allocate a rookie.
He had done it. He could remember, still, the smell and taste
of the sacking, his panic at his inability to breathe deeply,
and the fear of what would happen next. He had had on
ear protectors when the storm came, blank rounds and
thunder-flash grenades. He had been hustled out, the hood
had been lifted off, and no one seemed to have much time
for him: interest was in the 'bad' guys, who were wasted,
and the 'good' guys, who were heroes.

'I assume that's Eddie Deacon.'

Lukas made his first contribution. 'It is.'

'He has been beaten.'

'He has.'

'If he still lives, he is on the third level of the Sail building
in Scampia. It is not my expertise but I would suggest there
is no more difficult place inside the state from which to
extract a prisoner.'

Lukas said, 'I don't intrude, gentlemen, I don't push or
impose my opinions. I'm here to give help if I'm asked for
it.'

Castrolami said they would go in five minutes, not a
suggestion but a demand.

Lukas knew them now by their familiar titles. The bustle
broke around him. He had little to take, nothing of
consequence other than his laptop. Some that he knew of

made occasional trips into Baghdad or Bogotá, for the FBI, DoD or a contractor and travelled with their bespoke flak vest, blood and sterile dressings. Lukas had never bothered. Neither did he have manuals to refer to because everything he needed, and half a ton more, was in his head, but he regretted that he had no fresh socks or underwear in the rucksack.

They had discarded their given names, were identified by those their colleagues used for them. The Tractor, the Engineer and the Bomber were loading big kitbags. There was no more talk of military survival kit, water-resistant socks, small strengthened hacksaw blades and fishing hooks. Lukas had learned how they would operate at the first wave of an ROS assault. The Ingegnere would take off a door or blow out a window for entry. The Bombardiere would put in a handful of XM84 stun grenades, the 'flash and bang' gear – the flash was up to seven million candela and the bang 180 decibels. The Trattore would lead the storm guys inside. Lukas had seen it done in practice and for real, sometimes the practice was fouled up but the actual thing went a treat. At others the practice was perfect and the actual a disaster. What the Tractor, the Engineer and the Bomber did was a definition of the old 'inexact science', but so was Lukas's work.

Lukas hung back in the annexe. He heard Castrolami talking in the operations room. The small team, which would fit into one large minibus, would travel to Scampia ahead of a larger squad. Only when the initial group was in place would the numbers for securing a perimeter be deployed. Lukas understood. It was about security, about maintaining secrecy. He thought it a harsh world in which police officers and paramilitary men couldn't be trusted – might have a place on a gang leader's payroll.

A last brief act was played out in the annexe. The psychologist announced defiantly that he could monitor, observe, contribute from the operations room. The collator gave as his opinion that he was better employed close to his big computer and his archive. Lukas felt that the reputation of the Sail lay on them. He was not invited. Neither was it suggested that he should find a quiet corner and get involved in basket-weaving. He wasn't accused of imposing himself. Lukas was on board.

He thought, and it suited him well, that he was barely noticed as they hiked out of the annexe and skirted the side wall of the operations room, the far side from the banks of screens and the illuminated map. Castrolami was given a brief bear-hug by a superior, while others slapped the arms and shoulders of the ROS guys in encouragement. Lukas was offered no warmth, no good will, and flitted out. Apprehension burgeoned. He had seen the face, in monochrome, of his opponent. Had been there so often, looking into a face and wondering which well-trodden path to take to consign the face to the rubbish heap. Had been there so often – was concerned, again, that the magic moment was dulled. God, let it not be said that, almost, he was bored with all the faces.

There was a driver and the driver's escort, big men, armed with filled holsters and belts that sagged with kit. There was a communications kid, looked no more than nineteen, who carried a steel box and Lukas saw that it was chained by the handle to his wrist. There were six ROS, and Castrolami. A pecking order existed as they loaded into the minibus. The driver and his escort were together. The communications kid and Castrolami were side by side, the link and the decision-taker, there were the men who would make an entry, if it came down to the desperate uncertainty of a storm, and there was Lukas, who was without status and quantifiable expertise and had been there so many times before.

They left piazza Dante.

Gerald Seymour

Lukas sat across the aisle from Castrolami and the communications kid. A map of the Sail was spread out across the investigator's knees and he used a pencil torch. Lukas gained an impression of the enormity, complexity and threat posed by the building. He did not wish to talk.

He turned away from the map and stared out of the window at the passing streets. It was, he reflected, a city with some of the finest architecturally designed churches in Christendom, which contained some of the greatest works of art, sculpture and painting ever created. There was the beauty of the bay behind them and the crude majesty of the mountain. Sophistication, intellect, culture and glory encircled the minibus. All he had seen of them was the view over the rim of the crater when he had received the warning of hidden and violent danger. There were no such contrasts in Baghdad, or in the mountains and jungles of Colombia, or on the great plains of Afghanistan. The cafés seemed full, and the bars, and outside two restaurants he saw people standing on the pavement in what apologised for a queue, waiting to be given a table. It was so goddam normal.

Castrolami pushed the map of the Sail towards the communications kid, left him to fold it. He asked Lukas, 'When we get there, what do you want?'

'To be as close as possible.'

'What do you do first?'

'I try to make some calm,' Lukas said. 'It's not always easy but it's a good place to start.'

Castrolami looked into Lukas's face, and a slow smile spread. 'Do you have that buzz in you, the adrenalin pump? Is it going? Riding towards the location, not knowing what you'll find, and . . .'

Lukas shrugged, then said, droll, 'Worst you can find is a dry house. A dry house is where they were, it's the one they've quit. Sheets and blankets, a hell-hole for a cell, food and mountains of cigarette butts, but gone. That's a dry house. I don't often get sex, don't often fire a handgun, and I'm a small-town boy from a trailer park with a mongrel's pedigree, so I guess riding towards the location is sort of ecstasy, orgasm and cartridge discharge. Yes, the pump's going a bit.'

'Do we have a good environment or a bad one?'

He looked out of the window again. The road was clogged with traffic and a horn blasting wouldn't have helped, or a siren, or the lights. The driver wove, looked for weaknesses in the jam, and the ROS guys didn't talk but worked on their kit.

Lukas said, 'If it isn't a dry house, and if the boy's still alive, the location's about as shit as it gets – but, then, none of them comes easy. A big deal? You have the girl nailed down. None of them comes easy.'

18

When there wasn't much worth saying, Lukas usually stayed silent.

Castrolami seemed tight, knotted, and would have had cause. They had left the city and climbed on to the plateau area inland, to the east, and the dense housing was behind them. The ground opened: scrub, rubbish, abandoned construction, more scrub, more rubbish, more half-finished projects, and more scattered lighting. The traffic blockages of the old city were back down the hill. Lukas saw the towers.

He was near to making progress calls on his mobile, but not yet. He was not one of those who went off radar and only called in when he had success or failure to report, but he wouldn't call unless he had hard information. At Ground Force Security they paid his wage and put a roof over his head; if he didn't have them, he might just have to ship out and go back to Charlotte, a trailer park, a wife who might tolerate him if he was around to do handyman jobs and a son who would ignore him. He'd eat doughnuts and fries, drink grape juice, maybe hike some Carolina trails, and worry about a Bureau pension that had been cut short in contributions and would keep him light on cigarettes. He wouldn't walk away willingly from his employer, and he would call when he had information.

The towers speared up and alongside them there were big shoeboxes laid on their sides. Way back, when he was young in the Bureau and there was a shortage of personal-

protection guys for an overseas detail, he had taken a short
straw and had gone in the director's entourage to a terrorism
conference in west Berlin. There had been a chance of a day
across the other side: they'd been bussed through the Wall,
and he had seen the forests of towers on the outskirts of the
eastern sector. Lukas could live in an attic apartment under
the eaves off the rue de Bellechasse in the heart of a great
old city, or he could live in a cabin up high in a treeline –
like the guy at Ruby Ridge had. He couldn't have lived in
a tower block in east Berlin, or one out on the darkened
flatlands east of Naples. Castrolami had hold of his sleeve
and tugged at it, then pointed at the map. The pencil torch
caught the outline of the big block, and Castrolami pointed
out through the window. It was massive. It was indeed a sail.
The towers now seemed dwarfed by it. The lights from
windows etched in its shape. There seemed to Lukas to be
a hull to the building, then what was almost forward decking
and then twin sail shapes rose, climbed high.

They were close now.

What Castrolami had not asked him: could he maintain
the same hunger for his work as in the past when his reputation
was made? Did he have the same fascination for the
techniques that would undo his opponent?

Inside the minibus there was the murmur of the comms
kid's voice as he spoke into a button microphone. His metal-
lined case was open and dials were lit. Twice a separate
microphone was passed to Castrolami and enveloped in his
ham fist as he spoke. There was the scrape of weapons being
armed. He thought the Tractor was the leader, the Bomber
was the joker, and that the world's roof would have to collapse
before the Engineer contributed.

A contested entry was a disaster. Lukas knew it – they
would all know it. He thought the place would be, from
Castrolami's plan, like a gopher warren of tunnels and entries,

exits, climbs and descents, like the ground squirrels used. The navigation was done by the driver's escort, who would lean back and whisper into Castrolami's ear. He had said, himself, that he needed to be as close as was possible to the hostage and the hostage-taker, and he didn't think it needed saying again. He had seen a sign, crazily askew, for the via Baku: he wondered what the connection might be between an asshole corner of southern Italy and the capital city of Azerbaijan, but doubted it mattered. Another sign told him they were on the viale della Resistenza. The torch flashed on the map and the pudgy finger pointed to the location.

They were slowing.

Lukas felt the tightness in his gut – always there when the action came near.

Castrolami said, quiet but breathy, 'It is unlikely we will be met with armed resistance, but it is possible. If we are, stay close to my back. You do not show anyone your voice, your accent – damn Yankee. We may be confronted with passive opposition, crowds, abuse, heckling, man-handling. Stay close to me, hold on to me. I expect barricades, steel gates, blocks to slow us – the Ingegnere will deal with them, and for hostile people we have the Bombardiere. We attempt speed, but we do not know what we find and we do not have the luxury of time for reconnaissance. What do you wish to say?'

'I'm here. I can give advice if it's wanted. I don't impose.'

Castrolami punched his arm, a good hard jab, made it hurt, and it seemed to Lukas a gesture of affection – might have been respect. There was no call for respect.

The minibus came to a stop.

They had rocked on to a pavement and the weight had broken a slab. The roll had barely stopped when the Trattore had slid back the side door and was out. There was a stampede.

Lukas had never jumped with a parachute. He had been on an aircraft from which men had jumped, at night, over a targeted farm where a contract worker was reported to be held. What had lasted with him was the sight of the dispatcher by the open hatch as he booted the guys out and into the void. The driver's escort had that job. Half of the ROS guys, then Castrolami and the comms kid, the rest of the ROS guys, and Lukas. The escort's fist caught him, as if he was the runt of the damn litter, threw him forward and he cannoned first into a big backpack, then the one with the bolt-cutters damn near speared him with a handle. He steadied himself against Castrolami's backside and most of the wind was squeezed out of him. He gasped. He was in his forty-eighth year – did that matter? Maybe not the statistic, but he didn't run on pavements or do gym sessions, and guys with a childhood heritage of trailer parks didn't play tennis. He'd never had the time or inclination to learn golf, and mountain hiking was more a dream than real. He felt old. He sucked in air – felt old, feeble, but there was no young bastard pressing up against him. Why could Ground Force Security rent out the services of Lukas, a hack who had seen better days? Because negotiators and co-ordinators were happy to work a Stateside beat or to be in London or Berlin, but declined postings to Mosul, Jalalabad or Medellín, any goddam place where there were shit, flies and a building like the Sail – and a wretch who was looking at a knife or a pistol.

They were running, except the driver and his escort who were left behind.

Lukas didn't play at heroes, was separated from Castrolami's back by a cigarette-paper thickness. He saw, past the big shoulders, the shadows in a dark doorway. Lukas thought, then, there was brief negotiation, a few seconds, two or three exchanges, and the shadows were done and the way ahead was clear. There were pounding feet, and he imagined the heavy boots encasing water-resistant socks, and more boots behind him, which was as welcome a sound as any. The Tractor had a flashlight in one hand, turned it on. In the other he held a handgun. He wore a vest, and had a machine pistol slung on a strap looped at his neck. His chin jutted. No debate, negotiation or discussion. The Tractor led them through – as if he was crossing a water-filled ditch or rode a sand berm – and men made way for them. Lukas was given no explanation, but he factored that their entry on to a staircase was not impeded. That was a little victory, minimal, but a victory of sorts.

The smell of the place hit him.

The flashlight, used intermittently, guided him up.

He would do the best he could – had no more to offer.

It was as if a signal had been given from the base of the stairwell and sent on up to the floors above. The flashlight caught men and women, children with them. They were dressed, the smaller children in night clothes, and carried cases and bundles. One child had a puppy clasped to his chest, and others had prime toys. He sensed the mood of evacuation – as if a deck was cleared. There was no eye-contact between those on the stairs coming down, stumbling under their loads, and those going up, bowed under the weight of the kit. Two groups not acknowledging each other. Lukas thought he did dirty work: it was work that decent people should not be asked to perform. He went up the stairs and Castrolami's shoulders bounced in front of him.

Eddie wondered where the noise had gone. Salvatore talked. 'They pay me well – because I am the best. I am expert and I am valuable. I have accounts in banks in Switzerland and in Liechtenstein. I do not know where that is. There is another account in Andorra. I have never been there. I am twenty-four years old and I have much money and many accounts.'

He should have heard noise. The keenest sounds he had heard had been when he was brought up the staircase, hooded, and when he was taken down a long corridor and voices had been muffled behind doors and windows, with televisions and music. Men had shouted, women had laughed, kids had squealed and dogs had barked, yapped. He had heard less when he had run and realised that the corridor was a walkway, an aisle between boxed apartments. There was a knife on the table near the door, close to Salvatore's hip, and he had a pistol in his hands.

'I can buy what I want. I can go to any shop in Naples and I can buy anything. I want jewels for a girl, I can buy them. I want a suit, I want shoes, I want a car. I have the money in banks. They pay me because of my worth. They want me, the Borelli family. They can have me but they must pay. I think I have a million euros in accounts, and perhaps it is more. One day I will go to the coast, not Italy. One day I will go to France – they have told me, the family has, of Cannes and Nice, and I will go there. I think I will have many girlfriends when I go to France, because I will have money and I can buy anything.'

He could not recall so clearly the sounds of the walkway when he had fled along it before he saw – under the washing – the barred gate, closed. Eddie, then, had been on his toes and running at speed, despite the stiffness in his legs, knees and hips from being tied down, and the burden of the chain and ankle shackle. He had heard sounds then: shouts of pursuit, the gasp of his breath, doors slamming in his face, a kid's obscenity as he charged past a window – and there had been the loudness of the television in the room where he had taken refuge. Now he could hear nothing. It was as though quiet carpeted the air round him. Salvatore's shoes slithered on the flooring and his voice droned in the accented English as he played with the pistol and aimed it at points on the wall. Eddie thought there was in the eyes something demonic or manic or lunatic, something that was plain bloody mad. He realised it: he was the only audience the man had, maybe had ever had.

'I will go to France, to the Mediterranean, and I will buy an apartment – a penthouse – with cash and I will go to a showroom and buy a car and again I will use cash. In the morning I go to the bank and I sit down, and I authorise transfers from Liechtenstein and Andorra and other places, and then they go to get my money from their store in the basement and we fill a suitcase with my money and then I go to the real-estate office and to the showroom. I will find new friends and new girls. Maybe this is in one year, or three years, and maybe it is tomorrow after I have . . . I will go to France. I speak good English – the best, yes? I will speak good French. I have many enemies here, but they will never find me when I have gone to Cannes or Nice. There I will be unknown and I will have much, very much money. I have the money because of what I do well. I kill well.'

The shadow spun on its heels and the feet came close to Eddie's face and the shadow crouched. A little of the light from a window, thrown up by a streetlamp, orange, caught the pistol's barrel and rested on it. It was three or four inches, less than six, from Eddie's forehead. He stared at it and kept the focus of his eyes on the needle sight at the end of the barrel and could see the finger, just, on the bar protecting the trigger, and the finger slipped from the bar to the trigger stick. He wondered then if his bladder would burst, whether the urine would squirt into his trousers, fill the groin, make it steam hot. The finger moved from the trigger. He did not know if the safety catch had been on or off. What had he thought of? Had had a modicum of seconds to reflect. Had not thought of his parents, or his house friends, or anything noble, had not thought of Immacolata – had worried that he would mess his trousers. Had hated the bastard, and anger caught in him.

'I think, when I have gone to France, that many in Naples will remember my name. The kids will, women will. They will remember that I was a big man in Forcella and in Sanità and here in Scampia, and that I had respect. No one in Naples, I promise it you, would ever dare not to give me respect. I will be written of for many years, in the *Cronaca* and in the *Mattino*, and I will let them know that I live – go to Germany and send a postcard, go to Slovakia and send another. The police do not have the brains that I have and they will not find me. I will be written of in the papers and they will put my photograph there, because I have importance, and I have respect. I will never be taken. Do you understand me? I will not be taken alive.'

Eddie was still lying on his side. He had lost sensation in his hands from the tightness of the plastic at his wrists, and he thought the welts at his ankles were raw and his vision was through the slits of his swollen eyes and his lips were broken and the bruises throbbed, and he hated and felt the growing anger. The man, Salvatore, circled him, held the pistol in two hands and aimed it down, but the shadows of the fists were too dark for Eddie to know if the finger was on the bar or on the trigger, and the man laughed – cackled. Eddie thought Salvatore didn't hear the silence around them. Himself, he didn't know why the quiet had come.

The first gate on the walkway of the third level was chained and padlocked. Washing had not been taken off the wires, some of it still sodden and some of it nearly dry. The wet sheets, towels and shirts clung to their faces as they went forward. It was as if the evacuation was complete. Nobody came and nobody moved: no men from a clan, no families quitting, all gone, faded into the evening, and most of the lights with them. The clothes and bedding hung out to dry threw long shadows. No radio had been left on, and no television. They were wary of the silence, and the Tractor went on the balls of his feet.

Lukas saw, looking past Castrolami, a cola can lying abandoned on the walkway a few yards short of the steel-barred gate that had chains and a heavy-duty padlock securing it. The cola can was in the centre of the walkway. He was in Baghdad. There was a street, emptied, silent, where kids didn't play, men didn't stand on steps to smoke and talk. There was a street with a Sprite can tossed on to the path, and the patrol would use that path. There was a private, first class, of an airborne outfit and he was point on the patrol, and the Sprite can was in front of him and he was near to it. There was a first sergeant leading the patrol, walking with Lukas – doing acclimatisation – and the man's yell had damn near shredded the clothes and the vest off Lukas's back, and had stopped the private, first class, dead in his tracks. It had been explained – an empty street, no people, no traffic, was the tell-tale sign of an ambush. A trashed can was on a path and grunts always, did it *always*, kicked a can that was in front of them. A can could hold a quarter-kilo of plastic explosive and a detonator operating off a tilt switch could fire it when it was kicked, and it could take a leg off the point man and the balls off the one following him, and maybe some eyes . . . Lukas burst forward.

He shoved Castrolami aside. He sprinted as near as he could.

He went past the Engineer and the Bomber.

He caught the Tractor's arm. He held it, stopped him.

He panted – couldn't find a voice to speak. He pointed to the can.

They went on, and Lukas again had taken his place behind Castrolami, and each of them stepped with care round the can, until the last ROS guy squatted down, then went on to his knees and shone a torch into it. Lukas had turned and could see him under a kid's towel. Then the guy stood up and kicked the can to hell. It rattled away.

The warning he had given, his caution for a can, was not ridiculed – he had respect.

The Engineer took big bolt-cutters from his bag, opened the blades and put the loop of the padlock between them, flexed and used his strength, and the padlock broke apart. The gate was pushed open by the Tractor. Beyond it, the washing hung thicker and made a fog; it could not be seen through.

Lukas knelt. He could see under the washing, and the walkway stretched to a darkened infinity and had no horizon. Nothing, nobody, moved.

They used the long tunnel from the Palace of Justice to bring Immacolata to the Poggioreale gaol. She could have gone by car and entered through the back gates, but when offered the choice she took the walking option and did it briskly, with a good stride, Rossi and Orecchia at either side of her. The deputy prosecutor was in front, the *carabinieri* liaison officer behind.

The air around her was close, dank from the dribble of a water leak, and was ill lit. Prisoners were brought by small bus from the court to the gaol and the fumes hung, trapped.

Immacolata did not show relief when they reached the steps, when a door was unlocked by a guard, when fresh air wafted over her.

She was told by the deputy prosecutor how long she had. She shrugged, and answered that she did not need that much time.

The gaol was not yet shut down for the night and the clamour inside it filled her ears. She had no doubts. She was led to an interview room. At the door she was told her brothers had not been informed that they were to meet her.

The door opened. They had their backs to it. There were four officers in the room and cigarette smoke rose towards a single barred light. She saw that Giovanni lounged, had tipped back his chair, and Silvio was hunched forward, his head resting on his joined hands. They were manacled. She was led round the table and recognition broke. Shock from Giovanni, confusion from Silvio. She smoothed her skirt and sat down. Two of the officers flanked the table and two were immediately behind her brothers.

Immacolata said, 'I'm here to tell you – in person, because I'm not frightened of you – that I intend to continue collaborating with the state, and to give evidence in any criminal trial that follows the information I provide. I will not be deterred and—'

Big hands rested on Giovanni's shoulders. He spat, 'Bitch! You're the walking dead – and the boy you fucked will be sliced.'

'I won't be deterred and my decision is irrevocable. I'll be a witness in court, whatever is done to those who have been close to me.'

Silvio did not have to be held and his shoulders shook. He blurted, 'I loved you, you were my sister, I did whatever you asked me. I never told our mother I drove you to Nola. Why have you done this to me? Please, why?'

'To break the power of our family. I'll put that power under the heel of my shoe and grind it to dust. Whatever happens, my mind will not be changed.'

She stood. She was the queen of the moment and the audience was completed. Silvio – sad, inadequate, a worshipper – wept into his hands. She started to move round the table and Giovanni lunged. The hands, held together by manacles, were in her face, the fingers outstretched and the nails exposed, as a cat's claws would have been. One nail caught the tip of her nose, and as the blood welled he was thrust back into his chair. He spat, but it fell short of her. Then a hand was in his hair and locked his head still.

Silvio sobbed, 'I thought you loved me. I thought you were my friend.'

Giovanni snarled, 'They'll slice him slowly. They'll send you his dick. Keep looking over your shoulder, and know that you'll be found.'

She left. Her escorts would have hustled her out, but she went at her own pace.

She heard, outside the room – as inside Giovanni fought an unequal battle and Silvio howled – Orecchia ask Rossi, 'What did Caesar say?'

And heard Rossi's answer, 'At the Rubicon river, as he prepared to ford it and march south, he said, "*Iacta alea est!*" "The die is cast." She can't turn now.'

'She understands the consequences.'

'She understands – and has cut herself free of them.'

Orecchia said, 'God be gracious and protect us from principles.'

She didn't turn her head and tell him she'd heard what he'd said – and didn't think of Eddie Deacon, but of Nola and a cemetery.

They went past the agent's door. Easy to recognise: there was a light on inside and the room, seen through the broken door, and the clean window, was wrecked. It had been searched systematically and then, Lukas thought, trashed in vengeance. He knew now what had happened to the agent, about the fall and the dog that had been shot. Lukas was big on agents – assets – and he recognised their value more than most. In any city he worked, or any strip of jungle, or up any goddam mountain, he would ask about intelligence assets and probe for what they were able to bring to the table. It was not for him, an outsider, to criticise the unwillingness of an agency to share – well, not out loud and not for quoting. He could have said that the agent might be alive, might enjoy a glass of a local wine in a safe-house, if his material had been shared and he'd been lifted out. He could have surmised that many agents had been 'lost' – euphemism for slaughtered – because they'd been kept in place beyond the sale date. The agent had cheated those who had come to his apartment, had plunged from a window and so denied them the chance of the beating, the kicking, the burning with cigarettes, maybe the use of electrodes and waterboarding. For cheating them they had wrecked the place.

Lukas could see, also, the cables that hung from the ceiling and dropped down from the cavities in the plaster where they had been hidden, the hole through the wall and the place where an attachment for the hook that held a washing line in place had masked the exterior lens. He couldn't have sworn to it, but he thought that Castrolami's arms moved, saw the jerk of the elbows, and reckoned the investigator had crossed himself. If the boy survived – *if* Lukas's best effort was sufficient – *if* an apartment further up the walkway was not dry, then that life would be owed to the asset who had died. Sobering – yes. They went on, quiet, fast and wary, but not stampeding. Each took fistfuls of the washing and dragged it down, thought little of dumping it in the dirt at the side of the walkway. Sometimes it was women's underclothes they snatched, but there was no laughter. They hustled forward, momentum with them. Lukas thought he liked serious men, that they were good to be with when advancing towards what his jargon called the 'termination phase'. Then not even outsize knickers or a frilly imitation lace brassière made for humour.

The second gate was locked, with a large lock box welded to it. More delay. Lukas thought the gates, barricaded against them, were the sign that they were tolerated for an evening here, on this level alone – the limit of that cursory negotiation at the bottom of the stairs – but they had no automatic right to access.

Again, Lukas did not have to be told. Bolt-cutters could do chains and a padlock, but not entry through a locked gate. He wondered what they would use. The Engineer had turned, crouched and unhitched the straps of his bag. Eyes must have met. The Engineer told him that it would be T4 – an abbreviation for an impossible-to-pronounce formula name that ended in 'trinitramine', a compound of nitric acid and hexamine, with a blast velocity of 8750 metres per second and . . . Lukas had not heard him speak before. He had known enough technical screwballs in his time, and doubted they were different people from those who stood on platforms and noted train numbers, or had binoculars to see the registration on aircraft fuselages coming in to land and taking off. The Engineer worked fast, and his description of the power he was manufacturing fell on Lukas's deaf ears. It would be a crucial moment.

Along the empty corridor was an apartment – wet or dry. If it was wet, the hostage target was there and a psychopath, a lunatic, had to be talked out of killing him. What counted was to get close by covert approach. There was nothing secret about a blast of T4-type plastic explosive. Horrible stuff, colourless, and in the Engineer's hands, about half an ounce, less than a golfball. Then a stick detonator, the wiring, the waving of them back, taking shelter in doorways, the playing out of a cable and the clips going on to a box – and *if* the apartment was wet, they did not know which was its door.

'We go through. We look and we find. I speak. I ask for

the boy, and I ask for surrender. Maybe the boy gets killed, maybe I'm shot at. Then it's your chance. You want it different?'

'The way it is, that'll be fine by me.' Lukas took the chance offered him and hit Castrolami's arm – not as hard as he had been hit but with what force he could manage.

They waited for the Engineer to count them down.

Eddie boiled.

'You know, each time I do a hit, it is the next morning in the newspapers, and I buy them. They write so much about me. They make up much. I had thought of calling some of the reporters to meet me, and tell them that they must be exact and tell truths, they should treat me with greater respect. I read all the newspapers the morning after, and they carry the conferences of the police and they talk about me. I think they do not make much money, the reporters. They would be as easy to buy as police are. I earn in one week what a policeman makes in one year . . . They have nothing. I have money in the bank.'

The anger burned. Those who knew him would not have recognised Eddie's voice, and the crack of contempt in it. 'Maybe you don't.'

'What do you say? What?'

'Maybe you don't have money in the bank.'

'I do, I know it.' Gabbled, but irritated.

Eddie said, 'Maybe they've taken it all, fleeced you.'

'What is "fleeced"?'

'What you do – "fleece" is steal . . . They open the accounts for you?'

'The lawyer did, for Gabriella. Before her it was for Pasquale Borelli. The lawyer did what they instructed.'

'They'd have fleeced you. Did you ever see the statements?'

'They cannot send them. I was told the statements. It is a million euros, near.'

'If there was ever money there, which is doubtful, now it'll be gone.'

'I have their word.'

'Their word? Like your word? A word is a guarantee? In fucking Naples? I bet you—'

'What do you bet?'

'I bet you that your accounts, if they ever existed, are empty. I reckon you were easy to trick, to deceive. I reckon you're just some animal they employ, then put back in a cage. There's no money, I bet it.'

He was hit across the face. Salvatore had crouched low over him and used the barrel of the pistol as a whip. The blow made more blood, opened the wounds that had almost sealed, and scraped away more skin. It hurt bad. He thought he wanted the fucking show on the fucking road, wanted it over. He was finished with lying trussed – cut and bruised, in pain, his ribs throbbing – and helpless like a goddam chicken going to slaughter. No sirens, no goddam help. What made it easier – like a mouthful of codeine, paracetamol or ibuprofen, even like bloody aspirin – was that in his anger he had challenged the bastard on his money, had hit the open wound, had put salt on it. Wanted it over, and the triumph preserved. The victory was proven by the wild slashing strike on his face.

'Fuck you,' Eddie said, in his face.

He had pushed himself up, ignoring the pain. He sat upright. He looked into the wide eyes, could see them in the slack light. There was silence, and he didn't know why. Wanted it done.

He heard the scrape as a lever on the pistol was moved, thought it the safety. Heard the weapon cocked, metal scratching on metal. Could almost smile, saw the barrel wobble as if the bastard couldn't hold the aim steady. Needed it finished. Heard the explosion.

Maybe the front door of the apartment, on to the walkway, had not been locked because it opened and light flooded in. A window flew into the outer room, Eddie smelled smoke.

The door swung hard, slowed and flapped, then was still, but open.

He was pulled up. Because his ankles were fastened he couldn't move. He was dragged to the door, propelled into the walkway, and could feel the pistol's barrel, a pencil's width, against the back of his neck where the hair reached to.

Eddie was a shield.

He saw them, and, fifty paces up the walkway, wreathed in smoke, the frame of the barred gate, which had been open when he had run. Now it was half through a window. Doors near to it hung askew, unhinged, windows were out, and washing was stripped or shredded.

The men were through the gap. All huge. Three leading. Black suits, black masks, black weapons. He was wrenched round. He looked momentarily up the walkway, in the other direction, and a gate there was fastened shut.

The men had stopped. Weapons were up, aimed. Eddie felt Salvatore's breath on his neck, beside where the pistol barrel dug. They had come, and about fucking time and . . . all anger gone.

A blast in his ear, deafening.

Too fast for him to react, blink. A puff of concrete dust came off a wall near the gate, high, and the men scattered. One on his stomach, one in a right-side doorway and one in a left, with a rubbish bin for further cover. More men were behind them. Eddie saw one, large, wore a suit. Incredible, yes, a goddam suit, and there was a small guy beside him, who looked old, out of place, and crouched and— Eddie was dragged back inside.

They had come.

What had changed? It was that Eddie wanted to live – because they had come. Almost overwhelmed him, the sight of the men in their black kit, the guns and masks, the quiet around them, and the emptiness, and a man in a suit, and a man with short pepper-coloured hair and a lightweight windcheater. More behind them. Eddie trembled. Then his ankles were kicked hard and his feet went out from under him. He was felled, collapsed, and couldn't break the impact. He wriggled towards the far wall. He cursed himself for having provoked the bastard to anger, didn't think it smart – hadn't known they were coming.

He wondered who they were, what sort of men had come, who had sent them – what they knew of him.

The silence hung heavy. The quiet settled. He wanted to live, wanted nothing more.

The door to the walkway slammed shut. There was scraping as the table was dragged across the floor, then wedged into the outer doorway, chairs used as props to hold it. It was the older man he could picture best.

'I have had a short eyeball on the target hostage, Echo Delta Delta India Echo. He is held in an apartment of the Sail building, third level, Scampia, a Naples suburb. Initial indication is one hostage-taker, armed. Unlikely to be a covert exit point. Nothing by way of escape is negotiable. Target seemed from brief sighting at approx forty paces to be bound, had facial marks of abuse, but did not appear to have life-threatening injuries. Taker, my opinion, is unstable and unpredictable. Time to go to work. Out.'

He closed the call.

A waiter came to the table with the wine list, and Roddy Johnstone waved for it to be given to his guest.

'You all right, Duck? You look a bit pale. Got a ghost showing up?' the guest asked.

He shook his head. It was a decent restaurant, close to his office, and it was usual for him to bring prospective clients here, and convenient – halfway on foot between Grosvenor Square and Berkeley Square – for most. He asked his guest, who would be talking detail in a contract for the security of an oil-drilling programme in Georgia's Taribani Field, zone fourteen in block twelve, which could be worth fifteen million American dollars over ten years, to select a wine and choose from the menu for both of them. He apologised for having been distracted by the call.

He went outside. He stood on the pavement and the doorman lit a cigarette for him. He had seen Lukas's name come up on his mobile, had allowed him to talk, had not interrupted, had allowed him to ring off, had not spoken a word. Thoughts clouded his mind. He saw Lukas, saw a waste mass of concrete floors and walls, saw men with armed, aimed weapons, saw a young man who had gone off to get his girl back, had walked as an innocent into a snake's nest, had been beaten and had had a gun barrel against his head, and he saw an idiot who would have pledged – because they all did – that he would not be captured alive, and again he saw his man, Lukas. He flicked the cigarette towards a drain cover and watched it gutter.

Not something he would have wished to do, but not something to be avoided. He dialled. He did it because a kidnapping was involved, and a boy had been brought into the extended family of Duck's world. He would have cheapened himself had he not made the call then, there. He had no shame in admitting to himself that he cared.

He heard a call ring out, and heard it answered.

He said, 'Mrs Deacon? Mrs Betty Deacon, yes? . . . It's Roddy Johnstone from Ground Force. I won't beat around . . . This is a holding call. The position is that I've just received confirmation of what we call an "eyeball". It means that my man has seen your son, seen him physically, at a distance of about forty paces. He's in reasonable physical condition . . . Mrs Deacon, we're a long way from the end of this road. Eddie's held by an armed man in a housing complex. The authorities are there, and my colleague is with them. He's very good at what he does. Mrs Deacon, as soon as I have further news I'll give it you . . . I shall hope for the best and I shall hope for it very soon, but we're in uncertain times. Goodnight, Mrs Deacon, and my regards to your husband.'

He saw them too, winced, and wished he'd lit a second cigarette. He went back into the restaurant.

'Everything all right?' his guest asked.

He smiled. 'Probably, perhaps – about as all right as it can be. Now, what have you ordered for us?'

Immacolata had been given pizza in the prosecutor's office. She was not privy to events. He had been called out by his assistant three times, left his inner office, gone into the outer, took the phone and kept his voice at a pitch subdued enough for her not to hear what he said. She sensed that finality approached and that she was not invited to share it. Each time, when he came back, he had a deeper-cut frown on his forehead and then – as if he remembered its presence – would force a smile and attempt to wipe anxiety.

She ate the pizza and drank aerated water. She thought, in truth, they didn't believe in her resolve. She cleared her plate and emptied the bottle. Immacolata said, and did her sweet, warm smile, 'You need not be concerned for me. My mind is made up, and it's not for changing.'

He looked at her quizzically, as if he didn't yet understand her. 'I work in this room, Signorina for six days out of seven every week, for a minimum of ten hours every day. I strive after successes, but they are rare and elusive. To arrest a de Lauro or a Lo Russo or a Licciardi or a Contini classes as success. Maybe once a year we take one. Because of you, the evidence you bring, I have been able to close down an entire family – not an individual but a whole clan . . . Does that then defeat the criminal conspiracy? No. But it halts the advance. In my terms, to halt an advance, to stop a flow of Vesuvio's lava, is a success. Such are the crumbs off the table from which I survive. If you capitulate, Signorina, success is snatched away and the advance – irresistible – continues.'

'I won't capitulate.'

'You will not say – now, at this moment – that the life of the boy matters more?'

'No.'

'Say it to me again, please.'

'No . . . His life doesn't matter more.'

'Thank you.'

She stood up and let the pizza fragments fall from her lap on to his carpet and desk. She brushed the lap of her skirt, then took a little handkerchief from her bag and wiped the ring on the desk that the bottle had left. She touched her hair. She faced him. 'I'm ready for my next test – yes? It's a matter of giving proof? Where's Eddie?'

'In Scampia, in the Sail, at the mercy of your father's killer. Salvatore controls him.'

'Will you save him?'

'We'll try to.'

'Could I save him?'

'Of course.'

'And the price would be my evidence?'

He shrugged. He didn't have to give her his answer. She walked towards the door. It was as if she was an actor, on a stage, caught in a pool of light, and she knew the lines would not be spoken again, the questions and doubts would not be reiterated. She would not be thanked. She did not expect gratitude, and she thought humanity – what had been a variety of love – had been squeezed out of her, existed only in a padlock abandoned on a bridge. She said, 'I am ready to go to Posilippo now, to give you proof and serve you the crumbs, success. Can we move? I hope your best is good enough for Eddie's life.'

'It's only advice, not control.'

'Yes, of course,' Lukas answered. 'I give advice and you – obvious – are free to take or ignore it . . . It's the way, friend, it always is.'

He saw a wry smile spread on Castrolami's face – almost Lukas grinned, as dry as the skin of a tomato left out in the midday sun, what they sold in a supermarket – and Castrolami asked, 'What would be the first item of advice?'

Lukas squinted, looked up the length of the walkway. Two ROS guys, including the one they called Franco, the sniper, the *franco tiratore*, had gone up to the fourth level, had tracked along it then come down and were now hunkered in front of the far barred gate on the third level. The washing in front of him had not been torn away and it was only as he lay on his stomach that he could see the doorways and windows, the one door and the one window. He thought the section of walkway was now evacuated; if it wasn't, if some had been determined to stay behind, they must take their chance. There should not be the distraction of bawled commands, or requests, on a bullhorn for people to get clear. Always difficult to make the last few shift – they had a sick relative who was bedridden, a dog and four cats, a stick insect and a snake, a programme was coming on the television that they never missed, they feared they'd be looted once they'd gone. What now to advise?

He lit a cigarette. The Tractor had just started one, and the Engineer had just stubbed one out . . . From what he had seen and heard in the hours in the annexe off the operations room at piazza Dante he knew a little of the men around him. They talked girlfriends and sex, wives and arguments, kids and schools, mothers and food – and the psychologist made mobile calls to his partner, Maria, Spanish, and was concerned about the progress of her PhD thesis, while the collator was bothered that his son was on left-side defence in the café soccer team for the under-nines and should have been on the right. Castrolami had made one terse call, not more than ten seconds' duration, to a woman, hoping her work had gone well and stating that he would not be eating with her that evening.

Lukas's only communication had been with Roddy 'Duck' Johnstone, and had been short, brief, factual and without emotion. He had no one else to call. He never called his mother, Amy, and never called his father because he didn't know his name. Never called his one-time wife, Martha, who knew him only because a lawyer in Charlotte, out of a smart office block on the city centre's West Trade Street, sent her a small donation on the first Friday of each month, a couple of hundred dollars that had once been to look after the kid and had never been cancelled. She didn't acknowledge it. Never called his boy, Dougie, who did real estate out of premises on North Tryon Street. There was no one he knew, other than Duck – and that was professional – who would give a damn whether he called or not . . . Not even the artist on the riverbank or the man who had the grocery off the rue de Bellechasse, or the woman who sold him ice-creams outside the museum, or the waiters in the cafés would care greatly if he returned to their territory or not. He wasn't maudlin. It was the way he wanted his life to be. He didn't have ties that tugged at him. He was only bonded, so he was told, to his work. He lay on his stomach with his upper body jutting out of the recess of a doorway. He could see the distant shapes of the Sniper and his partner, the door they focused on, and the window, and he could see half of Castrolami's shoulder. Lying in the filth of the walkway would screw Castrolami's suit. What advice was on offer?

The walkway was secured at both ends, so no advice was needed on sanitising the perimeters of a designated siege area.

Nothing was negotiable on free passage out for a hostage-taker and his victim.

The renunciation of evidence would not happen. An exchange – witness statements ditched in return for a life given – was not an option.

Clemency for a killer – unlikely. Leniency – improbable.

'Right now I don't have advice to give,' Lukas said. 'I can tell you what I want and what I don't want.'

'Tell me.'

'I want to stabilise the atmosphere, cut the tension, get it stable. Make it so tedious that everyone wants to go to sleep – like it's taking the drama out of the show. The hostage-taker, what I have on him, he's young and he's used to immediate acceptance of what he says, and he'll reckon himself – saying it vulgar – the dog's bollocks. He sees himself right now as a central figure in a big theatre. We have to get him down to the ground, and calm him, bleed the adrenalin out of him, then keep him cool. That's the stabilisation. He'll threaten to kill because he has no other currency to chuck at us. Cool and calm is what we aim for. The priority for the boy is to have him walk out in one piece. Agreed? We do an assault by your people and we're on uncertain ground – may win, may lose. An assault is last-chance stuff. The hostage-taker, where's your priority for him?'

'Taken alive.'

'Most of them, ones fitting his profile, want what we call "police-assisted suicide". It's easy and quick, and they have a delusion about a legend being born. Alive, and he's just another number in another cell block, rotting and forgotten. Alive, then, is my aim point.'

'Do you do timetables?'

'Try not to.'

'I don't have for ever.'

Lukas understood. A deal already in place. Part of a walkway cleared. A clan leader ordering his people to stand aside on this limited patch of territory, and an understanding that the law-and-order guys do their work, hurry, look for nothing else, do not disrupt, get lost. A deal that called for a long spoon, supper taken with devils, not a nice deal, one that stuck in a gullet. A deal that was understandable.

'It'll be over by dawn,' Lukas said. He had the feeling he was regarded as an oracle, had done little to diminish it, and that he knew solutions to whatever problem areas were thrown up. But hostage negotiation, hostage rescue and hostage co-ordination were not exact sciences. Some people lived their lives on certainties, down to a level of decision-taking on whether to replace with a bayonet or screw-fastening bulb. He knew of no two cases where hostages had been taken that exactly mirrored each other, but, there were basic patterns, enough for him to make up expertise on the hoof. What Castrolami had not asked him: did he have the same excitement as years back? Did he find the processes repetitive and was the light in his eye dulled? 'I have that feeling, and . . .'

The shout came down the walkway, hacked into the night air.

'. . . it'll be finished by dawn. What did he shout?'

Lukas strained to hear the voice better and Castrolami had a hand cupping his ear.

He heard the obscenity. The feet came back across the floor and Eddie was heaved upright. He stood, tottered, was supported. The man was at his back and wriggled in his hips and pelvis but stayed close to him. Eddie felt the belt looped round his own waist, then buckled across his stomach. They were a single item, Siamese. One hand was round Eddie's chest, above the belt, and the other held the pistol against his neck.

His feet, from behind, kicked. He could manage a hop, and went forward. More hops and the space between the inner and outer door was crossed.

Halting, in English, at his ear: 'They do not answer me. They see you, they will answer me.'

What to say? Nothing. Eddie bit his lower lip. It was broken where his teeth closed on it, and swollen to double size and the pain, brief, was pure. His ankles were trussed, his wrists too, and he could only move at a snail's pace. He was driven forward . . . and, God, he wanted to live. He prayed silently, but the bitten lip moved, and they would not shoot. He could feel the body of Salvatore close against him and they were indivisible. The door was pulled open. Eddie blinked.

There were gaps between the sheets, towels, shirts, underwear and dishcloths. None of them stood.

Eddie did. Eddie was exposed. He looked left, saw the barrels of rifles and felt that each aimed at the centre of his chest, above the belt, below the arm, and zeroed – Eddie reckoned – on the place where his heart beat, bloody pounded. He didn't know if he could hold his bladder. His body was twisted a quarter-turn and he looked to the right and up the other section of the walkway. Light reflected back from the telescopic sight mounted above the barrel and another black-suited figure was prone beside the marksman and had binoculars. The binoculars' aim and the sight's and the barrel's were not on Eddie's chest but his head. He could feel the pressure of the second head, Salvatore's, against the back of his scalp, and the forehead moved, made little motions, bucking his own forward and back. Eddie read it. A rifle's bullet would enter and exit, would not hit one of them but both, and the movements of Salvatore's head dictated that the sniper's aim fluctuated between their two skulls. From the other direction, up the walkway, the rifle bullets would go through one chest – one ribcage, one set of lungs or one heart – then into the other.

Prayed again – 'Don't let the bastards shoot.' Realised it: 'the bastards' were the marksmen. A fucking jumble in his mind and the marksmen were the risk to his life, not the man hugging him close and holding the pistol to his neck.

The voice boomed in his ear, had stayed with English, and Eddie didn't know why: 'I walk out. I walk past you. I walk from the Sail. When I walk I have the guarantee that the whore, Immacolata Borelli, the *voltagabbana* – the turncoat – retracts evidence. You have a half-hour. Look for the time on your arm. Half an hour. In half an hour, no promise of retracting evidence, he is dead. Believe me, dead. You have a half-hour. You decide.'

Eddie shivered. The cold was on his skin, but the warmth of the night made him sweat. It was a new cold, and it came from fear. The rifles, he saw, never wavered in their aim and were on his head and his chest, and he was perhaps forty paces from them, and they would have a killing range of a quarter of a mile.

He sucked in great gasps of air, would have collapsed if the arm and the belt had not held him.

A man among them pushed himself up. He had been flat on his stomach, went to his knees, then used his hands for leverage. It was the man who was slight and inconsequential, who wore a creased, dusty shirt and crumpled trousers, and who was unshaven and had the short pepper-coloured hair. His face was weathered and worn and had the texture of hardship. He stood at his full height, then arched his spine as if to get stiffness from it . . . Salvatore breathed hard on Eddie's neck, beside the pistol barrel. The marksmen had not shifted, nor a big-bodied man who wore a suit and held a pistol loosely, uselessly, in his hand.

Eddie watched the man who stood, saw him cup his hands across his mouth, as if that was the way to be heard.

'Do they believe me?' a shrill whisper in Eddie's ear. Then the firearm's blast near his ear, and the hair above it was scorched, the stink of firing on his skin. Concrete dust came down and settled on his face. Eddie blinked, squeezed his eyes shut, opened them again, and the rifles were still aimed at his head and chest. 'I think, now, they believe me.'

The man had paused, as if at an interruption. Now he stood his ground and called to them.

19

'My name is Lukas. I'm a friend of Eddie's parents, not a policeman. I'd like to help.'

He twisted a little, lowered his head and murmured to Castrolami below him, 'This is advice. If you ever incline to hostage-taking and a jerk says, "I'd like to help", my advice is to shoot him, and fast.'

Lukas had that mischief in his face, but then his head rose and it was gone. He was sober, sombre. 'I'm here to see if I can help,' he shouted, throwing his voice down the walkway.

The mischief was off his face but it stayed inside him. First time the mischief had taken root since he had been at the forward airstrip in the mountains beyond Bogotá and the captain, Pablo, had asked for advice and it had been suggested that the assault team go in: there was not much else in Lukas's life that pumped excitement.

The tip of a directional microphone lay in front of his trainers, and by his ankle the comms kid took off his headphones and gave them to Castrolami.

He yelled again: 'Would be good if I could help to sort this out, and that's what I want to do – if you'll allow me.'

Because he now stood square in the centre of the walkway he could see far down it. There had been an accident in the hanging of the washing so there was an avenue of vision for him. He had manoeuvred himself into a position where he had a good eyeball on the boy and on the hood who held him.

'My name, I'm saying it again, is Lukas. What I'm looking to avoid is anyone getting hurt, and any way I can, I'll try to help prevent that.'

What Lukas saw: every few seconds, the hood's head moved and took the boy's with it, and he rated it as a hell of a hard call for Franco, the sniper, to have a zero on the small piece of skull that was visible as a target. And the bodies were locked together, like they were in stand-up sex out in the yard at a kids' party. He didn't rate the chances of the sniper getting a clean shot. And the pistol was against the back of the boy's head, and Lukas could see in the available light that the finger was inside the loop and against the trigger bar. Most likely a shot to the head – a killing shot – would induce a muscle spasm through the body. Most certainly, a chest shot – whether fatal and into an organ or a wounding shot – would set off a decisive twitch through tissue and ligament and it would go to that finger. A spasm, a twitch, would be sufficient to depress the trigger bar . . . wasted exercise. They had taught the siege-busters at the Quantico training unit to do a double tap in the head, close range, pistol if possible. Two shots to the brain *might* suppress a spasm.

'I told you what I want. I want it. Now you have twenty-five minutes. You use time.' The voice came back, reedy.

Lukas thought the hood was exhausted. God alone knew how long it had been since he'd slept in a bed. Maybe not for two nights or three. Exhausted and hungry – wouldn't have eaten proper cooked food. Exhaustion and hunger, to Lukas, balanced out. The hood would be irrational and unpredictable. He would make mistakes and be subject, big-time, to judgement errors. They were the equations Lukas worked on, were what he knew.

Castrolami, below him, beside him, murmured, 'We have a feed through, the psychologist hears this. He says that

Salvatore would dream of a legend – was never taken, killed
with honour, will already know that nothing can be negotiated
and that he is boxed. Salvatore knows it. He is a killer, he
expects to kill. More important than anything to Salvatore
is the belief that woven into the legend will be respect. The
psychologist says—'

Lukas said, 'I have his drift. Thank him.'

'What do you do?'

'What I *try* to do is get up close, talk a bit, get the pistol
off the boy's neck, take it from there. Do you want to indulge
the hood, give him police-assisted suicide – his legend – or
do you want to fuck him?'

'Charge him, convict him, hear the key turn and lose it,
smell the decay as he rots and the years go by. That is a
better message than giving him respect.'

'Harder to achieve, but a goal . . . Just watch me, just be
ready . . . as they say, on a wing and a prayer.'

He moved forward but slowly. Like he was the tide coming
in. Short, crabbed steps and he was gone from Castrolami
and the comms kid and was, in a few steps, separated from
the Tractor, the Engineer and the Bomber.

Lukas could see the boy's face, part of it. There was bruising
in rings, multicoloured, round the eyes, the cheeks were
scarred, the lips grotesque, and there were blood smears
from a wound on the forehead and from the nose, and more
blood was caked where it had dribbled from the mouth. The
boy wouldn't be standing if he hadn't been held by the belt
and the arm. There had been just blind fear on the face
when he had first seen it, but there had been a change, subtle.
Like hope was born.

There were many burdens on Lukas's back and shoulders.
The one he liked least was that he gave little packages of
fragile hope to hostages when he approached them.

He saw the increasing agitation on the hood's face, and

The Collaborator 499

went slower. He did short steps that were barely the length of his shoe . . . If the mother-fucker moved the pistol from the boy's neck, if the mother-fucker moved his own head clear of the boy's, then he made an opportunity for Franco, the sniper, to shoot with the Beretta M501 rifle. Lukas reckoned, through a 1.5-6 × 42mm Zeiss scope, that the sniper would have a good view, wounds and warts, of the two faces . . . It would be Castrolami's call before the sniper fired, and that was not the goal set.

He did not, of course, but he would have liked to offer more of his advice to Castrolami. Would have stopped and turned and the advice would have been: 'If a little guy who says he's just there to help ever starts walking towards you – and you're a hostage-taker – and has a decent, honest smile on his face, and looks concerned for you, just shoot him. Don't hesitate. Shoot.' He must have reached close to halfway from the start point to where the boy and the hood were. Would have been about twenty paces from them.

Lukas felt the crisis moment was on him.

The scream: 'Stop.'

The pistol did not move off the neck and the heads did not separate.

A second scream: 'Stop. Do not come close.'

At twenty paces, Lukas could be almost conversational. 'You don't want me nearer, I'm not coming nearer. Like I said, I'm just here to help. Let's make a start. I'm Lukas, and I'm not a policeman. I'm a friend of Eddie's mother and father. I want to help them, and help Eddie, and I want to help *you*. I want this to end with everybody winning. It's where I'm headed – everybody wins. You don't want me closer, I don't come closer. You're called Salvatore, yes? Good name. The Saviour, Il Salvatore – it's a great name to have. Right, I'm going to start doing some helping. Salvatore, what do you need? Do you need some food? We can get pizza up here. You need water? We can do water that's still or with gas. Cigarettes? Tell me the brand and I can get it.'

The pistol hadn't shifted and the heads hadn't separated. It was early. Lukas had time.

'I will help you, and you can trust me . . .'

There were some of them, dumb and stupid, exhausted and hungry, who believed they could indeed *trust* the little guy who came close and offered help, food and drink and cigarettes, and they either stared up at a cell window or were dead, buried.

'Tell me what you want and I'll get it for you.'

He realised, now, many things. Clarity swamped the mind of Salvatore. The walkway was sealed at either end. The apartments fronting on to it were either evacuated or locked and barred. He had no freedom of movement, was as a rat in a corner – with teeth – without anywhere to run. He wondered at what stage Fangio had slipped away on his scooter. No mention made of Immacolata and whether she would retract evidence. No appeal, grovel or beg for the life – safety – of the boy he was close against. If he killed the boy, Eddie, who had slept with Immacolata and was her lover, then he himself was dead. Maybe half a second after he had pulled the trigger, he was dead.

Was it his destiny? Did he crave death?

Didn't know. Had no one to tell him. Didn't have Pasquale Borelli, who had taught him to read, write, shoot and kill. Didn't have Gabriella Borelli to tell him whether he wanted to die, be shot down, and didn't walk behind her and follow the sway of her hips. Had no one, was alone . . . He had seen so many. They didn't lurch back when shot, as the movies showed it. They fell. They were like the cattle in the abattoir that the clan owned. They subsided. And they twitched. Chickens did, they flapped. Men's muscles moved. While the blood flowed, the fingers fidgeted, tried to catch dirt or the concrete on a pavement, the vinyl tiles on a bar floor. He had seen it. Death was frozen on a face, that last expression. Laughing? Never. Happy? Never. Supreme? Never. Etched on to a dead face was, at the last, fear. Did he want it?

He saw a television cameraman who filmed and smoked, then heaved the camera off his shoulder, dragged a last time on the cigarette and threw down the filter. It would be on the walkway near his head. He saw two reporters and heard their laughter, as if they were the latterday crowd in the piazza Mercato when the aristocrats were hanged, and maybe the laughter was about the filth of his clothes and the smell of his body, and he saw children who stared blank-faced at the blood. He didn't know how long his photo would stay on the screens of the kids' mobiles.

'One step more, and I blow his head away,' Salvatore yelled. Didn't have to, not to be heard twenty metres away. If he did, if he squeezed the trigger, he was dead a half-second later. Knew that, realised it.

The voice was so calm. 'Because I'm here to help, I need to know the type of pizza we can order, and if the water should be still or with gas, and the brand of cigarettes. Look, we're not in a hurry. You think about it, give me an answer when you're ready – what's on offer is food, something to drink and cigarettes. Take your time, Salvatore – we have all the time you need.'

And the face was so reasonable, and it smiled at him. He had no one to ask, to tell him whether he wanted to eat and drink and smoke, to die or to live, and the hands of his watch moved – couldn't be stopped.

Three raids, supported by arrest warrants . . . In the via Forcella, a good-sized crowd watched as Carmine and Anna

Borelli were led out through the main door of the block, escorted past the stall, empty, where the fish-seller traded. They didn't look fearsome. Anna Borelli carried her teeth, had not inserted them in her mouth, and wore a pink night wrap over a white gown and had on fluffy pink slippers. Carmine Borelli looked confused and his hair was wild. He clutched his stick and wore striped pyjamas. A police officer followed them with two overflowing bags of day clothes. They had not been given time to dress because the police had feared a riot when they were taken away, but it didn't happen. No riot, neither were they handcuffed. Two insults, both hard to stomach. To prompt no reaction in Naples was to be dead, irrelevant.

In an alleyway off the via Tribunali, the section running to the west of the via Duomo, the lawyer was arrested. He fared worse than the old clan leader and the old brothel keeper: he was handcuffed and the photographers of *Cronaca* and *Mattino* were there to poke lenses in his face. He was ashen. He wore the previous day's socks, shirt and underwear, and had to hold up his trousers because he had dressed at such speed that he had forgotten his belt. The crowd jeered because it was a sport to see a big man taken down. He was headed now for the foul, faeces-smelling cells reserved at Poggioreale for prisoners arriving late at night. It was the ultimate insult to him that he was not ferried to the Questura or to piazza Dante, but to a common cell.

Near to the Palace of Justice, behind the Holiday Inn that rose in the business zone of the city, there was an apartment block that was a target only for the most successful to aspire to. It was – had been – the home of Massimo, the lawyer's clerk and nephew. On a table in the kitchen area there was a fulsome letter of apology to his family, of explanation to the prosecutor, of pleading to his God. He apologised for the disgrace bred from greed. He explained the link between the kidnap of the English boy, the Borelli veterans and the hitman, Il Pistole. He pleaded that he should not be eternally damned for carrying a sentence of death. One of the police officers who found him suspended from a skylight in a smaller bedroom by a sheet had had experience of hangings. He said that the signs on the neck showed that the young man, having kicked away the chair, and choking, had tried to save himself, and failed; weals at the neck showed the efforts he had made following his change of heart.

The net closed around a clan, stifled its breath, strangled it.

Her mother spat at her.

Gabriella Borelli had been given an officer's coat to drape over her shoulders but, with or without it, she gave no sign of cold.

No response from Immacolata.

They had thought, at the palace, that she would lecture her mother in her conversion from the clan's culture. She did not. She said nothing. The tactic, employing silence, had been determined in the car that had brought her round the bay, along the coast road and through the gaol's gates.

The spit was on Immacolata's cheek and her chin and she did not wipe it.

There was a table between them. Two women guards were behind her mother, but Immacolata sensed they would intervene only if there was a physical attack. She thought them in awe of her mother. Rossi and Orecchia were behind her. Her mother, before spitting, had used different avenues to demonstrate her disgust, contempt for and loathing of her daughter: the shame to the family of a collaborator, the betrayal of her relatives, the treachery of siding with the prosecutor against her own.

She had not flinched. She had stared back at her mother,

had ridden the punches as a boxer did. She had been taunted: where would she live, who would befriend her, could she live a lie for the rest of her life? Did she understand what it would be to cringe each time on a darkened street if she heard a footstep behind her? Did she know how much bounty money her mother and father in joint enterprise had placed on her life? Did she understand that she would never be forgiven?

There was the spit, then her mother's final throw: 'You sleep with a boy, you curl your legs round him, you take him into you, you fuck him, and you kill him . . . I never betrayed your father. You took the boy into your bed, and he means nothing to you. You kill him. It is not Salvatore who kills him, it's you. I love your father and I love Vincenzo, Giovanni and Silvio, and they love me . . . You cannot love. The boy comes, searches for you, will give his life for you. You cannot love because you're cold. You're not a daughter. You have the cold of a whore. You don't know what love is, what loyalty is. The boy did. You're cold, not of Naples. You kill the boy. It's as if you fire the shot or hold the knife. Do you imagine that one of our family, if there was love, would turn away and condemn to death? Perhaps you fucked him like a whore does, were cold . . . You will never love. You're not capable. You're not your father's daughter, not my daughter. You're not your brothers' sister. All of our family have warmth, can love, not you. The proof of it? You killed the boy.'

Her mother swung round, did not spit again, and strode to the door. As if she was a monarch, the two women officers scurried to get to it first and to open it for her. They stood aside so that she could pass through. Immacolata heard more keys jangle in harmony, more doors opened and closed in slammed timpani, the distant trill of her mother's laughter, as if she deigned to share a joke with her escort. Then the voices, the footsteps, the music of keys and the percussion of doors faded, were gone.

Her chin trembled.

They had set Immacolata hurdles to leap, she understood that. She had cleared them all, except this one. Here, she had stumbled.

She looked at her watch – had no reason to but did – and saw that the minute hand showed five to the hour. The watch was in a gold setting but discreet. It had been her father's present to her on her twenty-first birthday, one of many presents, and had become part of her. She had worn that watch in the telephone kiosk on an east London street when she had made the international call, and in an east London park when she had met the enemy of her family, and on a flight to Rome and in a car that had carried her south and home. It was five minutes to an hour, and the time had no significance to her. The watch was part of an old life. She took it off, opened her fingers, let it fall to the concrete floor of the room that had been made available to them in the late hours while a prison slept. She had been wounded, and knew it. Deliberately, Immacolata put her heel on the watch face, and killed it at five minutes to an hour.

Rossi pulled a handkerchief from his jacket pocket, unfolded it and – without fanfare – wiped the spittle off her face. Orecchia took her arm.

She left the watch behind her, for a cleaner to find or a trustee prisoner, as she had left behind a padlock on a bridge.

'Do we have long?' she asked.

'Not long,' Orecchia answered.

She said where, now, she wanted to be taken. Rossi shrugged. Orecchia said it would be done. She thought they humoured her because of what her mother had said. She didn't know the importance of a watch stopped at five minutes to an hour.

*

He did not want food. He did not want water. He did not want cigarettes. It was five times now that he had been asked if he wanted to eat, drink, smoke. He yelled it back at the small man who sat cross-legged on the walkway. Nobody listened to him. Why did nobody listen? In Forcella, in Sanità, men listened when he spoke. He didn't have to raise his voice. He could whisper and men would crane forward to hear what he said, and others would hush those at the back. If he was angry, men were fearful. If he made a joke, men laughed.

'I don't want anything.'

'It's just that it's a long time since you ate or drank, Salvatore. Myself, I could do with a cigarette and—'

'Anything except that you look at the time. Look.'

The man had a gentle voice. 'Use my name,' he said. 'It's Lukas. What I always say is that a guy's name is the most important thing he owns. I'm Lukas, you're Salvatore, he's Eddie. I don't want to be hustled by time.'

'Look at your watch.'

'All right, easy, all right. Can I say something, Salvatore? The gun. Can the gun be moved from where it is? Eddie's head? You're tired, course you are. Can you just shift the gun a little? They frighten me, guns do.'

'Look at your watch – see the time.'

'How about you move the gun and I look at my watch? Is that reasonable? You're tired, that situation, your hand might slip. Maybe you have a hair trigger. We don't want an accident.'

'Look at the time.' He couldn't now see his own watch. Hadn't seen it since the man had come forward and offered food, then sat, and Salvatore hadn't dared to move, not a centimetre, and the guns' aim was on him. The way his arm was across the boy's chest, and his own head was half buried in the hair at the back of the boy's skull, didn't allow him to see the face of his watch . . . but now he heard the chime, distant. A church's clock, a church's bell. Could have been the Church of the Resurrection he had passed on Fangio's pillion. Midnight's strike . . . If a player of importance, a figure who was respected, let a given deadline drift, allowed an ultimatum to slip, then face – authority – was lost, could never be regained.

'That is fair exchange, Salvatore. You move your pistol, shift it a little, and I'll check my watch. Listen, friend, all I'm here to do is to help.'

He screamed. He heard his own voice, detached from it, as if it was another who howled in the night, a cat's cry. 'Where is she? Where is her statement? Where is the retraction? Answer me.'

The gentle voice was so reasonable, and there was a shrug, helpless, from the small shoulders and the hands gestured it. 'Way above my level, that sort of decision, Salvatore. Nobody tells me anything. The jerks who make that sort of decision, they'd have gone home long ago. People like us are left out of bed, no food and no water and no goddam cigarettes, and there'll be no decision from them till the morning comes. Better, Salvatore, for you, for me and for Eddie, that we sort this out ourselves, and I can go home, and Eddie can, and you can go get some sleep.'

It was like honey, the voice, sweet and cloying and satisfying, and he knew the deadline of an ultimatum had gone and could not be clawed back . . . If he killed the boy then he, himself, was dead, and he could see the light reflected from the scope's lens. He couldn't clear it from his mind: did he want to die?

He cocked the pistol, scraped metal on metal, and the sound echoed along the concrete of the walkway and filtered through the washing lines, and the hammer was back. He had no hatred of the boy. He had no love for Gabriella

Borelli, or loyalty to Pasquale Borelli who had created him. He loved the respect that was shown him. A slow gathering smile came to his face but his stomach growled and his throat was dry, and he craved to smoke, and his finger tightened on the trigger stick, squeezed on it.

The watch face was in front of his mouth, and it looked as though Lukas examined the time it showed and had difficulty in that light. He murmured, lips barely moving, 'Don't shoot. Don't respond.

'You were asking me the time, Salvatore, about five minutes past—'

The shot was fired.

Lukas saw the flash and the recoil of the weapon, and saw the boy flinch, cringe, sag, but he was held up by the arm and the belt. There was no blood.

He knew that if a second shot was fired it would be a killing shot.

What a fucking way to live, what a fuck-awful job to have . . . He had stood once in a corner of the board room of Ground Force Security, had been a day back from Baghdad and had come out with a freed hostage, and Duck had led the directors in celebration drinks – Lukas wouldn't have been there had there not been delays at Heathrow from the baggage handlers. He had been sober and his employers had not. One had quoted, declaimed it, a Shakespeare speech: their King Harry on the eve of the battle. 'And gentlemen in England now abed Shall think themselves accursed they were not here . . .' Not if the 'here' was a mud-wall village beyond the conurbation of Ba'aquba. Likewise, not if the 'here' was a stinking, foul, dirt-laden walkway on the third level of the Sail. Bullshit . . . And any right-minded person, valuing sanity, should have been 'now abed'. But it was what Lukas did, and was all he knew. He had slipped out of that boardroom and doubted that any of them had noticed that he, the cause of their celebration, had quit on them. He had the watch again in front of his face.

'Next time will be for real. I'm not usually this much of a glory-hunter, but I fancy it's time to go and do some walking.'

There was no answer in his earpiece. He didn't expect it. It was the side show. It was the B flick. The main event was Miss Immacolata and her denunciation, and the boy was rated as secondary. He could do what he damn well pleased.

He called forward, 'I think I have that message, Salvatore. You should trust me. I am here to help, and best for all of us – if I am to help – is that you give me trust. Watch me.'

Lukas stood. He had seen so many men, women and children with a knife close to their throats or wired explosives round their bodies or a pistol against the soft skin at the back of an ear. He had seen mute terror on the faces of the old and the young, and sometimes he had been far back from them, linked only by a closed-circuit camera or binocular vision, and a few times he had been close and they had seen him, and the burden was goddam near intolerable then because of the dependence on him focused from their eyes, as if he was a final chance. Maybe most of those people – intelligent or stupid, experienced in the world or innocents – had been side-show material or B-flick fodder. There were some he'd lost and they'd had a half-minute of fame, posthumous. There were some he'd helped to save and they might, just, have secured a full fifteen minutes in the limelight. Only an idiot without a life, without an idea of a proper job, without a bed, would have been there, midnight gone, and the next bullet drawing blood, and feeling the night cold in his knees. What Castrolami had not asked: would he ever, all these years in, forget the basics that underpinned success, lose the mischief and excitement, and ever just get – so

simple – goddam bored, been there and seen it? Questions
not asked were those not needing answers. He flexed – so
damn tired . . . Not a long time left for the resolving of it.
Folk in Charlotte went up into the hills and hiked trails at
weekends, on public holidays and for their summer vacations.
They took cabins, and the last morning there was a cut-off
when the cabin had to be vacated and them gone, forgotten,
no sign of them left behind. Lukas thought that by five,
before the dawn, they would be off the third level, out of
the Sail and driving away down the road from Scampia. He
appreciated the agreement made, through third parties,
between Castrolami and the local big-shot player. By first
light, the ROS team would be gone and the dealers would
be back, and Salvatore was either in handcuffs or dead, and
Eddie Deacon was either in a body-bag or walking free. It
wasn't a big window of time but more than sufficient for
Lukas to climb through. What bothered him, this time, he
cared about the target – which was shit. Didn't do concern
and emotion, except . . . Saw the face and the fear, saw the
hair and the pistol barrel, saw the eyes and the bruises and
the lips and the swelling and the cheeks and the cuts.

He said it again, pleasant, like he talked to a friend, a trusting
one. 'Just watch me, Salvatore. Watch me very carefully.'

He bent and pulled loose the knots on his laces, then
kicked off his trainers and used his toe to shift them to the
side. Then he ducked down again and pulled off the socks.
He couldn't remember how long he'd worn them, and smelled
them. He dropped them on to the trainers and stood in his
bare feet.

'Just as I say, Salvatore, keep watching me.'

He did it as a palming motion, slipped his hand past his
ear and extracted the gear, moulded and flesh-coloured. He
hadn't expected Castrolami in his ear, or wanted it, and he
admired the investigator for not burdening him with queries,

hesitancies. The palm went into the pocket of the lightweight windcheater, then Lukas shed the coat and tossed it on to the pile. He had never done a strip before, but the tiredness ate him and he sought to push the matter on – force it. His shirt went next, unbuttoned, taken off, discarded.

'Watch me, Salvatore, watch me all the time and have trust in me. I'm here to help Eddie and to help you.'

He did everything slowly, nothing suddenly. His hands went to his belt and unfastened the buckle. He was not self-conscious, never had been. Almost, because of the way his mind worked, he shared the agony of self-doubt inflicted on the hitman. In seminar talk it was 'police-assisted suicide', but in any canteen in Paris, Berlin, New York or London it was 'suicide-by-cop'. It was the easy way, lifted the decision-taking out of the equation, had somebody else do the dirty stuff. Didn't have to climb on to a parapet on a wide-span bridge or go up a crane ladder and feel the wind swaying it as he went higher, and didn't have to sweat on whether there were enough pills in the bottle and he'd come to, alive and vegetable-brained. And easier than turning the firearm on himself, feeling the ugliness of the barrel in the mouth and the foresight in the roof above the tonsils. All about self-doubt, and all about the selfishness of a bastard who thought of himself only; most certainly did not think of the poor guy, police marksman, who blew him away, then went on to trauma counselling. It was a fucking awful place to be, and a fucking awful job – and Lukas had always said he would fight bare-knuckled any man who tried to take it off him. He did the zip on his trousers, let them fall and kicked them off, used a bare toe to move them aside and shove them with the heap.

'Just keep watching me, Salvatore, and know that you can trust me. It's all going to be fine. You and me, we're going to sort everything.'

He took off his undershirt.

Not a fine sight, he thought.

Damn near twenty years before, the medic from the Bureau's recruitment programme had taken a sight of that chest, the concave bit between the bones, the spindly arms sprouting, and failed him. He was told afterwards, when all the rest had gone well, that he presented, next to naked, a poor example of young manhood, and it hadn't improved in two decades. He chucked aside the undershirt. Might have killed then for a cigarette and might have killed as well for a shower, long and hot, and soap. Not right for him to shiver and he didn't. They watched him, as they were supposed to. Didn't think that seeing him would give too much comfort to the boy. Didn't think, looking at him from twenty paces would summon up too much suspicion and anxiety in Salvatore. Their eyes, the two sets, were never off him.

He heard, alongside him, a door open. He said, in his mind, bawled it: Fuck me, do I need that? Do I hell? He turned his head, not full on and used the periphery of his vision. An old woman stood in a doorway and she had a goddam cat in her arms. She looked hard at Lukas and shoved the cat down. It yowled, and she kicked it hard with a gnarled foot that was half in and half out of a slipper, and the cat flew behind him. The door slammed and a bolt was drawn. Silence. He thought the old woman had either refused to move or had been too deaf to know of the evacuation, the cat wanted to pee or crap and had roused her. End of story. I was near, God believe me, to a damn coronary. Don't do it me again, please. He had his arm up, scratched above his ear, and could say to his watch face, 'I don't aim to make it easy for the shite. We want him rotting.'

He wore navy boxer shorts. They had seen better days and the colour had faded from rich to dull and the elastic in the waist had lost the snap, and the shorts hung slack on his belly.

The pistol barrel had not moved, was in the boy's hair.

'I can't abide shouting, Salvatore, so I'm coming a bit nearer. There's sensitive things to talk about and I don't want the world knowing what our business is.'

There were good goose pimples on Lukas's skin. Mustn't shiver. Mustn't show fear. All bluff. He took the first step forward. All a bluff, and an opaque mist chucked over the reality. If the mist was blown away, the bluff called, he was dead and the boy was dead and Salvatore had achieved his bus-pass ride to the angels. The smile was good. It was a rare talent: Lukas's smile never looked as if it was pasted on his face, and it was calm, quiet and as sincere as it came. He was on the fourth and fifth steps, stretching them.

'I'm not a danger to you, Salvatore, I'm a friend, and I've come to offer help. Trust me.'

He didn't know how much of what he said was understood, and was unable to gauge the Italian's comprehension of his message. Lukas thought his bearing more important than anything. His nakedness and his lack of physique proved he threatened nothing, nobody. He heard behind him a soft but strangled howl, and wondered if the bloody cat was nuzzling its damn face against a rifle barrel, and if the animal had been hit with the heel of a hand. Had done ten paces, then twelve. The eyes of Salvatore seemed wider, the lower lip jabbered and the jaw wobbled. He had no voice. Lukas thought he tried to speak and couldn't.

A hell of a way to spend a night. Good damn thing he looked down because there was syringe glass on the walkway concrete, and shit from a dog – not the cat's. A hell of a place to be ... He kept the smile in place. An instructor for the training of the Critical Incident Response people had said it was the best smile he'd come across and asked why it couldn't be carried from the role-play scenarios into the canteen when they ate together. It was an act, had no truth.

Fifteen paces taken, then sixteen. Always smile. The boy gazed at him like he was a messiah.

'You have my word, Salvatore, and my word is my bond, that you can trust me, and that way nobody's hurt, and we get to go home, and you get a proper bed and some sleep and a meal. What I'm working at, Salvatore, is that every one of us is a winner. You know about winning. You win because you're smart, Salvatore. I can see that. You're a big man and smart, a winner.'

He could see more of the boy's face than the hood's. Shouldn't have allowed a personal feeling to intrude in the work – had done, and Lukas saw that as a failure. A small one, but failures totted. Too many small ones and there was weight enough for catastrophe. Catastrophe was the pistol being fired, blood spurting, bone splintering . . . The boy had a good face. Assault teams, negotiators and co-ordinators all wanted to believe that the target for rescue was worth saving, was of gold-plated value. Found half the time, after a rescue, that they were creeps, useless – some too fucking arrogant to offer gratitude, not that Lukas wanted thanks. Wanted a job done well. Had counted them, had done twenty-one steps, was level with the doorway. It was a good face and a terrorised face.

'I appreciate you letting me up close, Salvatore. An idiot wouldn't have, but you're a smart guy. Can I call you "friend"? I'd like to.'

He wasn't certain. Lukas stood in the centre of the walkway. The boy and Salvatore, wrapped together, like one, were in the doorway. The pistol had not moved from the back of the boy's head and he saw that it remained cocked, the finger inside the guard, resting on the trigger bar.

'I want to talk with you, hear you, and that way I can best be your friend, and I can help you.'

He was not yet certain that the hood would not shoot.

Inexact sciences – whether, when, why a gunman would pull the damn trigger. One of many sciences for which there could not be textbooks, only a bedrock of experience, was getting into the mind of a holed-up gunman and anticipating whether he wanted to be in a warm, cleaned-out cell or hankered after a one-way ride to Valhalla. Lukas didn't know.

He did a little roll of his eyebrows to Salvatore. 'I doubt he means anything to you, that Eddie, anything at all. Doesn't mean anything to me. Not smart like you, friend, not a winner. Means a great deal to his parents. Pretty ordinary people, and that's why I said I'd try to help. They're not winners either – not like you are.'

He put his hands on his hips, as if he was standing in a bar, talking with a man he knew and respected, and sent a message big and clear, and spoke a confidence.

'He – that's Eddie – doesn't know that the bitch – the woman he came to find – wasn't prepared to lift a finger for him. I'm not supposed to tell you this . . . She couldn't care less for him – could have sent signals, could have opened up channels. She's not changing her mind. You could have sent bits of him back to her, or all of him dumped on her doorstep, and she wouldn't have changed. Only word for her, "bitch", but he, that's Eddie, has only found that out these last three days, whatever. Hurting him, Salvatore, won't change her, won't alter a hard bitch . . . It's just what I'm thinking.'

They were in the doorway. From where he stood, he couldn't have touched the boy. Would have had to take a couple of steps to be close enough, then could have tousled the boy's hair, pinched his cheek or slapped his upper arm for encouragement, but he hadn't yet convinced himself that the hood wouldn't shoot. It all happened, in these situations, so damn fast – was so damn unpredictable.

He thought that at least five rifles were aimed at the little part of Salvatore's body protruding from the doorway's recess. Not enough to give the marksmen an aim and have them shoot, and the pistol remained at the boy's neck. It would be one word, or a short sentence, one movement or gesture that could change it, and the pistol might be moved and might be fired. Lukas didn't know. He stood, near naked and cold, fighting the urge to shiver, and couldn't know whether what he said or did would win or lose it. The lips moved. He strained to hear.

'They will never take me . . .'

They all say that, friend, he murmured in his mind, and kept the smile. And I don't know whether I believe you. Have to find out, don't I? The smile clung to his face.

'They will never take me as a prisoner.' His voice seemed to growl from deep in his throat. The breath hissed on the back of Eddie's neck.

He didn't know whether the smile, six or seven feet from him, was real or manufactured.

'Not me, not a prisoner. One step, I shoot.'

Eddie felt himself a spectator. The man's arm was tight round him and the man's fingers were hard in a fold of his T-shirt, and the man's bones were against his buttocks, the chest against his back, the head against his own. A spectator, a voyeur, a watcher. He could not relate to the incoherent babble of the man and the breath on his neck and the wet spit coming with it.

'I kill him. One step closer, dead, him.'

Almost, Eddie thought, the man cried tears, and edged to hysteria. And he was a spectator also when he gazed into the calm face of Lukas. He could see each hair on his head and face, the stubble growth, what was in his ears and nostrils, the curled hair on his chest and at the base of his stomach, visible because the boxers drooped.

'I shoot him. Do you not believe me? You will.'

The skin was broken by the force used to press the pistol barrel against his neck and Eddie could feel the wet there. Lukas had not moved, had not gone back or forward, and his hands were still on his hips. They were not flexed and there seemed no strategy of deceit about the posture. Lukas was, Eddie believed, in control.

'You believe me when I shoot him. Not one step.'

He felt comfort given him. The man, Lukas, oozed competence and experience. He didn't have to speak. He had the calm of a parent while a toddler rages, knows the child will quieten. He'd had an old teacher at school, sixth-form English, forty years in the job and a new headmaster, half his age, had trashed the veteran's ideas: 'Experience often clouds judgement, best without it.' The pupils had thought it bullshit. Eddie valued experience. Valued it big when it was in a smile from a man who masked any trace of fear. A weedy little beggar. No strength to him, no muscle, spindly legs, arms almost emaciated, and that burn mark on his lower lip that came from smoking cigarettes to the filter. Seemed to offer no threat.

'I tell you, you believe me, I will shoot.'

'What I believe, friend – I want to call you that, OK? I believe, friend, that you're a big man, a smart man. Too big and too smart for an accident. I think, friend, you're hurting Eddie with the barrel. Can we do something about that? Not hurt him . . . That's good.'

The barrel was less pressured on his neck, Eddie knew. It no longer gouged. It had an indent, but less force was used.

'That's good, friend, and it's generous. I appreciate that. We have to figure a way out of this.'

'I shoot. I have no fear.'

'You have no fear, of course you don't. Fear is for little

guys. Him, Eddie, he's fit to shit his pants, but he's not a big guy.'

'You come no closer.'

'I'm not moving.'

Maybe there was cramp in Salvatore's hand – maybe it was, ironic, bloody *generosity* – but the pistol had moved again, imperceptibly but a further lessening of the pressure. Eddie didn't move, was one of those guys with painted faces and robes who struck statue poses at tourist sites. He realised that Lukas, too, had moved, edged closer. Eddie knew it because he could match the window-sill across the walkway with the corner of Lukas's right elbow, and there was less of the sill to see, and a big paint flake was obscured by the arm. Eddie knew, standing and held upright, with the pistol in his skin and the tiny sounds inside his ear from the firings, where all the paint scrapes and flakes were on the window opposite. It could have been a full pace closer – could have put him, damn near anyway, with a lunge, in touching distance. Eddie reckoned Lukas knew what he was doing and the comfort in him grew.

'You don't move.'

'I don't move . . . What I care, friend, is how we come out of this, before there's an accident.'

'They don't take me.'

'Not a surrender, no . . . Not paraded like some damn chimpanzee in a zoo cage. Absolutely not.'

'You call me *scimpanzé*? Do you? A *scimpanzé*, chimpanzee, cannot shoot. I can. I am not taken.'

'How about, friend, you try to shoot? *Try*. Not Eddie, not worth the cost of a bullet. You *try* to shoot me. You jam and—'

'What is "jam"?'

'It is "block". Malfunction, does not fire, but you tried . . . a smart guy, you know about weapons. There could be dirt in the ammunition, dirt in the pistol with a build-up of cordite in the barrel, dirt in the magazine mechanism. It can be the extractor bar breaking. The automatic blow-back can fail. For many reasons it can block and jam . . . the word gets passed.'

'I will not be taken.'

'Yes, yes . . .' Eddie thought then that he heard the first wisp of impatience. Like it had been a good game, and an interesting experience, and it had run its course, and the first twist of boredom was there, and a little of the confidence slipped in him. 'What is important is your prestige and dignity, friend. You *tried*. You did not surrender. You were good to your word. It was just that the damn machine, the pistol, the kit, failed you. That message gets put around. Nobody can say that Salvatore, big man and smart man, bottled out. Not him. It was the pistol that failed. There's another thing.'

Eddie could watch the eyes of Lukas. Every feature of his body was unremarkable, stunted, without authority, except his eyes. There was less of the window to see and the gap between Lukas and the two of them shortened, and it would only have been a short lunge for the touch. The eyes were extraordinary. They were locked on the man who pressed his body against Eddie. They had the quality to hold and mesmerise. Eddie did not think that he, himself, held interest to Lukas, only Salvatore – the *friend*. He didn't know how it would end, but knew it would be very soon. A minute or two minutes. His comfort bled because he thought he recognised impatience.

'The other thing . . . You get a good lawyer. You're intelligent and you have the resources, and you get a top man to front up for you. You pull a prosecution case to pieces: not difficult because they're always second rate. Maybe you walk at the trial. Maybe you go free on appeal. It doesn't last, locked up. Show me, Salvatore, that you're a big guy and a smart guy, and I already know you're a generous guy.'

'Do what?'

'We all have some food. We all get some sleep. There's no accident. What do you say, friend?'

Lukas had moved again, could have touched. Two bright flashes on the dirt and the concrete, which caught in Eddie's glance. Two discharged cartridge cases. Two shots fired and two cartridge cases thrown out – no fucking jam, play-acted or otherwise . . . The comfort had gone and he felt the stress build again and his body was rigid.

'You did not listen.'

'Course I did, friend. I listened well. Heard all you said. Just giving you the good back way out and—'

'You did not listen.'

The pistol was off Eddie's neck, gone from his skin. It was out in front of Eddie's face, and the arm was loosed that had been across his chest. Two hands on the pistol grip. Eddie understood. Should have taken longer . . . maybe too tired, maybe too hungry, maybe just bored pig-sick with a thug with a gun, maybe done it all before and so many times . . . saw the shock spread on Lukas's face, like disbelief.

Eddie heard, 'God, did I do this, did I?'

And then the pistol blast and the cordite dust flashed in his face, and the bright brass of the cartridge was ejected, fell, bounced and rolled. Blood came back at him, a fine spray, and there was more behind. He saw the slight ugly knees bend, then falter, then collapse, and saw the shock on the face, preserved, like the scale of a mistake and its consequences were the last thought that . . . He did a sort of hop. Eddie had no legs free to kick backwards. As he jumped up, held by the belt, he hacked his heels behind him and felt them hit and hurt, and he could punch with his hands, all done in one crazy, uncontrolled moment – his clenched fists hit the belly.

The pistol arced, fell and clattered.

They went down. He was underneath Salvatore and his

head was held, gripped, and his face was beaten into the concrete . . . and they came. His eyes were closed, shut tight – couldn't absorb more.

Nightmare engulfed him. He was crushed. Weight on him squeezed out the breath from his lungs. His head was in blood. He couldn't move, see or breathe. There were voices, muffled and indistinct, and he didn't understand what was yelled. He felt himself sinking, then falling, then lost, and the abyss closed over him . . . and the weight was lifted. Eddie dared to open his eyes.

He was ignored.

He lay in a smeared strip of blood that now sank into the porous dirt of the concrete. Two figures, huge in vests over black overalls, with firearms hooked on their shoulders, took turns to work on the chest of the man who had called himself Lukas. They pounded on the chest and didn't stop until the door behind him, where he had been held, was kicked flat, then used as a litter. Two more of them took him. Hoisted on the door, Lukas was carried away. Eddie didn't know whether it was boredom or impatience, or just shit luck that had failed Lukas.

He didn't move his head. Beyond where Lukas had been, Salvatore lay on his stomach as his hands were hitched behind him and fastened with ties. One more of them in the black overalls and the masks stood over Salvatore and had a dirty boot across his neck, and Eddie knew he was alive because the chest heaved and there were small yelps of pain when the boot was shifted or pressed harder. Eddie was glad he lived. He thought it a worse, more severe punishment to live than to be proxy shot.

Last they came to him.

A big man towered over him, wearing a suit that now had rents at the knees and elbows and was stained with the dust of the concrete; a vivid tie was loosened at the neck and a collar button undone, and his hair was a tangled mess, and there was blood on his shirt and jacket. Eddie might have been wrong, but he thought he saw wet glisten in the man's eyes. A short-bladed knife was used to cut the ties at his ankles and wrists.

He was turned over.

The man in the suit stood back. Another, whom they called Tractor, crouched over him and felt his face with mittened fingers, then lifted each of his arms and flexed them, did the same for his legs. There were cuts, abrasions and bruising on every part of his body that the hands touched but he didn't cry out. The Tractor stood and backed away, as if he had no more interest. Another, and he was called the Engineer, stood over Eddie and reached down.

Eddie took the hand, the fist closed over his wrist and he was heaved up.

The suit led . . . The Tractor followed, then their prisoner with men close around him. Eddie trailed, and the one they called the Bomber was behind him. The cat that had been shut out scratched at a door but was not admitted. They went past the broken apartment he had run into and he saw the wreckage and didn't ask about the man who had opened his home to a fugitive. They went through two barred gates, one open, one destroyed, and down three flights of stairs.

There was a crowd at the main entrance of the block.

He was not jeered or jostled. He was stared at. The black overalls were close round their prisoner and hustled him to the transport, but the crowd didn't push or surge. Eddie thought they wanted either their beds or to get back to their work and trade. It was a far place that he had come to and he didn't know them and they didn't know him, so he gave them no greeting or acknowledgement.

The suit stood beside the door of a minibus. The prisoner was in already. The suit waited for him.

Eddie came to the door.

The suit said, 'I'd known him for less than one week. He was the best . . . What are you? Are you worth the life of the best? But you didn't think of that . . .'

He climbed in. He was driven away.

20

It was still dark when they left the hospital, a great cavern of a building on the edge of the Scampia district. The *pronto soccorso* section was as grim a place as Eddie had known and he had been left with two black overalls on a plastic seat in a corridor, and the world had gone by him – beaten-up tarts, overdosed druggies, knife-wound victims, complicated pregnancies. He had known it was a formality but had sat still, and a nurse had come with a bowl and a towel and had cleaned his face wounds and had stitched, expertly, his lips, and he had had sutures under his right eye. He had not mentioned the pain in his ribcage, had thought it disrespectful of Lukas's injuries. A little after the American consul had arrived, with a phalanx of security around him, Castrolami had emerged from behind the swing doors. It had been obvious when they had gone in that the injuries were terminal, that Lukas was dead, but Eddie supposed it necessary for them to go through the procedures of resuscitation and fail. Castrolami – the suit had given his name in the minibus in a curt growl and had not offered a hand for the greeting – had walked up to him in that wide corridor outside the emergency section, and had flicked his fingers as a gesture for Eddie to follow him and had kept walking. He might have been the damn dog.

They did not use the minibus. There were hugs and cheek-brush kisses between Castrolami and one called the Tractor, another called the Engineer and a third called the Bomber, and the one who had a sniper rifle – uncased – made a joke of complaining that he had not been given the opportunity to shoot. Eddie realised then that the prisoner was gone, would have been transferred to a different wagon and taken away. Beside the minibus was a marked *carabinieri* saloon, with a uniformed driver and an escort, and the engine idled. He was put into the back and Castrolami slumped beside him.

They left the hospital where a body would now be wheeled towards the mortuary building.

Not much to talk about. *He was the best . . . What are you? Are you worth the life of the best?* There was no warmth on offer, nothing that soothed the jumbled confusion in his mind. He supposed that, by now, a telephone call would have been made to England, to a corner of Wiltshire, to a bungalow in a lane, and that lights had flashed on in answer to the persistence of a bell, and that his parents now sat on their bed, in their night clothes, in shock and relief – his mother might have gone to make two mugs of cocoa. He couldn't face making a call himself – would have to, but later. They sat silent and they looked out of their different windows.

The light grew, came slowly.

He did not ask where they went, why. *What are you?* Wasn't prepared to try to answer, and the blood of the 'best' was caking his T-shirt and jeans. They didn't go towards the city, but drove away from it and the first light, soft gold, was above distant hills.

There was no beauty, no majesty alongside the road.

They went by homes and small farms, scorched orchards, compact factory units and ribbon developments of advertising hoardings. He thought of the orderly, managed greenery of the village where he had spent his childhood; here there was anarchy. The sun peeped a fraction higher, and the first glimpse of a segment, still gold, was over the hills' horizon.

Castrolami had taken from his pocket an old leatherbound
notepad, with scuffed corners, and had started to write busily.
It would have been his memory jottings for his report on
the death of the 'best'.

Eddie was, and he realised it, an intruder, not wanted.

He felt no anger at this but accepted it and sat deep on
the seat, and the car was driven fast on empty roads. He
had, of course, no watch, but if he craned forward he could
see the dash in front of the driver, and thought they had
been travelling for a little more than half an hour.

There was a sign beside the road, and the driver slowed
and the escort studied his map, then written instructions.
The place was called Nola.

They went into the heart of it, past a cathedral-sized church.
The low sun was nestled on the tower, the road was rough,
the pavements worse, and a very few hurried to be at work.
Eddie thought the place desolate, as if hope had gone.

He did not ask why they had come here, for what purpose.

Nobody had fed him, nobody had offered him coffee or
water, or a beer. He saw more churches, and the road took
them along the perimeter of a hospital's grounds. Then they
veered off a main route and headed on narrower, meaner
streets.

The driver stopped a few metres short of a cemetery's main
gates. They were of heavy ironwork and closed; Eddie assumed
they were locked. There was a pedestrian's door at the side . . .
He could have played hard. He could have sat in the car and
demanded explanations. A man was dead, the 'best' man. The
man with the caved chest and the chair-leg-thin arms and the
knees that had nothing pretty to them was in the mortuary.
He followed Castrolami out of the car. He was led.

First light bloomed inside the small gate. A man was lit
as he swept dried leaves, and when he saw them, he eased
himself on to his witch's broom and Castrolami must have

asked the question with his eyes because the sweeper gestured to his right and watched them.

There was a girl's statue on a plinth, life-size, and a single rose slotted by her hand. She had the sadness of youth snatched and her name, carved in the stonework, was Angelabella. He went through avenues of small chapels, all with artificial flowers flourishing, and some had candles burning and displayed photographs of the long-deceased when they had lived and enjoyed health. A great piazza for the dead opened in front of him and Castrolami. He was considered responsible for the loss of the 'best'. He queried nothing, was obedient.

Between concrete paths there were gravestones, more flowers, more candles and more sepia photographs. At the far end of the square of the dead there was a wall with five layers of sealed shelves each large enough to take an adult's corpse, and more flowers decorated it. Two men stood against it and the sun caught their faces.

One waved to Castrolami, who acknowledged and switched course.

He saw her.

She would have noticed the two men's reaction and she stood, her hand across her forehead to shield her eyes from the sun, low and growing in intensity.

She did not run towards him. He followed Castrolami, kept Castrolami's pace.

In his ear: 'She wanted this. Myself, I would have thrown you on the plane, the first. She wanted to be here when news came of whether you had survived or not. Her friend is here, her most valued friend. Her friend is here because of the toxic pollution of what we call the Triangle of Death. The pollution is by the Borelli family, in part, over many years. It is why she has collaborated. It is in memory of her friend, a tribute.'

'I was second to her friend?'

'You were second, Eddie, to her friend. You could not compete . . . It is ludicrous to be here, but we are. You do not have long.'

Her arms were not outstretched, welcoming. They were behind her back. The light on her face did not flatter and there were bags under her eyes, lines at her mouth and a frown of worry. He thought her drably dressed – a plain grey skirt, a blouse that seemed darker – her hair was uncombed and she wore no lipstick.

Castrolami moved aside. The two men behind her edged clear.

He was in front of her. He was as far from her, and from the bulge of the blouse, as he had been from Lukas when he had thought the 'best' man was impatient, might have been bored and looked tired enough to drop. It was the face of the girl he had slept with and laughed with and . . . He was not certain he knew her, and he let his hands hang and hers were behind her back.

'You survived?'

Not the moment for the trite or the sarcastic. 'Yes, I survived.'

'You are hurt? You have wounds.'

A shrug, a grin that dragged on the sutures. 'I'm fine – like if I walked into a door.'

'I couldn't help you.'

'You could have helped me. You chose not to help me.'

'It was not easy.'

'You made a choice.' Eddie gazed into her eyes, held them. 'Do you understand the choice?'

'I understand that my life was of secondary importance.'

'Eddie, that is so pompous. Can you not . . . ?' She looked away, broke the intensity of the contact.

He said, 'Sort of puts me in my place – second place.'

'Should we talk of what's been, the past?'

He smiled, almost managed to laugh, and the pain was in his ribs at the thought of letting his chest heave. 'In the past, here – in this damn country, in Naples – there were people of quite outstanding courage. Top of the list, he was called Lukas and he tried to save me – he's my past. There's a fish-seller down via Forcella and he gave me the warning before the bastard bounced me, which was big – he's in my past. A man in that block, when I'd broken free and was running and the dogs of hell were after me, he opened a door for me. I don't know what happened to him, or the fish-seller, but Lukas died and I lived and . . . What bit of the past do you want to talk about?'

'I put a padlock on a bridge in Rome, and I threw the key in the river,' Immacolata said. The sun was in her eyes, worse than before. It made her squint, and took more of the prettiness off her.

'Don't know what you're talking about. Am I supposed to be impressed? What's special about a padlock on a bloody bridge?'

She shrugged.

Eddie grimaced. 'Do I get to see the padlock – whose significance escapes me – that doesn't have a key?'

'Maybe.'

'When is "maybe"? Some day, some time?'

'Perhaps . . . Go home.'

He swung on his heel and his trainer ground at the gravel chips on the avenue between the headstones. He walked briskly and Castrolami had to stretch his stride to catch him. The sun had now risen, up and flush on him.

Castrolami said that if they used the light and the siren they would be at Capodicino in time for the first flight of the day and to buy a new shirt.

*

An hour later . . . Marco Castrolami wore the suit that was kept on a hanger in a cupboard of his work area, a clean shirt and tie, and he escorted Salvatore, Il Pistole, from the front entrance of piazza Dante. Men of the ROS section held the arms of the prisoner – the Tractor and the Bomber – but their identities were obscured by balaclava masks with eye slits. The camera flashes exploded in the hitman's face. He winced and turned away, which gave an impression of fear that would be frozen irrevocably in the digital memories. Castrolami saw a reporter he recognised, an eager young woman, but couldn't remember her name or whether she was employed by *Cronaca* or *Mattino*, or an agency, and he murmured as he passed her: 'He always threatened to kill himself rather than face arrest. In fact, confronted with firearms, he didn't choose suicide-by-cop but surrendered without a fight – hardly a hero's end.' He would not normally have spoken to what he usually termed the 'vermin pack', but the day was not usual.

He had dropped his charge at the airport, in time for the first London flight out of Capodicino, had shaken the hand formally and muttered gruffly something about 'good fortune for the future' and 'better to cut Naples out of any future travel plans', had cuffed his shoulder in an awkward gesture, had not mentioned Lukas's death, and had seen the boy met by his consul, who would do the ticket, then take him in search of the shirt, and had left him.

He had not, in years, allowed himself to be photographed for the Naples dailies, but it was not a normal day. With the hitman on his way to a life sentence, he would go back to piazza Dante, clear his desk and cupboard, then write the letter to his superior. His personal effects would be in a plastic bag and he would drop off his ID at the front desk and slip away. No fanfare, no party . . . He would not be in Luciano's trattoria that night where the ROS men were due to eat, finally, swordfish steaks. He would be out of Naples by the end of the day.

Salvatore was driven away in a convoy of sirens and lights, *en route* for Poggiorcale. What had Castrolami's years in the city of magnificence and squalor, beauty and rank ugliness, glory and shame achieved? He would go up north, maybe drive a taxi or work in a cheese shop. Perhaps he had achieved something, perhaps he had not – more could not have been asked of him.

A day later . . . Men from the Misso clan spread out in the Sanità district, through the little businesses where the carved-wood madonnas watched trading from behind screens of lit candles, and called at the shops and bars that had been under the protection and control of the Borelli family. And men from the Mazzarella clan came to the via Forcella and the via Duomo and the via Carbonara, and walked in freedom and safety on the narrow alleys. Guns were carried and remained hidden. Premises were not earmarked for petrol bombing after dark. It was a seamless transfer of authority in all the areas that had been the fiefdom of the Borellis – grandfather, son and grandsons. Most of their foot-soldiers embraced humility and offered themselves to the new masters, and the few who had picked fights in the past with Misso people and Mazzarella people, or traded insults, or had slept with their women, were gone in the night and by midday might have reached southern Germany or western Austria or the Mediterranean coast of France . . . At Poggioreale, Giovanni was pushed from a lunch queue and Silvio dared not leave his cell, and Carmine sat, trembled and waited for a doctor to see him – and at Posilippo, Anna and Gabriella were in the same exercise yard but did not deign to let their eyes meet. They had known power and it was stripped from them, and they could focus only on their hatred of the young woman who had brought them low, Immacolata, who shared their blood.

A week later . . . He was lucky that his job was still available, the principal had told him. Eddie had been dutifully grateful. He had thanked him.

Outside the staff room, he shared a cigarette with Lottie and she – inevitably – asked him about the love of his life, the Juliet story, and he'd said something about 'just didn't work out', and nothing about a concept of justice being bigger than the value of his life. And near the end of that shared smoke she'd looked into his face, where the bruising was yellow with mauve traces and the swelling on his lips was still prominent and the scrapes had scabs and the stitches needed to come out. She'd asked. He'd said that the memory was a bit dulled: might have been a door he'd walked into and then again it might have been a set of stairs he'd fallen down, anyway that's what he'd told the principal, and he'd managed to laugh.

She quizzed him. In Naples, while he wasn't walking into doors or falling downstairs, had he taken a coffee in the Galeria Umberto I, built to revitalise the city after the 1884 cholera epidemic? No, he had not. Had he wandered in the state rooms of the Palazzo Reale, completed in 1651 after a half-century of work? No, he had missed out on that experience. In the Capella Sansevero, had he circled the Veiled Christ, the work of the eighteenth-century sculptor, Giuseppe Sammartino, regarded by many as the élite art work housed in the city? No, he had not been able to. Had he been to San Lorenzo Maggiore or the Pio Monte della Misericordia or the Gesù Nuovo or had he been to the ruins of Pompeii, or had he climbed to the rim of Vesuvio? No . . . no . . . no. 'Not my business, Eddie, but what did you do there? For God's sake, Naples is one of the wonders of the world – did it just pass you by?'

He'd shrugged. She would have thought him an imbecile and a Philistine, and the roll of her eyebrows seemed to suggest he'd have been better off in Milton Keynes or Welwyn Garden City. When the cigarette was finished and he'd stamped on it and she'd ground her heel on it, she asked, 'That address we worked out, what was there?' He'd said there was a couple of old people, the girl's grandparents, and he'd smiled and just seemed to tell her that the subject area was closed. No talk about the Sail, and about a pistol in the neck and the gouge it had made and shots fired and a man who was the 'best' killed. No war stories.

A bell rang in the corridor.

Neither did he tell her about a cemetery, with the sun rising, and about a girl who looked drained and wan and near broken, and was dressed drably, and who had spoken of a padlock and . . . He said to Lottie that it was good to be back in the comfort zone of Agatha Christie, and Poirot and Jane Marple, and *The Body in the Library*. Well, for a bit – grateful for the work but no one should bet their shirt on him not moving on. He thought that Lottie had believed nothing he had told her, but was too polite to quiz him further.

He went into his class. Of course, same walls and same posters of tourist Britain, same desks and same students as there always were for that day of the week at ten in the morning, and the same table for him to spread out his notes. Nothing changed – except there was a private emptiness and he did not know how, whether, it could be filled.

A month later . . . They were gathered on a viewing platform in the Crowders Mountain State Park. It was out west from Charlotte, beyond Gastonia and along Route 85, and was a favoured place for those seeking good rock-climbing conditions. The family were there, and a man from the New

York office of Ground Force Security, and another represented the Federal Bureau of Investigation. Those men held back and allowed the mother, the wife and the son of Foster Lukas to do their bit with the small veneer wood casket. It could have been a short experience of dignity and respect, but Ground Force had realised early that the blood relatives gave not a damn once a will had been produced that left all worldly chattels to a clinic that helped military veterans acclimatise with their new artificial limbs, and the Bureau had come up with the idea of scattering the ashes at a place of natural grandeur. Trouble was, the wind was wrong. The FBI man was retired as an agent, but was kept as a freelancer on the payroll for the funerals of those who had long left the Bureau but required recognition. 'What I heard, there was burnout: too much work, till it had gotten to obsessional levels and no hobbies – Lukas didn't give himself time for women, for golf, not even for wall-eye fishing. Wasn't that old but the work levels and the places they took him sort of left him crisped.' The wife had the top off the small casket, supplied by a crematorium in London, and the mother tilted it, but the goddam wind was wrong. The Ground Force man said, 'Our evaluation, from the debriefs of those who were closest to him, he'd gotten careless. Happens with burnout cases.' A good handful of the ash blew back over the viewing platform rail and became embedded on the son's trousers and provoked a barely suppressed oath. The Bureau man responded, 'There were two factors that killed him. The one was that carelessness which comes from having done something so many times that it's clockwork, but the other was involvement, emotional involvement. We say that any form of involvement is a road to failure and worse than "careless", but emotional involvement is the pits. That's the combination that killed him. But I reckon "careless" was bigger.' Mother threw some more and a little went into the wife's eye, and a sprinkling of it on to her coat.

The two men walked away, left them bickering about the wind and about a dirty coat and a pair of trousers that would need cleaning and a mote in the eye, and both thought their work done . . . It was indeed a hell of a place with a hell of a vista, and the Ground Force man said, as he fished car keys from his pocket, 'He felt for the boy he was trying to bust out of a bad time – wasn't just a dreary routine. Lukas was the sort of man you need in that kind of scrape – difficult, taciturn, lacking in social skills, and as good a type as we throw up. The boy was lucky to have him on the case.' The family had finished and had turned away from the platform. They both waved at them, and called out their good wishes – which were not acknowledged. The Bureau man said, 'The boy was indeed lucky, and will probably never know how lucky.' They parted, would drive in their own hire cars to the airport at Charlotte and the flights would take them back to DC and to New York City, and neither could have pictured the Sail building and a walkway where the washing hung, and a little runt of a guy naked except for his boxers.

A year later . . . The senior judge thanked her.

She bobbed her head. She stood. She turned for the aisle and the double doors. The prosecutor had told her that the sentences would range between *ergastolo*, life, for the younger men, except her juvenile brother, thirty years for her mother, twenty years for the advocate, ten years for her grandfather who would die in Poggioreale, and eighteen months at Posilippo for her grandmother.

In the cage, no one looked at her. Her mother and her three brothers, her grandfather and grandmother, the lawyer who had known her since she was a babe in arms, and the hitman, all looked away as if that co-ordinated gesture demonstrated their contempt of her. It was a wasted effort. She never glanced at them. On earlier hearings the abuse from the cage – particularly from Giovanni and Anna Borelli – had blistered across the court room, and on her fourth day in court Vincenzo had come to the front of the cage and spat venomously at her, and her mother had declaimed that Immacolata would rot in a living hell, and on many days Silvio had wept. Her evidence was completed after a month of daily testimony. She had forsworn cosmetics and dressed in lifeless colours for her appearances. That day, her last in court, she was different. She had brought, almost, a possessive smirk to the face of Orecchia and a bounce to the step of Rossi when they had collected her from the safe-house and driven her early to the Palace of Justice. They, alone, were privy to the transformation.

Rossi and Orecchia had taken her the previous evening to the boutique salon in the back-street on the seaward side of the piazza dei Martiri. Her mother's account? Of course it would be on her mother's account. Who would have refused her? The owner faced an investigation from the Guardia di Finanza, so easily arranged, if Immacolata Borelli and her escorts were turned away . . . and the account was still open because her mother needed fresh underwear and required the changes of plain clothing that might, to a court, indicate a misunderstood and guiltless woman. That day, her daughter had been driven to court in the bulletproof and armour-plated Lancia in clothing that was chic, elegant, styled. Her jacket and skirt were Asian silk, sea blue and severe, her shoes were white, with low heels, her blouse was cream and hung loose. She wore no jewellery. Also, the night before, the wife of a court security guard, had come to the safe-house, cut and styled her hair. She had turned heads in court, all except those of her family and her family's closest confidants. It was as if a trapped bird had escaped a cage.

She went down the stairs from the court, through guarded

double doors into a concrete underground cavern, and was led to the Lancia.

It was time there, beside the car, for a brief moment when the professionalism of the Servizio Centrale Protezione was abandoned, thrown to the winds. Orecchia took her hand and kissed it lightly. Rossi kissed her on each cheek, cool lips. She knew them, knew of their families and their problems, their excitements and their moments of despair. They were, perhaps, her only family.

She sat in the back, encased by the dark privacy windows, and accepted now and did not query the vest that was laid on the seat beside her. Orecchia drove, for this final journey, in the middle of an October afternoon when light rain fell on the city and the mountain's summit was hidden in gloomy cloud. Beyond the tunnel, the road ahead was blocked by police motorcycles, and they were given a free run on to an open road. She would never see the city again, knew it.

At the airport gate, Rossi laid his machine pistol on his lap, rummaged in his briefcase, produced her airline ticket and passed it to her. He said, quietly, that the aircraft was due to leave five minutes ago but was held for her. Then he gave her the new passport that carried the new name. They were at the terminal's Departures door. Orecchia turned and faced her, then tapped the top of his head. She took her cue and lowered the dark glasses from her hair, covered her eyes with them and her upper face.

Rossi said, 'At the gate they're expecting us. We'll be taken straight to the aircraft. I'm with you until the hatch closes after you . . . You'll be met?'

'I don't know.'

Orecchia frowned. 'You said you were coming?'

'I did it by text. The number he used to have. What flight, where we should have dinner. I don't know whether he has

a different mobile . . . I didn't call, maybe for fear of what I
might be told.'

'Are you sure of this?' Rossi demanded of her.

'Very sure – I've not had a text back but I'm sure . . . I
hope I'll find him.' She paused, then said softly, 'After what
I did to him, what else – now – can I do? I must look for
him – at the airport, in a restaurant we used, in the bar he
liked. I owe it to him to look.'

Orecchia scribbled on a sheet of his notepad, then ripped
it off. 'Call me and tell me if you've found what you're
looking for.'

She smiled at them, and treasured them for their loyalty.
'You'll get one word, *fatturato*. In English that's "turnover".
Then you'll know I found him.'

Orecchia changed – was the professional, the guard. 'You
don't stop, you follow Alessandro, you keep close to him.
Goodbye, Signorina Immacolata, who is finished. Goodbye,
whoever you have become, and today you are beautiful. I
hope you're met.'

The car door was opened for her.

She walked well. The gate closed behind her. She didn't
know if he would be there. She had a brisk stride and
remembered a park, a bench and a young man, and a question
put in innocence – and a great wrong done to him, and to
others, in a faraway place.